He Lowered His Mouth to Hers.

Sarah had been expecting the kiss. She had even anticipated its hard demand, its confidence. What she had not anticipated was its effect. Without a moment's hesitation, without a moment's thought, she was clinging to him. He caught her bottom lip between his teeth, bringing her a quick thrill of pain, a sharp shaft of need. There was more here than she had ever imagined, more passion than she had ever known. Wanting still more, she ran her hands up his back until they gripped his shoulders.

There was nothing soft about him. His body was taut, his mouth bruising hard. There was no comfort here, no easy enjoyment. Here was danger and excitement. Here was a kiss more intimate than any loving she had ever known.

NORA ROBERTS

Promise Me Tomorrow

PUBLISHED BY POCKET BOOKS NEW YORK

Another *Original* publication of POCKET BOOKS

POCKET BOOKS, a division of Simon & Schuster, Inc.
1230 Avenue of the Americas, New York, N.Y. 10020

ISBN: 0-671-47019-1

First Pocket Books printing February, 1984

10 9 8 7 6 5 4 3 2 1

POCKET and colophon are registered trademarks
of Simon & Schuster, Inc.

Printed in the U.S.A.

To Ruth and Marianne,
for reading and listening.
But especially for making me laugh

Promise Me Tomorrow

Chapter One

It was a clean and balanced structure. The first five stories spread out and were banded by an unbroken ribbon of windows. From this base rose a tower of glass. Its translucence caused it to appear fragile in spite of its fifty stories. Slicing through the azure sky, it seemed unsupported.

Under the white blaze of the sun Sarah stood, one hand shielding her eyes, her head tilted back so that she could see the topmost story. Her face held the look of concentrated admiration one sees on an art student viewing an old master. She saw art in the delicacy of the sleek glass tower, the grace of the horizontal base, the perfect balance of form and function. There was elegance in the height and slenderness, and there was strength. She recognized the power. Sarah respected power whether it belonged to an inanimate object or a living being. She had cultivated her own throughout her life.

She had been born of quietly average parents. James Lancaster had been a pediatrician, a tall, spare man. He had been thirty-five when Sarah was born. He had rusty brown hair, clever eyes, a long thin nose, and a wide thin mouth. Sarah remembered him as a man with gentle hands and quick smiles. A man without guile.

Penelope Lancaster was a woman who balanced her checkbook monthly and to the penny. She was ten years younger than her husband. She kept a tidy house in New Rochelle and painted the shutters herself every other year. Though tiny, she had surprisingly long legs and firm, well-developed breasts. Her face was classically oval and rosy, her eyes wide and green. She had a casual blonde prettiness that promised to remain appealing into old age. She clipped coupons every Thursday from the newspaper.

From these two pleasant, attractive people had sprung a sparkling, skyrocketing beauty. The genes had been right at the moment of Sarah's conception. Her face was the shape of her mother's, her complexion a melding of her father's fairness and her mother's rosiness. Her mouth was wide, with a passionate fullness in the lower lip. Her nose was elegant, sharp and straight, giving her profile an Egyptian look. Her eyes were arresting, big and almond-shaped with odd green lights. Her hair was the color of a young fawn's, an elusive brown with shade upon shade of variation.

Beautiful children possess power, though it often remains dormant unless they are clever as well. Sarah had always been clever. More, her intelligence had matured early. It had often disconcerted her parents to see such ripe intelligence in a child's face, to detect adult understanding in youthful eyes. Her habit of looking straight into another's eyes and searching for the whole person had begun as a young girl. Her mature, questing brain might have alienated her from her contemporaries, but she was saved by a sincere affection for people. Flaws didn't bother Sarah. When she found them, she accepted them, at times appreciated them for their uniqueness. It was monotony she detested, not human weakness. She was also one who enjoyed not only having her way, but the journey getting it.

From babyhood, she had used charm as a weapon. It was natural and effective. When it failed, as it did from time to time, she simply shifted her tactics. She was capable of intimidation, she had a temper, and she was stubborn. She never used tears. Women who used tears as a weapon, in Sarah's opinion, traded equality for short-term victory. Convenient tears were hypocritical. Sarah had never been a hypocrite. In any case, she knew her dry-eyed lancing look was worth an arsenal of tears.

Now she used it to study and dissect the Haladay Building. Architecturally, she felt the structure was a superior work, both practically and aesthetically. It had always been Sarah's purpose when she sat at a drawing board to consider both these aspects. The Haladay Building suited Phoenix. It was as clean and light as the desert air. Maxwell Haladay was, in his own way, as outstanding as the building which had been created for him. He was shrewd, savvy, and self-made, all of which appealed to Sarah. She liked the earthy quality of Haladay's struggle for success and was sentimental enough to enjoy a happy ending. Moreover, the secrecy surrounding his personal life during his half-century rise to power stirred her imagination.

She knew Haladay had made the move to Arizona some thirty years before because of his wife's failing health. After her death the main branch of his organization remained in Phoenix though the Haladay tentacles stretched worldwide. Sarah hoped the man was as interesting as his building. She finished her outside examination of the fifty stories, then glanced quickly to the right and left before crossing the street against the light.

The lobby was spacious and degrees cooler than the sidewalk. The mosaic floor sparkled under a dozen silver chandeliers. Spaced along the walls were paintings of Arizona scenes: deserts, mountains, plains, canyons, and a particularly good charcoal sketch of an old Navajo woman. The artist in Sarah was drawn to the portrait while the city dweller was vaguely intimidated by the openness of the landscapes. There was also a selection of cacti, an assortment of flowering plants, and several chairs and sofas, but essentially the lobby offered space and coolness. An army of elevators lined a wall done in discreet beige.

It's time, she told herself and pretended there was no tension at the base of her neck. There's nothing more discourteous than being late for an appointment. A tiny leather purse was strapped crosswise over her jacket, and she shifted it to her hip as she approached the elevators. Pushing a button, she prepared to wait.

"Excuse me, miss."

Turning, Sarah found herself confronted by a uniformed security guard. He had a square, lived-in face and tired eyes. Sarah had a weakness for tired eyes and greeted his professional sobriety with a quick smile. "Hello, how are you?"

She had a fantastic face. He ignored her question. He did, however, suck in his stomach. "Who would you care to see?"

"I have an appointment with Byron Lloyd."

"And your name, miss?"

"Sarah Lancaster." Briefly she scanned his nameplate, then smiled into his eyes.

The smile did it. It was sincere and charming. "Fiftieth floor. I'll call up and let them know you're on your way."

"Thanks, Joe." As an afterthought, she asked, "Do I look okay?"

Her hair was plaited into one thick braid and wound in a circle at the base of her neck. Her vested suit of pelican gray was given a flamboyant touch by a shocking pink blouse.

"You look real nice."

Accepting this as Joe's highest form of praise, Sarah flashed him a fresh smile before she stepped into the elevator. "Wish me luck," she demanded and heard him do so as the doors closed her in. "I think I'm going to need it," she whispered, then took a deep breath.

This interview was the most important thing to date in her professional life. At this point all of Sarah's energy was focused on her career as an architect. She wanted to work for Haladay. The New York interview had gone well, she reminded herself as she watched the small red numbers telling her she was getting closer to the fiftieth floor. Phase one, the résumé, had been a success. Phase two, the initial interview with the head of the Manhattan branch, had been a success. Phase three had to be a success as well. It followed, didn't it? Sarah chewed on her bottom lip. When it was convenient, she liked to think that matters moved in a logical order. One, two, three, no detours. Phase three was Byron Lloyd. In the gargantuan Haladay organization, only Maxwell Haladay himself held more power than the man on the fiftieth floor.

Sarah's natural confidence was waning as the numbers climbed higher. A position as an architect with Haladay could make the difference between a moderately successful career and a brilliantly successful career. It could make the difference between designing buildings and designing *important* buildings. Sarah wanted to build, and while she was about it, she wanted to build something big. Ambition had driven her through college, phase one; into a well-established New York firm, phase two; and now to Haladay Enterprises, phase three. Simple mathematics, she thought and bit her lip again. Sarah knew she had the talent to make phase three work. What she needed was the opportunity. As she watched the numbers move into the forties she wondered if Byron Lloyd would give her that opportunity.

So much depended on the next half hour. I can't afford to let nerves take over. It's important that Byron Lloyd see that I'm capable, confident, and poised. And I am . . . most of the time. This would be easier if I didn't want the job so badly. Sarah sighed, knowing she wasn't going to want it any less when the car reached the fiftieth floor. As the doors slid open she lifted her chin. She was going to get it.

The reception area on the fiftieth floor was carpeted in gold. The pile was so thick that Sarah decided no shoe had ever touched bottom. Before any of the three secretaries in residence could do more than make a cursory survey, Sarah was approached by a small brunette. She wore her hair in a smooth, chin-length pageboy that set off her features and round green eyes. She moved well, but Sarah decided her grace was practiced rather than natural. As she drew closer, Sarah caught a quiet whiff of Arpège.

"Ms. Lancaster, I'm Kay Rupert, Mr. Lloyd's secretary." Kay extended a hand. "I hope you had a pleasant trip."

"Yes." Finding Kay's palm too cool, Sarah broke contact. "I like flying east to west." She glanced at her watch and adjusted for the change in time zones. "Of course, flying west to east, you lose all the time again, so nothing really changes, does it?"

Kay's brow rose ever so slightly as Sarah flashed her a lightning smile. "No, I suppose not. Mr. Lloyd's expecting you. If you'll just come with me."

The perfect secretary, Sarah decided. Thank God she isn't mine.

She followed Kay through double glass doors that led to a wide corridor. The walls were pearl-toned and well lacquered; they made an excellent background for the paintings that lined them. To Kay's annoyance, Sarah stopped to study a Matisse. "Part of Mr. Lloyd's collection," Kay told her briefly.

A man of taste, Sarah mused, nibbling on her lip. And means. The analysis brought fresh butterflies to her stomach. A collector. She turned back to Kay. Their eyes met. Because it was her habit, Sarah studied the secretary openly. She made no attempt to hide the probing, nor did her smile fade as she sensed the other woman's growing discomfort.

"It's lovely," she said simply, joining Kay again.

Kay turned and continued down the corridor. That one, Sarah thought, will be a smashing business success and no fun at all. After a brisk knock, Kay opened a single panel and stepped over the threshold. "Ms. Lancaster is here, Mr. Lloyd." With the unobtrusiveness Sarah had known she would possess, Kay melted back, then disappeared behind the closed door.

For a strange, frozen moment Sarah saw nothing of the room. Her vision narrowed and focused on the man who rose from a large ebony desk. As he crossed to her, she had a vivid sensation of cold fear so sharp it brought a shaft of pain. As from a great distance, she heard him say her name, and his voice seemed to touch some chord of memory. It flashed through her mind that if she accepted the hand he offered, there would be no turning back.

"Ms. Lancaster, are you all right?"

Sarah shook her head like a diver breaking water and forced air in and out of her lungs. Nerves, she told herself. And too much sun. "Yes, yes, I'm fine," she murmured. Like an offering, she placed her hand in his. His grip was warm and real. "I'm afraid I stood too long in the sun looking at the building." She smiled, hoping to eradicate the awkwardness of her entrance.

He said nothing. Her hand was cold in his. For a moment they stood studying each other.

He was taller than she had expected, with an animal type of leanness in both his face and body. His hair was the deep black she knew would show touches of red in the sunlight. It grew in thick loose waves. Over the bones of his face, his skin was stretched tight and tanned. It was the narrow, angular face of a warrior or a scholar. Somehow she thought it at odds with the perfectly tailored suit. The contrast appealed immediately. His brows arched, then lifted slightly at the tips while below, his eyes were large, heavy lidded, and surprisingly blue.

"You're not at all what I expected," Sarah said. She smiled, waiting for him to release her hand.

Byron inclined his head, but kept her hand in his a

7

moment longer as he felt warmth flow back into it. "What did you expect?"

"I haven't gotten that far yet."

He gestured to a chair, then led her across the room. She settled into an overstuffed chair of ivory leather.

"Would you like something?" he asked.

A trip to Greece, a Mercedes 450 SL, and a frost-free refrigerator. Sarah ticked off the first three desires that sprang to mind and felt better. "No," she answered, then smiled with easy charm. "Thank you."

Byron saw the quick flash of humor but made no comment. As he took his seat behind the desk, Sarah watched the air of command settle over him. Now he was what she had expected. Authority suited him, she decided.

"Dave Tyson of our New York branch speaks well of you." His voice was low-key and smooth, like well-aged Scotch. Sarah noted that his hands were wide-palmed and long-fingered like a musician's or a surgeon's. They remained still on the surface of the desk as he spoke. She brought her attention from his hands to his face. It was a sharply attractive face, frankly sensual, with eyes that compelled because they held secrets.

"I'm glad to hear that," she said. Allowing her spine to relax against the chair, she tried to imagine that she was settling in for a friendly chat rather than an important interview. "I suppose I have him to thank for being brought out here to meet you."

"Your résumé was a large factor," he commented. "Mr. Haladay was pleased with it." He continued speaking while she mulled over the wonder of Maxwell Haladay actually reading her résumé. "Haladay Enterprises is, of course, the largest and most diversified building corporation in the country. We maintain high standards and hire only the best professionals. Mr. Haladay was impressed by your designs and by the buildings you've been associated with. Tyson's recommendation is another mark in your favor. He feels the work you've done for Boumell and Sons has shown imagination and skill.''

''That's a nice boost for the ego.'' Sarah's brows drew together in a brief frown. ''I had no idea Mr. Haladay did such extensive personal research on prospective employees.''

''Mr. Haladay takes a personal interest in all his employees,'' Byron assured her. ''Why do you want to leave Boumell and work for Haladay?''

Sarah had been expecting such a question, but she hadn't expected it to be so blunt. She was pleasantly surprised. ''Because I want to build important things, and I'll never have the chance at Boumell. I will at Haladay.''

''Are you ambitious or dedicated?''

''Both,'' she answered instantly.

He studied her for a moment without a flicker of expression. Sarah wondered if her answer had been too quick. Perhaps she should have used tact instead of honesty.

''You worked under William Turhane at City College in New York. He also speaks well of you,'' Byron said.

''Does he?'' She smiled. ''He didn't always when I was his student. I think 'exasperating' was his pet word. It was an accurate one, I'm sure.'' Sarah paused for a moment, then decided to take the plunge. ''Perhaps you could clear something up for me. When word slipped out that Haladay Enterprises was looking for a new architect, you must have been swamped with résumés. I'm certain dozens of applicants had more experience than I do. How did I get this far?''

Byron hesitated a moment. He took a gold cigarette case from his jacket pocket and offered it to Sarah. She refused with a shake of her head. In the space of seconds he reevaluated her. Her beauty had stunned him for a moment, as had the brief glimpse of vulnerability he had seen when she had first entered the office. From reports, he knew that Sarah Lancaster was single, a left-wing Democrat more interested in art and old movies than politics. She was considered brilliant, talented, and mildly eccentric. He saw for himself that she was also direct. Though he sensed her nervousness, it pleased him that she controlled it without any visible effort. Leaning back, he laced long fingers together.

"You were in the top five percent of your class at City College. Your record with Boumell shows potential and imagination. The work you did on the Unitarian Church in Buffalo was particularly impressive."

Sarah listened with lifted brows. She was not flattered, for he was as impersonal as a computer, but she was interested. The design of the Unitarian Church had been completely her own.

"We've been told you're a bit unconventional." He paused, watching surprise flicker across her face. For a moment her normal defenses slipped and Byron caught a brief glimpse of insecurity. "Actually," he continued, deciding to press the moment to see how she would handle it, " 'eccentric' was the term."

For a heartbeat Sarah said nothing while her mind raced. Who, she wondered, had spread that rumor? There had been absolutely nothing in Byron's voice to tell her if being eccentric was a demerit or a point in her favor. Should she deny it? Should she casually agree? She knew jobs were easily lost for one wrong answer.

" 'Eccentric' sounds like someone's maiden aunt," she returned and hoped she sounded unconcerned. "Unconventional might be true, depending on one's definition of the word. I've heard it said that Maxwell Haladay is an unconventional man."

Still Byron's eyes gave away nothing. He's a cool one, she concluded. Is any job worth all this? she asked herself as she kept her eyes steady on his. Oh God, yes. This one was. She forced her shoulders to relax.

Slowly Byron crushed out his cigarette. Behind him the

sun slanted through the tinted glass and fell onto his desk. "I'm sure Dave Tyson gave you a thorough explanation of the financial aspects of this position."

His change of subject nearly threw Sarah off balance. "Yes, he explained the company benefits and the salary."

Byron's brow lifted at her casual dismissal of lucrative company benefit plans and a ten-thousand-dollar-a-year raise.

"Other terms are of more concern to me. I'm curious about how much creative freedom an architect has and how much control she retains over a building she has designed once it's under construction."

Byron watched her. He noted the smoky quality of her voice, a night voice. He took account of her hands, which gestured, narrow-boned and graceful, with the nails unfashionably short and unpainted. She was, he decided, a set of contradictions. The conventional suit, the flamboyant blouse, the sultry voice, the nun's hands. He approved of her directness but reserved judgment on the woman.

"First," he began, "creative freedom depends upon creative output. Mr. Haladay retains final approval, but if he didn't respect the judgment of those on his staff, they wouldn't be on his staff. Second, architects are required to oversee certain phases of construction on a project of their design."

Sarah rose. "I see," she murmured as she began to wander around the room. His answers did not wholly please her, but, she reminded herself, he had answered. That was something. "Calm colors of authority," she stated as she ran a finger down a fabric-covered wall. "The ivories, the creams, the biscuits." Sarah gauged the office to be roughly a hundred square feet and completely organized. She felt that little of the inner man was to be seen in the neutral colors and smooth surfaces of his office. Intuition told her he was neither neutral nor smooth. We might have something to say to each other outside of this room, she reflected, without the nifty business suits and leather chairs. "I think your home is decorated differently," she said, letting her thoughts rise to the surface. Sarah turned back to Byron, then gave him a long level look. She was weary of the chess match. If she was to be checkmated, she would go down boldly. "I'm not very good at small talk," she said, "but I'm a good architect."

"And a very young one," Byron returned, unwillingly intrigued. He saw the quick annoyance in her eyes.

"Guilty." Her voice was cool with a hint of anger beneath. "I'm twenty-six, which means I barely have the schoolroom chalk from under my nails."

"No need to apologize for your age, Ms. Lancaster. Your youth is among the reasons Mr. Haladay wants you for this position."

The words jolted Sarah. "Do I understand you to say you're offering me this position?"

"No," Byron corrected. "Mr. Haladay has offered you this position."

Turning to the window, Sarah waited for her thoughts to come to order. Her initial shock was replaced by a combination of joy, triumph, excitement, and fear. The fear was unexpected. It told her, *Now you've got your opportunity, Sarah; the rest is up to you. Don't blow it.*

"Could I ask," she began, surprised at the calmness in her own voice, "when Mr. Haladay decided?"

"Last week."

"Last week," she repeated stupidly. She remembered vividly the agony she had lived through in the past week, the torment of doubt during the flight from New York, the last-minute attack of nerves in the elevator. All that suffering for nothing! She blew out a long breath. "Why didn't you tell me right away instead of letting me sit there agonizing?"

"Mr. Haladay wanted my impressions. If you had already known, my questions would have been academic."

Excitement was beginning to dominate her other emotions. Sarah suppressed it. She wanted it for later, when she could savor it. Byron was speaking again. She forced herself to listen quietly.

"I think you'll like Phoenix, Ms. Lancaster, once you've made the initial adjustments."

"Phoenix? I thought the offer was for a position in the New York branch." Her voice trailed off to a murmur. "I hadn't given any thought to moving to Phoenix."

"Is moving a problem?"

She stared at him a moment as her mind repeated his question. A problem? Is it a problem? Sadness briefly haunted her eyes, then was gone. "I can have things cleared up and be in Phoenix by the end of the month. I will meet Mr. Haladay after I've settled in, won't I?"

"You move quickly, don't you?" Byron watched her go from wistful to practical to eager in the space of ten seconds.

"God, yes. And if I move quickly enough, I can catch the afternoon flight back to New York." Sarah crossed the room. "I've got a project to finish up before I can sever my professional ties, and too many personal dealings to think about. A month is barely any time when you think of it, and May has only thirty days."

"Thirty-one," Byron corrected automatically, moving with her to the door.

"Well, what's one day?" Sarah turned to him, giving him her long, direct look. What was it going to be like working with him? It was difficult to say from the interview.

"Good-bye, Mr. Lloyd," she said briskly, offering her hand. "I'll be in touch."

He kept her hand in his, placing his other hand over hers as it rested on the doorknob. It was an odd and total connection. She only just resisted the urge to jerk away. For some reason she felt both in tune and at odds with him.

"Contact Dave when you're ready. The company will have your things shipped." His voice was businesslike, but Sarah caught a fleeting, enigmatic flash in his eyes.

"All right," she agreed. "Is there something else?"

His gaze did not waver from hers. It occurred to her that not once during the interview had she seen him smile. "Have a good flight," he said as he opened the door.

Chapter Two

THREE WEEKS LATER, CLAD IN AN OLD TERRY-CLOTH robe, Sarah sat cross-legged among a pile of boxes and cartons. The windows of her apartment were open wide to bring New York inside on her last night. Eight floors below, it throbbed and pulsed. Minnelli was opening on Broadway, two vagrants counted their day's take by a fountain across from Radio City, Bloomingdale's had a new shipment from Gucci, and a history teacher was being mugged in Central Park.

In the kitchen, pouring wine into jelly glasses, was Benedict Eager, a Fifth Avenue psychoanalyst. They had been comfortable lovers for nearly a year. The adjective was Sarah's own. Their relationship was a shoes off, feet on the table affair that required no frills or flowers or candlelight. They saw each other clearly; no soft focus. Sarah could relax totally with Benedict.

He was a small, spare man in his late thirties who sported a thick brown beard that he felt suited his image. He wore round, wirerimmed glasses, and his speech still hinted of Boston though he had lived in Manhattan for ten years. He liked Woody Allen and Tolstoy and was Sarah's best friend.

"Sarah, my dear." Benedict came into the living room

bearing two glasses. "Would you prefer Elmer Fudd or Daffy Duck?"

"Daffy Duck." She reached up to take the glass. "You're much more Elmer Fuddish than I."

"Thank you." He perched on a carton opposite her.

"I'm going to get quietly drunk, Benedict," she announced, lifting her Daffy Duck glass and watching the wine slosh into his bill and out again. "Then I'm going to crawl into that sleeping bag over there and spend my last night in New York under a cloud of apple wine." She inclined her head and sipped. "You may join me if you like."

Benedict scratched the top of his head and grinned. One of the things that had attracted him to Sarah was her attitude toward sex. She was the warmest woman, and the most interesting, he knew in bed or out. Making love with Sarah was a constant adventure. He lifted his glass. "That sounds delightful."

"It was the right decision," she muttered, then took two long swallows of wine. Knowing the way her mind worked, Benedict was aware that no answer was expected of him. For the moment she might as easily have been alone, yet she drew some comfort simply because he was there. "There's no reason to cling to New York just because it's where I've always been. Now that Mom and Dad are gone . . ." Sarah shut her eyes and rubbed the bridge of her nose between her thumb and forefinger. Did time really heal all wounds? Three months hadn't dulled the ache, the vague unexplainable feelings of guilt and betrayal. She wondered if a twenty-six-year-old woman had the right to feel like an orphan.

Sipping wine, Benedict remained silent as Sarah brooded. Her expression told him she was completely involved with her own thoughts. She knew the position with Haladay had come at a perfect time. It would give her something to throw herself into, something to keep her mind charged while grief was still raw inside her. The interview with

Dave Tyson had been scheduled little more than a month after her parents' sudden death.

When the shock had passed, Sarah had known a range of feelings from sorrow to loneliness to fury. Her love for her parents had been a steady, comforting fact. One day her parents had been tucked cozily into their New Rochelle split-level with three years left on the mortgage and new wallpaper in the kitchen. The next day they had been gone. The fire had taken even the house, leaving nothing but a shell. None of the small treasures of a twenty-eight-year marriage remained: no photographs, no chipped cups, no stairs that creaked on the left side coming down. Gone, Sarah reflected and felt the familiar edge of pain and anger. Gone as though it had never existed. At odd times she would remember her mother's brisk, practical voice or one of her father's silly, harmless jokes.

Why did the chicken cross the road? Because the light turned green.

Oh, Dad, you'll never change.

And, of course, he hadn't. There hadn't been time. I should have gone to see them more. I should have spent more time with them. You think you have time, all the time you need, then it just comes up and cuts you off at the knees. Goddamn time. I'm going to beat you. I'll leave a mark. Nothing's ever going to wipe me out as though I had never existed. The fury came, but she pushed it aside. Don't look back, she told herself. Look ahead, straight ahead. Working for Haladay was the biggest break in her career, and it was only the beginning.

"When you're given an opportunity like this, you've got to take it," she said aloud. Benedict looked at her with affection. He made no effort to really understand her. He preferred simply to enjoy her.

Glancing up, she stared into his eyes. That look, he reflected. It doesn't miss much. Clean as a scalpel. Sarah held up a hand for him to grasp. Her artist's fingers were firm in his.

She wanted, needed, the same devotion she gave. People who kept themselves apart or who doled out their emotions miserly puzzled her. She thrived on human contact: the touch of a hand, the spoken word, the brush of shoulders in a crowded elevator. She gripped Benedict's hand tighter, clinging to the familiar.

"It would be different if we'd fallen in love. Really in love."

He gave her his small, ironic smile. "Would it?"

A frustrated breath rushed out. "Damn it, don't play shrink with me." Sarah rose and paced the room before stopping to add more wine to her glass. "God knows we should be in love; it's absolutely ridiculous that we're not. Maybe we are and don't know it. We've both seen *The Maltese Falcon* thirty-two times—that should count for something." It isn't just a move, she thought wildly. It's an amputation . . . a total severance from everything familiar. What do I know about Phoenix? What do I know about working in a huge organization like Haladay? What makes me think I can handle this the way I handle a weekend trip to Long Island? She tossed back some wine and paced the room until her thoughts began to slow. Stopping in front of Benedict, she sighed and rested her forehead against his. "Good God, what will I do without you?"

"Everything." He gave her a companionable pat on the bottom. "You're just nervous; it'll pass." He thought briefly that he had yet to deal with the hole her leaving was going to put in his life. "You know this is exactly what you need, and what you want, or you wouldn't be going. You've been waiting for this turn in the road for a long time."

"I do want to go," she admitted. "I need to go. You're so smart."

"Ah, you've been talking to my mother again."

Her chuckle delighted him. With her glass in her fingers, she linked her hands around his neck. "No one in Phoenix knows what makes me laugh or how I like my back rubbed or where I lose my keys."

"Is that where my charm for you lies?" Benedict gave her a quick kiss, changed his mind, and gave her a lingering one. His hands moved to her hips. "Your charms are too diverse to mention."

Resting her cheek against his, she spoke quietly. "I never would have made it through the last few months without you. You did more than keep me sane after the fire, you kept me whole. Every time I started to fall apart, you were right there."

"You're a strong lady, Sarah," he said as he combed his fingers through her hair. Her scent wafted around him and he frowned. The hole was going to be bigger than he had anticipated. "You would have landed on your feet with or without me. I just made the impact a bit softer."

"No." He felt her head shake briskly. The arms around his neck tightened. "I don't think so. I think if you hadn't been a part of my life when my parents were killed, I would have ended up needing you professionally instead of personally."

He kissed her ear. "My fees are outrageous."

"Capitalist," she murmured.

"You know the problem, Sarah? We like each other too much. We're too compatible." Cheek rested against cheek. "There's never been any spark, nothing to make either one of us uncomfortable. Love, passion, they need a bit of desperation. A few bumps and bruises."

For a moment Sarah stood still, enjoying his warmth and his familiar scent. He's right, of course, she thought. They had always been more like friends than lovers. Their lovemaking had been pleasant, never desperate. There had been no wild, painful surges, no urgency, only an easy enjoyment. She was a little afraid to make love with someone else, she suddenly realized. It might not be so easy.

"I do love you, Benedict," she murmured. After patting his beard, she straightened. "And I hope you find someone incompatible one day." Her eyes were serious as she bent to kiss his cheek, then she smiled, her slow smile that involved each of her features one at a time. It was the smile Benedict loved, and uniquely Sarah's. It gave everything in a matter of seconds and demanded everything in return. She watched him answer the smile before she turned and walked away. It was time, she decided, to begin thinking about tomorrow instead of yesterday.

At the window she stared down at the street below. One cab cut off another at the light. The sound of screeching tires, blasting horns, and quick cursing rushed up to her. It was a hot night. Sarah could smell the city through the screen.

"I've done some probing into the history of the first mate of the Haladay ship," she said.

"Oh?" Benedict slipped out of his battered Wilson tennis shoes.

"Mmm." Sarah watched the traffic chug its way up the street. Her shoulders moved restlessly. "He intrigued me. There's something rather . . ." She searched for a word with a circling movement of her hand. "Piratical about him." With a laugh, Sarah shook her head. "Maybe I'm stretching the analogy too far. Anyway, I wondered about someone so young being second in command. He's only thirty-six."

She found she very much wanted to put her thoughts on Byron Lloyd into words. "He started working for Haladay when he was sixteen. Haladay was always ahead of his time, and offered educational benefits for his employees. Byron worked construction, but he took every course he could squeeze in. Somehow or other, he caught Haladay's attention." She pushed the hair away from her face to look earnestly at Benedict. "I'm told not much escapes Haladay's eye, so I can imagine that a teenager who was working his ass off during the day and cramming his brain at night would interest him. He obviously saw potential, because he personally put Byron through engineering school." She remembered his cool, unsmiling eyes and thought he might indeed be part computer, part slide rule.

"Gradually he was promoted. He worked at virtually every job, except perhaps the typing pool. He did his time as an apprentice." Sarah lifted her glass and sipped. The wine was cold and tart on her tongue. "He worked his way up to vice-president before he turned thirty."

"No small accomplishment," Benedict commented when she paused and stared into space. "But then it appears his ambition started young. I've known others similarly inclined." He grinned.

Sarah shot him a look. "Have you?" She continued. "He's supposed to be brilliant, shrewd, cool." Frowning, Sarah swirled her wine and remembered her impression of Byron. Controlled and dangerous. Perhaps the control adds to the danger. There had been something about him that had left her vaguely disturbed. After three weeks she still had not been quite able to throw it off. Thinking about him now brought on the faintest unease. Sarah resented it.

"He's also supposed to be a great connoisseur of women," she went on.

"Busy man," Benedict commented. Sarah scowled at him. With a laugh, he rose and lifted the half-empty bottle. "He obviously made quite an impression." After filling her glass again, he put down the bottle and then untied the belt to her robe. The terry cloth parted obligingly.

"He made an impression," she agreed, then linked her arms around Benedict's neck. "I'm just not sure what kind."

"Think about it tomorrow," he suggested as his hands slipped around her waist. He moved his hands to her breasts. They were small and firm under his palms. Sarah turned her head until their lips met, then sighed with the pleasure of his knowledge of her. He knew where she wanted to be touched. His beard brushed her shoulder as he lowered his mouth to her neck. When her nipples were taut, he let his hand roam to her thigh, just feathering his fingers over the soft mound of hair. Sarah gave a quiet moan, nipping at his ear as his fingers entered her.

"I am going to miss you, Benedict," she murmured, then pulled loose the snap of his jeans. In two quick tugs she had them past his hips, then took him into her hands. A wave of regret washed over her, and she buried her face in his shoulder. Closing her eyes, she pushed away all thought and let herself ride on the pleasure his hands and mouth were bringing her. His fingers were moving in and out of her quickly now, while his free hand brought her closer as her body shuddered in response.

"Come on," he said, tickling the opening of her ear with his tongue. "I want to show you some things about a sleeping bag that aren't in the boy scout manual."

The wing of the plane dipped. The ground seemed to rise crookedly toward the sky. Sarah's stomach shifted with the movement. She pushed sunglasses on her nose and groaned. Her head was throbbing. In addition to the hangover, which she accepted, was the dragging weariness brought on by a restless night, which she resented. The hangover had been brought on by her own free will, but she had had no choice regarding the insomnia. Neither the wine's comfort nor Benedict's lovemaking had helped her sleep.

For hours she had lain awake listening to the street sounds that had been a part of her life for eight years. She had wondered how many days and nights she had been in that apartment never hearing the life surging outside her window. It was a constant motion she had taken for granted, as she had taken the two comfortable people in New Rochelle for granted.

The plane touched down, bouncing twice and then settling. She vowed never to take anything for granted again. The trick was to be prepared for anything. There was a whole new life waiting in Phoenix, and she was going to be ready for it. As the plane shuddered to a halt she considered checking into a hotel, downing three Excedrins, and tuning out for the next twenty-four hours. She pulled a floppy-brimmed emerald-green hat over her hair and unfastened her seatbelt.

Byron watched her disembark. He wondered how anyone could wear such a ridiculous hat with such aplomb. The buttonless jacket she wore was the same vivid green worn over a calm ivory blouse and skirt. None of the other women who deplaned had the same look of casual perfection.

Byron kept to the back. His height enabled him to keep sight of her over the crowd. She moved smoothly, rapidly. He didn't signal her, but waited until she was nearly upon him before he touched her arm.

Stopping, she looked up. "Mr. Lloyd, this is a surprise."

"I came to meet you."

Sarah studied him from under the brim of her hat. Her lips curved in a smile. "I'm honored; I was expecting a minion." She pulled off her glasses and scrutinized him.

In her gaze Byron saw candor, good humor, and an unexpected vulnerability. As with the first time, the vulnerability made him wary. There were also faint traces of mauve under her eyes, which spoke clearly of her restless night. "No hand luggage," he said at length, then glanced down at the small clutch she carried.

"I travel light." Did he ever smile? Did he resent her or was this just his way with people?

"Fine. I've arranged for your baggage to be sent along to your hotel. Would you care to check in there first or go by the office?"

Sarah resented his aloofness. Crisply, she matched his tone. "Putting me to work already?"

"I thought you might like a tour of the building." Byron

seemed unperturbed by her change in manner. When he took her elbow and began to lead her through the terminal, she rebelled.

"What I'd like is a pharmacy and a cup of coffee." The sun flashed as they emerged outside, and she pushed her tinted glasses back on her nose. Her headache pulsed.

"For now, why don't we just tour a few floors of the Haladay Building?" Byron opened the door of a pale gray Mercedes. His tone was calm. Sarah started to get in, then turned to face him with the opened door between them.

"Are you trying to irritate me?"

"Why would I try to irritate you, Sarah?"

"Maybe it's just your nature," she concluded, then turned away. His hands gripped hers on top of the opened door, surprising her with their strength and their insistence.

"You're very young," he said quietly. In that moment she saw that she had been right about the danger beneath the control. "I haven't much experience entertaining children."

"Children?" She took several deep breaths. "I'm not a child, and I'm not asking to be entertained."

"Good. I think we'll get on well enough." Byron released her hands, and she slipped into the car.

Byron pulled into his space in the underground parking complex and sat in silence. He knew that behind the floppy-brimmed hat and oversized sunglasses, Sarah was enjoying a morning nap. He studied her profile, the sharp nose and cheekline, then rolled down his window and lit a cigarette. He would wait until she woke. Patience was a virtue he had learned to cultivate.

Byron Lloyd had grown up hard and quickly, without a father and without money. He had learned to survive by using his back, his wits, and his patience. Patience had been the most difficult. He had worked and studied. He had let his contemporaries enjoy their rebellion against what they would be in a decade. He knew what he wanted. Power.

Byron had worked for his position in Haladay Enterprises. He had traded his youth for it. He knew hundreds of people on a first-name basis, thousands less intimately. He trusted only two without reservation. One of them was Byron Lloyd.

He shifted and drew deep on his cigarette. It was not often that he thought of the past. There was something about Sarah that had reminded him. Perhaps it was that she radiated what he had once passed over: youth, innocence. Yet he saw in her what he had seen in himself: ambition, a thirst for power.

For a moment he studied her profile again and remembered what he had felt when he had first seen her. Desire. It had been instant and sharp and unexpected. There had been times he had lain with a willing woman and not felt a need as keen as he had felt then. He had slept with dozens of beautiful women, imaginative women. He had had his first at sixteen in the cab of a Haladay pickup. The night before, he had slept between satin sheets with a concert pianist with clever fingers and full, milk-white breasts. He had enjoyed her, used her, given her pleasure. She meant no more to him than the long-ago girl in the cab of a borrowed truck. Throughout his life Byron had never mixed emotion with sex. To do so would have invited complications he had no time for. He varied the women he slept with and generally avoided those he worked with. He respected his secretary for her intelligence and capabilities, saw that she was well compensated, and never considered taking her to bed.

Byron knew about Sarah's relationship with Benedict and thought about the fact that she had taken only one lover during the past year. They had not been living together, so she would have been free to enjoy other men. Byron drew meditatively on his cigarette. *Loyalty.* A useful trait, he decided, particularly if it extends to other areas.

The report in his files on Sarah was inclusive. She would have been appalled and angry had she known of its existence.

To Byron, the report was a tool, nothing more. He would use it as he would a slide rule or a calculator. But it contained facts only, and was, therefore, incomplete. Byron's files didn't include Sarah's feelings, her thoughts and fears, her dreams. For all his knowledge of her credit rating, political affiliation, and shoe size, the woman beside him remained a stranger, a stranger who would not fit comfortably into any pattern.

"That was great."

Byron turned his head to watch Sarah stretch. Her shoulders came up, then circled down in one slow, luxurious movement. Pulling off her sunglasses, she sent him a smile. The nap had mellowed her mood. "How long have you been politely waiting for me to resurface?"

"Not long." He noted that she dropped the glasses into her purse without reaching for a mirror.

Sarah sighed and stifled a yawn, grateful that both the headache and the fatigue had vanished. "I haven't made a very auspicious start, have I?" It was more a statement than a question or apology. "Am I fired?"

"You're not on company time yet." He leaned across her to unlatch her door. It was her scent, he discovered, some melding of wildflowers, which had been teasing his senses all morning. Desire washed over him again. He felt it flare even as he saw the recognition of it in her eyes. On impulse, he, a man who never surrendered to impulse, lowered his mouth to hers.

Sarah had been expecting the kiss. She had even anticipated its hard demand, its confidence. What she had not expected was its effect. Without a moment's hesitation, without a moment's thought, she was clinging to him. The kiss was hungry from the first touch of lips. There was no testing, no initial exploration, but an instant understanding. Tongue met tongue. Sarah moaned as the kiss grew deeper. He caught her bottom lip between his teeth, bringing her a quick thrill of pain, a sharp shaft of need. The muscles in her thighs went lax as she felt the ache spread from her stomach until it tingled in her fingertips. There was more here than she had ever imagined, more passion than she had known was available to her. This was the agony of pleasure that had never touched her. This was the missing ingredient whose absence had made Benedict more friend than lover. Wanting more, she ran her hands up his back until they gripped his shoulders.

There was nothing soft about him. His body was taut, his mouth bruising hard. There was no comfort here, no easy enjoyment. Here was danger and excitement. Every other kiss she had known was bland in comparison. Abruptly, Byron ended the kiss and stared down at her. In his eyes she saw no question, no answer, only her own reflection.

"You know," he murmured and ran his hand down from the curve of her shoulder until it cradled her hip, "if we'd gone to your hotel first, we'd be making love now."

"What a pity you're so efficient."

He lifted his brows at her blunt honesty. A wisp of hair fell over her brow. He resisted the urge to brush it away. "Perhaps it's for the best. I don't think going to bed is a wise way to begin a business association." His tone was conversational now.

Still vibrating, Sarah was careful with her words and her inflection. The kiss had been more intimate than any loving she had ever known. The intensity of her own desire astonished her, but she was not naive enough to make a present of her thoughts. She arched a brow. "No, I'm sure you're right, but then you did initiate it."

"Agreed. You're a very beautiful woman and very much aware of your effect on men."

"Perhaps." Sarah watched his brows lift and slipped from the car. She stretched again as she stood, waiting for Byron to join her.

"We'll take the private elevator," he announced as he slipped a key into the slot. A single door slid open.

"Very handy." Sarah stepped inside and took quick note of the deep red carpeting and smoked-glass walls. "I had noticed the doors in your office, though they're very well concealed in the molding. Who else has access?''

''Mr. Haladay.'' Byron pushed a button on the front wall, and the doors closed silently. ''The car runs up through my office and his. There's an entrance on each floor, but a key is required to release them. It also goes to the vestibule in the penthouse. I keep an apartment there. It's more practical than making the drive every day.''

''Are you always practical, Mr. Lloyd?'' She was smiling, but she shook her head before he could speak. ''No, don't tell me, I'd rather find out for myself.''

Byron pressed another button. The elevator began to rise.

Chapter Three

THE DOORS OF THE ELEVATOR SLID OPEN. As THEY stepped from the car into a wide hallway, Byron took Sarah's arm.

"I'm sure you'd like to meet Cassidy, as you'll be working with him directly. He's in charge of the Architecture Department and your immediate supervisor."

John Cassidy. In quick order, Sarah ticked off six of his most important buildings. The Peoples' Building and Trust in Seattle remained her favorite because of its basic simplicity and strength. Yes, she thought as she let Byron lead her, I very much want to meet John Cassidy.

At the end of the hall, double glass doors separated at Byron's touch. Sarah brought herself back to the moment. In the center of a large reception area sat a sprawling desk occupied by three phones and one woman. She had beautifully full white hair waved away from an angular face. New England cheekbones, Sarah mused, admiring them and the pearly luminescence of the woman's complexion. The smile she gave them was polished.

"Good morning, Mr. Lloyd." Sarah heard Katharine Hepburn flow through the woman's voice. But unlike Kate, there was no searing wit in the woman's eyes.

"Good morning, Mrs. Fitzwalter." Byron nodded as he paused in front of her desk.

What are you doing here, Sarah? she demanded of herself as she glanced around the tastefully decorated, antiseptic room. What the hell are you doing here? Moving up, she reminded herself. With my bridges still smoldering behind me.

"I'd like to see Cassidy if he's free."

"Yes, Mr. Lloyd." Mrs. Fitzwalter's voice was coolly professional. "He's in his office. Please go right back; I'll ring through."

As they crossed the room and passed through another set of glass doors, Sarah turned to Byron. "She's very efficient, isn't she? That sort of person rather terrifies me."

Byron glanced down at the green eyes. "I doubt that."

Sarah grinned. "Perhaps 'baffles' is closer to the truth. My secretary at Bournell giggled and dyed her hair."

Byron made a noncommittal sound and threw open a door. There was a new impression of space and clutter, confusion and tobacco. Sarah relaxed.

"Ah, Byron, so you've brought her."

A thick-armed, wide-bellied man with a florid face and shocking red hair came across the room. He wore a plaid shirt, wrinkled slacks, and scuffed Hush Puppies. He looks, thought Sarah, like a leprechaun who's taken up weight-lifting. She liked him on sight, forgetting for a moment the genius behind the gnomelike grin.

"Sarah Lancaster," Byron began. "John Cassidy, chief architect."

"Hello, Mr. Cassidy." Sarah smiled into a face as round, hairless, and chubby as a Botticelli cherub's. The scent of tobacco seemed to float around him.

His handshake was warm and firm. "Welcome, Sarah Lancaster. What do you think of our department?"

"This is only the first stop on the tour," Sarah said. "But so far I like what I see."

The candor of her stare flustered Cassidy. He cleared his

throat and continued. "Glad to hear it. You'll hear I'm a hard man and rightly so. Nothing is built in the Haladay name except the best. There'll be times I have to fight that one for you." Cassidy waved the back of his hand at Byron with avuncular affection. Sarah was surprised to see a smile warm Byron's face. "He is an engineer, after all."

Sarah felt the easy flow of affection between the two men. It puzzled her, as there seemed to be so many intrinsic differences between the two. "I've tried not to hold it against him," she said.

With a chuckle, Cassidy approved her. He turned and lumbered to a drafting table. "Come," he invited. "Have a look. This one's my baby. A man can't administrate all the time. Dries up the juices." He settled himself with a few sighs and wheezes on a high stool. Sarah peered over his shoulder. The drawing was half completed but already revealed a simple dignity, a solidity, a permanence.

"Do you have the sections?"

Cassidy let out a rumbling laugh. "Caught your eye, has it?" He winked at Byron over his shoulder. Sarah was too involved to notice.

"You've heard of J. T. Orwell?" Byron asked as he crossed the room to join them.

"Publishing," Sarah muttered as she concentrated on Cassidy's drawing. With the one word she summed up a two-hundred-million-dollar empire.

Byron watched her. She was completely absorbed by the drawing. He could feel her eagerness.

Cassidy's gaze roamed over both man and woman, then dropped to the drawing. "This is the J. T. Orwell Memorial Hospital." He scratched a point just under his chin, considering. "The site's in his hometown in Illinois. You'll have to wait to see the sections until you report for work."

"Bribery's a crime, Mr. Cassidy," Sarah murmured. The one-dimensional skeleton of the building called for further study, but she brought her eyes back to his.

"Is it?" Cassidy gave her a bland, broad-faced smile. Yes, definitely. She would do.

Sarah was still thinking of the drawing as they passed by Mrs. Fitzwalter and through the glass doors. "I'll show you your office," Byron offered and steered her to the right.

"Ah yes." Sarah brought her attention back, then tilted her face to his. Her look sharpened a moment. Byron noted two faint lines appear between her brows. "He's very fond of you."

"You sound surprised."

"I am."

The simple honesty of the two words left no room for comment. Still, they annoyed him. As they passed, a door opened and out strode every woman's image of the California dream. Tall, bronzed, blond, with a surfer's body in a Brooks Brothers' suit, he paused and shot Sarah a grin. The grin was casually sexy.

"Sarah Lancaster, Evan Gibson. You're associates."

"So, this is the new architect from the east." Evan took her hand, giving it an extra squeeze. His eyes moved quickly down and up, so quickly, it might not have happened at all. Sarah felt the assessment. Careful, she thought and gently freed her hand. This one's not as harmless as he looks.

In his cheeks were creases that had been dimples in his early youth. His eyes were blue, but paler than Byron's. As though, Sarah thought, two or three shades had been washed away. Though his suit was impeccable, there was a looseness, an informality about him that was not in Byron. His grin said *trust me,* while Byron's eyes said *keep two paces back.* Though Evan spoke to Byron, he kept his eyes on Sarah. "Have you been giving Ms. Lancaster the grand tour?"

"The small one. Ms. Lancaster's a bit tired after the flight. The grand tour will have to wait."

Sarah decided that the time to state her independence had

come. She never permitted anyone to talk around her. "Ms. Lancaster," she said dryly, "is starving due to the time change and a sub-edible airline breakfast. Can I interest anyone in a hamburger?"

Both men shifted their eyes to her, but before either could comment, the doors of the private elevator slid open. The man who stepped out was tall, perhaps three inches more than six feet. He had the shoulders of a halfback and the chest of a Brahman bull. Sarah's first impression of Maxwell Haladay was of strength. Pure strength. His hair was white, growing thick and brushed back from a high brow. There was a trim mustache. His eyebrows were two heavy horizontal black lines. There were fine, spreading lines from his eyes to his temples, and deep creases on either side of his mouth. His skin had the bronzed, ageless look of the very wealthy.

Sarah felt Evan come to attention. In Byron, she sensed no change whatsoever. She concluded that he came to attention for no one.

Haladay stopped in front of them. He neither smiled nor spoke. His eyes narrowed fractionally as he made a long, careful survey of Sarah. Maxwell Haladay was closing in on his seventieth year, but he looked ten years younger. Power suited him, she thought. Observing the nose, which had been knocked out of alignment some fifty years before by a fist, and the thin scar along his temple, she decided he had earned it. No one had handed success to Maxwell Haladay. She liked him for it, respecting the broken nose more than she would have respected capped teeth.

"Maxwell Haladay, Sarah Lancaster." Byron paused briefly in the introduction, letting his eyes rest on Haladay's. "Your new architect."

Haladay turned his attention to Sarah. "The one we stole from New York." His voice was like a gravel pit, deep with rough edges. To Sarah, it was instantly appealing. She smiled and extended her hand.

"I'm very pleased to meet you, Mr. Haladay." The hand

that enveloped hers was thick and beefy, but the skin was surprisingly dry and smooth.

"I've heard that you're ambitious and smart." His eyes slid briefly over to Byron. "I like people with brains and ambition. One without the other is annoying. Why aren't you married?"

"Is that an offer?" she returned and heard Evan gently suck in his breath. Haladay's laugh echoed down the hall.

"This one's got guts as well as brains," he said to Byron. "She might give you some trouble."

"No doubt," Byron said mildly.

"I'll give you a week to settle in, Ms. Lancaster, then I'll see you in my office. Finish showing Ms. Lancaster around, Gibson." It was the first remark Haladay had made to Evan. "I want you upstairs, Byron." Without waiting for agreements or good-byes, he turned and walked back to the elevator.

Byron turned to Sarah. "Report to Cassidy in the morning," he told her. "It might be best to check in with Personnel before you leave today."

"All right." Sarah nodded. "I'll do that."

"If you have any problems, let me know." Turning, he moved down the hall to join Haladay. The elevator doors clicked closed. Inside the car the men exchanged a look before Byron pushed the button for the fiftieth floor. They did not speak.

A formidable man, Sarah thought. Two formidable men, she corrected herself. Tucking a stray wisp of hair behind her ear, she turned again to Evan. "Tell me, Evan, is Mr. Haladay always like that?"

"Always. He never changes."

Sarah said nothing, remembering the age in Haladay's hands. She felt a quick surge of regret. *Time.* With all of his power, all of his money, all of his vitality, he still couldn't beat time. She shook off the feeling and recalled that her first impression had been one of strength. For the moment she wanted to believe that Maxwell Haladay and all he stood for were indestructible.

Evan took her fingertips in his hand.

"I hope you weren't busy, as it appears I've been dumped on you," she said.

"I've been waiting a lifetime to be dumped on like this."

She withdrew her hand. "In that case, you won't mind showing me my office." She shifted her purse to the other hand and glanced around. "Then maybe we can talk seriously about that hamburger."

Obligingly, Evan led her down the hall. He began to calculate how long it would take him to get her into bed. Sarah began to calculate how long it would take before she was given her first big assignment.

Over the next few days Sarah learned the routine of Haladay's Architectural Department. During this time she did not see Maxwell Haladay at all and saw little of Byron. Most of her working hours were spent with Cassidy or Evan Gibson. She found Cassidy kind, but demanding and volatile as well. The words "nine to five" meant nothing to him, and a lunch break was a luxury that could be dispensed with if a project required attention. When he stopped treating Sarah as a woman, which took about a day and a half, he relaxed the restraints on his language and his temper. Sarah appreciated his imaginative cursing, enjoyed the bite of his temper, and was grateful for his informality. Invariably, he looked wrinkled and smelled of tobacco. Sarah came close to adoring him within the week. He was also undeniably brilliant.

Understanding Evan took little time. He was good looking, talented, and spoiled. Women came easily to him, and he was as devoted to the game of pursuit and conquer as some men are to golf. Sarah came to understand quickly that Evan thought all women fair prey. His attitude would have caused her to dislike him intensely had he not redeemed himself by his good humor.

With Evan, Sarah shared a secretary, a small redhead with an amazing amount of freckles and an index-file mind. She had been christened Marguerite Jean Childress, but had been Mugs since childhood. She was efficient, reliable, and prompt. She wore her hair in a friz that drooped into her eyes, bit her nails, and read trashy paperback novels on her breaks. Sarah wouldn't have traded a dozen Kays or Mrs. Fitzwalters for Mugs. With her help, Sarah soon had a working knowledge of the file system, the phone system, and company politics.

Relocating, Sarah discovered, was a long and complicated process. For the fourth night in a row she left her office after seven. She spotted Mugs slouched at her desk, a paperback with the dubious title of *Wild Nights in the Laundromat* in one hand and a half-eaten banana in the other.

"Mugs." Sarah balanced her briefcase on the corner of the desk and waited for her secretary to drag her eyes from her book. "You didn't have to stay."

"That's okay, Ms. Lancaster." Mugs gave her a cheerful smile, then blew the fringe of friz from her eyes. "I didn't mind. You might've needed something."

"It's Friday night," Sarah reminded her with a quick glance at her own watch. "You must have a date."

"Sure." Mugs grinned. "Jerry's picking me up downstairs; he's in Accounting. Just pizza and a movie, no big deal."

For a moment Sarah envied Mugs her Jerry from Accounting with his pizza and movie. With a sigh, she picked up her briefcase again. "Come on, get started on your weekend. I've got to get up bright and early and renew my search for an apartment."

"Did Personnel give you a list?" Mugs asked as she swallowed the last of her banana. She dropped the peel in the trash, the book in her purse, and rose.

"Yes, but so far . . ." Sarah trailed off with a shrug.

While Mugs began switching off lights, she moved to the door.

"Let's have a look."

Sarah tugged the list from her case as they walked toward the elevator. She glanced at the door to the private car and wondered if Byron was up in his penthouse. He wouldn't be alone, she mused, then frowned at the path her thoughts had taken.

"This one," Mugs stated, drawing back Sarah's attention. She pointed one unpainted, uneven nail at an address on Sarah's list. "That's the one for you, Ms. Lancaster. Take my word for it." Mugs pushed the button for the elevator before handing the paper back to Sarah.

"I'll go there first tomorrow," Sarah promised Mugs. Suddenly she was tired. The thought of a long quiet evening by herself seemed inviting. She heard the rumble of the rising elevator and turned back to Mugs. "Mugs," she began in a curious tone. "What exactly can happen in a Laundromat?"

Mugs rolled her eyes from floor to ceiling. "You wouldn't believe it, Ms. Lancaster. You just wouldn't believe it." They stepped into the car while she thumbed through the pages.

Sarah had been focusing her search for an apartment on the center of town. The core of the city, the noise, the traffic, were familiar. On the edges of Phoenix stretched wide, baked lands. The mountains were distant. Between them and the city was the desert; open, dry, empty. There were buttes and canyons, caves and cacti. Warm colors, space, quiet. To Sarah, the transition from east to west had been enough to adjust to. She was not ready to confront the vastness.

She had known a suburban childhood. As an adult she had lived in one of the most populated cities in the world and had thrived on it. In her life there had always been crowds of people and almost constant motion. Thinking the desert would be too empty, too quiet, too still, Sarah decided to avoid it.

Though the apartment complex Mugs had recommended was closer to the outskirts of town than Sarah would have liked, she decided to take a look. Already she had located and rejected six possibles on her list and was willing to move on someone else's suggestion. Still, as she walked down the hall toward the vacancy, she was far from optimistic. Why should this one be any different? It would either be too small or too big and the oven would be a reject from 1952. Sighing, she jingled the keys in her hand. She paused for a moment in front of 612, then tossed her hair over her shoulder and thrust the key in the lock. After pushing open the door, Sarah stood on the threshold in silence.

"God bless Mugs," she murmured and leaned on the jamb. The empty room was drenched with sunlight. Oak-planked floors and freshly painted walls bounced rays generously back and forth. On the south wall was a wide glass door that led to a balcony with black wrought-iron railings. Sarah could see it crowded with pots of flowers and tangled with vines. No drapes, she decided, letting her eyes roam to the windows. Shades . . . bamboo or wood slats. With a quick calculation, she estimated the area of the living room to be ninety square feet. Her footsteps echoed hollowly as she entered and wandered through it. The west corner of the room was a pool of light. A latticed breakfront would separate her working area from the rest of the room. She pulled a measuring tape from her purse, tossed her purse on the floor, and began to plan. She saw bookshelves lining the north wall, her maize mat spread on the floor. As she measured wall space and window length, the room became hers.

"Jesus Christ, you're beautiful!"

Sarah whirled around. In the doorway was a tall, slim woman in faded denim cutoffs and a T-shirt. Her legs were long and slim and tanned, her feet bare, her toenails painted dark copper. Her elfin face was framed by a curly mop of russet hair. Sarah saw something of both Puck and Titania and was intrigued. Her eyes were heavily mascaraed, cloudy gray, and uncompromisingly assessing. "Thanks. Come on in," Sarah invited, allowing the measuring tape to dangle from her hand.

"Just look at that hair. It's a sin for all that to belong to one person!" The woman entered, her movements quick and energetic. She made a circle around Sarah. "Goddamn size seven with hair right down to your buns." She put her hands on her straight hips and shook her head.

Sarah grinned and waited for the inspection to be completed.

"Well, there might be an advantage in all this."

Amused, Sarah met the shrewd gray eyes. "You think so?"

"Yeah. I can take care of your overflow. The men you can't handle can just slip across the hall." She grinned engagingly. "I'm Dallas Darcy." She stuck out a slim, long-fingered hand. "Are we going to be neighbors?"

"Sarah Lancaster." The handshake was firm and warm. "Yes, I think so." Sarah tossed the measuring tape over her shoulders. If the apartment had not already decided her, the woman facing her would have. "I haven't even seen the bathroom yet, and I'm in love."

"I'll play guide," Dallas offered, then turned and moved to the hall at their right. "The bath's through here. Please try to keep up with the tour and feel free to ask questions. This is a Haladay building, so we have only the best in pipes and porcelain." She opened the door to the bath and gestured. "I should know, I'm a loyal employee."

"No kidding? So am I. That is, I'm an employee. I don't suppose I could be considered terribly loyal after a week." She turned the tap and watched hot water steam into the sink.

"What department?" Dallas leaned on the door and

concluded that should the occasion arise, she could probably fit into Sarah's clothes without too much of a struggle.

"I'm an architect." Sarah turned off the tap.

"Oh." She separated the word into three syllables, low, then high, then low again. Sarah was to learn that it was her response for a variety of situations. "So you're the one." Straightening, Dallas ran a hand through her curls. They sprang back in the same disorder. "I'd heard we were getting some talent from the east. New York, isn't it?"

"Mmm." Sarah slid open one side of the double-doored medicine cabinet, found it empty, then closed it. Dallas repeated the procedure on the other door. In the mirror their eyes met and held. There was no measuring this time, but a mutual appreciation.

"You're supposed to be brilliant," Dallas accused. "Brilliant people give me nothing but trouble."

"Vicious gossip," Sarah assured her, then turned away to find the bedroom. "Is there anything in the lease about wallpaper?" she asked. "I really want to paper some of these walls and part of the ceiling in here. What department are you in?" She pulled the tape from around her shoulders and handed one end to Dallas. "Here, hold this." She measured the space between the closet door and a window.

"I really hate to tell you this so early in our relationship. I'm the procurement manager. Everyone hates the procurement manager."

Sarah wound up her tape and made a sympathetic purse of the lips. "Oh, surely not everyone."

"Everyone. Creative minds have no appreciation for procurement procedures."

Sarah grinned. "It's a dirty job, I imagine." She stuck the measuring tape in the back pocket of her jeans.

"Oh, filthy," Dallas agreed cheerfully. "I love it." They passed through the living room on the way to the kitchen. "I suppose you'll be working closely with Evan Gibson."

"Hmmm . . ." Sarah stopped the mental arrangement of her furniture and looked up at Dallas. "Do I detect a note of interest?"

Testing a window, Dallas sent her an engaging grin over her shoulder. "I've been working on Evan Gibson for over a year. Maybe I should try candy and flowers. Could be he's old-fashioned."

Sarah gave Dallas her long, thorough look. "You're entirely too intelligent for Evan, and he's entirely too dull for you."

The look and the comment surprised Dallas into turning completely around. "I have this weakness for fantastic bodies, white-toothed grins, and sun-streaked hair," Dallas confessed. "Fun and games and good sex. Others prefer the dark, mysterious type."

"Like Byron," Sarah concluded as she finished her inspection of the oven. Self-cleaning.

"*Byron?* Jesus, don't tell me you call him that face-to-face?" Scandalized and impressed, Dallas hoisted herself onto the counter as Sarah prowled through empty cupboards. Her long legs dangled.

"That's his name. What else should I call him?"

"Oh, I don't know." She shrugged her thin shoulders.

Sarah pulled open the refrigerator door but her mind drifted back to the man she had thought of too often that week. What is it about him? she demanded, shook her head, and slammed the door. "What do you call Mr. Haladay?" Sarah asked, turning back to Dallas. "Imperial Leader?"

"I don't call him anything at all. I simply lower myself into the prostrate position as he passes by."

"Must be hell on your hosiery bill."

"I'm going to like having you for a neighbor." Dallas linked her fingers and stretched her arms to the ceiling. "I don't suppose you picked up any nifty clothes while you were in Gotham City?"

Sarah took another moment to study Dallas's gamine

face. Sometimes friendship requires no time at all. If I had special-ordered her, Sarah thought gratefully, she couldn't be any more right. "I have a Halston that makes even the most hardened critics lust after procurement managers."

"Oh my God." Dallas slid from the counter and grabbed Sarah's hand. "Let's go sign your lease and start unpacking."

Chapter Four

Maxwell Haladay had started at the bottom of the ladder. He was, in fact, fond of saying that he had dug the footings for the ladder. At the age of thirteen he had quit school and taken a job mixing cement on construction sites. It was a hot, tedious job that required sheer brawn and did nothing to tax his intelligence. For hour after hour, six days a week, Haladay blended sand, mortar, and water for sweaty, tobacco-spitting bricklayers in southern California. Even at thirteen he had been shrewd with a dollar and with his time. In between batches of cement Haladay had done odd jobs for other laborers. He had watched carpenters and electricians and learned to separate those who had a craft from those who had a job. When engineers or architects came to the sites, Haladay found a reason to be close by. He listened, absorbing their terms just as he absorbed the more earthy terms of the laborers. He learned quickly and he remembered.

For four years he roamed from building site to building site. By the time he was seventeen he had reached his full adult height and weight and had moved up to bricklayer. No one questioned him when he claimed twenty-one years. He was six foot three, two hundred and twenty-five pounds, with shoulders like a tank. Who would have questioned?

Haladay gave part of his wages to his mother to help maintain the house they rented on the outskirts of L.A. He had never known his father and had never felt shame at the term "bastard." Instead, he appreciated the fact that it meant he belonged to no man and, therefore, was obliged to no man. A man had slept with his mother and given him life. Haladay was certain he could handle the rest on his own. His successes then would be his, and only his, just as his failures would be. He didn't plan to have many of those. From childhood, he believed that a man was master of his own fate. As soon as he was able, he set out to prove it.

As he approached the end of his teens, Haladay was big and handsome. The fair, rosy skin he had inherited from his Irish ancestors was bronzed dark by the California sun. He was smart enough to use his tongue to avoid a fight and strong enough to use his fists when necessary. He gained a reputation as a good-natured brawler who wasn't afraid to work for a living. He slept only with prostitutes, as he wanted no emotional entanglements or accidental offspring. He gained a lasting respect for women in business.

He had been eighteen when he had gone to work for Farmore Construction as a mason. Farmore watched him, saw that he had brains and the ability to command, and gave him more responsibility. Haladay asked for more money and got it. He struck up a friendship with the bookkeeper and learned from him. The only thing he regretted at this part of his life was his lack of formal education and the knowledge that it was unavailable to him.

The Depression hit. The building industry, like everything else, was thrown into chaos. Through the lean, desperate years Haladay worked for Farmore when there was work and hustled odd jobs wherever he could. Haladay learned how to live tight and how to make an extra dollar at a time when extra dollars were fantasies. When he wanted a woman, he did without supper. He lined the bottoms of his shoes with newspaper and made do. For a month one summer he worked as a bouncer in a grimy roadhouse and earned the thin scar that Sarah had noted on his temple. A broken bottle and six stitches.

During the Depression, Haladay had lived more in the future than in the present. He saw that in a time of hopelessness, fortunes could be made by men who had brains and guts. He had both.

He invested small sums from his savings in a still shaken stock market. His mother ran off with an out-of-work musician and disappeared from his life. Alone, Haladay moved from the rented house and slept on a bench in Farmore's office. The money he saved in rent, he invested. From time to time he ran whiskey over the Mexican border. He kept his mouth shut and invested the profits. In 1932, with the end of the Great Depression in sight, Haladay had turned his hard-earned savings into five thousand dollars.

He let his money ride. While his contemporaries watched the racing forms, he watched the stock market quotes. By the time he was twenty-five, he had amassed over ten thousand dollars. He saw his chance and took it. In 1935 Maxwell Haladay bought Farmore Construction, married a local beauty named Laura Winters, and began to build his empire.

Decades and two hundred million dollars later, Haladay sat in his mahogany-paneled office. There was an early Picasso oil on the wall, a Rodin sculpture in an eighteenth-century curio cabinet, and half a dozen bottles of Napoleon brandy in the bar. He wore a charcoal-gray suit hand-tailored in fine, soft wool. His shoes were Italian leather, costing more than he had earned the entire year of 1929. His watch was gold and Swiss, his tie silk and French. Still, Haladay was thinking more of the future than the present.

"I want them to break ground on schedule next week," he barked into the phone. "If there's any problem, send it to Legal and have a report on my desk in the morning. Stupid bastards," he grumbled as he hung up. "Why are there so many stupid bastards in the world?"

"Didn't you say once it was the stupid bastards who held

the world together?'' Byron spoke idly as he flipped through a thick contract.

''What kind of bullshit is that?'' Haladay frowned and crushed a peppermint between his teeth.

''Your kind, Max. I don't like this phrase in paragraph eight. The wording'll have to be cleaned up.'' Byron circled the offending phrase before he looked up. His eyes were calm as they met the fierce green ones. Maxwell Haladay was the other person Byron trusted without reservation. ''The construction on the Ridgefield project is going well. The work's on schedule, and so far, within budget. You might want to fly to Chicago and take a look. Maybe it'll improve your mood.''

''Smart-mouthed young son of a bitch.'' Haladay grumbled again, but the corners of his mouth twitched. He stroked his mustache to conceal it. ''You know I don't give a shit when a project's on schedule and within budget. It's the ones that're off schedule and over budget that keep the blood pumping. Without the screw-ups my arteries would be like grade one cement.''

Byron leaned back in his chair, relaxed and without his usual cool reserve. Could Sarah have seen him now, she would have found him less of an enigma.

''Tell you what,'' Byron said. ''Why don't you take a look at the cost overruns on the hotel in Madrid? I've got to fly out and nail someone's ass to the wall as soon as things are tallied on this end. Perhaps you'd like the pleasure.''

''I gave up carpentry when I made my second million.'' His brows lowered, however. ''How bad are the overruns?''

''Bad enough.'' Byron glanced back down at the contract. ''You'll get a report.''

Haladay pursed his lips in thought. ''Madrid, Madrid. Wasn't there a dancer in Madrid? Rosa, Isabelle? Nice ass.''

''Carmen,'' Byron corrected as he made another note in the margin. ''A singer. But you have the rest of it right.''

"My memory is infallible."

"And selective."

Grinning, Haladay answered the buzzer on his desk. "I've always admired your taste," he added to Byron. "Yes," he growled into the speaker. "Sarah Lancaster?" He paused and met Byron's eyes again. "Yes, send her in. Stay." Nodding, Byron put aside the contract. He straightened in his chair. Both stood as she entered.

Sarah's first impression when she walked through the door was that for two men who looked so dramatically different, there was something essentially the same about them. It was, she decided, the air of command. There was a tangible force that seemed to flow from both. I'd hate to come up against both of them at the same time, she reflected. Winning would be impossible, survival doubtful. She decided that if there were ever a need to attack, she would divide them first.

"Good morning, gentlemen."

Haladay returned her smile; Byron ignored it. His look acknowledged her but stopped short of a welcome.

"I hope this is a good time, Mr. Haladay. You did say a week."

"I did indeed." He gestured for her to sit. "How are you settling in?"

"Quickly. I'm already used to Evan's coffee." And to evading his advances, she added silently. She sat in a buckskin-colored leather chair, noting out of the corner of her eye that Byron settled in its twin. "Mugs has briefed me on office routine, Cassidy's drilled me on procedure, and I'm anxious to get to work."

"In a hurry to start, are you?" Haladay leaned back in his custom-made chair and watched Sarah over laced fingers.

"Yes." Sarah leaned back and crossed her legs. Fleetingly, she thought it odd that the man sitting beside her intimidated her more than the man behind the desk. Because I can understand him, she realized. I can see who he is. I

47

don't know who Byron is. She pushed him out of her thoughts. "I hate being in between projects. I've never had patience with intermissions."

"I see." He narrowed his eyes. "I'd like to ask you a question, Sarah."

"Of course, Max," she replied so casually that it took him a moment to react. His brows lifted, furrowing his forehead with deep grooves. Sarah waited, keeping her eyes steady. Abruptly, he tossed back his head and roared with laughter. Sarah let out a long, quiet breath.

"She's got as much nerve as you," he told Byron. "And nearly as much as me." He grinned at her. "We're going to do well together."

He added in a more businesslike tone, "All right, Sarah, what do you want to do?"

"To build."

"For me or for yourself?"

Fair question, she thought. "You own the art gallery, Max, but I want to paint the pictures. I want my signature in the corner."

"Good enough." He liked her directness. He nodded, then the lines deepened in his forehead again. "I get top-quality work from my staff. Haladay buildings stand on that reputation. *My* reputation." Sarah heard the stress on the pronoun. "Materials are always, without exception, first grade. Building codes are followed to the letter. There's no skirting the law. If I find out any member of my organization hasn't followed the rules, he's out." Haladay ran a gold pen through his fingers as though it were a cigar, then impatiently put it down on the desk. "There's more to this than avoiding fines or bribes. It's a matter of pride. As long as I run Haladay Enterprises, there are no kickbacks, nothing under the table."

Sarah folded her hands. "I don't have any problems with your standards, Max. I have my own."

He studied her for a moment before he shifted his eyes to

Byron. Sarah saw the look pass between them, quick and private. "Byron will speak to Cassidy about a project."

"Good." Though her nerves began to flutter, she pushed ahead before she could be dismissed. Keep the momentum going and pretend you're absolutely sure of herself. She acted quickly on her own advice. "Your bid's been accepted on the Delacroix Center in Paris."

Haladay brushed at his mustache with his forefinger. Byron recognized the gesture and knew he had been taken by surprise. "You're well informed."

"I realize, of course, that there's a great deal of legal work to be cut through—contracts, schedules, penalty clauses and whatnot. It should be about three months before the project gets to the drafting stage." Deliberately she turned to Byron and spoke to him directly for the first time. "Is that about right, Byron?"

His eyes were impassive as they studied her. "That's about it."

"I want to design the theater." Once it was said, Sarah felt more at ease. She let the silence build around her.

"That's a very big, important project." The furrows in Haladay's brows deepened.

"I know." There was a touch of arrogance in her tone.

"We have a staff of architects in our Paris branch."

"I know that too. But the Paris branch is considerably smaller than the Phoenix, and your chief architect there is involved in another extensive project in the south of France."

"Is there anything you don't know?" Haladay demanded.

Sarah smiled serenely, shifted in her chair, and recrossed her legs.

"You also undoubtedly know that Byron handles assignments of this nature," Haladay said with a trace of irony.

"Yes, I know. I thought it best to mention the matter now, as I expect you'll both want to think about it." Rising, she added blithely, "Have a nice day, Max. Good-bye, Byron." She walked swiftly from the room, leaving a faint scent of wildflowers in her wake.

As the door closed behind her Byron stood. "I'd like to talk with her."

"Are you going to give her the project?"

"Is that what you want?"

Haladay again picked up the gold pen on his desk and scowled at it. "We agreed I wouldn't interfere."

"I'll get back to you," Byron said. He overtook Sarah in the corridor. Surprised, she turned to face him. "You've impressed him," he said without preamble.

"Have I? I only said what I felt."

"It's not what you said as much as that you had the nerve to say it. You're quick and you've got guts. Max admires both."

She had done it. It was over . . . for now. She remembered that she had yet to discover Byron's weakness. "And you, Byron, what do you admire?"

A moment passed as they watched each other. Then he surprised her by giving her one of his rare smiles. "Corot paintings." He took her arm and began to walk again. "I owe you a lunch."

Sarah acted on impulse. Demurely, she tilted her chin to the side, slid her eyes to his, and looked up from under her lashes. "Is that an invitation or an observation?" They were both aware of the meaning and the power of the look and she waited for his reaction to it. A ghost of a smile parted her lips. Byron thought of the taste of her mouth and the smoothness of her skin. Desire shot through him and he pushed it aside. If he took her, he was determined that it would be in his own time on his own ground.

"It's both," he stated as he punched the down button on the elevator. "We'll stop by my office. Kay can let your secretary know you'll be out."

Chapter Five

O NCE SEATED IN A CORNER BOOTH OF THE PHOENIX Hilton, Sarah slipped off her shoes. Out of the office Sarah was inclined to think of Byron as simply a man and not as one of the upper echelon of Haladay Enterprises.

Her eyes paused a moment on lobster salad. "Is the quiche good here?" Glancing up, she found him studying her. Sarah propped her elbows on the table, cupped her chin in her palm, and stared back. "What do you see?"

"That you have a remarkable face."

"So do you." She felt he had spoken with more spontaneity than was his habit and was pleased. "I make a study of faces," she told him. "Your bone structure's good. Is it Indian or Celtic?"

"My mother's Navajo." Byron's voice was expressionless, but as he reached inside his jacket for his cigarette case, his eyes remained on hers. He expected one of the familiar responses: speculation, curiosity, patronizing comments, or the withdrawal he remembered from his youth.

"That explains it." Sarah folded her menu and set it aside. "I'm supposed to get my cheekbones from some wild Celtic strain. Now, about the quiche."

None of the responses Byron had anticipated would have

occurred to Sarah. "The quiche is good here," he told her, and signaled the waiter.

Sarah watched him as he ordered the quiche and chose a Chablis. His manner was smooth. She found she admired him for it more because she sensed something unrefined underneath. Something reckless in his eyes made her want to dig beneath the surface. She wanted to sort out Byron Lloyd and learn what made him different.

He is different, she mused, listening with half an ear as Byron spoke to the waiter. *Smooth and calm on the outside, but there's something bubbling underneath. I wonder if he takes orders as well as he gives them.* She thought of Maxwell Haladay and frowned. There was an intimacy between them, an understanding that required no words. For a moment she wondered who really ran Haladay Enterprises. Byron turned, catching the look of frowning concentration on Sarah's face. He lifted a brow and waited for her to speak.

"I'm wondering who you are," Sarah told him. "I'm wondering what you are."

He smiled, and his smile was a challenge. *Find out,* it told her. *If you can.* "Are you settling into your apartment?" he asked after a pause.

"Yes, I'm beginning to." The Chablis was brought to the table, poured, and tasted. She let it rest a moment, cool and dry, on her tongue. "My furniture's being sent over tomorrow. We've been doing some redecorating in the evenings."

"We?"

"Dallas and I. Dallas Darcy, your procurement manager." Byron had a vague recollection of a tall woman with a mop of fox-colored hair. "She likes my swag lamp but insists I add some local pottery. My decor, it seems, is entirely too eastern." *And so am I,* she thought on a quick flash of homesickness.

"You miss New York." His statement brought her eyes

back to his. Sarah moved her shoulders restlessly, annoyed with herself.

"I've learned in the past few months that I don't acclimate to change quickly."

"Acclimating easily wouldn't suit you."

"I suppose you're right. I do like to feel in control. We have that in common."

"Is that why you want to head the Delacroix project?"

Not answering immediately, Sarah twirled the stem of her glass between her fingers. She watched the liquid dip and sway. She had known he would ask sooner or later. Her eyes lifted and locked on his.

"I want the Delacroix project because I know I can do it, and I know I can do it well. At Boumell I was treated primarily as a designer. More accurately, as a glorified decorator. I'm an architect, Byron, and a goddamn good one." Sarah paused a moment, then deliberately set down her glass. "I was given the assignment on the Unitarian Church Max admired because I had a friend who pulled some strings." She let out a quick, impatient breath as her distaste reflected on her face. "I never like admitting that."

"No, I can see you don't." Byron scanned her face. "Why did you?"

"Because we're going to be working together. Because I want you to understand." Her second statement had been spoken before Sarah had realized she had had the thought. "Boumell would never have given me that job if I hadn't been asked for specifically. I knew the project was perfect for me, and I knew it was the sort that would gain me recognition. I was hungry. I used a connection."

"It's been done before." Byron's answer was calm, in direct contrast to the temper that flared in Sarah's eyes.

"I know that, but I don't have to like it. Damn it, is that the only way I'll ever build anything important? The general consensus at Boumell was that I was young and had plenty of time. But that wasn't all; I had three strikes against me. I'm a woman, and women are primarily designers. I'm young, and youth lacks discipline and judgment. I'm considered attractive, and there are still plenty of idiots who believe that if an attractive woman advances in business it's because she's sleeping with the right people."

"You have a point, but it doesn't apply at Haladay. Max doesn't consider that brains have a gender."

"Yes, I've heard that." After a long breath she leaned on the table again. "That's one of the reasons I wanted this position. Listen, Byron, we both know the strides women have made in the professional and business worlds, but architecture is one of the last male-dominated strongholds." Her brow furrowed again. "I didn't study architecture to prove a point."

"Why did you study it?"

"Because I want to build. I want to make buildings that serve not only aesthetic purposes but practical ones, buildings people can live with and enjoy."

"Sounds reasonable."

Byron paused in the act of pouring more Chablis into her glass. Her eyes when he met them were friendly and generous.

"I've been waiting for a project like the Delacroix Center. I know you have a great many things to consider before you assign the architect, and I don't expect to get the assignment simply because I asked for it. But if I'm good enough, and I am, and if I earn it, and I will . . . I want it."

"You don't lack confidence, do you?"

"I can't afford to." Sarah shrugged. "I'm impatient."

"Are you confessing a fault or a virtue?"

"Your choice," she said and added a lightning smile.

"You were thinking of opening your own firm when we contacted you." Byron watched the smile fade away into surprise.

She wondered how much the man across from her knew

about her. This, she thought, was something I hadn't bargained on talking about. She swallowed some wine, then stared into the glass. "I had come into some money," she began in a steady voice, but her fingers tightened on the stem of the glass. "My parents were killed, and there was some money from the insurance." Her stomach muscles knotted and pain flashed in her eyes. Such a neat, tidy little check, she remembered. Pay to the bearer all that's left of James and Penelope Lancaster. "I considered opening my own firm or perhaps finding a partner. I probably would have done one or the other if I hadn't gotten the position at Haladay."

"Why did that change your mind?"

"I had to choose between my vanity and my profession. Working for Haladay, I know I'll be designing real buildings. Working for myself . . ." Sarah shrugged. "Who knows if anything I conceived would ever be fact? I'm a good enough gambler to know which is the best hand."

"It appears you don't run strictly on impulse after all."

Her laughter was quick and warm. Briefly, Byron's eyes lingered on her mouth. He remembered her lightning response to his touch. He caught himself wondering how she would look with her hair down and her clothes off.

"Impulse, ambition, ego . . ." Sarah continued. "I think both of us have our share. Still, we're both working for him, aren't we?" Her lips curved as she brought her fork to them. "You were right about the quiche, Byron. It's marvelous."

Sarah's office had a good southern exposure. To decorate the glass wall behind her desk, she had hung plants at varying levels. Sunlight streamed through the clear glass, bursting through empty spaces and filtering through leaves.

The walls of her office were covered with white-on-white paper. The carpet was a pale green. She had taken down the full-length drapes when she had hung her plants and felt less hemmed in without them. Here and there, she had added touches of her own to what was otherwise a coolly efficient room. There was a deeply etched black vase for a glass-topped table, a jarring Dali print matted and framed, a long narrow mirror. A bowl of multicolored gumballs sat on a high stool and a delicate Dresden shepherdess posed on a single shelf. The office was now as uniquely hers as her apartment.

Cassidy paced from plants to Dali, from gumballs to Dresden. He moved with his hands locked behind his back and his head bent, hair flopping over his brow. His breath puffed in and out with each step. Occasionally he wriggled his fingers. Sarah sat at her desk and watched.

"The rich are a mystery, that's the truth. Why Harrison Reed needs a guest house when he lives in a fifty-room mausoleum, I don't know. Not to mention the poolhouse we built for him five years back. It's big enough to house a family of four with a dog. Show people!" He made a series of clicks with his tongue. "But then, it's his money. It's a small project, Sarah, but a good one for you. Five bedrooms, three baths, living, dining, and game rooms. It's all in the file." He waved a hand toward the manila folder on her desk. "They're photos of the site, and some of the main house. Jesus, what a place! It makes me shudder to think of it. He says he wants to keep the guest house simple." Cassidy snorted. "Simple to that crazy bastard means ten Grecian pillars instead of twenty." He blew a stream of air through his nostrils.

Sarah enjoyed watching Cassidy run through his paces. She had listened to his words and enjoyed his theatrics. Now she shifted her attention to the folder on her desk. Opening it, she leafed through the photos. "Don't worry, Cassidy. We'll give Harrison Reed exactly what he wants." She glanced at the two shots of the main house and turned to the pictures of the site. "I'll work up some preliminary sketches, then fly out to California and discuss them with him. I want to see the site firsthand."

"Have Mugs make the arrangements," he told her with a

brisk nod, but at the door he paused and turned back to look at the blonde head bent over the photos in the file. His face puckered into a frown. "Watch out for Reed, Sarah. He gobbles up little girls like you for breakfast."

Sarah glanced up. There was genuine concern and a touch of embarrassment on Cassidy's face. She smiled. "Don't worry about me, Cassidy. I'm tough. He won't get past the first nibble."

Cassidy made a quick hooting sound before he pulled open her door and lumbered out. Sarah forgot the warning as the door shut behind him. Rising, she went to her drawing board. It might not be Cassidy's hospital or the Delacroix project, but it was a start. She propped the shots of the site on a shelf at eye level, half closed her lids, and stared at them. A good start. She picked up her tools.

For the next two hours Sarah sketched freehand. This was the time she could let her mind flow; creating, imagining. The thinking on paper . . . doodles, drawings, bits and pieces of her own concept of a guest house on a woodsy little site in southern California. She could see the space, the division of it, the filling of it. There were no complicated technical problems to solve. It was a simple project. She could make no specific calculations until she had seen the site and Harrison Reed firsthand.

Of the four sketches she had completed, Sarah already had a favorite. Now she had to make it Reed's favorite as well. She decided to take ten preliminary sketches with her, feeling that if a client was given plenty of choices, it was easier to lead him to the right one. With a hard look at the photos of the site, and another at her own sketches, Sarah had no doubt which was the right one. As she spread out a fresh piece of paper, her buzzer sounded. She pushed the intercom with one hand, sketching with the other.

"Yes, Mugs."

"Mr. Lloyd's here with Mrs. Woodloe-Winfield."

"Who?" Sarah stopped sketching and gave Mugs her full attention.

"Mr. Lloyd's here with Mrs. Woodloe-Winfield."

Sarah frowned and set down her pencil. "Do I know who Mrs. Woodloe-Winfield is, Mugs?"

"No, ma'am. I don't believe so, but I'll be glad to get that information for you."

Sarah's laugh was quick and appreciative. "For the moment, just send her in."

Wondering what anyone named Woodloe-Winfield had to do with her, Sarah slid off her stool and back into her shoes. Woodloe-Winfield sounds like a little old lady with blue-tinted hair and a Gucci bag, she thought as she buckled the ankle straps on her shoes.

She had been right only about the Gucci bag, she saw, when Mrs. Woodloe-Winfield entered with Byron. The blue-tinted hair of Sarah's imagination turned out to be a soft, strawberry blonde framing a young, heart-shaped face.

"Good morning, Byron," said Sarah.

"Good morning, Sarah. Gloria Woodloe-Winfield, Sarah Lancaster. Gloria is an old friend in need of an architect."

"Byron, good's so much kinder a word than old." Gloria's voice floated lazily over vowels.

Sarah instantly disliked her, then struggled against the unfavorable first impression. "Please, sit down." She waited until Gloria was seated in an armchair, then, seeing that Byron would remain standing, opted to sit on the corner of her desk. "How can I help you, Mrs. Woodloe-Winfield?"

"Why, I . . . perhaps you could explain it, Byron." Gloria laced her fingers and crossed her legs.

"Gloria was widowed last year and left with a four-hundred-acre ranch," Byron said. "The ranch house no longer suits her needs. She wants a smaller home built on a lot nearer town."

"A cozier house, if you know what I mean." Gloria gave

Sarah a girl-to-girl smile. "There are too many rooms and too many memories in the old house. I must begin to put that behind me."

"Of course. Perhaps you'd give me an idea of the type of house you have in mind? The size you want, the type of living and entertaining you plan to do, any firm preferences you have as to style or materials."

"Oh my," Gloria said plaintively. "I just don't know a thing about it. Why don't you draw something for me?"

"Now?" Sarah narrowed her eyes.

"That's what you do, isn't it?" Gloria smiled. "Draw things?"

A quick surge of temper rose and was swallowed. Professionalism was important to Sarah. "It's not possible to draw anything viable, Mrs. Woodloe-Winfield, unless I have an idea as to the type of house you have in mind." It was hard for Sarah to keep sarcasm from her tone; she was sure Gloria's ignorance was a pretense. "Once I know the size you'd like, the number of rooms, the location and topography of the site, we can move from there."

"Oh dear, that all sounds so very technical. Don't you have little pictures or samples?"

"Perhaps you could give me a better idea as to what you're looking for?" Sarah asked patiently.

"I've simply no idea about buildings." A helpless gesture with her hands was combined with a melting glance toward Byron.

Sarah shot her a straight uncompromising look. "You might find the Renaissance period appealing. Or perhaps Gothic, French Gothic with a flying buttress." Sarah caught Byron's warning glance. The hell with him, she decided. "I've always had a soft spot for Art Nouveau. Of course, I could just let my own creative juices flow and create a home for the woman I perceive you to be." She smiled, seeing that she had made her point. "Now, how many rooms had you in mind?" She picked up a notepad and waited.

"Six bedrooms, three baths, with a dressing room and additional bath off the master." She added a parlor, maid's room, and summer kitchen.

"That's very helpful," Sarah said. This time there was no disguising the irony in her tone. "I'll need to see the site, then we can discuss precisely the best location for the house. Is it already landscaped, or do you plan to have it done?"

"You'll be working with Dutch Kelly on that," Byron said coldly. "He'll be in touch with you."

Sarah ignored the irritation she saw in his eyes. *I was justified*, she told herself, *and I'd do it again.* "Fine," she said aloud. "I'll check out the site and have some sketches ready next week."

"Well." Gloria looked down at her perfect nails. "I suppose if you can't work any faster, that will have to do."

"I appreciate your patience." Sarah contrived to sound humble and sarcastic at the same time.

Gloria rose and held out a hand to Byron. "Now I'm certainly ready for that lunch you promised me. I've done enough business for one day." She turned to leave.

Sarah rolled her eyes to the ceiling. Over Gloria's head, Byron watched her. "I have one or two things to discuss with Ms. Lancaster. Why don't you wait for me in my office?"

"Don't be too long," Gloria admonished, rising on tiptoe to kiss Byron's cheek. With an excuse of a nod for Sarah, she glided from the room.

"Do you make it a habit to be rude to clients?" Byron asked when the door had closed behind Gloria.

"I'm sure," Sarah said mildly, "I don't know what you mean."

"The hell you don't."

"Why, fiddledeedee, Rhett." Sarah flounced to the window, tossed her head, and batted her eyes. "No gentleman uses that tone with a lady."

If he had not been so angry, Sarah's uncanny mimicry of Gloria would have amused him.

"I'm not dealing with a lady, I'm dealing with an architect."

"Your point." Sunlight dappled around her as she fiddled with the leaves of a spider plant. "All right, Byron, I'll give your little southern transplant her Arizona Tara. I'll even manage to make it cozy because I'm very good at what I do. But I'm not an illustrator, and I'm not in mass production." Her temper began to surge again, springing into her eyes as she turned to face him. "If she wants model home 321A, she's come to the wrong place."

Byron's voice became cooler, a dangerous sign. "Mrs. Woodloe-Winfield is simply not aware of how your profession operates."

"Oh, bullshit," Sarah interrupted. "She doesn't have to know the technicalities to know you can't order a house the way you do a side of beef or a pair of drapes." She crossed the room until she stood toe to toe with him. "She's not as air-headed as she pretends, and we both know it. You saw through that I-need-a-man-to-guide-me act. If your ego needs that sort of thing it's your problem. Go play macho with Miss Scarlett and let me get on with my job."

He took her arm as she started to turn away. The pressure caused her to suck in a quick breath of air. He took a step forward, and she retreated as far as his grip would allow. The fury in his eyes alarmed her. There was a violence in him she had not expected.

"Don't give me orders." The warning whipped out at her as he tightened his fingers on her arm. Sarah's heart hammered. "I don't take orders. I don't tolerate comments on my personal life, and no one turns her back on me."

Their faces were close, their bodies just touching as he held her still. He watched fear flutter in her eyes. Cursing himself, he released her arm. It had been a long time since he had come that close to losing control.

He saw that she was pale and that her hand had reached for the spot where he had gripped her as if to restore circulation. It occurred to him that her arm was slender and that he had held it tightly enough to insure bruises. Her eyes were dry as she glared at him, but her breathing was ragged. He cursed himself again, vigorously.

"We don't beat employees for insubordination these days, Sarah." He was pleased to see color flow back into her face. "That's better." He gave her a nod of approval. "I don't like to use intimidation."

"What a pity," she tossed back. "You're so good at it."

Byron turned and walked to the door. "You've got a busy week ahead of you," he said brusquely. "You'd better conserve your energy."

"Engineers!" The word exploded from her as he opened the door. Outside, Mugs lifted an eyebrow.

"I'll expect sketches in ten days." He closed the door firmly. A few moments later the door swung open again and Dallas strode in.

"Ready for lunch? I've been starving in the other room waiting for you to get rid of Mr. Lloyd. Hey, you look fit to kill. I guess I better forget the idea of talking you into buying lunch."

"Byron Lloyd," Sarah said by way of an answer, "is an arrogant, officious bully and a rotten son of a bitch."

"Of course he is, love. That's why he's at the top." She glanced in the mirror, brushing at disordered curls. "He's also got a great body, or haven't you noticed?"

"So does a 1966 Corvette." Sarah reached for her purse from the bottom drawer of her desk.

"I suppose this is a bad time to charm you into fixing me up with Evan." She watched Sarah's expression in the mirror, catching the quick squint that meant she was about to do something she disliked.

"Dallas," Sarah began carefully, "Evan's nice enough, but he's superficial."

"Everything I see on the surface looks terrific. I'm not

interested in thoughts on nuclear energy or his preference in twentieth-century novelists.'' She sent Sarah a grin.

"How long have I known you, Dallas?'' Sarah asked.

"About three weeks.''

"Practically a lifetime.'' Crossing the room, Sarah stopped when they stood close, but continued to speak. "Evan's mind isn't broad enough for yours. He'd never appreciate you.''

Dallas considered a moment. "Possibly not,'' she conceded. "I might just have to give up the idea of marrying him and having his baby. Can I settle for dinner and a night of wild passion and mindless sex?''

A sigh of frustration escaped Sarah. He'll hurt her, she thought, and already felt responsible.

"I'm indestructible,'' Dallas told her, reading her eyes. It touched her that Sarah would care, and once again she smiled. "Impervious to pain. Do you see this spot here?'' she demanded, touching a forefinger to the inside of her left elbow. "This is the only part of my entire body that isn't invulnerable.'' Her heavily lashed gray eyes laughed as she saw Sarah smile. Pressing her advantage, she turned and linked her arm through Sarah's. "You wouldn't want me to pine away night after night, alone in a dark, cheerless apartment with only reruns for company, would you?''

"Okay, you win.'' Blowing out a swift breath, Sarah accepted defeat.

"I knew you'd see it my way.'' Dallas patted her cheek and began to lead her from the room. "Now what did Mr. Lloyd do to rile you so?''

Chapter Six

IT WAS JUST PAST FIVE WHEN SARAH FINISHED HER sketches of Harrison Reed's guest house. They satisfied her. Her reward for her lingering temper was a nagging headache. When Sarah argued she liked to win. With Byron she had lost hands down. His potential for violence had taken her by surprise. She would be prepared the next time, and not so easily frightened. She didn't enjoy the picture of herself cowering before angry eyes and a few harsh words. Not my style, she told herself as she reached beneath the collar of her blouse to rub at the tension. Forget it . . . better, she corrected herself, forget *him*. Sarah lifted her interoffice phone, but before she could speak into it, Evan Gibson strolled through her door.

"Greetings, fair lady. Your workday is done."

"Not quite," she countered mildly as he walked over and perched on her desk. "You'll have to learn to knock, Evan," she told him. Then, because matchmaking for Dallas made her uncomfortable, she dove in quickly. "How do you feel about redheads?"

"I'm partial to blondes." Evan reached over to pinch a loose strand of her hair between his thumb and forefinger.

"But you haven't any prejudices, have you?" Sarah gave him a winning smile. "I hope not, because I know the most delightful redhead. I might just be able to convince her to go out with you." Her eyes were guileless and friendly. Maybe they'll be good for each other, she thought. "Yes, I probably could," she continued out loud. "Dinner might be a good idea. She likes Chinese."

"Sarah." Evan enjoyed the way her blouse draped over her breasts. For a moment he allowed himself the pleasure of imagining himself taking it off her. "I want to spend time with you. We can start with dinner."

"Oh no, I like Italian," Sarah said quickly. She scrawled on a pad, tore off the sheet, and handed it to Evan. "I'll give you a good recommendation," she promised. She pushed Mugs's signal. "Damn, isn't Mugs at her desk? She doesn't answer."

Evan scanned the name on Sarah's note, then stuck it in his jacket pocket. "I sent her home." He bent his head a moment to study the drawings scattered on her desk.

"You might have checked with me first." Sarah frowned at the top of his head.

"Oh, sorry. Did you need her?"

Sarah shrugged. It was too much of an effort to be angry. "It's nothing. I can make the call without her." She began to search through the file for Harrison Reed's number.

"Nothing's so important it can't wait until tomorrow." Moving behind her, Evan slipped his hands onto her shoulders. His thumbs ran lightly up the nape of her neck.

"One or two things," she mumbled, absorbed in the file. She was caught totally off guard when he dragged her up from the seat.

His mouth was on hers so quickly, so passionately, Sarah had no time to act. The heat of the kiss surprised her. She had known he wanted her, but hadn't realized how intensely. At first, stunned, she didn't struggle.

He ran his hands down her once, swiftly, then found the zipper of her skirt. Sarah felt his fingers and managed to free her mouth. "Evan," she said breathlessly. "Time out." Her continued struggles ultimately caused him to stop

65

and look down at her. Realizing that she had placed herself in a dangerous situation, Sarah cursed herself. "I'd like you to let me go now."

"I'm going to make love to you."

His voice was unsteady and caused her to experience her first trickle of real alarm. "No, Evan." She kept her tone calm and quiet. "You're not." Her hands were on his chest, and she gave it one hard push. After breaking away, she put the desk between them. "Evan, I'm sorry." She shook her head, then pushed at wisps of loosened hair. "I shouldn't have let that happen. I have no intention of letting it go any further."

"I didn't think you were the type to play games, Sarah."

"I'm not." Her voice was firm now and cool. "I hope you aren't going to play the fool and start chasing me around the desk." Her words stopped him cold.

"Goddamn it, Sarah. You know where to plant your foot, don't you?"

"Evan, I'm—" The door swung open and Cassidy burst in.

"For Christ's sake, where is everybody?"

"Doesn't anyone knock anymore?" Sarah complained. Cassidy sensed the tension. Assessing the situation at a glance, he continued to bluster.

"I've been buzzing you for fifteen goddamn minutes," he told Evan. "You've got to fly to Boulder and smooth out some problems with the Martindale Lodge. Get your briefcase and grab an extra pair of shorts. Your ticket's at the airport."

"What's the problem?"

"You'll be briefed on the other end." Cassidy cast a meaningful look at his watch. "Your plane leaves in forty-five minutes. Get moving."

"I'm halfway there," Evan said. In the first instant his eyes met Sarah's, she saw the anger, then it was replaced by his more familiar charm. He gave her a brief salute and was gone. She sank into a chair, surprised at how deeply the incident had shaken her.

"As long as you're here," she said to Cassidy as she pushed at the papers on her desk, "you might like to see my ideas for the Reed house."

"Are you all right?"

Sarah glanced up. She didn't want to speak about Evan's behavior any more than she wanted to confess her own poor handling of it. Cassidy's eyes were too shrewd and too direct. "Yes." Her hands turned over and her fingers spread. "It was nothing."

"Bullshit." Cassidy stood on the other side of her desk, his thick arms folded over his chest, his chin lowered. Sarah sighed. "Evan got a bit out of line. Part of it was my fault."

Cassidy snorted. "I'll speak to him," he said.

"Oh no, please, Cassidy." With a quick shake of her head, Sarah rose. "Don't do that. We'd never be able to work together again comfortably." She pushed pins more securely into her hair, then found her shoes. Her nerves were already settling. Perching on the desk, she worked on an ankle strap while keeping her eyes on Cassidy. "Evan's ego's just a bit dented. He'll get over it. I could have handled it a lot better than I did."

Cassidy frowned. Gibson's brains are below his belt, he thought angrily. Goddamn nuisance worrying about screwing around when there's buildings to be built. "I won't speak to him. If," he added as she started to thank him, "you'll tell me if he bothers you again."

Sarah patted his cheek. "All right, Papa." When his wide face creased into a frown, she switched to an Irish brogue. "Mr. Cassidy, will you be defending me honor and keeping me pure?"

"You're a sassy one, you are, Sarah Lancaster. I'll wager there's some Irish in you somewhere," he muttered.

"Isn't there in all of us, Cassidy? And will you be escorting me to the elevator?" she asked and took his arm.

"Smartass," Cassidy grumbled, but his arm remained linked with hers as they walked from the room.

By seven that evening Byron had put in a twelve-hour day. Years of cramming a day's work and a day's study into twenty-four hours had toughened him. He knew he was a bit too serious, a bit too exacting. Circumstances had made him so. Brains and ambitions when mixed with poverty can be hell.

Byron had had no time for adolescence. He had broken into an adult world at sixteen and never looked back. He had known his first woman while his contemporaries were still struggling with bra hooks in the back seat of Chevys.

Maxwell Haladay had given Byron the things he needed to reach his goals: money and opportunity—and the most important ingredient, education. He had gambled on the boy and had watched his investment pay off in the man. From the beginning of their relationship, they had dealt with each other as adults. Still, one had never had a son, the other a father. They filled needs that neither was consciously aware of having.

Over the fifteen years of their association, Byron had developed a taste for good wine, French painters, and beautiful women. He was in a position that inspired petty jealousies, but his workingman's rise through the company had made him a folk hero among the rank and file while ability had gained him the respect of other engineers. He was at home with board members and bank presidents. But lingering always in the back of his mind were the years of poverty, of growing up as neither white nor Indian. The term "half-breed" can leave a scar even in the twentieth century. He had learned early that to succeed in Haladay's world, he had to control his emotions. His temper, set free, was brutal and dangerous. He kept it on a choke chain.

Sarah had come close to breaking the chain. He didn't like remembering the incident. He didn't like admitting that she had gotten past his guard more than once. Perhaps that was why he had lost his temper so quickly. He knew he had frightened her badly, yet she had not reacted as he expected a woman to. She had not run or wept or cringed, but had stared at him with fear in her eyes. He respected her for that, and for her immediate resilience.

As he rode the elevator to his apartment atop the Haladay Building, Sarah was still firmly entrenched in his mind. Though weeks had passed, he remembered the feel and taste of her mouth, the softness of her body, the scent that surrounded her. Women were not permitted into Byron's mind unless invited. Sarah was a gate crasher.

Byron moved directly to the bedroom when he entered his private quarters. It was a sophisticated room, yet warm enough to surprise some of the women who had slept in the wide-striped platform bed. The walls were an inky indigo blue. Bamboo blinds allowed the sun to filter through to a pair of thriving ficus trees. The floor was natural wood, polished to a high gloss and covered with one long Navajo rug.

Byron stripped quickly, tossing his clothes carelessly onto a chair before he moved to the adjoining bath. For fifteen minutes he stood in the shower, starting with the spray blistering hot and moving gradually toward icy cold. His muscles relaxed, and for the first time in twelve hours, so did his mind. After toweling, he pulled on a short silk kimono and walked back to the bedroom.

Lying naked on her stomach, her ankles crossed in the air, was Gloria Woodloe-Winfield. Byron hesitated for only a heartbeat, then completed the knot in the belt of his robe. "Hello, Gloria. How did you get up here?"

"I told the doorman downstairs that you were expecting me. He's seen us together." Gloria propped her head on the heels of her hands and allowed her hair to pour over her shoulders. "I wanted to surprise you."

"You succeeded." Byron moved to the built-in bar in the corner, then poured a brandy. He made a mental note to speak with the doorman. Turning back, he surveyed his guest from the bottoms of her feet to the crown of her head. Her skin was milk white, without a trace of tan lines. Her legs were short but well formed, leading to a rounded bottom and gently arched back. Her breasts were as full as her hips promised, and darkly tipped.

"Brandy?" he asked conversationally, then toasted her with his snifter.

Gloria rose languidly. She paused to toss her hair behind her back. Her round breasts swayed. She kept her eyes on his as she moved toward him.

"When Jack was alive, you wouldn't touch me. I never told you that I wanted you, because you were his friend. Jack's been dead for six months." She slid her hands up his kimono, resting her palms on the damp mat of hair on his chest. When she spoke again, her voice was husky. "I can't mourn forever, Byron. Jack wouldn't want me to."

Byron carefully removed her hands from his chest and took a casual drink, then set down his glass. "You didn't mourn six minutes much less six months. Jack took you out of a steamy swamp in Louisiana and gave you a handful of credit cards. All he ever wanted was to keep you happy and show you off. He was an old man with a weakness for toys. You stuck out a five-year marriage because you wanted to get your greedy little hands on the rest of his money."

Gloria lowered her eyes. She had wanted Byron too long to risk losing him now. She had spent nights sweating beside the old man thinking about Byron Lloyd. "Byron, please." Her lips brushed his chest where the panels of the kimono met. Just barely, she controlled the urge to run her tongue along his skin. Her fingers worked at the knot in his belt. "I've been so lonely. I need to be loved again."

With his hand, he jerked up her chin until their eyes met. "You've been *loved* dozens of times since you buried Jack, and undoubtedly a discreet few while he was alive. I've known hundreds like you."

Furious, she pulled back, but he grabbed her arm. Her

helpless, little-girl face was transformed by temper. The calm blue eyes were as hard as diamonds.

"You know what you are, Gloria. You should appreciate the fact that I know too and don't give a damn. In fact"—he pulled her closer until her breasts yielded against his chest—"I like you better without the act. You came here looking for something; let's call it what it is."

Her head fell back, and she tossed it to free her face of strands of hair. She smiled, and it was no longer innocent or helpless. She preferred it this way. She would rather be treated like a cat than a kitten. After five years of being an old man's fantasy, she wanted the excitement of being a young man's reality. "All right." She slipped her hands under the silk of his robe and ran her fingers down his ribs. "I came because I want you. I've wanted you for years, from the first minute I saw you. It's a well-known fact that you don't sleep with married women. I had to wait. Every time I took a lover, I pretended he was you. I dreamed about you and what we could do to each other. You won't be disappointed," she added in a whisper as her hands moved to his hips. "I'm really very good."

"I'll just bet you are," he murmured.

A narrow shaft of sunlight fell across her face. He watched her features become fine and delicate. Her lips grew fuller. Her eyes went from blue to melting brown streaked with green. The sudden scent of wildflowers threatened to smother him.

"Damn you," Byron swore. "Goddamn you." He buried his mouth against Gloria's throat and tasted Sarah.

Chapter Seven

DALLAS OPENED ONE EYE AND GLARED AT THE SUN pouring through her undraped window. Moving only her head, she glared at the alarm clock beside the bed. "Aw, shit." She rolled over, prepared to ignore both of them.

"Hey, Dallas." Dennis Houseman grumbled and removed the point of her elbow from his ribs. "Watch it, will ya?"

With a yawn, she propped herself up on her forearms and stared down at him. Dennis Houseman was sliding toward forty and had what she considered the perfect dash of gray spreading back from his temples. His face was nice, not gorgeous, but definitely nice with its square dependable jaw and wide forehead. Even asleep, without his horn-rim glasses and calculator, Dallas decided he looked like a CPA. He was what Dallas termed one of her standbys. She could always depend on Dennis for a meal or a movie and a night in bed. The one thing that separated Dennis from her other standbys was that he wanted to marry her and asked at regular intervals. Though she had no intention of obliging him, she was fond of him. They slept together three or four times a month during tax season and double that during the slack. The system had been in progress for three years and continued to appeal to Dallas's sense of humor.

He was not the youngest of the men she saw, nor the most handsome, nor the wittiest. Neither was he the best lover. Despite all that, he was her favorite. Looking down at him now, with sleep creases in his cheek and a night's growth of stubble on his chin, she tried to figure out why. He certainly didn't make her blood pressure rise like Evan Gibson, and he wasn't as expert a lover as the young Italian crane operator she had shared linguini and passion with the week before. He didn't have the IQ or the body of the assistant D.A. What he has, Dallas concluded as she blew a curl out of her eyes, is solidity . . . sweetness. In a burst of affection, Dallas decided to wake him up. She rolled on top of him, then bit his shoulder.

"Jesus!" His eyes snapped open with a look of glazed surprise. "Dallas, what the hell—"

She stopped his complaint with a long, intense kiss. He gave a quiet grunt as her tongue awakened his mouth, then his hands moved to the cheeks of her flat bottom. He was hard before he was fully awake.

"Hi." She lifted her mouth from his and smiled. Her angular face was pale without makeup, and her hair was disheveled. Naked, her body was all angles and straight lines, with the breasts of a twelve-year-old. Yet Dennis, as did a long line of other men, thought she was one of the sexiest creatures he had ever known. Her appeal was partially her total lack of inhibitions, her lack of apology. He was desperately in love with her, but realistic enough to know he would never hold her. He was also careful enough to hide his feelings, knowing that she would stop seeing him if she understood.

"What time is it?" he asked. He moved his hand up the long length of her back, then down again. Dallas snuggled up to him.

"The alarm's going to ring in fifteen minutes." The scent of their night together lingered on his skin. She bit his lip, then began to move her hands down his sides. "I promised to take Sarah to the airport this morning."

"Sarah?" He felt lazy and warm and continued to massage her bottom.

"The architect across the hall who I'm keeping away from you because you'd fall for her and toss me out the nearest window."

"In a pig's eye. If you'd marry me, you wouldn't have to worry about Sarahs across the hall."

Dallas recognized the seriousness in his tone, though he had tried to keep the words light. For a moment she was swamped with regret and buried her face in the curve of his shoulder. *This is a good man. What the hell's wrong with me?* She shut her eyes tight until the regret faded.

"I think you really mean it, Dennis," she murmured, flicking her tongue over his skin. She slid her hand between them and took him in her long fingers. "Show me."

"God, don't you ever wear down?" Already his breathing was shaky.

With a laugh, she opened her legs and slid down, taking him inside her so quickly that he could do nothing but groan and let her lead the way. When the alarm rang, he was fully awake, drenched with sweat, and exhausted. Dallas stretched her arms to the ceiling, gave him a quick kiss, and strolled off to the shower. There was, she decided, no better way to start off the day.

Within the hour Sarah was speeding toward the airport in the passenger seat of Dallas's garishly orange TR3. The top was down. The dry wind blew the driver's fox-colored hair back from her thin face, then up toward the sky. It pulled ruthlessly at the pins in Sarah's hair, but she leaned back on the seat, enjoying it.

"You really didn't have to do this," she shouted over the wind. "You're going to be late for work."

"Everyone cheers when the procurement manager's late for work." Dallas downshifted and took a corner with a scream of tires.

"God, Dallas, you drive like a maniac."

Laughing, Dallas turned her head, automatically pushing loosened hair from her eyes.

She looks terrific this morning, pleased with herself, Sarah decided. There could only be one reason. "You could get a job hacking in New York," she said aloud. "They're always looking for the odd maniac."

"It's the car." The road straightened and the speedometer hovered at ninety. "If I were driving a station wagon with wood-grained paneling, I'd never go over fifty, and I'd stop for a full minute at stop signs whether I needed to or not."

Sarah tried to imagine Dallas driving a station wagon. She failed. "I don't know why I have to bother with the airport," she commented as the needle on the gauge inched higher. "You could drive to L.A. as quickly as I can fly there."

"Don't tempt me. I'd love to get a firsthand look at Harrison Reed. Architects get all the breaks." She took her eyes off the road for a dangerous three seconds to scowl at Sarah. "You will remember everything, won't you?" she demanded. "And I don't mean about the house. I want to know what he looks like. *Really* looks like. Up close. I want to know the exact shade of his eyes, his shoe size, what he smells like, what he looks like naked. Jesus, I'm driving myself crazy!"

She threw a grin at Sarah before she continued. "I'm going to want details, my love, very specific, firsthand, nitty-gritty details. God, that marvelous voice. They say he won't speak a word before noon."

"They?"

"I read it in the gossip columns."

"Dallas." Sarah turned completely around in her seat. She was laughing as the wind yanked one of her hairpins out and tossed it onto the road. "You don't really read the gossip columns."

"Me? Oh no." Blithely, Dallas waved one hand in the air and steered around a curve with the other. "I just happened to catch a word or two when I was lining my birdcage.''

"I see." Sarah nodded. "I'll do my best on details, but I won't be there more than a few days. I doubt I'll be in the presence of the magnificent Harrison Reed for more than a couple of hours.''

"Do you have any idea what can be accomplished in a couple of hours?'' Dallas's grin widened as she recalled the productive ten minutes that morning. "They say he has a voracious sexual appetite. You'd better watch it, kiddo.''

She jerked the car to a halt in front of the main terminal.

"Thanks for the advice.'' Sarah slipped from the car, grabbing her briefcase and bag from the back. "And for the lift.'' She leaned toward Dallas a moment, keeping her voice low. "Watch out for cruising state troopers on the way back.''

"Why?'' Dallas's brows rose into her tumbled curls.

"They say they have voracious sexual appetites.''

"Yeah?'' Dallas beamed and put the car in first gear. "I better get started. Have a nice trip.'' She was off like a shot. Sarah watched her weave her way miraculously through airport traffic before turning to enter the terminal.

The air conditioning hit her like a wave. Shivering and wondering why no one was ever satisfied with a reasonable seventy-two degrees, she walked directly into Byron. People buzzed around them, the loudspeaker announced departures and arrivals, but she only stared up at him, losing herself for the moment in his eyes.

He had taken her arms when she had turned into him, and still held them lightly. Something about her surprised, absorbed look gave him a twist of pleasure. Something passed quietly in the silence, but neither acknowledged it. The entire incident seemed timeless but took no longer than ten seconds.

Byron broke the eye contact and allowed his gaze to run over her. "You look as though you've come through a wind tunnel.''

Sarah stepped away from him, feeling his brief hesitation before he released her arms. "I took the high-speed shuttle in from town. I didn't expect to see you here."

Byron reached for her bags. When she held firmly onto the handles, he glanced back down at her. "I'm not going to steal them, Sarah," he said. "I'm simply going to carry them for you."

"They're not heavy." They stood face-to-face, with his hands over hers on the handles. His palms were hard on the back of her hands, harder than one would think looking at him in the perfectly tailored black suit. Sarah blew the hair out of her eyes. "Listen, Byron, I'd just love to stand around and chat, but I've got a plane to catch. Do you mind?"

The loudspeaker announced the boarding of a flight to Houston. "The ticket for your commercial flight's been canceled," he told her. "We're sharing a company jet. I'll drop you off in L.A. before I go on to Madrid."

"Nobody told me."

"I'm telling you now."

For several seconds neither spoke. Byron noted that the rose deepened under her skin and the green in her eyes grew brighter. It occurred to him that he could fire her on the spot and get her out of his professional and personal lives. It occurred to him a moment later that he had no intention of doing so.

"Perhaps you'd rather walk to L.A. than sit in the same plane with me."

Sarah opened her mouth, then shut it again without making a sound. The smile started slowly, beginning in her eyes. "I'm sorry."

Both the smile and the apology disconcerted him. A moment passed before he realized that her hands had relaxed under his.

"I'll carry the briefcase," she told him. "It has all my vital possessions in it, like my hairbrush and metric converter." When her hands were freed from his, she

77

relinquished possession of her suitcase and took his arm to walk through the terminal.

On board, Sarah took a long survey of the main cabin. There was a thick blue carpet and oyster-white chairs, a long sofa and a built-in bar. All the comforts of home. Swinging back to Byron, she dropped her briefcase on the sofa. "It's very elegant. Very tasteful. No hot tubs, first-run movies, or live entertainment?"

"Only on the big jet we use for P.R." Byron gestured for her to sit. He waited until she was settled and strapped in before taking the chair across from her. With a flick of a switch, he signaled the pilot. Sarah heard the whine of engines and felt the surge of power under her feet. She glanced out the window to watch the takeoff. She loved the sensation of having the ground drop away below her.

"I heard you had some trouble with Evan Gibson."

Sarah turned quickly toward him. His face, as usual, told nothing of his thoughts.

"It was nothing." Damn Cassidy, she thought briefly. She changed the subject. "What's happening in Madrid?"

"Did Gibson make advances?"

"Oh, Christ, Byron, do you know how impossibly Victorian that sounds?"

Byron waited while the plane climbed and leveled off. "I asked you a question."

"Cassidy shouldn't have bothered you—"

"Cassidy knows he damn well better bother me."

"Byron, it was nothing. It was a misunderstanding. Evan . . ." She hesitated. "I hadn't made myself very clear, I'm afraid. Evan got the wrong impression."

Byron saw her nibble on her bottom lip. He remembered the gesture from their initial interview.

Sarah gave an exasperated sigh. "Please, Byron, drop it." She unbuckled her seatbelt and rose immediately to wander the cabin. He watched her jam her hands into the deep pockets of her skirt.

He stood, and her head tilted back so that her eyes would

remain direct. "If Evan makes a mistake like that again, I want to hear about it."

Sarah narrowed her eyes but before she could respond he surprised her by smiling. Then he walked into the adjoining galley. "Coffee?" he asked as he set up a percolator.

The smile totally undermined her. She walked to the doorway of the galley to watch him set out cups. "How many women have you charmed with that?" she asked abruptly.

Byron turned to face her. "Hmm?"

"With that smile." Sarah tilted her head. "The one you pull out so unexpectedly. It's a killer."

For a moment she thought he wouldn't answer, then his features relaxed. "I stopped counting." The humor in his eyes brought the instant response of her laughter. Shaking her head, she turned back into the main cabin.

"I believe you're a first-rate bastard, Byron."

"You are perceptive."

"I went out to the Woodloe-Winfield site yesterday afternoon to meet with Dutch Kelly. Gloria joined us."

"Was the meeting productive?"

"It took us three hours, but we decided on the positioning of the house." She thought back on Gloria's yes-no-maybe attitude. "Oh, yes . . . she wants two dozen azaleas. To remind her of her childhood.

"I've started on the drawings." As she spoke, Sarah absentmindedly ran her hand through her hair.

The pins securing the knot at her nape, already loosened during the drive to the airport, fell out. Her hair tumbled to her shoulders, then cascaded down her back and over her arms.

The words Byron had been about to say vanished. His hand reached out, then his fingers of their own volition buried themselves in the masses of her hair. For the moment he was totally captivated. Sarah felt a pressure in her chest, then realized numbly that she was holding her breath. Air shuddered through her lips as she released it. She had not expected to see need in his eyes. She had not expected to feel need in return. She wanted to touch him, to reach out to him.

Byron continued to look down at her, totally absorbed, her hair wrapped around his fingers. The fragrance of wildflowers overwhelmed him. It was then that he remembered how her scent had come to him while he was making love to another woman. He dropped his hands and stepped back. For the first time in years he felt foolish. The moment shattered like crystal. In frustration, Sarah watched the gap between them widen. Better this way, she reminded herself as she took a slow, steadying breath. Much better this way. "When will you be back from Madrid?" she asked.

"A week."

He turned back to the galley. The coffee was perking fretfully, waiting for attention. Sarah began to roll her hair into a fresh knot.

"Don't." Byron spoke from the doorway. Sarah turned to face him with her hands still full of hair. "Leave it down." He carried two mugs of coffee across the cabin, offering one as he stopped in front of her. "Please."

After only a moment's hesitation Sarah lowered her arms, then accepted the coffee. It was, she discovered, both hot and excellent. After a second sip she sat again, cradling the mug in both hands. "You make great coffee." In a fluid motion, she tucked her legs under her. "I use mine to clean furniture."

Byron sat down. "I saw your ideas for the Reed site. They're very good."

"Thanks. Cassidy thinks he's going to balk at the simplicity. I like to think I can persuade him." The beginnings of a smile touched her lips as she thought of the next phase of the project. She was going to enjoy meeting Harrison Reed. She caught Byron's look of inquiry. "I've given him the space he wanted. The outside's simply an envelope. Mine's the right one for the site and the purpose." Lifting her coffee, she sipped and watched him over the rim. "Which drawing did you like best?"

"Number three," he said. Sarah grinned. It pleased her that they had both chosen the same one.

"We might be able to work together after all," she said. Her mind leaped back to the Woodloe-Winfield project and Gloria. "I have some rough sketches for the W-W site. I should have something more refined for you next week. If you're not back, shall I deal with her directly?"

"It's your project."

The pilot's voice crackled over the intercom. Sarah slid her feet to the floor and pulled on her safety belt.

Later Byron watched from the window of the plane as she walked with her quick dancer's step toward the LAX terminal. Her hair swung loose over her hips. When he turned, he saw her hairpins on top of the leather-padded table. He lifted one and held it in his fingers a moment. He would have sworn her scent still lingered. Annoyed, he tossed the pin aside and signaled the pilot.

Chapter Eight

EVEN THE DIRT IN CALIFORNIA WAS CLEAN. AROUND her, as Sarah drove from the airport toward Harrison Reed's estate, the hills were a soft wash of color. The air was balmy, not dry like Phoenix, not close like New York. Southern California smelled green and lush—and wealthy. Sarah decided that before she returned to Phoenix she would whip into Beverly Hills to buy something outrageous and expensive for Dallas.

She liked being able to buy something outrageous and expensive now and again—and being able to rent the sleek little Mercedes for the trip from the airport to the site. Sarah enjoyed the financial rewards of her profession and, even more, she enjoyed dealing with an important client. Harrison Reed was a famous actor. She knew that if the guest house was admired, her name would be linked with it.

She was smiling when she pulled up to the tall wrought-iron gates of the Reed estate.

She disliked the gates on sight. They made her think of a prison. She slid from the car, slamming the door lightly behind her. A man stood on the other side of the gate frowning at her.

He was, she estimated, roughly thirty, just under medium height, swarthy and stocky in a sleeveless black T-shirt and tight jeans.

"Sarah Lancaster to see Mr. Reed," she said.

He stared suspiciously at her. "You the architect?"

He had not been hired for his manners, she reflected. She nodded.

Without a word, he walked to a small structure inside the gate. Through the window, his eyes remained on hers while he spoke on a phone. Seconds after he replaced the receiver, the gates soundlessly opened. He came to the doorway, made a come-ahead gesture with his arm, then somehow managed to hook his thumbs in the front pockets of his skin-tight jeans.

Sarah moved back to her car thinking fame had its price.

The road wound and curved through grounds thick with trees. There was a scent that she identified after a moment as citrus. It seemed that Harrison Reed had a grove of orange trees. Gently, the road came to a crest and then leveled off. It was here that the main house first came into view. Sarah put on the brake, turned off the ignition, and stared. It was worse in three dimensions than it had been in the photos. No wonder Cassidy had snorted. For a man with his sense of balance, the conglomeration up ahead was cause to weep. To Sarah it was a nightmare the snapshots had only half prepared her for.

The original structure, she noted, had a certain amount of ostentatious charm, but ells and wings had been added, sprawling up and sideways until the ridiculous became the grotesque. Closing her eyes a moment, she breathed in the scent of oranges. The image of the house was etched on the back of her lids.

"Damn," she muttered as she switched on the ignition again. She thought of the beautiful, clean sketches in her briefcase and stepped on the gas. "Maybe Cassidy didn't do me a favor after all."

She parked the car near the entrance and mounted two

levels of stone steps, then paused at the front door to use the large brass lion's-head knocker.

The woman who answered was dressed in a conventional gray maid's uniform and white apron.

"Ms. Lancaster."

"Yes." Sarah tried a smile. "Hello."

Silently, the woman backed up to allow Sarah's entrance, then immediately turned to walk on silent crepe-soled shoes down a wide hallway. After glancing at the enormous crystal chandelier and the curving staircase, Sarah followed. There were sudden archways and rooms with carved lintels shooting off here and there unexpectedly. The housekeeper made an abrupt right turn and took them into one.

"Mr. Reed will be right with you."

"Thank you," Sarah said as she moved in a slow circle around the room. She was both appalled and fascinated by its opulence.

There were low brocade divans with satin pillows piled in calculated disarray, heavy gold overdrapes with thin sheers at the windows, and a huge gilt-framed mirror over a white marble fireplace. Next to the fireplace sat a tall brass urn, ornately carved, containing sprays of peacock feathers. Sarah moved to the red velvet bar and, finding a bottle of vermouth, poured a glass. She was taking her first sip when Harrison Reed made his entrance. Sarah knew immediately that Dallas would adore him.

He wore buff-colored riding slacks with a wide-collared silk shirt full at the sleeves. He was trim and bronzed, with his famous mane of chestnut hair perfectly disheveled. His features were classic, made more appealing by deepening lines, his dark eyes as molten as she had seen them on the screen. He looked unquestionably closer to forty than the fifty she knew him to be. The fountain of youth, she decided, is money.

"You're Sarah Lancaster, my architect?" He didn't have

Promise Me Tomorrow

to affect the surprise in his voice. She was not at all what he had expected. "The last one Max sent me to do the poolhouse was skinny, middle-aged, and balding."

"Carl Masters," Sarah answered, recognizing the subject of his description. "He's working on a project in Washington State." She extended her hand, enjoying the craggy planes of his face. He did no less than she had expected by taking her hand to his lips. The gesture suited him.

"How fortunate for me."

"I hope you feel that way after you've heard my ideas." Skillfully she removed her hand from his. "I hope you don't mind," she added, lifting her glass. "The room seemed to call for it."

"Not at all. Please . . ." His arm movement was only slightly theatrical. "Sit down."

"Thank you, but I'd really like to see the site right away." After a last sip Sarah set the glass back on the bar. She sensed that he was accustomed to deference and softened her request with a smile. "I hope you'll have the time to discuss the drawings I've brought with me. I think you'll find what you want among them, but it's much easier to know what's needed after seeing the site. Can you show me now, Mr. Reed?"

"Harrison, please," he invited. Immediately he decided to take an active interest in the designing of his guest house.

Beyond the sloping lawns, past the clay tennis courts, out of sight of the circular pool and just before the stables, was a narrow plot of land flanked by a grove of orange trees. Sarah walked over the grass. Her hands were in her pockets, her eyes narrowed as she focused on producing an image of the guest house on the empty site. For the moment, Harrison Reed was forgotten entirely. She could see it already and knew she'd need only a few changes in the original freehand sketch.

Harrison watched her. He saw that he had been wrong to

85

think her simply young and attractive. She knew what she was about. He reminded himself that she worked for Max. Max doesn't hire age or looks, he mused. He hires brains. He grinned at the hip-length hair and slender carriage. The old son of a bitch probably never noticed that she has a terrific ass.

Sarah continued to walk around the site, oblivious to Harrison. She could feel the excitement growing out of the certainty that she could transform the empty space without destroying it. The front window would face west to catch the sunset, and the kitchen east to get the morning light, she decided.

Harrison. For the first time in ten minutes Sarah sensed him behind her. She hoped that she wouldn't have to convince him that he didn't have to build a basilica to make a statement.

"I know people who would kill for a plot of land like this. I'm one of them," she told him.

He followed the sweeping gesture of her arm. She saw that the lines around his eyes were more noticeable in the sunlight, but there were only a few wisps of gray through his hair. "Actually, it was my recently departed third wife who convinced me that this was the spot for a guest house."

From the cynicism in his tone, Sarah deduced that departed meant divorced and not deceased. "Then you have at least one thing to thank her for."

Harrison glanced down quickly at her tone, then broke into a grin. "There are others, I suppose."

Sarah tucked her arm in his and pointed into empty space. "It's perfect, Harrison. Can you see it? A little hideaway in old brick with a covered porch and a flagstone patio off the back. Lots of small sashed windows with shutters, white shingles on the roof, and smoke coming out of the chimney. And inside, oak floors and exposed beams; small, interesting rooms with lots of sunlight. A stone fireplace with a raised hearth on the north wall." Sarah raised her eyes as she spoke. He was following the gestures of her free hand, but his expression told her he was far from convinced.

"It sounds a bit primitive."

"Not primitive, Harrison," she corrected. She turned to face him fully. "There must be a lot of pressure in your work, in the lives of the people you know. Sometimes the answer is to forget all that and go for something simple and uncomplicated." Her eyes were serious as she studied him. "You know many people who are constantly surrounded by luxury. You could offer them something else."

Harrison studied her in silence, then said thoughtfully, "Let me see your sketches."

Sarah grinned, enjoying the taste of victory.

Later, standing barefoot on a rose-pink carpet, trying to ignore the matching canopy bed, Sarah put through a call to Cassidy in Phoenix.

"Well, Sarah. What's your progress?"

As his voice boomed in her ear, she cradled the phone on her shoulder. "I'm just about to have an afternoon swim and an iced margarita. How are you?" She adjusted the strap on her black maillot.

"I've just come out of a two-hour meeting with a group of engineers."

Sarah grinned but made a sympathetic noise into the phone. "Listen, Cassidy, Harrison is ready to sign a contract."

"How much gold leaf do we have to import?"

"Not an ounce." She was pleased with herself and took no pains to hide it. "It's to be a simple brick house, two stories. Outside dimensions thirty by thirty."

"No shit?"

Sarah laughed. "No shit, Cassidy. He's asked me to stay until tomorrow, and I'm obliging him. You can reach me at home if necessary tomorrow afternoon and Sunday."

"I wouldn't let a daughter of mine stay the night in that place," he grumbled.

His words brought Sarah a quick surge of affection. "Cassidy, stop worrying and take two Excedrin for the headache those nasty engineers gave you."

"Smartass," Cassidy mumbled before he broke the connection.

Grinning, Sarah replaced the receiver, grabbed a short white robe, then strolled from the room. It took her over ten minutes to work her way through the house and the grounds to the pool. Harrison was already there, lounging in a canvas chaise. He was, she decided with a glance at his trim, brown body, in astonishingly good shape. He rose at her approach and went directly to a portable bar that stood fully stocked under a striped umbrella. Sarah hadn't mentioned to Cassidy that her host had worked his way through a batch of martinis during their discussion of the sketches. Still, though she watched him critically, she could detect no sluggishness in his movements. She thought he was one of those rare creatures who could drink steadily and not become drunk. She wondered too if he was ever really sober.

"The lady ordered an iced margarita," he announced as she came up beside him.

"The lady did indeed," she agreed, accepting the cold glass. She sipped and approved. "Wonderful."

As she turned away to look at the pool and palm trees, Harrison studied her. She had less ample curves than the women who normally appealed to him, but there was something in the slender, almost boyish build that attracted him. He had thought her face exceptionally beautiful when he had first seen it, but now he recognized that there was more. This was not a woman who stood at a mirror and looked for flaws or perfection.

When she turned back to him, her hair swayed and caught glints of sunlight.

"You're in the wrong profession," he said as he took a step toward her. "I could make you a star."

Sarah laughed. "But I'm going to be a star, Harrison, in my own field." She was smiling as she took another drink, but he saw that she meant what she said. He had heard that tone, seen that look on the face of an actor beginning to climb. She'll make it too, he decided. He watched as she shed the robe and sat down.

"Where the hell did Max find you?"

Sarah was enjoying the sparkle of the sun on the water and the feel of its warmth on her bare legs. "New York," she answered, feeling sleepy and content. "I've always lived in New York."

Harrison downed his martini. "God, what a city." He shook his head. "I did some of my best and worst acting in New York."

"I saw you do *Richard II*."

"Christ, you must have been in diapers."

"It was only ten years ago. You were magnificent. I cried when you crowned Bolingbroke."

His eyes looked past her, then focused. " 'My crown I am; but still my griefs are mine: You may my glories and my state depose, but not my griefs; still am I king of those.' " He paused a moment, then stared down at his empty glass. "Ten years," he murmured. "Christ." He filled his glass again.

"You're still magnificent."

He glanced down at her, recognizing her sincerity. Taking her hand, he pulled her to her feet. "How old are you?"

"Twenty-six."

"Jesus, my son's older than you are."

Sarah laughed. "Harrison, I'm going to tell you the truth and hope you'll accept it. If you weren't a client, I'd very much like to go to bed with you. But since you are"—she paused long enough to take the martini glass from his hand—"I suggest we take a swim."

"Sarah." He sighed. "Max knows how to pick them, the old bastard."

"I'll tell him you said so," she promised.

The hotel suite in Madrid was quiet and elegant. The brandy in Byron's hand felt warm and smooth. The business that had brought him to Spain had been speedily and successfully concluded with only minor points to be tied up in a morning meeting. By noon the following day he would be on his way back to Phoenix. He felt no satisfaction. Instead he felt a restlessness, a need to slip away from his Haladay image. His eyes brooded as he sipped the brandy. He wanted something, and for the first time in his adult life, he was not entirely certain what it was.

As she walked in from the adjoining bedroom, Carmen studied him. She recognized the absorbed, private look on his face. She was well aware that there were many facets to the man and that he would allow her to know only a few. Her relationship with Byron was a long one, spanning years and other lovers. She knew, and was pleased, that she was closer to him than any other woman. Perhaps she came the closest to being his friend. She understood his drive and respected it because of her own ambition. Carmen had only one constant lover—her career.

In the ten years they had known each other, both had risen in their respective fields. Both were successful and both remembered poor beginnings. Neither had relaxed with success.

Moving to him, Carmen waited, then smiled when his eyes lifted to hers. "You're quiet tonight." Her face was arresting, with its dark eyes, full wide mouth, long nose, and prominent cheekbones. It had been painted over and over again. Her hair, the raven black of her country, was parted in the center and worn loose over her shoulders. The gold of her skin shone through the thin white silk of her lounging pajamas. She sat beside him and took the brandy from his hand and sipped. "Did you enjoy the performance this evening?"

"You were marvelous, as always. Your voice never ceases to amaze me." He watched Carmen's tongue trace the rim of the snifter. "I heard that you begin a tour of Europe next month."

"City to city, country to country. Fast, fast." Her shrug was typically Spanish. She smiled and sipped again. "New people, more people. More applause. Do people like you and me ever stop being hungry, Byron?"

His gaze passed over the cluster of rubies at her ears. "No," he said.

"No," she murmured as she sat back and looked up at the ceiling. "How long have we known each other?"

"Ten years."

"Ten years. *Dios,* no wonder I feel I'm constantly in a race. How well I remember the first night we were together." She made a lazy, languid movement. "I was singing in Barcelona. I still enjoy having you in the audience." Carmen laughed over the rim of the snifter. "And having you later." After setting down the brandy, she began to unbutton his shirt. "Did I thank you for the roses?"

"Yes, but you can thank me again." He wound a lock of her hair around his finger and remembered the feel of Sarah's.

"Caro." Carmen ran her hands over his chest, inching closer as his arms came around her. "You have a woman on your mind."

Byron found the zipper at her throat and pulled it down. Her skin was warm and pampered smooth. "You're right," he murmured against her ear.

She laughed quietly as she felt his lips move to her shoulder. "But, *caro,* the woman in your arms is not the woman on your mind." He stiffened, but she tilted back her head until their eyes met. "Ten years, you said, *querido.*

There are few illusions left between us." Carmen resisted the urge to ask for a name; instead she brought his hand to her lips. "I shall make you forget about her for a little while."

Her body was full and curved and magnificent. Byron reached for her. He knew her skin would taste like her scent, musky and dark. For the moment, that was enough.

Chapter Nine

When Sarah entered Haladay's office on Monday afternoon, she was riding on a wave of exhilaration. She had spent her weekend closeted in her apartment, refining the drawing to scale the blueprints for the Reed job. The finished project gave her a great deal of pleasure. Phase one had gone perfectly from beginning to end; now she was itching to break ground on phase two. She felt more than ready for her afternoon meeting with Haladay.

"Hello, Joe." She stopped, as was her habit, and smiled at the guard. "How's Rose?"

"Hello, Sarah. She's just fine." Joe returned her smile before he noticed who had followed her into the building. "Good morning, Mr. Lloyd."

"Oh, hello, Byron. How was Spain?"

"Hot," he said briefly and, taking her elbow, led her past the cluster of public elevators. "I'll take you to your floor."

"Fine." She watched him insert his key. "I much prefer this elevator. I hate elevators that sing. Did everything go all right in Madrid?"

Byron pushed the button for her floor, then turned to look at her. She frowned at the coolness in his eyes, remembering that they had parted on friendly enough terms. "Are you always so personal with the guards?"

"What?"

He watched the lines appear between her brow as she concentrated.

"Do you mean Joe?" She shifted her briefcase onto her left hand. "Are you serious?" Her eyes widened. "God, you *are* serious." Anger rose quickly. "It must be very difficult being so far above the common man. You've probably never done more than grant an occasional nod to that man. And I'm certain you don't know he's worked here for ten years, that he has two kids, one who'll be going into college in the fall, and a wife who likes to bake lasagna."

Byron eyed her coolly. "I'm certainly aware of all that fascinating information now."

"Damn you, don't you be condescending with me." She forgot the potential violence of his temper, forgot his position and plunged ahead. "What right do you have to split people up into classes? You've dug your share of ditches, Byron. Don't forget where you came from."

His hand closed over her arm, but this time Sarah held her ground.

"I know where I came from," he said. "I don't need you to remind me."

"And I don't need lessons in deportment from you. Your authority ends with my job." She wrenched her arm from his hold. "Don't you ever . . ." She took a moment to steady her voice. "Don't you ever criticize my personal conduct outside of the office again."

The doors slid open, and she turned her back on him and walked away.

"Morning, Ms. Lancaster." Mugs set down her latest paperback and glanced up. Recognizing fury when she saw it, she cleared her throat and began again. "Want some coffee?"

"Hold my calls for the next few minutes," Sarah ordered briskly as she passed by the desk and into her office.

"Yes, ma'am."

"*Bastard!*" Sarah exploded the moment the door shut behind her. Tossing aside her briefcase, she stormed around the room. How could I have possibly thought I liked him? She folded her arms as she stared through a space in her plants. Because she wanted her emotions to level off, she shut her eyes and stood absolutely still. Gradually her anger cooled. Get busy and forget it, she ordered herself. Turning, she lifted the phone and pushed Mugs's buzzer.

"Yes, Ms. Lancaster."

"Mugs, get me a stat writer and see if Cassidy has time to check over my final drawings for the Reed project." Sarah dropped into her chair as she spoke, then picked up a pencil and began to scribble. "And find out if Dutch Kelly's free to discuss more formalized plans for the W-W project . . . maybe sometime this afternoon. What time's my meeting with Mr. Haladay?"

"Twelve thirty. It's for lunch in his office. He'll probably have a cold buffet."

Sarah frowned, noting down on her pad the order of her day. "Will Mr. Lloyd be there?"

"It's usual."

"Shit," she whispered under her breath, but Mugs had sharp ears. "Okay, take care of the stat writer and Kelly. I'll call Cassidy myself. And Mugs . . ."

"Yes, Ms. Lancaster?"

"I could use that coffee now, if you don't mind."

"Sure thing."

"Thanks." Sarah set down the phone, took a long breath, then rose to pick up her briefcase.

When Sarah entered Haladay's office, both men were behind the massive desk. Haladay sat with Byron standing behind him. Whether it was the positioning or the light or the angle, Sarah noted that Haladay's age seemed more marked with Byron beside him. She had a moment's regret for the old man and the inevitable change.

"Hello, Max." She shot him a quick smile as she crossed the room. "How was your weekend?"

"Weekends mean an entirely different thing at my age than they do at yours," he said dryly. "Let's see the blueprints."

After settling her briefcase on his desk, she flipped the top open and handed them to him.

"Fix us a drink, Byron," Haladay said as he pulled the blueprints from their tube, "while I take a look at what she's done." He rose and began to spread the drawings across his desk.

"Martini all right?" Byron asked.

"Please."

He turned, nonplussing her with a smile. "Dry?"

"So you have to blow the dust off it."

He poured two martinis, then chose a bottle of sherry and half filled a third glass. When he held out her drink, Sarah reached for it, and for a moment they both held the stem. She lifted her eyes, then was suddenly reminded of the first day in his office when his hand had closed over hers on the doorknob. She had felt a message pass then, as she felt one now. Still, she could not decipher it. Then her hand was alone on the stem and he had withdrawn again.

"It appears you've done a good job," Haladay commented.

Distracted, Sarah turned from Byron and brought her thoughts to order. "I *have* done a good job," she corrected, then crossed over to him. She sipped at the martini as Byron joined them, handing Haladay the half glass of sherry. Haladay scowled at it, downed it, then set the empty glass on his desk.

"What do you think?" he demanded of Byron, then gestured with a sweeping arm over the blueprints.

Byron leaned over the desk and systematically went through the prints and stats. "It's very good," he said at length and straightened. "I see no problem."

"Glad to hear it." Sarah's voice was as dry as her martini. "It's perfect for the site, Max," she said.

"What'd you think of Reed?" Haladay demanded.

"I thought he was a very nice man. And a talented one."

"He's a lush," Haladay said. "But I like the son of a bitch."

"He likes you too," Sarah returned.

"I've been to that monstrosity he lives in. Cassidy won't set foot in the place."

Sarah laughed. "No, I don't suppose he would. Not even for you. I've never seen anything like it." She shook her head. "I'm still having nightmares."

Haladay gave her a long, hard look. "Given Reed's taste, it's difficult to imagine you persuading him to agree to something small and simple."

Her eyes narrowed. She set down her glass. "I didn't persuade him in bed. I don't entertain clients that way. I simply hit the right key at the right time. Now if you'll excuse me." Sarah turned on her heel, but Haladay put a hand on her shoulder and stopped her.

"Short fuse," he commented to Byron. He grinned as he squeezed her shoulder. "Have some caviar," he suggested. Turning back to the buffet, he spread a cracker.

"You wanted me to be angry."

"I like to know my people have integrity."

"No," Sarah corrected. "It's your ego." She gestured at Byron. "Our integrity reflects Haladay integrity."

"You're a sharp one."

"Oh, not as sharp as you, Max, and not half as devious." She gave a low laugh. "But I'm going to work on it."

"Here, have some caviar. It's one of the few pleasures left to me." Over her head, he caught Byron's eye and scowled. "Byron and the doctors have a conspiracy to make my remaining years as dull as possible. You saw that pitiful excuse for a drink he gave me, didn't you?" Haladay demanded of Sarah. "And who the hell has it arranged so they only serve me that fake coffee?"

"Decaffeinated," Byron corrected, lighting a cigarette.

"Not only here," Haladay continued, "but at home. And even on my own goddamn plane. No cigars either. And my diet. Jesus Christ." He took an unsalted cracker and devoured it.

"Max's diet is sensible," Byron stated.

"Horseshit!" Max tossed a shrimp into his mouth. "What the hell does he know about food? It's only when a man reaches full maturity that he really appreciates food." He picked up a carrot stick and broke it in half. "Until he hits sixty, a man's too preoccupied with sex to understand food. You'll notice," he pointed out, "he hasn't eaten anything."

"If you don't need me anymore," Sarah said as she moved to his desk to gather her papers, "I've got a meeting with Kelly on another project."

Byron rose and crossed to her. "I'd like to speak with you about that."

"All right." After snapping her briefcase shut, Sarah looked up at him. "In my office? I have some preliminary sketches there."

"Fine."

She looked past Byron to Haladay. "Good-bye, Max."

"Good-bye, Sarah."

Sarah waited only until Byron had rung for the elevator. "It's his heart, isn't it?" she asked, as they stepped in.

"Yes."

"How bad?"

"He had a massive coronary last year."

"Damn." Sarah breathed the word, then leaned against the wall of the car. "Damn." She stared at the red numbers over the door. "So he's not indestructible after all. I wanted you to tell me he was."

Mugs glanced up from her typewriter as they passed her desk.

"Ms. Darcy from Procurement called."

"I'll get back to her." Sarah went directly to her desk

and set down her briefcase, waiting until Byron shut the door before she spoke again. "You've kept this very quiet."

He walked to the desk. "That's how Max wants it. He doesn't like to be fussed over, and bankers and other people in the industry tend to get nervous when they hear about heart attacks."

"Byron, his job . . . the stress . . ."

"The job is what keeps him alive," Byron said. "He'd dry up without it. I spare him as much as possible."

She searched his face, understood, and nodded. "Yes, that explains quite a bit. He accepts it from you. He'd hate it from anyone else. He doesn't like weaknesses, does he?"

"Particularly his own."

"Who else knows?"

"Cassidy, his secretary, his lawyer."

She lifted her eyes. "Why have you told me?"

He took his time with his answer. "Let's say you have integrity."

A smile touched her eyes and reached her mouth. "You're a very clever man, Byron." She turned to walk to the file cabinet and pulled out a folder. "The W-W project, sketches enclosed." She handed Byron the folder. "I'm fairly certain they're what she's looking for."

Without commenting, he opened the folder and began to page through the sketches. She had given Gloria a taste of the South with wrought-iron railings and individual balconies, yet the general structure and style fitted into the Arizona landscape. Inside she had allowed a touch of flamboyance in the master bedroom and given Gloria two walls of recessed clothes closets in the adjoining dressing room. Looking over the sketches, Byron decided that the house suited Gloria to perfection.

"You don't seem to have missed anything," he commented, then closed the folder and handed it back to her.

Sarah gave him a disgusted frown. "I hate negative compliments."

Byron tucked his hands in his pockets as she returned the folder to the file. "You used the English Bond for your bricklaying in this, but Flemish in the Reed prints. Why?"

With a quick gesture, she pushed the file drawer closed. "The Flemish looks more Old World to me. The English Bond suits her. It's more distinct than the Flemish and more decorative than the American." She leaned back against the cabinet and folded her arms. "What do you think of the sketches?"

"I think they suit her."

"Damn it, Byron." In frustration, she tossed up her hands, then began to pace. "Must you always be so objective?"

"Yes," he said simply.

"Well, do you want to take the sketches to her after I meet with Kelly, or shall I have her come in?"

"Have her come in."

They're lovers now, she concluded, *but he's already getting restless.* "All right. I'll arrange a meeting for Wednesday. Do you want to be included?"

"That won't be necessary."

She grinned at him and lifted her brow.

"You know, Byron, Max was right. You didn't eat a thing."

He acknowledged her teasing smile with a nod. "I wouldn't take Max's theory too seriously."

Her eyes shone with amusement as she laughed. "Is that a warning?"

Surprising both himself and Sarah, Byron raised his hand to her face and caressed her cheek. Looking into her eyes, he moved his thumb over her lips.

Without giving herself a moment to consider, Sarah stepped forward and into his arms. Their mouths met with instant heat and instant pressure. There was a desperation in the way their lips parted and met again, clinging, avid and hot, as though there would never be enough time to draw all that was needed.

Her body longed to know his, to feel the warmth of skin against skin. She pressed against him, inviting, requesting, as his hands moved to cradle her hips. She felt a need for him that she had never felt before for any man. She wanted him, wanted to spend hours discovering and being discovered by him. She seemed to grow softer wherever he touched her. Briefly he crushed her against him before he pulled away.

Looking down at her, Byron saw the same vulnerability on her face that had been there in the first moments he had seen her. She was without defense and, he knew, his for the taking. With his hands on her shoulders, he could feel her trembling lightly. He dropped them and stepped back. "It seems our timing continues to be poor."

Sarah's breathing was unsteady. No glib response would come, no casual smile. As she watched, he turned and left her.

Chapter Ten

THE PHONE RANG JUST AS DALLAS HAD WORKED THE shampoo into a lather. She squinted one eye open.

By the time the phone had rung the third time, she was out of the shower and grabbing a towel. "Shit," she muttered, wiping lather out of her eyes as she tried to work the towel around her body. "Bet it's a wrong number." She hooked the end of the towel between her breasts as she lifted the receiver. "Hello."

"Hello, Dallas. Evan Gibson. We work together at Haladay."

A grin spread from one of Dallas's soapy ears to the other. "Gibson?" she repeated in a voice that hesitated and questioned.

"In the Architecture Department," he explained. "We have a mutual friend, Sarah Lancaster."

"In Architecture, sure." Shampoo dribbled cold down her back and she shifted her shoulders. "We've had some dealings now and again." Dallas ran the tip of her tongue over her teeth, then adjusted the towel as it began to slip. "And of course, Sarah's mentioned you. How are you?"

"Fine." Evan moved on smoothly. "I don't get many opportunities to get down to Procurement."

"They keep me behind bars there." Dallas rubbed dripping water off her leg with the bottom of the opposite foot.

"Sarah tells me we have a mutual interest."

"Oh?"

"Chinese food."

"Oh." She split the word into three syllables before she laughed.

"Why don't I pick you up in an hour?"

"Hour and a half." She hung up the phone. It's about time, she thought and ran a hand through her shampoo bubbles. Before she could move down the hall into the bedroom, a knock sounded on her front door. She pulled open the door and grinned at Sarah. "Hi! Come on in, you can help me pick out an outfit." She scrambled into the bedroom.

Sarah closed the door. "Glad somebody's in a good mood," she muttered, following Dallas into the bedroom. Dallas was already routing through her closet. "Who's in the shower?" Sarah asked as the sound of running water came through the open door.

"Oh, shit, I am." Like a flash, Dallas darted into the bath.

With a sigh, Sarah tossed herself onto the bed. Her thoughts drifted back to the afternoon and Byron. She was annoyed that he should be so constantly on her mind.

The spray of the shower stopped abruptly. "Hey, Sarah," Dallas called from the bath. "Do you think I should wear the Hermès scarf you brought me back from California?"

Sarah glanced toward the sound of the voice. She could see flashes of Dallas through the opening as she hustled around the bathroom. "Where are you going?"

Dallas stood naked in the doorway, rubbing a towel briskly through her hair. "To do Chinese." She grinned and tossed the towel on the floor. "With Evan Gibson."

"Oh, he called?"

"Yes." With her quick, nervous gestures, Dallas came back into the bedroom and began digging in a drawer. "I know, I know, you're afraid he's going to debase my body, mess up my mind, and break my heart. I'm just working on the first part." She wriggled into stockings, then began to dig again.

Sarah studied the sharp points of her shoulder blades. For a moment she chewed on her bottom lip.

"Dallas," she began, then stopped and sighed. "Oh, shit."

"What's the matter, love?" Dallas adjusted the straps of a black silk teddy over her shoulders, then sat on the edge of the bed.

Sarah sat up, folding her legs under her. "Dallas, last week . . . Evan came on pretty strong in the office."

"Oh?" Dallas's brows rose.

"A great deal of it was my fault, I suppose, but he took me by surprise. Goddamn it." Sarah frowned. "I didn't exactly fight him off at first."

"No?"

Sarah winced at Dallas's smile. "We didn't part on the best of terms. I bruised his ego, and I'm afraid he might still have it in his head that he needs to convince me of what I'm missing."

"You've really been letting this bother you." Dallas shook her head and rose. She began another search through her closet. "Sarah, I'm a big girl, I know how to take a fall. Besides . . ." She tossed a grin over her shoulder. "While he's fooling around with me, he won't be bothering you."

"Dallas." Sarah stood to make her final attempt. "He may be fun to look at, but he's shallow and egotistical."

"So am I." She pulled two slinky dresses out of the closet. "Which one will look better with that scarf?"

The Arizona sun is white in August. The wide straw hat Sarah had pulled over her ponytail shaded her eyes. The

T-shirt stuck to her back and had a streak of dampness down the center front.

She watched the laborers raise the roof. To a man, they were stripped to the waist, their backs brown and gleaming. Sarah pulled her own shirt away from her back and longed to follow their example. She swiped a hand across her forehead, then hooked her hands in her back pockets and listened to the clatter of hammer against wood.

During each stage of construction Gloria had haunted the site. From Sarah's experience and from the reports that trickled back to her, Gloria was an obstruction to the work. She was constantly changing her mind and coming up with new ideas.

New ideas, Sarah scoffed. She watched a beam slide into place and prayed that Gloria would spend the day at the hairdresser's. I will not complain to Byron, she thought. We've managed not to cross swords for over a month; no way I'm going to start anything by bad-mouthing a client.

A drop of sweat trickled down the back of her neck and continued down between her shoulder blades. Sarah ignored it. The house was little more than a shell, but it took no effort for her to visualize the finished product. A bulldozer hummed off to the west where Gloria wanted her formal garden. Over the racket Sarah could hear an occasional shout or obscenity.

It was going to be a fine piece of work. Sarah put her hands on her hips and smiled broadly as the sun beat down on her. With a nod, she worked her way across the dirt and into the shell of the house. Over her head, men sweated and pounded on beams.

"Springer!" She spotted the foreman standing with a carpenter in what would be Gloria's dining room.

He turned as she called, then with a jerk of his thumb dismissed the other man. The red bandanna he wore around his bald head was soaked, his shirt patched under the arms. He was a native of Oklahoma, a veteran with Haladay and a man Sarah liked to work with. His arms were hard and roped with muscles, and his thighs were as wide as Sarah's waist.

He spoke in a surprisingly soft voice. "Ma'am."

"The new shipment is in, the white brick Mrs. Woodloe-Winfield wanted for that garden wall."

"Fine and dandy."

"You know how to keep on schedule, Springer. Everything here seems under control. I'm going back to the office; you don't need me."

"I heard the lady was coming by this afternoon." He plucked a cold drink from his cooler and offered it to Sarah.

"I'm definitely going back to the office," she murmured as she held the iced bottle to her forehead.

"Women should stay off construction sites," he commented, choosing another bottle from his cooler. He twisted off the cap and chugged down half the contents before he brought his eyes back to Sarah's. He grinned when he saw her expression. "Of course, that's not meaning women in the business. One of my best masons's a woman. Don't even notice it when she's got a brick in her hand. Nobody around here even thinks about you as a woman."

Sarah took a long pull from her bottle. "Shut up, Springer," she suggested. She wiped her mouth with the back of her hand. "Let me know if you have any more problems with my client."

"Yes, ma'am." Springer watched her walk away. Smart lady, he thought. He dropped his eyes to her hips, enjoying their movement under the faded jeans.

With her long, elegant legs neatly crossed, Kay Rupert sat facing Byron. In her practiced, well-modulated voice, she outlined his schedule for the following day. As Byron's secretary, she perhaps more than anyone else in the vast network of Haladay Enterprises knew how much of the old man's power now rested with him. She was not a very perceptive woman, but she was ambitious.

She had not done her best over the years to make herself indispensable to Byron Lloyd just to remain his secretary. Her plans were bigger than that. Byron was a prime catch, and she more than any of his lovers knew how prime. She had made it her business to be his right arm, or as near his right arm as he would permit. She knew his taste in women and catered to it. She was a patient woman and she wanted Byron Lloyd.

Never once had she made a move that could be construed as an invitation. Kay was well aware that the wrong step could cost her her job and her chances. Getting Byron into bed meant nothing; she wanted his name on a marriage license. When Haladay was gone, Byron would move up. Kay fully intended to move with him.

"After the ten o'clock board meeting, you have lunch with Pia Stromberg. He's going to make a pitch for an addition to our Amsterdam offices; all pertinent information is in the file. Your afternoon appointments begin at one thirty. O'Keefe, to finalize the disposition of some suits against the company, then Bryden and Shodell representing the bank, Cassidy with a report on the Orwell project. You have a dinner engagement with Mr. Haladay at his home at seven." Kay flipped over her pad. Byron stood at the window and stared out.

"Mrs. Woodloe-Winfield called this morning while you were in conference." Kay, her eyes on his profile, caught the brief tightening of his jawline.

"Any other calls?"

"Several. Fletcher from the AIA, Lou Trainer from the mayor's office, Carol Dribeck from KRJ-TV, and Marla Sumner."

"Get Fletcher for me, give Trainer and the reporter to P.R., and send Ms. Sumner a dozen roses. She's at the Hilton."

Kay meticulously noted the instructions on her pad. "And the color?"

"Red, I imagine." He shrugged. "Before you get Fletcher, check whether Sarah Lancaster is in her office. If not, find her. I want to see her."

"Right away." She rose to leave. The door closed quietly behind her.

From his window, Byron could see all of east Phoenix. He could easily pick out half a dozen buildings that stood because of Haladay. In cities all over the world it would be the same. Frowning, he turned from the window and returned to his desk to study Sarah's drawings.

There were copies of her plans for the Reed project and for Gloria's, for past projects with Boumell and still further back from her college assignments. He held up the preliminary sketches for the renovation of a local school she had recently been assigned.

Springer, a man whose opinion and ability Byron respected, had labeled Sarah a good architect. High praise indeed, Byron mused, for a man of few words. He wanted the Delacroix Center in Paris to have an architect who could work with a construction crew, was thorough and creative. He also wanted someone fresh. A new face, a new name, and an attractive woman wouldn't hurt the Haladay image.

Lighting a cigarette, Byron leaned back in his chair. He knew that sending Sarah to Paris was a gamble and for one last time he wanted to consider the odds. She was young, too goddamn young, but she was able. Byron blew a thin stream of gray smoke at the ceiling. And she had guts.

I'm tossing her in, he decided abruptly, taking another deep drag. If she's over her head, she'll have to swim. The risk, he concluded, was minimal.

The buzzer on his desk sounded briefly. "Ms. Lancaster is here."

"Send her in." Slowly Byron crushed out his cigarette.

Sarah entered Byron's office straight from the site. He surveyed her from straw hat to battered sneakers. "Hello, Sarah." He didn't rise, but continued to look at her as she crossed the room to his desk.

"Hello, Byron." She dropped into the same chair she had used during her initial interview.

Being summoned precipitately to his office irked her. She was tired. What she wanted was a drink and a shower.

"Is there a problem?" she asked.

"No." Byron saw the fatigue on her face. Abruptly he recalled that it was 102 degrees outside the building. "You've been out at the Woodloe-Winfield site?"

"Yes, I just got in. The roof's going up."

He rose and walked to the bar at the far end of the room. Opening the small refrigerator, he found a bottle of ginger ale, poured some into a tall glass, added ice, then came back to her.

"Thank you."

"I don't imagine you're used to the heat here." He stood over her as she drank. The sun, he noted, had warmed her skin but not quite tanned it. There was more blonde in her hair.

"No, I'm not. Will I ever be?"

"We won't be assigning you any new projects after this month."

"What?" Immediately Sarah sat bolt upright. Her hat tumbled down her back. She stood before he could answer. "What's wrong with my work?"

"To my knowledge, nothing."

"Then why are you putting a hold on my assignments?" she demanded. She struggled to keep calm. "I don't understand. . . ."

Silently he approved her self-control. "It will take you a few months to clear up your projects, or to get them to a stage where someone can take over for you. You'll be going to Paris the first of the year."

"To Paris." Sarah stood still. The expression on Byron's face told her nothing. She pushed back the flutter of anticipation in her stomach, afraid to acknowledge it, and took an extra moment to insure that her voice would be calm. "The Delacroix Center?"

"That's right. Your assignment will begin on location right after the first of the year. There will, of course, be preliminary meetings at this end beforehand."

"Byron, wait a minute." Sarah held up a hand to stop him. Part of her was afraid to put the question on a yes or no basis, but she took a deep breath and spoke quickly. "Are you making me the architect of record on the Delacroix Center?"

"Yes."

After letting out the breath she had been holding, Sarah closed her eyes. Oh God . . . oh God. She could feel her heart pounding at her ribs. Jesus, don't blow it by bursting into tears. Knowing her control was slipping, she turned and walked to the bar, carefully setting her glass down.

"You know, Byron, you have a talent for understatement. I don't suppose you know what this means to me."

"I have an idea," Byron replied. He was well aware of her struggle to retain her composure.

"Perhaps you do." She turned to face him directly. "Why?"

"Why?" he repeated.

"Why are you giving me Delacroix, Byron? There must be specific reasons."

He gestured to his desk. "There are some of them."

Sarah crossed over to look at the drawings on his desk. Her brow lifted when she noticed her college work, but she didn't ask how he had come by it. She brought her eyes back to his. "Why else?"

"I want someone who can work with a crew. Springer doesn't bitch about you. He would if you gave him cause." He paused to light a cigarette. "I also want someone fresh, comparatively unknown. And the press will like the fact that you're a young, beautiful woman."

"Shit," Sarah said softly. Shaking her head, she turned away. "I hate that." She placed her palms together and pressed hard for a moment. "I really hate that." Swiftly she whirled back to him, and he saw the flash of temper in her eyes. "It's all part of the game though, isn't it? There's always an angle."

"You go for the angles in business, Sarah, or you fold. When you've got an edge, you use it. It's easy to get chewed up out there if you make the wrong move."

She saw the ruthlessness, the cunning. Months before, she had recognized Byron's power; now she recognized that he would never easily relinquish it. "You know more about all that than I do," she said bitterly. "I'll have to learn." She moved to the chair and picked up her hat. Her voice and her face were calm when she faced him again. "I'm going to build that center, Byron, and it's going to be fantastic. If my being a woman gives me a political edge, good for me. There's one thing I can promise you—you're never going to regret giving it to me."

Chapter Eleven

SARAH WAS PLEASED WITH HER PARIS OFFICE. IT WAS L-shaped with mullioned windows, silk wallpaper, and an antique pecan desk. There was a huge, beautifully faded Aubusson carpet spread on the floor. The bottom slash of the "L" formed a sitting room with sofa and chairs and small tables. There was a silver dish of chocolate mints which her secretary kept replenished.

Madame Fountblane was a broad-hipped, matronly woman who wore a hairnet over her chignon and spoke precise English. Sarah responded to her friendliness and learned to accept her habit of serving chocolate and pastries every day at eleven.

Sarah discovered that the French conducted business formally, with a gracious politeness. She discovered too that they were shrewd, tough, and mercenary. During her first month in Paris the meetings seemed endless. Hours were spent with the group of businessmen who were funding the center, and more hours with zoning officials, safety officials, engineers, technicians, the public relations staff, the vice-presidents of Marketing and Construction. Then there were the reams of reports to be read and written. Sarah gritted her teeth and coped with politics and protocol. She had asked for the Delacroix Center knowing she would have to do more than design the building. The artist in her rebelled against the bureaucratic red tape and the endless paperwork. Her ambition drove her to master them.

The head of the committee for the Delacroix Center was André Ceseare. He was a short, red-faced man in his fifties with small black eyes and receding salt-and-pepper hair. Sarah had been immediately drawn to his quick humor. His English was uncertain but, though Sarah's French was above average, he insisted on speaking English. He spoke with his hands as effusively as she. Because she dealt most directly with him, Sarah found the transition to French life and business just a little easier.

The only prominent member of the Paris branch Sarah had yet to meet was Januel Bounnet. He ran the Paris section of Haladay, as Dave Tyson ran the Manhattan. There was no Mugs to give her information on Bounnet, and her own research had only produced a sketchy profile of a man of thirty-seven, ten years divorced. He had worked for the Haladay organization for fifteen years, had been the assistant to the head of Haladay Paris for three, and for the last five years had held the position himself. Because Sarah could find nothing in the Bounnet biography that brought him to life, she forgot him. The Delacroix Center was her primary interest.

Already, in her mind's eye, Sarah could see the finished theater; a low, sweeping building, glassed on the east end. The lobby would hold a central garden. She saw the building geometrically; the wide west end with no breaks in the precast concrete for glass, the main theater with its winding balconies on rising levels, the fluidity of a staircase, the long breezeways. She wanted to begin.

To curb her impatience until ground could be broken, Sarah spent long hours in the evening perfecting and polishing the accepted design. She pored over the stats. She worried over the amount of time it took for supplies to be delivered. More, she fretted over the need for forms and justifications and contractual procedure. Red tape, she learned, was red tape, in any language. As always, it frustrated her.

The light spilling through the window at Sarah's back had changed color. Shadows filled the corners of her office. Sarah had had the entire floor to herself for half an hour, but still she lingered. On her pad, she sketched her varied ideas for the interior of one of the center's smaller theaters. She wanted something intimate and understated in contrast to the grand elegance of the main theater. Theater was pomp and feathers, but also black tights and bare feet. She wanted the audience to smell the greasepaint:

As she sketched, her mind began to drift. She propped her chin on her fist, staring into space.

First New York, she reflected, and now the whole country. Who would've thought, a year ago, that so much in my life would have changed? She thought of the sendoff Dallas had given her the night before she had left for Paris. She remembered laughter and voices so typically American, the scent of American cigarettes, cans of Budweiser, the vintage Beatles records.

The apartment had been jammed with people, most of them more than a little drunk, and an ancient Flash Gordon serial had zipped by silently on the television. Wistfully, Sarah looked back on the scene with unexpected nostalgia. It hadn't been until she had lived outside the country that she had realized how American she was. And as she had told Byron Lloyd some months before, she did not acclimate easily.

There were adjustments for Sarah to make during her first month; not only the adaptation to a different culture, but the shouldering of new responsibilities. Before, Boumell and then Cassidy had handled the business matters; the meetings, the reports, the political maneuvers. Her authority to delegate had been minimal. Now Sarah was forced to learn fast or sink. She was the new kid on the block, but also a foreigner and therefore doubly suspect. There was constant pressure to prove herself.

She learned how to deal with bankers, with purchasing agents, with laymen who knew nothing about construction but wanted to keep close tabs on their francs. She began to develop a diplomacy she had never felt the need for before. She didn't always like what she had to do. She was learning to play the game.

Alone in her office in Haladay Paris, Sarah felt adrift and lonely.

"Damn it, Sarah, snap out of it." Tossing down her pencil, she sprang up and stalked to her window.

I'm in one of the most romantic cities in the world, she mused as she watched night fall. I've a whole weekend free, and I'm standing here feeling sorry for myself instead of making plans. Think of the buildings. Think of the incredible, the glorious architecture all around me. Think of the museums and the art. Her reflection smiled wanly back at her from the window.

"Oh God," she said aloud. "I've got to get to the Louvre."

"I think you'll find it closed."

With a gasp of alarm, Sarah stumbled back against the windowsill. The dark silhouette in the doorway blocked out the light from the hall. As she watched, it came forward and became a man.

"I'm sorry, I startled you."

"It's all right." She smiled. "Is there something I can do for you?"

"You must forgive me." With a light laugh and a shake of his head, he stepped into the room, then crossed to her. "I was certain you would be middle-aged with a strong chin and broad hand. I knew I would be intimidated. If I had known how wrong I was . . ." Pausing, he lifted one of Sarah's hands to his lips. "I would have cut my business short and returned much sooner." His breath was warm on her fingers. "I'm Januel Bounnet, your associate during your stay in Paris."

Sarah allowed her hand to linger in his. His skin was dry

and smooth against hers. His eyes were a different gray from Dallas's, lighter, almost translucent. She had never seen a color quite like it. "I didn't know you were coming back, not until next week."

"It pleases me to have arrived early."

Sarah lifted a brow and reluctantly removed her hand from Januel's. She had missed casual intimacies since coming to France. "A pity you didn't arrive sooner. You've missed a month of fascinating meetings."

The elegant shrug of his shoulders was essentially French. "You must fill me in and give me all the news from America. I'm sure I would find a less . . . crowded meeting more interesting." He saw the smile flash in her eyes seconds before her lips curved. Yes, he was definitely going to enjoy Sarah Lancaster.

"I might be persuaded to give you a condensed version," she answered, no longer feeling lonely, "though I'm not very enthusiastic about paperwork."

"Alas, producing it is part of my profession." He spread his hands again. "But I am keeping you. You have an appointment at the Louvre?"

"The Louvre?" Sarah repeated, puzzled. Her face cleared with a laugh. "No, I was thinking of all the buildings there are for me to study while I'm in Paris. I've been too busy to sightsee so far, but I'm still a tourist."

"A tourist needs a guide to see Paris properly." His eyes drifted to her neck. "I should like to apply for the job."

"I'd like that too." Sarah smiled. "But I warn you, I take lots of snapshots and look for souvenirs."

"Tomorrow we will find you key chains with dangling Eiffel Towers, but tonight . . ." He took her hand again, by the fingers. "I know a small café with dim corners. We will have supper and you will tell me all about Sarah Lancaster. Already I find her enchanting."

* * *

Dear Dallas,

Paris in February is chilly and damp and wonderful. I've gotten through the first month of homesickness and the purgatory of meetings. Now I'm starting to enjoy myself. I love the reruns of Bonanza. You haven't lived until you've heard Hoss Cartwright spout French. The traffic is hateful. My hotel room is cold. I miss my apartment and my noisy dishwasher and you. For several days I missed Sears, Roebuck. I've learned how incredibly American I am.

But I'm learning how to appreciate certain French delicacies. The pastries could put flesh even on your bones. The buildings. I get sweaty palms and ragged breathing just thinking of them. Who needs sex? I know, I know, you do, but then how excited can you get looking at purchase orders and requisitions? (I've been finding out.) Still, the most impressive French landmark I've come across is Januel Bounnet.

He runs things out here and is the most incredible-looking man I've ever seen. Pure classic features with fabulous gray eyes that are very light and absolutely clear. He's blond. And yes, he's got a nice body. He's slender, and though he hasn't the muscles of your crane operator, he's not soft.

Okay, besides the devastating exterior, he's kind and intelligent and has rather sweetly impeccable manners. We've been to Maxim's and the Lido and the Bois de Boulogne. He makes me feel like a teenager with a crush. As far as I can remember, I never felt like this when I was a teenager. He kisses my hand and sends me flowers. No one's ever treated me the way he does, and though I'm not certain I ever wanted to be treated this way, now it seems natural. I never considered myself a romantic, but perhaps I was wrong. He makes me feel very romantic, and I like it.

Let me know how Max is doing, and if Cassidy is

*managing without me. I miss them too, and Mugs.
Too bad she doesn't read French—they've got some
books over here even she wouldn't believe. Is Byron
doing anything interesting these days? Tell Mugs to
send me a memo.*

*By the way, the head of Procurement here is stout
and jolly with Santa Claus glasses. Everyone detests
him.*

*Love,
Sarah*

Recognizing Sarah's writing, Evan picked up the letter
from Dallas's coffee table. He frowned as he read it. The
more consistently Sarah had rebuffed his advances, the
more determined he had become to have her. He had
become obsessed with her, and though he knew this focus
on one woman was out of character, he was unable to stop
it. Her indifference fanned his desire.

As he read Sarah's thoughts on Januel Bounnet, he
pictured them together. He saw them in bed, Sarah naked
and willing, her narrow boy's hips working feverishly, her
soft, pale skin sheened with dampness.

Walking in from the bedroom, Dallas saw Evan with the
letter. She recognized the naked desire on his face, and a
swift rush of pain surprised her. It had been years since she
had been really hurt by a man. She'd been careful. For a
moment she stood stock-still, trying to analyze the sensation. After the first wave of surprise, came the anger.

"Interesting reading?" she demanded as she crossed to
Evan. As he glanced up, she tore the letter from his hand.
"Because I sleep with you doesn't mean you can monitor
my mail."

"If you didn't want me to see it, you should've put it
away," Evan said coldly. He walked over to help himself to
her gin. "Besides," he continued, adding tonic, "it was
Sarah who brought us together, right?"

Dallas ran the letter between her fingers as she watched him drink. "Oh yeah, we're both real fond of Sarah, aren't we?"

"Sure." Evan swirled the liquor, then drank. "Why the hell not?"

She's six thousand miles away, Dallas thought furiously. Six fucking thousand miles, and he's still drooling over her. She turned away, walking the room with Sarah's letter flapping against her palm. Goddamn it, why don't I tell him to pack up and take a hike? She dragged a hand through her cap of curls. Because I'm hooked. Jesus, I threw out the line, and I'm the one with the hook in my mouth.

Warned me, didn't you, Sarah? Dallas stared down at the dashing, looping lines that were Sarah's writing. For a moment she wanted to crumple the paper into a ball, to wish Sarah to oblivion for being right, for being whatever it was that Evan wanted so desperately. Until that moment, she hadn't realized how totally she had become involved with him. It had been weeks since she'd slept with anyone else. She had found excuses to refuse a simple dinner date with Dennis, knowing she hurt him. More and more, she was doing something she had promised herself years before she would never do. She was centering her life, her emotions, around one man.

Evan studied Dallas as she paced erratically. They'd had some laughs the past few weeks, he mused. She was fun and incredibly agile, and crazy about him. He had been aware of how deeply she had become involved long before she had. He didn't want to lose her yet, but he realized now he would have to be more subtle. She was still his connection to Sarah.

"Hey, you're not steamed because I read your letter? I figured you had it out to read to me anyway." He smiled disarmingly. "There didn't seem to be anything too personal in it. Besides . . ." He smiled again, setting down his glass before crossing the room to her. He traced her ear with the tip of his finger. "I figured you and I have no secrets."

Even as he smiled at her, Dallas recognized the calculation. Evan saw the surrender in her eyes. He slipped both hands under her blouse to take her small, firm breasts. "Not mad, are you?" he murmured as his thumbs flicked casually over the hard nipples.

For an instant Dallas hated him, but when he slid her shorts down over her hips and thrust his hand between her legs, she didn't object. He rubbed his palm back and forth over her while his other hand held her hip. His rhythm was unhurried, casual, as he continued to smile down at her. She came once, quickly, but their faces were still inches apart when she closed her eyes and began to shudder. Dallas dropped Sarah's letter to the floor and jerked down the zipper of Evan's jeans.

The letter was under Evan's back a few minutes later as they climaxed, but neither thought of Sarah.

Chapter Twelve

THE PANTHÉON. SARAH HAD SEEN PICTURES DETAILING every aspect of the eighteenth-century structure, but she was still not prepared for the reality.

"The stone dome at the intersection of the cross is triple shelled." She spoke not to instruct Januel, but to put her thoughts into words. "The outer dome is cut stone, unbelievably thin, five or six inches at the crown. Inches," she repeated, and made a sweeping gesture with both hands. "Incredible. Think of it, Januel."

She breathed deep, tasting the damp air. Looking at the building reminded her of why she had wanted to be an architect. Here was life in stone and wood. Here was a lasting accomplishment. It moved her as she knew it had moved, and would move, generations.

Turning, Sarah found Januel's clear gray eyes on her. "What do you see, Januel, when you look at a building like this?" After tossing her hair over her shoulder, she linked her arm with his so that they looked together. There was a need in her to share the magnificence.

"When you hear a song," Januel began, "you think: 'Ah yes, that's nice,' or 'No, no, I don't like that.' Or you don't think at all and merely enjoy." He turned to her to brush away tendrils the wind had set dancing in front of her eyes. "But I think when a musician hears a song, he hears all the separate qualities—the bass, the treble—and he judges. So, an artist studies the brushstrokes in a painting, a writer the structure of a sentence. I'm not an artist. I see a building, a magnificent old building like many others in Paris."

His answer frustrated her, and the quick gesture of her hand reflected it. "But don't you sometimes want to know why it's so right or so wrong?"

"I'm a businessman, Sarah." His shoulders moved carelessly before he took her hand. "I appreciate beauty naturally. When I see a beautiful woman, I don't question how or why, I'm merely grateful."

Sarah sighed. All too often she found Januel's responses maddeningly superficial, but he had many qualities she admired.

In the week she had known him, Sarah had come to respect Januel's mind. He was shrewd and quick. He handled what she had always considered mysteries of administration with ease and confidence. If she did not sense the same raw strength as she had recognized in Byron Lloyd, she sensed a more refined technique. She admired his flair for diplomacy. He used charm where she had seen Byron use logic. How did two extraordinarily different men succeed in the same business with such totally diverse styles? Ambition? She had asked herself the question more than once.

On a more personal level, Januel had, in the evenings they had spent together, filled a void Sarah had felt for months. He was a companion, a man to talk with, to touch both physically and mentally. He stimulated her, reminding Sarah of her own femininity, of needs that had not been filled since she had left New York. He reminded her that her work was not enough.

Though they were not yet lovers, Sarah had felt a comfortable pleasure in his arms. She had tasted a promise in his mouth. She wasn't certain whether he hesitated over intimacy or whether her own indecision held him off. She wanted him, but knew herself well enough to be aware that once she opened herself physically, she would open emotionally as well. When Sarah gave herself, she held nothing in reserve.

The sky was a deeper gray as they walked around the Panthéon. The clouds were dark and heavy. Abruptly Sarah leaned over and kissed Januel's cheek. "You're very sweet."

His brow lifted with a smile. "Am I?"

"You've let me drag you all over Paris to goggle at buildings you've seen countless times."

"Not sweet but selfish," he corrected as they walked back to his car. "I want you to myself. When Sundays are warm and dry, I shall drag you from the city for solitary picnics in the woods." He smiled, kissing her hand briefly as he opened the passenger door of his car.

"I'll look forward to spring." Her skin felt warm and soft where he had kissed it. Sarah watched him round the hood to his side of the car and was again struck by the classic beauty of his features.

The first streak of lightning split the clouds as Januel turned the key in the ignition. Thunder grumbled and lightning snaked again, but the rain held back. The air grew weighty and thick. Traffic charged and raced and swerved. Januel drove toward Sarah's hotel with the confidence of a man used to brushing people out of his way.

Sarah's mind was involved with the impending storm. The light took on a dim, eerie glow. More than the sun and the rain, Sarah loved the last few moments before the break of a storm. She could feel it tingling around her and saw it in the dark arrogance of the sky.

Above them the clouds rolled and bumped. The rain hurled itself against the windshield as Januel pulled the car to the curb across from Sarah's hotel.

"I've an umbrella in the back," he began, but Sarah was already out of the car.

She was instantly drenched. Her hair was sleek against her scalp, her jacket soaked through. The mauve skirt of her dress clung to her legs. Delighted, she stood with her face lifted and her eyes closed.

"*Nom de Dieu*, you'll drown in a moment." Januel pulled her under the cover of an English umbrella.

"Isn't it marvelous?" Her eyes were brilliant as another clap of thunder rolled above their heads. Drops of rain clung to her lashes.

For an answer, Januel grabbed her hand and rushed her across the street and into the hotel lobby. At the door he shook out his umbrella, then closed it. Breathless from laughing, Sarah leaned against the wall and watched him. He gave her an exasperated smile before taking her hand and crossing to the elevators. "You'll catch a chill."

"No, I'm disgustingly healthy." She brushed a few stray raindrops from his cashmere jacket. "I've always liked the rain, even on picnics." Her smile was open and happy. The rain had made her feel alive and vital. She wanted to share the sensation.

Januel kissed her nose as the elevator doors shut them inside. "Then perhaps we won't wait until spring for our picnic."

He saw by her quick grin that his answer had pleased her. Because she was aware of her soaking sleeves and Januel's fastidiousness, she resisted tucking her arm through his. Instead she began to search for her room key when they reached her floor.

"I've seen precious little rain since I moved from New York," she said as she groped through her bag. "It's possible this is the same rain I got caught in when I was running for the Fifty-ninth Street subway last year." When she located the key, Januel took it from her and slid it into the lock.

"Sarah." He laughed as he nudged her into the room. "At times I fear you are quite mad."

She ran her fingers through her dripping hair as she

grinned at him. "Maybe. There's brandy on the bar. Why don't you pour some?"

Sarah slipped into the bathroom to peel out of her jacket and grab a towel. When she came back, she stood in the bedroom doorway, rubbing her hair briskly with the towel and watching Januel fill the snifters. She enjoyed the way he moved, the gentle fluidity of his muscles. He too had taken off his jacket. His shirt and slacks clung to his body. She admired the sweep of his brow and the curve of his chin. Never had she seen features more beautifully balanced. He smiled as he offered her the brandy. Sarah slipped out of her shoes as she cupped the snifter in both hands. Outside, the thunder grew dim and the rain began a soft patter.

"It seems the storm's over," she commented. She held the brandy on her tongue a moment, savoring it. "I like them best when they're quick and furious. The air's always cleaner after." Glancing down, she pulled the clinging skirt away from her legs, then grinned. "I suppose I'd better change."

Januel set down his snifter, then took the towel from Sarah's shoulders. With long, gentle strokes, he began to dry her hair. The gesture set the blood pounding in Sarah's veins. His eyes met hers and lingered.

"You are exquisite," he murmured as he let the towel drop. "Your hair smells of rain." His hand slid around her neck as he feathered a kiss at her temple. With his free hand, he took the brandy from her and set it aside. With slow, whispering kisses he traced her mouth. She reached up to pull him firmly down to her, but he took her hands and continued to tease her lips with his tongue. "Sarah." He nipped her earlobe and felt her tremble. "We must get you out of these wet clothes." She felt his hand on the zipper of her dress and murmured in response.

He took his time undressing her. His hands wandered here and there without truly possessing as her wet dress dropped at their feet. "Lovely," he whispered as his hands caressed beneath the silk of her chemise. Taking her hips, he ran his thumbs down the long bones. Still without hurry, he slipped the straps of the chemise from her shoulders, then urged it down the length of her, letting his fingers trace over her skin. Sarah's heartbeat grew rapid and unsteady. At last Januel's mouth took hers, and she wrapped her arms around his neck as he led her into the bedroom.

She shivered at the cool spread under her skin. Her limbs felt heavy. She fumbled with the buttons of his shirt, wanting to feel him, wanting the warmth of skin against skin. The pleasure of being loved was nearly painful. Her breath was a sigh.

She heard Januel's murmurs, in beautiful, soft French, as they explored each other more freely. He was smooth and lean, with hands as clever as they were elegant. Sarah wanted to lie naked and tangled forever, being close, feeling tiny thrills pass along her skin. When he suckled at her breast, she cradled his head with one hand and ran her other hand over his back. She found a gentle play of muscles.

His palms were soft, running along her inner thigh and over her curling tuft of hair. He lingered there, until her movements beneath him became less languid. The scent of rain and wildflowers seem to cling to her everywhere. The pulse above her breast began to hammer. Januel tasted it. His breath came quickly, rushing to meet hers as their mouths joined again. . . .

Sleepy and content beside Januel, Sarah rested a head on his shoulder and traced her finger over the light spray of hair on his chest. She could taste the faintest trace of salt on his skin. The bottom of her foot rubbed over the top of his as she closed her eyes.

"Mmm, that was nice. It should've rained days ago."

Januel laughed as he kissed the crown of her head. Her hair was still damp and like silk under his hand. He ran his fingers through it, then watched it fall onto the pillowcase.

"Did you know that making love is more effective than brandy for warding off chills?"

Sarah roused herself enough to lift her head and smile at him. Her brow arched expressively. "I do now." He pulled her down to him for a short, satisfying kiss. Sarah pillowed her cheek on his chest and closed her eyes.

"It will have to be a very short nap before you have to dress, *chérie*," Januel commented and ran a hand absently over her smooth flank.

She stretched languidly. "Why do I have to dress?"

"We have tickets for the ballet," he reminded her. *"Giselle."* Januel glanced at his watch. "We must be at the theater in ninety minutes."

"Oh yes, the ballet." Sarah yawned, then ran a hand down his ribcage. "I don't suppose we could miss the first act, could we?"

Januel touched her shoulder lightly. "There is always after the theater, *mon amour.*"

Sarah sighed as she felt him shift away from her. She wanted more time, more intimacy. Something nagged at her, insisting that there hadn't been enough. But he turned and smiled at her. Because her heart had opened to let him in, she responded.

Chapter Thirteen

I<small>T WAS AT THE GROUND-BREAKING CEREMONIES THAT</small>
Sarah first captured the eye of the French press. Standing
beside the dapper figure of André Ceseare, she was immediate news.

She was wearing a stark black loose coat over a simple
white silk dress, and had managed to look both professional
and mysterious. An American, a beautiful female American, made good copy, particularly when she was designing
an important French building. And she was under the
Haladay wing; Haladay Paris was a prestigious, highly
respected firm.

When Sarah found herself surrounded by reporters, she
answered their rapid-fire questions patiently. The public
relations branch had drummed the advantage of good press
into her head. And she remembered Byron's brief comments the day he had given her the Delacroix assignment.
Sarah cooperated for Haladay and for herself.

Questions about the theater, the style of architecture, the
estimated time of construction, Sarah answered with no
evasions. Questions about herself, she answered more
discreetly. Every evening edition carried Sarah's picture
alongside the story on the Delacroix Center. Two celebrities
were launched.

Sarah was to learn how quickly her name had become known that evening at André's cocktail party. Packed into his antique-and-art-cluttered townhouse was the cream of Paris society. The air was ripe with perfume and expensive tobacco.

Men were dressed in everything from casual silk shirts and hand-made jeans to tuxedos. The women knew fashion and could afford to keep up with it. Sarah recognized flashy St. Laurents and classic Diors. Gold gleamed in abundance. Hairstyles ranged from prim to extravagant. Sarah had dressed to please herself in a black silk tanktop and narrow black pants, topped with a punched-gold sheepskin jacket. She left her hair loose and wore no jewelry.

The wealth and fame interested her; the casual drip of diamonds, the pampered faces. They lived differently, she knew, these people who could wear fortunes. Sarah enjoyed studying them. She would enjoy building for them. As for becoming one of them, she would enjoy the wealth and fame, but on her terms. She remembered the gates and the guard at Harrison Reed's estate.

"Have I told you how marvelous you look?" Januel murmured in her ear.

Sarah tilted her head, shooting him a sidelong smile. "Yes, but you can tell me again."

"You look like a young panther, lean and limber." His eyes roamed down her, then back to her face. It was not an appraising look, but an appreciative one. He knew her body very well.

They had made love often over the past weeks, and Sarah had found him a gentle, attentive partner. Her one disappointment was that he would never spend the night with her. Always, they made love in her hotel suite, and always, he left her to sleep alone. She missed the companionship, the continuation of intimacy.

"*Chérie*, everyone is impressed by you," Januel continued. "You enchanted the press this afternoon, and you intrigue the beau monde tonight." He leaned closer so that his words carried to her only. His cologne was light and appealing. "Do you know how difficult it has been to get you to myself for even a few minutes?"

Sarah tilted her head and smiled at him. "No, but we could leave, then you could have me to yourself for much more than a few minutes."

"André would roast me for stealing his centerpiece." Januel touched the rim of his glass to hers. "Now you must follow a social blueprint as the builders follow yours for the center. You'll be deluged with invitations to parties and requests for interviews."

Sarah moved her shoulders, glancing around as she sipped her wine. "It should be fun as long as it doesn't interfere with my work. I'll be pretty busy at the site for a while." She liked the notion of socializing, but not when she was working on a project.

"This is part of your work too," Januel reminded her.

Sarah made an absent sound of agreement and nodded. She remembered Byron's words. A young, attractive woman wouldn't hurt the Haladay image. She had agreed to learn the game and wanted the prize at the end. Success, power, fame—were they all the same? she wondered. I don't know, she decided, but I'm damn well going to find out.

"Sarah." Januel touched her arm to reclaim her attention. He waited until she had smiled, acknowledging him. "You must check with me before you refuse or accept any invitation, also before you grant interviews. We will outline the questions you can expect and your answers."

"Must I?" Sarah murmured. "Why?" She took no pains to conceal her annoyance.

Januel laid a hand gently on hers. "Sarah, you're still a relative stranger in Paris. There are people you should cultivate and people you should not." He watched her frown deepen. "It is quite possible that without the proper guide you could miss an opportunity or offend the wrong person. It is possible," he continued gently, "that a clever reporter could trick you into being . . . indiscreet."

"No one tricks me into being indiscreet," Sarah said. "And I cultivate gardens, not people."

Patiently, Januel took her hand in his. "Sarah, this is business. Things cannot always be as simple as you might like." In a public display of affection, he bent down and brushed her mouth with his. "Think about it, *chérie*."

The gentleness in his look and voice caused Sarah to feel that she had been childishly touchy. She sighed. "All right, I'll think about it."

"Dear Januel, how long it's been!"

"Madeline, as beautiful as ever." Januel brought her hand to his lips. "Comtesse Madeline de la Salle, may I present Mademoiselle Sarah Lancaster."

"Ah." The syllable was knowledgeable. "The architect, and more lovely than your photograph." Her eyes darted down to Sarah's toes, then back. "You have a fine eye for style, mademoiselle."

"Thank you, madame."

"Everyone buzzes about the theater and what a brilliant accomplishment it will be. You're to be congratulated."

"I'd rather have my congratulations after it's finished." Sarah smiled. "We've a long way to go."

The smile gave Madeline a moment's pause. It was surprisingly worldly. "I'm having a small dinner party next week. I'd like you to join me." Her eyes drifted across to Januel. "Both of you."

"Of course, Madeline," Januel answered before Sarah could respond. "We'd love to come."

Sarah looked at him inquiringly. His inference of possession both pleased and irritated her. Even as Januel met the look and smiled, she felt a touch on her arm.

"Sarah, *ma chère*, you must not hide in a corner," André scolded in his rapid-fire, stop-and-go English. "There is someone you must meet. I shall steal her from you, Januel."

"As long as you return her."

Sarah glanced back at him before moving to the other side of the room with André. "That makes me sound like a Christmas present that doesn't suit," she commented.

Madeline watched them thread their way through the crowd. "A pretty child," she stated, then ran her tongue over the rim of her glass. "And bright."

"Pretty and bright," Januel agreed. His teeth showed in a quick smile. "But not such a child, Madeline. Young, to be sure." Glancing over, he saw Sarah's hand being kissed by one of André's Swiss colleagues. "Young enough to be malleable," he added, bringing his eyes back to Madeline. "Pretty enough to be appealing, and bright enough to go to the top."

"And naive enough to take you with her?" Madeline added with a nod. She gave a low chuckle before she moved closer. Her full breast brushed Januel's arm as she smiled up at him. "Can she be all this and still feed your . . . generous appetite?" She smiled over the rim of her champagne, watching his eyes.

"Let's say Sarah hasn't your experience or your . . ." He paused, remembered. "Imagination."

She laughed again, then dipped a finger into his wine and laid it on her tongue. "Call me when you're bored playing with children," she invited.

Sarah sat at her drawing board. She had tied the curtains back from the window to allow the warm spring sunlight to spill through. At the moment she noticed none of it.

There were final changes to be made on the interior design of one of the theaters. Her work had her full attention. The chocolate and pastries that her secretary had brought to her two hours earlier sat cold and forgotten on the elegant coffee table across the room. The phone rang three times before she heard it, and twice more before she remembered that she had sent Madame Fountblane to lunch.

"Damn," she muttered and lifted the receiver. "Sarah

Lancaster," she said while continuing to frown down at her sketch.

"Hello, Sarah Lancaster." The low, gravelly voice was pure American.

"Max!" The surge of pleasure was instantaneous. She dropped her pencil and touched the phone with both hands. "It's good to hear an American speak American. Say something else," she demanded.

Haladay laughed, enjoying the quick excitement in her voice. "Don't tell me you're homesick."

"I was; I got over it." Until just now, she thought ruefully, then shook her head. "How are you, Max?"

"I'm fine." He passed a hand over his heart, knowing he exaggerated. "I hear things are going well for you, but I'd like to hear it firsthand."

For the first time that day Sarah noticed the sunlight spilling over her desk. She rose, taking the phone with her. "We're on schedule. Once we waded through the paperwork and broke ground, things picked up. Christ, Max, the formalities over here are incredible." The leaves on the trees outside her window were greening. Sarah cradled the phone on her shoulder and opened the window with her free hand. Spring rushed into the room. "The excavation crews had a lot of mud to deal with. We had a bit of rain over here. But it's been dry for several days. The frame's going up quickly."

"No problems?"

"I looked over a punch list this morning." Sarah wandered back to her desk and sat down. "Very minor stuff. It's going beautifully, Max. It's almost scary. André is very supportive and manages to keep the backers out of the way the majority of the time. Januel deals with the officials."

"Bounnet?" Sarah heard Max crunch a peppermint between his teeth. "He knows his stuff. Got your picture in the paper a couple of times."

Sarah grinned and leaned back in her chair. She should

have known he would miss nothing. "Maybe I'll start a scrapbook. Did Byron like the stories?"

"Good publicity," Haladay stated ambiguously. "Don't get too cocky."

She laughed. "Max, the center's going to be one hell of a building. Come out and see for yourself."

She thought she heard him sigh but couldn't be certain. "When it's finished," he said after a moment, "I'll take you to the opening performance."

"It's a date."

"Keep me posted," he instructed, falling back into a business tone. "I want to hear from you as well as Bounnet."

"All right." She sensed the dismissal. "Good-bye, Max."

Chapter Fourteen

On the site of the Delacroix project, Sarah in jeans and a T-shirt became as familiar as steel girders and concrete block. When Dallas sent her a Yankees fielder's cap, she added it to her uniform. Pictures of the woman amid the growing shell of the building vied with pictures of the woman in chic Paris society. Because Januel was always her escort, her name was linked with his, and their relationship was fresh cause for speculation in print. Sarah didn't read the tabloids in French or English. Most of the time she pretended they didn't exist.

Generally Sarah enjoyed the parties, the people, her own growing fame. Above all else, she enjoyed watching her designs take shape in concrete and steel. When construction was into its second month, she was on the cover of *Newsweek*. Sarah read the article and worried about the central staircase leading to the main theater. She found no time to truly savor the flavor of success. All her energies were involved with her work. I resent *wasting* time, she thought, as hands on her hips she inspected the mosaic floor in the completed east wing lobby. The walls were glass. Here, where Sarah paced, would be an exotic central garden. The plants had already been ordered; rhododendron, fuchsia, wisteria, weeping cherry, dozens of varieties of roses. She had worked with the landscape expert and together they had created something unique and exceptionally beautiful. The paths that would wind through the garden were already set into the floor, the two miniature fountains already operable.

In other parts of the building Sarah could hear the construction workers. It was hot, the air thick as mechanics worked with a faulty cooling system. Sarah had bundled her hair under her cap and tied her red cotton blouse under her breasts. Still, sweat trickled down her back in a slow, miserable stream.

Sarah passed the back of her hand over her forehead and pushed up the brim of her cap. If they didn't get the air working soon, they'd have to knock off. She began to walk toward the sounds of building. They were nearly a week behind schedule now. A week. To be less than a week behind on a job of this size was a miracle, but she was too much of a perfectionist to be satisfied.

She picked her way across the plastic tarp laid over the entrance to the west wing. Carpenters, stripped to the waist, were working on the main staircase. Slowly, they were molding the oak into what Sarah had pictured as a sweeping, liquid expanse of wood. The stairs would descend in an arch like a waterfall.

"*Pardon.*" Sarah interrupted one workman with the shoulders and arms of Hercules. Jesus, she thought as he turned to her. I should ship him home to Dallas.

"*Oui*, Mademoiselle Lancaster?"

She spoke in quick French. "Can you tell me where to find Monsieur Lafitte?" A quick glance had told her the foreman was not with this crew of carpenters.

"With the mechanics. They're still working on the cooling system."

One of his companions made a comment about the heat, something fast and colloquial that Sarah could only partially translate. She waited for the laughter to subside.

"If it's not fixed in an hour, we close down for the rest of the day. What's your name?'' She addressed the young Hercules as she pulled off her cap and used it as a fan.

"Jean-Marc, mademoiselle.''

"Jean-Marc, tell everyone to break for lunch. One hour today. If the cooling system hasn't been fixed in an hour, everyone goes home. You'll spread the word for me?''

"Oui, mademoiselle.'' He flashed her a smile as he unhooked his tool belt.

She left him slinging a shirt over his shoulder and calling out instructions.

Paul Lafitte was a small, wide man of fifty with curly gray hair and a curly gray mustache. In all the weeks they had worked together, Sarah had never heard him raise his voice. She liked his style, his intelligence, and his sense of fairness. More than once, they had shared a bottle of wine and a hunk of bread and cheese in a quick lunch break on the site. He took as much pride in the center as she did.

Sarah could hear him talking as she wound her way down labyrinthine corridors and staircases to the now nearly airless utility room. She saw Derille, the chief engineer, with Lafitte and three mechanics. Lafitte rubbed his damp, grimy handkerchief over his brow and softly cursed the immense unit which refused to cool the air.

"Paul.'' Sarah moved toward them.

"Sarah.'' He spread his hands in the gesture all Frenchmen learn in the cradle. "We have a problem," he said.

Beside him, Derille snorted and pushed back damp, dark hair. He was a foot taller than Lafitte and lanky, and he wore thick-lensed glasses. Sarah knew he was a good engineer and liked him well enough, though they had argued more than once over the center. "Lafitte has a genius for understatement. Perhaps if you had not insisted on so much unsectioned space in each wing—" he began with a grim smile.

"I design the building," she said, cutting him off. "Heating and cooling it are your problems, not mine.'' Because she knew he was as hot and edgy as she was, she tempered the statement by touching his arm. "Let's see what the mechanics come up with before we argue. I'll say one thing. This is one hell of a tight building."

She fanned herself with her cap, but the air she stirred was steaming and stable. Lafitte was talking to the mechanics. When he returned to her, he explained, "It's the coil, a defect. A replacement will be necessary."

"Merde;" she said distinctly.

Lafitte politely agreed.

"How long will it take to get one?" she asked.

He stuck out his lower lip as he shrugged. "It's difficult to say." Beads of moisture congregated just below his mustache. "Perhaps a week."

"Merde," Sarah said again, then jammed her hands into her pockets. "I'm not losing a goddamn week," she muttered. "No way. Where'd we get the unit?"

Derille answered. "Saint-Etienne. We'll have to contact the firm and order a replacement coil. The paperwork will take time—processing the order, shipping."

Sarah turned back to Lafitte. "Pick one of the men to fly to Saint-Etienne this afternoon. He can pick up the coil and fly it back. Make sure you get someone who can recognize the part. I don't want any foul-ups. I'll arrange the details. Give me an hour." After looking down at her watch, she shook her head. "No, hell, I might need two at this time of day. Bring a courier to my office in two hours. Make sure he's ready to move." With her quick, surefooted stride, she headed for the stairway. "Oh yeah, I gave the crews the rest of the day off. Get yourselves out of here too. No one can work in these conditions."

"Bien," Lafitte murmured, but she was already bounding up the stairs. He turned back to his men. "You heard the lady."

The air was kinder in Sarah's office; fresh and cool and lightly scented with fresh roses from Januel. Her hair still curled damply at her temples, but for the first time in three hours, the cotton of her shirt separated from her skin.

"Get me the manager of the factory in Saint-Etienne where we bought the cooling unit for the center." Sarah gave the order to Madame Fountblane as she swung through her office door. She pulled open the drawer of a file cabinet and began to rummage. "Then check out the quickest round-trip flight there and back and make a reservation. If there isn't anything suitable, get a charter." Sarah located the specs on the cooling system and whipped them out. "And see if Monsieur Bounnet's in."

Leaving her secretary dialing, Sarah spread out the specs. Her finger moved rapidly over the papers, her eyes following. With a quick scrawl, she jotted down the unit's code and model. The buzzer sounded beside her.

"Monsieur Brionne, the manager of the Gaspar Factory in Saint-Etienne."

"Thanks." Sarah changed lines. "Monsieur Brionne, Sarah Lancaster. We've a bit of a problem."

Fifteen minutes later Sarah signaled her secretary again. "Is Monsieur Bounnet in?"

"He's in a meeting at the World Bank and is not scheduled back until four."

"Damn," Sarah muttered under her breath, and tapped her fingernails against the desk's surface as she rearranged her thoughts. "It'll have to be Troudeau then. See if he's available, and send Lafitte in whenever he gets here."

Within ninety minutes Sarah had plowed her way through the paperwork and had a man on his way to Saint-Etienne. Now, with her office empty and her phone silent, she remembered that she had eaten no lunch. Her shirt felt stiff across the shoulder blades from dried perspiration. Leaning back in her chair, she allowed herself to relax for the first time that day. Overlaying her hunger and weariness was a sense of accomplishment. A problem had been handled with minimal fuss. A week's layoff had been avoided. Sarah knew the building had progressed far enough for her to consider going back to Phoenix. She pushed away the papers that littered her desk.

I absolutely refuse to file them, she decided. I'm going home and shower for an entire hour. Before she could push away from the desk, however, her door opened and Januel strode in.

"You're back early," she said, annoyed that he hadn't knocked.

"The meeting was over earlier than I expected." His tone was cool. "You've been busy," he commented.

"Yes." She straightened her shoulders automatically. "Is there a problem?"

"There is always a problem when a member of the staff oversteps his or her authority."

"Elaborate," she said, raising an eyebrow.

"It has just come to my attention that you stopped work on the Delacroix project this afternoon, and that you have arranged for one of the mechanics to fly to Saint-Etienne to pick up a part."

"Yes. Would you like me to give you the details, or do you already have them?"

"Troudeau tells me of a defective coil." Januel brushed the problem aside. "What concerns me though, Sarah, is that you seem to have forgotten who is in charge."

Puzzled, she stared up at him. This is ridiculous, she thought. He's concerned about his ego. "I haven't forgotten who's in charge, Januel," she corrected. "You weren't available."

"The entire matter should have waited until I was available."

"No." She rose then so that their faces were level. "We got the last flight to Saint-Etienne today. Time was important."

"So is the smooth running of a business."

"Goddamn it, Troudeau has the necessary authority, and I followed standard procedures as closely as was feasible. It was a clear-cut decision, Januel." She tossed up her hands. "The only other option was to lose days."

"That remains to be seen. The cooling system is only one

aspect of the project. And there is no doubt that you ignored several steps of purchasing procedure."

The hell with purchasing procedure, Sarah thought, but managed to hold her tongue.

"The crews are hired to work," Januel went on. "They expect to work and do so until I authorize them to stop. You overstepped yourself this afternoon."

"Perhaps I did." Sarah spoke with the calm of fury. She found it almost unbelievable that he could be so rigid. "Under the same conditions, I'd overstep myself tomorrow. I was there, Januel," she said, trying to excuse him, not herself. "You weren't."

"I am not in a position to spend my time wandering about building sites."

"No. But I am, and I'm telling you, the conditions today were unbearable."

"Construction workers are used to working under such conditions." Januel made a quick, elegant gesture of dismissal.

"Save your class distinctions," she shot back furiously. "I haven't the patience for them. And don't you tell me about construction workers. I've been with crews when it's been so hot they couldn't lay shingles because the tar burned their hands. They swill down salt tablets and gallons of water and sweat like pigs. I don't know how hot it was in that building today, but it was worse than hot, it was airless. What fans we had stirred around stale air. It was like being in a goddamn box. If you don't trust my judgment, talk to Lafitte or Derille. They were there too." She pushed her hair back from her face with both hands. "And if you don't like the way I handle things, take it up with Max. I don't work for you."

Januel had not expected this reaction. Her eyes met his without faltering. After a moment he spoke again. "I have no doubt you did what you felt was correct, Sarah. Indeed, it might prove to be so on further study. It was, however, impetuous. You must understand my position. Authorizing a break in the work schedule is a radical decision. Such a thing should be passed up the chain of command.''

"And if a couple of workers keel over from heat exhaustion while the decision's making its journey, that's the breaks." Incensed, Sarah shook her head. "No, I can't see the logic in that." She began to push together the papers on her desk. "If I've gone outside the proper channels, I'm sorry, but I feel I had no choice. People are more important to me than protocol."

"We look at this thing differently. You must build your building." He laid his hands on the back of her shoulders. "I must administrate."

Sarah stiffened at his touch, and though he felt it, Januel didn't break the contact. "Don't patronize me, Januel." She turned to face him.

"Very well." He kept his voice pleasant, and she could no longer see any signs of temper in his face. "I've told you my position on the matter, but as it's a *fait accompli,* there's no point in worrying about it anymore. I only ask, Sarah, that you limit your duties to your architecture and leave administration to me."

"And if you're not available?"

"I shall make certain I am."

"All right," she said coolly. "You've told me."

"And now . . ." He stepped toward her again. "We will put our business disagreement aside?" He touched her cheek with a finger and smiled. His eyes were again light and clear.

It was not a simple matter for Sarah to switch her emotions on and off. And her emotions had been involved in the defense of her position, not ego or pride. She made an effort to separate her professional and personal viewpoints.

"All right, Januel." Suddenly tired, Sarah rubbed the bridge of her nose between her thumb and forefinger. "I'll only be here for a few more weeks in any case. I doubt that the problem will come up again."

"But, my love, this is not the time to speak of your

leaving." Januel slipped an arm around her waist. "Let me take you to dinner tonight, the same little café where we ate the first night we met. There we will be only a man and woman who find pleasure in each other. We should have a table on the sidewalk." He brought her hand to his lips. "You like the stars."

Sarah looked into his eyes. She found it impossible to resent him. We disagree, she told herself. That's all. "With champagne and napoleons?" she demanded. When he laughed, she kissed him briefly, then wriggled out of his embrace. "I'd like that, Januel."

"Then you shall have it, my love."

Chapter Fifteen

HER WORK CLOTHES TOSSED INTO A HEAP ON THE closet floor, Sarah sat cross-legged on her bed, dressed in a skin-toned lace teddy. As she brushed her hair she thought about Januel.

Sentence by sentence, she went over their last conversation. His attitude puzzled her. It had not occurred to her that by acting on her own initiative, she had been undermining his authority.

Why should a man in his position, and with his talent, be so insecure? How could anyone so generous and kind be petty?

Maybe she had overreacted to the situation. Should she have waited and talked to Januel before dismissing the men?

No! Those men couldn't go on working in that oven. And by expediting the delivery of the coil, she had saved the company time and money.

She still couldn't understand why Januel had reacted so strongly. Could he actually believe that workingmen didn't deserve decent working conditions? She conjured up a picture of Januel in her mind; his smooth, even features, his pale blond hair, his clear eyes. I can't believe he could think that way . . . not really.

She shook her head. I won't think about it anymore

tonight, she thought. She pushed herself from the bed and went to her closet. The ring of her bell surprised her.

"He's early," she murmured as she scooped up a thin white robe. With one arm in the robe, the other struggling down its sleeve, she pulled open the door. "You're early," she began with a smile. "Oh." The smile turned into astonishment as she looked up at Byron Lloyd.

"So it seems." His eyes ran down the length of her before returning to her face. "Expecting someone?"

"I certainly wasn't expecting you," she said. "I thought you were thousands of miles away."

"I just got in."

"Well, welcome, traveler." She invited him in with a flourish of her arm. "I've drinks for your men and water for your horses." After closing the door behind him, she turned to find him barely a step away.

"Paris agrees with you," Byron commented after a moment. He made no move to back up, to make the distance between them conventional. She wore the same scent. He remembered it. Her skin was smooth and glowing without makeup, her eyes younger, more vulnerable. She had lost her Phoenix tan during the winter, and her coloring was as he had first seen it, pale and fragile.

"Thank you." The compliment surprised her. She knew how frugal he was with personal comments. A thought came to her abruptly. "Is Max all right?" Sarah reached out to take his arm.

Her concern was easily read. "Yes, he's all right." Byron felt her fingers relax on his sleeve. Just her touch reminded him of how much he had wanted her months before and how much he wanted her now.

Sarah dropped her hand and turned away. "What can I fix you, Byron? I have a bar of sorts. A little of this, a little of that."

"Try for a little bourbon, straight up."

"That's an easy one." She moved across the room and lifted two glasses. She poured bourbon generously into one glass and Perrier into another. "I didn't expect you. Shouldn't someone have sent up a signal? I hope there's no problem I don't know about."

"I had a meeting in London." Byron watched her hair lift and fall as she tossed it behind her back. "Since I was this close, I wanted to see the project firsthand." He waited until she had moved back to him. The robe shifted gently at her hips. "You've become quite a celebrity."

"Yes. I still can't believe it." After handing him his bourbon, Sarah touched her glass to his. The first shock waves of seeing him had passed. "You saw the *Newsweek* article?" She gestured for him to sit.

"That and others."

"The others are basically social nonsense. This party, that dress, who's where with whom." Sarah shrugged them off. "But the *Newsweek* thing was different. I think it was good publicity for Haladay and for architecture. And probably women in architecture. And"—she grinned and sipped again—"for me."

"P.R. is thinking of canonizing you." Byron swirled his bourbon.

"You called it, Byron, as far as the press angle goes."

Byron drank, watching her smile at him. "It appears Bounnet has been looking out for you."

Sarah's brow lifted. "I don't think that's the right choice of words." She cupped the drink in both hands, as he had seen her do with a mug of coffee. "No one needs to look out for me." He had less flesh in his face than Januel, more bone. The involuntary comparison annoyed her.

"The press enjoys linking you," he said casually. "You photograph well together."

Sarah knew when she was being baited. "Januel's a very attractive man," she said coolly. "I know it's good publicity, but I don't much care for being photographed every time I turn a corner."

"Don't you? It's always difficult to have it all, Sarah."

It was the first time he had spoken her name since he had come into the room. Hearing it, she smiled and set down her drink. "Why should I have to give up my privacy?"

"Because nothing's free." Byron finished his bourbon and rose. "Since I seem to have interrupted you in the middle of dressing, I'll leave you to finish."

Sarah unfolded her legs and stood. Her robe shifted, parting a bit more where it crossed over her breasts. "Don't go. It's been so long since I've heard anyone speak honest-to-God American. I've missed that. Talk to me while I dress." She turned toward the bedroom. "I'll leave the door open." Sarah went directly to her closet. Byron walked to the bar. "How long will you be in Paris?"

"A week or so." Byron added bourbon to his glass. He stood by the window gazing out at the setting sun. He thought of making love to Sarah as the sun set. He drank, letting the bourbon spread through him. There were sounds of hangers sliding over the closet pole. "Have you had any problems with the project?"

"Problems?" Sarah thought of the coil and nibbled on her lip. "Nothing important, no."

Byron noticed the slight hesitation but let it pass. Tomorrow, he decided, was soon enough. "I'll want to go through both the building and the paperwork tomorrow."

"Mmm." Sarah remembered the total disorder of her desk and the heat-trapped interior of the building. "How's Cassidy?"

"He's fine." He heard the door of the closet shut. "His fifth grandchild was born last month."

"Boy or girl?" she asked, rummaging through her jewelry box.

"Boy, eight pounds. Matthew Lloyd Cassidy. I'm the godfather."

"Oh." Genuinely surprised, Sarah tried to picture Byron Lloyd holding a squirming infant. "Cassidy must be very pleased."

"Naturally. Do you want your drink?"

"What? Oh, yes. I'm G-rated at this point, if you don't mind bringing it in."

Byron paused at the doorway to watch her standing with her weight on one bare foot, struggling with the clasp of a silver chain. "Damn," she muttered, blowing the hair from her eyes. She saw Byron in the mirror. "Give me a hand, will you? I can't get it."

Byron set the glass on the dresser. "Turn around." He placed his hands on her shoulders. It was the contact of his palms on her bare skin that told Sarah she had made a mistake. This was not a man to ask casual favors of. "Lift your hair."

She obeyed, trying to ignore the increased rhythm of her heart. Byron's fingers brushed the nape of her neck and she shuddered. Sarah met his eyes in the mirror.

Silently he took her hands in his, bringing them down to her sides so that her hair tumbled free again. Their eyes were locked in the glass. She shook her head and watched him smile. She tried to draw her hands away, but his closed over them.

Still not speaking, he turned her to face him. He took her earlobe gently between his thumb and forefinger. Sarah's breath trembled.

"Emeralds," he said quietly. "You should wear emeralds. They'd catch the green in your eyes." She remembered the sensation of his mouth on hers. It had been hard and demanding and exhilarating. When the doorbell rang, neither of them moved.

"That's Januel," she managed, then swallowed. He moved his hand, and then was no longer touching her. "Would you like to join us for dinner?" She wondered if the invitation sounded as ridiculous to him as it did to her.

"I think not."

Sarah moved quickly past him into the next room. "Are you staying in the hotel?" she asked, knowing how strained her voice sounded.

"Next door. Eight sixteen."

"Oh." She opened the door to Januel.

"*Chérie*, enchanting as always." Sarah watched his smile fade as his eyes traveled past her.

"Byron's come to see how our project is doing," she said.

"Byron." Januel stepped forward and extended his hand. "It's good to have you with us. If I had known you were coming, I would have met you at the airport."

The handshake was brief. These two, Sarah noted instantly, did not like each other.

"A drink, Januel?" she asked brightly.

"Yes, thank you, Sarah."

Byron noted that Sarah poured from a bottle of vermouth without asking his choice.

"I've asked Byron to come with us," Sarah said as she brought Januel his drink. "But he turned me down."

"We're dining at a small café Sarah and I are particularly fond of." Januel smiled at Byron as he touched Sarah's shoulder lightly. "It's very quiet and informal. We'd love you to join us."

The hell you would, Byron reflected as he met the smile dead on. Without speaking, he turned to Sarah, noting that she was staring hard at both of them. She wore the same concentrated look he had seen on her face when she studied a set of blueprints. It would be simple to agree and foul up Bounnet's plans for the evening. He'd enjoy that.

"I appreciate the offer," Byron said, "but I'll pass. I have a few things to catch up on before the meeting tomorrow."

Chapter Sixteen

SARAH COULD SEE THE SUN RISE FROM HER BEDROOM window. A pearly rose was spreading over a sky still misted with night. Far to the west, there were lingering stars. Opening the window, she let morning into the room. She was wide awake and pleased with herself. Ten minutes before, the phone had awakened her from a dead sleep. She had her coil, and Lafitte was already at the site overseeing the repair. Work would continue with little more than a ripple in the rhythm. She took a deep, relieved breath before heading for the shower. As the steam rose around her she thought over her evening with Januel.

Januel had been distant and preoccupied throughout dinner. Sarah had wondered if his aloofness stemmed from their disagreement in the office or Byron's presence. She had felt the strength of his dislike for Byron and wondered if it was personal or professional.

She turned off the shower and grabbed a towel. I like Byron, she thought. It's the physical attraction that worries me. It's there, she admitted, remembering the feeling that had coursed through her when their eyes met in her bedroom mirror. There's no use pretending it isn't. But we'll be working together for a long time. I'll simply have to ignore it.

Still naked, and slightly damp from the shower, Sarah walked back into the bedroom. In a quick, practiced rhythm she wound her hair into one fat braid and let it hang down her back.

This morning, she decided, I'll take him through the center. I want to know what he thinks of the building. This afternoon, she added as she pulled on a T-shirt, I'll turn him over to the paper pushers. That should keep him out of my way.

She glanced at her watch—seven thirty. Well, if he isn't up, he should be. Swinging a leather bag over her shoulder, Sarah strolled from her room down the hall to 816.

Byron heard the knock as he rinsed off traces of shaving lather. *"Entrez,"* he called out as he reached for a towel. He continued in French as he pulled on a robe. "Just leave it on the table," he ordered, then belted the robe before walking out of the room.

"Morning, Byron." Sarah gave him a friendly smile. "What would you like me to leave?"

"A pot of coffee to begin with."

"Sorry, fresh out," Sarah told him. "I didn't know you spoke French."

"Only a few phrases. You're up early." He turned and disappeared into the bedroom.

"I like to get to the site early. I thought you might like a lift." Sarah wandered around the room, dropping her bag onto a chair. There was nothing of Byron Lloyd to be seen anywhere.

"Have you had breakfast?"

"I never eat breakfast." Moving to the window, Sarah compared his view with hers.

"I do."

She wrinkled her nose at the flat finality of the statement. "All right, I'll wait, as long as it's not a five-course meal with brandy and cigars. That must be it," she continued as a knock sounded at the door.

"I could do with the coffee."

"Okay, just a minute." After instructing the waiter to leave the tray, Sarah poured the coffee from pot to cup. "Black," she said, crossing to the bedroom. "It looks strong enough to cut rock."

He stood next to the bed, naked to the waist, with low-slung jeans fitting close over his hips. His torso was bronzed, with no sign of a tan line where the jeans hugged. The mat of dark hair narrowed on its journey to his waist. His frame was narrow, but his arms were roped with muscles. Where Januel was slender, Byron was lean. He had the disciplined body of an athlete.

She moved to him and held out the cup. "Here you go," she said and struggled to keep her voice at a natural level.

Byron held a denim shirt in one hand and accepted the coffee with the other. Eyes steady on hers, he lifted the cup and sipped. She could smell the faint fragrance of shaving cream and soap on him.

What would happen, she wondered, if I took just one more step?

"Why don't you find out?" Byron suggested.

Furious with the ease with which he had read her, Sarah turned and walked from the room. "Your breakfast is getting cold," she called over her shoulder.

Sarah guided Byron through the west wing to the completed theater in the round. It was one of her favorite rooms in the center.

It wasn't grand, but more along the lines of a good college theater with a relatively small seating capacity. It was an actor's theater, without frills.

"The acoustics are great." Sarah's voice echoed from wall to wall as she moved around the stage. It seemed to hang suspended in the air. "Le Claire, the playwright, is on the founding committee. He told me that actors would love to perform in this theater. 'Then to the well-trod stage anon . . .'" Sarah declaimed, then laughed, turning a full circle.

"How long did you study dance?" When Sarah gave him a puzzled look, he continued, "No one moves the way you do without training."

Sarah wondered, for the first time in her life, how she moved. "I was six when I started. I can't remember a time when I didn't take lessons. My mother wanted me to try for the New York City Ballet. I majored in architecture at NYCC. I disappointed her. . . . Anyway . . . the seating capacity in this theater is three hundred fifty . . ."

"Sarah." The touch of his hand on her shoulder surprised her. It was the first purely gentle gesture she had seen him make. "You shouldn't feel guilty for being who you are."

"I know. But I do. Come on." Her smile was warmer as she turned away again. "You'd better have a look at the dressing rooms before we push on. I'm saving the best for last."

Over an hour passed before they crossed the covered breezeway into the east wing. Overhead, thousands of tiny pin lights were tucked into the ceiling, to be turned into stars by night.

"If we don't have any major problem, we should finish very near the projected date." Sarah glanced down to see the crews working below. "Now that we've got the coil for the cooling system, we're back to normal."

They passed a crew of painters as they turned down a corridor in the east wing. Sarah called one of them by name, then neatly caught the apple he pulled out of his pocket and tossed to her. Sarah laughed, polishing it on the seat of her pants. "He's always bringing me fruit," she explained to Byron.

"You were telling me about the coil."

"Oh." She frowned, tossing the apple from palm to palm. "Well, we had a defective coil. The cooling system shut down and turned this place into a closed box yesterday. I had the crew stop working after lunch." She glanced up at him, waiting for some criticism.

"And?" he asked, noting the challenge in her eye.

"And, they stopped. I went back to the office and put a rush through to the factory at Saint-Etienne. I had a man fly down, pick up the part, and fly back." Sarah paused a moment, lifting her brow. "I ignored a great deal of office procedure and paperwork."

"Yes, I imagine you did," Byron said. "Would you like me to give you a pat on the head?"

Unexpectedly she laughed. "I'm glad you came, Byron," she said. "I didn't realize how much I had missed you."

Making a sharp right, Sarah led the way into the main theater. She moved directly to the wall switches and flicked them all on. Overhead, a dozen teardrop chandeliers trembled into life. Light showered over the royal-blue carpet.

"Very impressive." Byron took a few steps into the theater and turned a slow circle. He noted the elegant overhang of the balconies, the grace of the arches. He had seen the design on graph paper; now he saw the reality.

"Doesn't it ever amaze you that people can take wood and stone and turn it into this?" Sarah said as she let her eyes roam around the theater. "I don't think a building has to be old to have ghosts. This room has already been touched by dozens of hands."

"And by the spirit of the architect."

"And by the mind of the engineer."

She smiled. Their eyes met in perfect understanding.

Sarah had admired the graceful, fluid lines of Madeline de la Salle's home the first time she had seen it. It was an ancestral home the Frenchwoman had inherited through her late, titled husband, and it seemed to Sarah quintessentially French. She had also found it cold. Now, on her second visit to the Château de la Salle, her impression remained the same.

She liked the drawing room with its heavy drapes and ornate cornices, its white fireplace with marble mantel and carved cherubs, and the fussy rococo furniture that so suited the room and its mistress. She was not certain whether she liked Madeline de la Salle, but she felt that she too was superbly crafted.

Over the marble mantelpiece was a gilt oval mirror. It made the relatively small room appear enormous. Tucked into a corner, Sarah could observe everything and everyone without totally separating herself.

In a room crowded nearly elbow to elbow with bodies, she felt little warmth. There was laughter and conversation, but she had no desire to mingle. She preferred to watch the faces.

An actress she had met briefly moved past, trailing a fingertip over Sarah's arm in greeting. Impulsively, Sarah gave her a "Hello, darling" smile. She got a flash of capped teeth in return.

When her gaze passed over a champion soccer player, she tried a quick, bubbly, cheerleader smile. Her eyes met Byron's in the mantel mirror. She grinned, lifting her glass in a private salute.

He wove his way through the crowd, evading several people who called him or touched his arm. It was the first time Sarah had seen him in a social situation. He moved well, confidently, avoiding capture here and there with a quick word.

"What were you doing?" he asked when he had finally reached her.

"Playing the game. I'm glad you're here."

"Are you?"

"Yes, I've never seen you bored." She let her gaze drift from him to roam the room. "These people . . ." Her face showed distaste.

"They have money," Byron said flatly.

"So I've noticed." She brought her eyes back to him.

"But then, I rather like money. I plan to have quite a bit of it."

"You visualize a hundred million, two hundred million in a building, in a structure. That's the way your mind works."

Sarah lifted a brow. He's right, she realized.

"Can you really imagine it in your own bank account?" He smiled. "I don't think so. Once you've passed the first few million, does it matter? How much can a rational person spend in a lifetime? More often than not, you end up seeing people who care only about making money, or who already have it and don't know how to enjoy it."

"You make poverty sound appealing."

"There's nothing appealing about being poor," he said. "Once you've been there, you can always taste it. But you do learn to value money for what it is—an absence of poverty—and you'll push just a bit harder because you know you're never going back."

He had dropped his guard without being aware of it. She saw that Byron's weakness was his sensitivity about his past. No matter how firmly he turned his back on it, it remained with him. She had always believed shadows still existed in the dark. You just couldn't see them. She wanted to comfort him, to touch him, but she held back, aware that he would detest sympathy.

"Do you know how revealing your eyes are?" he murmured.

"Yes."

"Sarah, did you think I had abandoned you?" Januel appeared suddenly at her side. He lifted her hand to his lips. "Forgive me for being away so long . . . Byron." He gave a faint nod with his smile. "I didn't know you were here."

"Bounnet."

Madeline swept over to them. "Byron, you don't mingle," she scolded, resting a hand on his forearm.

"Madeline, as ravishing as ever." His lips hovered over

her hand a moment before he released it. "It's been a long time."

"Too long," she said. "We must watch you with our young architect." Madeline turned to smile at Sarah. "Be careful with this one, Sarah. He's a devil with women."

"Is he?" Sarah allowed her eyes to drift toward Byron. "Yes, I suppose he is."

Chapter Seventeen

SARAH DID NOT ARRIVE AT THE SITE IN THE BEST OF spirits. She had spent her morning at a board meeting. But more, there was the letter from Dallas she carried in her bag. The words were all there, but the tone had changed. Sarah could sense the shift in their relationship and knew the cause of it.

Evan Gibson, she thought resentfully as she pulled her cab to a halt in the center's parking area. Son of a bitch. She jammed her hands in the pockets of her skirt after she slammed the car door.

I should have stayed out of it, she told herself for the thousandth time. *I should have followed my instincts and stayed the hell out of it.*

Stopping, Sarah ran her eyes slowly over the center. She was pleased with her work. *It looks just right*, she thought. *It'll look even better when the landscaping is finished.* Mentally, she placed the remaining trees and shrubs and flowerbeds. *They don't need me here anymore.* She sighed, feeling herself being tugged in opposing directions. She thought of Januel and the building, of her apartment and Dallas and Maxwell Haladay, of Benedict and everything that was New York.

Sarah stood in the warm Paris spring and felt that she belonged nowhere and to no one. Quickly she moved toward the building, wanting noise and activity.

She found Lafitte in the first-floor west wing theater. Here the level of noise was all but deafening. Some men bolted down seats while others worked on power boxes behind the stage. Overhead, more men stood on scaffolding, installing grids for stage lighting. Because Lafitte's attention was focused on them, Sarah had to touch his arm before he turned his head in her direction.

"Paul?"

"Ah, Sarah." His mustache curled over his grin. "Your meeting went well?"

"It went," she told him, wrinkling her nose. "I'll never understand why I can't just build without having to hassle with budget committees. What difference does it make what it costs if it's right?" She ran a hand over the back of her neck before encountering Lafitte's amused eyes. "Go ahead and laugh," she said, smiling for the first time that day. "You don't have to barter your soul for Honduras mahogany. And they're the ones who wanted me to add the rooftop restaurant."

"And you so cleverly obliged them. We have another inspection this afternoon."

"Yeah, that's why I wanted to be here. Everything going all right?"

"*Comme ci comme ça.* Mr. Lloyd is backstage with the electricians."

"Damn." Sarah jammed her hands into her pockets. "Why does he spend so much time here? It makes me nervous." Her eyes brooded on the stage, then came back to Lafitte. "Why isn't he back in the office wading through the paperwork like an administrator?"

"Mr. Lloyd is very thorough," Lafitte answered with an easy French shrug.

"What do you think of him?" she asked suddenly.

Seeing Lafitte's expression change, she spoke impatiently. "Damn it, don't get discreet on me, Paul. What do you think of him?"

Lafitte shifted his weight onto one foot and frowned. He tugged on his left ear, as Sarah had seen him do before when thinking through a situation. Normally she would have been amused by his plodding step-by-step caution.

"He's smart," Lafitte began at last. "He knows building and he's objective." He looked back at Sarah again and found her eyes searching his. "Some are governed by their feelings; he's not one of them."

"Yes," Sarah agreed after a moment. "I believe you're right. But why is he here? Why is he spending so much of his time in this building? Why hasn't he gone back to Phoenix?"

"Why don't you ask him?"

"I don't know." Sarah's voice trailed off as she shook her head. "But I have an uneasy feeling that you know why he's here and you're not telling me." Her eyes whipped back to his. "Why do you suppose I have that feeling, Paul?"

Lafitte shrugged, then looked back to the ceiling. "You'd do better to speak to Mr. Lloyd." He frowned. "Why the hell is Dupres working alone? There are two men to a grid."

"You might as well go up yourself," Sarah told him moodily. "You're not helping me any."

Lafitte turned and gave her a quick smile. "I like you, Sarah. I like you because you are ruled by your feelings."

She gave him a long, level stare. "Go on up," she told him. When he turned and walked toward Dupres and his scaffolding, Sarah watched him. She'd seen something in his eyes. An evasion.

"Sarah." Byron had waited to speak her name until he stood directly in front of her. The noise was pitched high around them. It echoed from the walls and off the ceiling. Sarah, still wearing the skirt and jacket she had worn to her morning meeting, and with heels and thin silk stockings, felt out of place. Byron was dressed more like a laborer than an administrator in jeans and a chambray work shirt.

"I didn't think you'd be here today," she said.

"Didn't you?"

Byron hooked his thumbs in the front pockets of his jeans. It was a gesture she didn't associate with the vice-president of Haladay. "Do you have any objections?"

"Not objections," she countered. "Just questions. The first one being, are you here as an administrator, an engineer, or an interested observer?"

Byron kept his eyes on her face. "Yes."

"Don't be amusing," she snapped and took a step nearer as she tossed up a hand to point at Lafitte. "Paul knows more than I do."

Casually, Byron looked up to watch Lafitte in conversation with his man at the top of the scaffolding. "About what?"

"Byron, would you tell me if there was a problem?"

"What makes you think there's a problem, Sarah?"

"Oh, Christ!" She turned away. For a few moments she watched Lafitte work with the ceiling grid. "I wish to hell you'd go back to Phoenix and get off my case!" she shouted. The noise prevented everyone but Byron from hearing her.

He looked at her, and his voice was calm when he answered. "I wasn't aware that I was on your case."

"It feels like you are." She whirled around. "Like you're looking over my shoulder. I don't need a goddamn proctor, Byron. If you'd just give me some straight answers. Or if Paul would talk to me." Infuriated, she tilted her head back to the ceiling again. For an instant her heart stopped.

She saw the grid swing loose, watched as it fell on Lafitte. At her stunned expression, Byron looked up in time to see the grid crash into Lafitte's skull and knock him over the scaffold railing.

"Oh, God!"

Sarah was halfway down the aisle before Lafitte and the grid reached the floor. The noise masked the sound of his fall. Degree by degree, it grew quieter, until there was silence. Sarah was almost to the scaffolding before Byron caught her.

His fingers wrapped tight around her arm, stopping her. "Paul. Oh, no. Oh, God, no."

Byron took her shoulders to keep her still, using his body to block her line of vision. Beneath his hands, he could feel her trembling even as she tried to push him away. He shook her once, hard, then again, until she looked up at him. Her eyes were wide, dry and terrified.

"Go call an ambulance," he ordered, knowing it was too late.

"Paul," she said again and shook her head. It couldn't be true, part of her brain insisted. "Byron, let me . . ."

"Go call an ambulance," he said again. His grip tightened until he knew by her indrawn breath that pain had registered. "Now." Her eyes continued to cling to his. "Now, goddamn it." Roughly, he spun her around and pushed.

Sarah fled up the aisle without looking back. Byron waited until she had swung through the doors before he turned around. "Keep everyone out of here," he told a burly electrician beside him. "That means Mademoiselle Lancaster too." He pushed his way through the crowd to Lafitte.

It seemed as though hours had passed. Sarah had heard the insistent, two-toned wail of the siren, had watched the attendants hustle into the theater with their equipment, then had dealt with the silence. She knew Lafitte was dead. She had known it from the instant the grid had crashed down on him, but she wanted to deny it. She wanted to go back to their conversation, to see him grin at her again, to keep him on the ground with her.

There were birds singing outside. She watched them fly from tree to tree on the south end where the landscaping was all but completed. The sun was warm on the nape of her neck. She covered her face with her hands.

"Sarah." She whirled around to find Byron directly behind her. "Go home," he said simply and took her arm. She resisted, turning back to face him.

"Byron, please . . ." She shook her head and tried to swallow. "Is he . . ."

"He's dead. There's nothing you can do here."

She made a quiet moaning sound as her eyes closed. For a moment she leaned on him, again lifting her hands to her face. "No." She shook her head, denying it. "No, God . . . oh, please, no." He heard the desperation rise in her voice and took her shoulders.

"Go home, Sarah. I don't need a hysterical woman on my hands." His voice was curt. He watched her swallow the need to weep, but her breath still shuddered.

"How?" she demanded, forcing herself to ask, to listen. *Don't fall apart*, she commanded herself, hurt by the coldness of his words. *Don't fall apart.*

"I'm not certain." Byron released her shoulders to light a cigarette. She could still feel the pressure of his fingers. Sarah watched him through the veil of smoke. "It seems he hadn't secured the grid properly, and when he let go of it, it swung loose. Go back to the hotel; have your calls screened through the switchboard. Once the press hears about this, they'll be hounding you for a statement."

"I don't give a shit about the press." Sarah grabbed at his arm. "Byron, Paul has a family; his little granddaughter's five. She can count to twenty. I told him to go up there." Her voice began to catch on jerky breaths. "I told him to go up. If I hadn't, maybe . . . maybe he'd be all right. Maybe he'd . . ."

"You're being egotistical," Byron said coldly.

Sarah flinched as if he had struck her. Any hint of color drained from her skin. "God," she said softly. "How I hate you." She spun around and ran to her car, fumbling the key from her purse.

Byron watched her pull out of the parking area and dart into the street. "Fuck," he said briefly, savagely, then tossed aside his cigarette.

The sun was hot the day of the funeral. The scent of freshly turned earth was warm and strong. Standing well in the back of the crowd of mourners, Sarah tried to think of the excitement of breaking ground on a new site, of a garden plowed and ready for seed. She could only see Paul Lafitte breaking off a hunk of crusty bread to share with her.

There were faces in the crowd she recognized. Concentrating on them, Sarah blocked out the prayers and the weeping. There was Derille, grim and composed, and several laborers she knew, some crying openly, others mouthing responses to the priest. She found the aroma of fresh flowers nauseating. Over dozens of bowed heads, her eyes met Byron's.

His presence there surprised her, and she continued to stare at him after the prayers ended and the crowd began to thin. For three days they had given each other a wide berth. Now Sarah saw him walk to Lafitte's widow. He bent and spoke to her, and she gripped his hand in both of hers, speaking rapidly. Sarah turned away, then began to cross the well-trimmed grass. She felt him behind her before she had gone a hundred yards, but waited to speak until he was beside her.

"I didn't expect to see you here," she said without looking at him.

"Did Bounnet bring you?"

"No." Her eyes were shadowed by the wide brim of her hat. She glanced briefly at Byron, then straight ahead. "He had some meetings. So did I; he covered for me."

"I'll take you back."

"I have my car."

"I said I'll take you back." He stopped her with a hand

on her arm. "Give me your keys." He took the keys from her hand. "Wait here." He strode away and spoke briefly to one of the mechanics from the project.

Sarah said nothing when Byron came back and took her arm again. When they stood beside his car, she glanced past his shoulder back across the cemetery. Lafitte's family moved away from the grave in a dark semicircle. Sarah lifted her eyes to Byron.

"I hate funerals."

Turning, she slid into the car and closed her eyes as her head touched the back of the seat. She listened to the engine catch, then felt the quiet movement of the Daimler. When he lit a cigarette, the scent of tobacco drifted to her.

"I hate accidents." She kept her eyes closed, shaded by the brim of her hat. "Death is ugly enough but an accident. . . . I apologize for saying I hated you. I don't, or I only did for that moment. I wanted you to hold my hand and let me cry on your shoulder."

"I know what you wanted."

Sarah drew off her hat and tossed it into the back seat. "You're so much more controlled than I am. Paul called you detached. It's a good description. I get too attached. Byron—" Abruptly, she noticed the world outside the car. "This isn't the way back to the office."

"No."

Sarah closed her eyes again. Depression had made her unbearably tired. The car purred on with its driver and passenger silent. When they stopped, Sarah opened her eyes and glanced from the window.

To her right was a park full of blooming flowers and noisy children. She saw a dog race across the grass and leap on a blue ball. Without speaking, Byron leaned across her and opened her door.

"Why are we here?" she asked. Their eyes met, and she recalled vividly the first time he had kissed her in the garage area beneath Haladay.

"Why not?" he asked. "It's a beautiful day."

He got out of the car, then crossed to the grass. Slowly Sarah followed. When she reached him, he held out a hand. Surprised, she simply stared down at it a moment, then, looking back up, she smiled and placed hers in it. She felt herself relaxing for the first time in days.

Life throbbed around them. Children laughed and squealed, darting along the paths. Couples strolled with arms linked around waists. An old woman with a scarf knotted under her chin threw crumbs to bored pigeons. Sarah watched two art students, their pads and pencils forgotten on the grass, kissing passionately under the shade of an elm.

"Would you do me a favor?" she asked.

"What?"

"Would you hold me for a minute?"

Byron brushed a stray wisp of hair from her cheek, then slipped his arm around her waist. He could feel the contour of her face as she dropped her head against his shoulder. She relaxed on a soft, long breath.

"You're a strange man, Byron," she murmured. "But I'm beginning to understand why Cassidy is so fond of you." She brushed her lips over his cheek, then drew back. "Thank you."

Chapter Eighteen

SARAH SHED HER BLACK BLAZER WHEN SHE RETURNED TO her office. She wanted to get right down to work. After the walk in the park, she found it easier to think about life than about death.

With the afternoon came the threat of a thunderstorm. Shadows shifted in Sarah's office, and there was a distant groan of thunder from the west. Her work had piled up since Lafitte's accident, and now she began to sort through it. There were the final changes the board had agreed on for the rooftop restaurant. Sarah wanted to finish them, to tie up loose ends. Once that was done, there would be no reason for her to remain in Europe.

Sarah felt she had learned a great deal in the past six months. She knew she could handle a position of authority, and that she liked it. She discovered that being able to devote her talent to a single job for an extended period of time was extremely rewarding. Her desire to build had increased with the success of the Delacroix Center.

"Sarah."

Her head snapped up from the scatter of papers on her desk. Janciel moved to her and took both of her hands between his.

"Sarah, you shouldn't have come in today." His voice

was soft and understanding. Sarah squeezed his hands as she rose.

"No, I wanted—needed—to work."

"I know how dreadful this has been for you." Bending, he kissed both her temples. "You were close to Paul, and to have been there . . ." He sighed, bringing his hands gently to her shoulders. "I wish I could have spared you that."

"His wife looked so small today," she murmured. "So lost." She thought of the little woman in black.

"She'll be well taken care of by the company," Januel told her. He pressed her shoulders once before releasing them. "You mustn't worry about her."

Sarah looked up at him a moment, then turned away. There was a sudden vivid memory of her parents' insurance check. She could remember the grain of the paper. "Death benefits," she whispered. "There's something obscene about the sound of it." She shook her head quickly and tried to recapture the feeling she had experienced with Byron in the park. Life went on.

Walking to the window, she stood and watched the clouds boil. "I'd like a good storm," she said suddenly and tossed up the window. "I'd like a really good storm." The wind whipped in and shivered over her blouse.

"Yes." Januel came up behind her, again laying his hands on her shoulders. "I recall your fondness for the rain."

Sarah leaned back against him, remembering the first time they had made love, the gentle contentment. "I'll be leaving in a few days," she said quietly. "I'm going to miss you, Januel."

Januel turned her to face him, then cupped her face in his hands. His eyes were clear and beautiful. "Don't talk of leaving, Sarah." He kissed her once, lingeringly. "It's just as simple to stay as to go."

"I'm not needed anymore." She started to shake her head, but he stopped the movement with another kiss.

"I need you." He brought her hands to his lips, turning them over to kiss her palms. "Stay in Paris, Sarah. Marry me."

Stunned, she stared at him. This was something she had not expected, and, unprepared, she had no words.

"My love." He pressed his lips to her forehead. "I hadn't planned to ask you so abruptly, or in such a setting." He smiled, still holding her hands. "I forgot myself when you spoke of leaving. Don't answer now." His hands tightened on hers as she started to speak. "Let me court you as a woman should be courted." He drew her close. "I will ask you again, properly. Only for the next day or two, think about staying rather than leaving. Will you do that?"

"Yes." She rested her forehead against his shoulder before drawing away. "Yes, I'll think about it."

"Will you let me take you to dinner?"

"No." With a confused laugh, she lifted her hands to his chest. "No, please, I want to work late in any case, and . . . you've tossed me a curve, Januel. I need some time."

"I won't pressure you tonight." He kissed her, then looked down into her eyes. "Tomorrow?"

"Yes, tomorrow."

Sarah waited until the door had closed behind him before she sat down. She heard the rain begin.

When a building is empty of people, all its whispers and wheezes become audible. The older the building, the more vocal. Sarah sat alone in her office, listening to the whiz and pop of the air conditioner, the yawning of boards, the fizzle of rain on closed windows. Her work had long since been completed, and she had, uncharacteristically, set her desk to rights. I've got to think, she admitted when she had run out of delaying tactics. Propping her elbows on the desk, she rested her head in her hands.

"Marriage," she said aloud as if testing the word. Then, more specifically, "Marriage to Januel." No images formed in her mind, and she rose, frustrated. Damn it, why should she draw such a blank on this?

Obviously, she decided after a moment, she'd never given marriage enough thought. She wandered the office in her bare feet, stopping to stare through the rain-splattered window. Januel is kind, she thought. He's intelligent and gentle. She smiled, resting her forehead against the pane. He makes me feel good.

She thought of her parents, then of Paul, and how quickly a life could be snuffed out. Somehow everyone took life for granted until suddenly faced with its end. Death frightened her, its finality. There was so much to be done, so much to have before it was all over. Paul had been young when he had climbed the scaffolding to his death. Now he would never be old. How many dreams and wishes had he put off, thinking there would always be a tomorrow? Once Sarah had vowed to beat time at its own game. Professionally she had kept that promise. Now she wondered what she really wanted as a woman—and how long she could afford to wait.

"I'd like a home," she murmured, then stopped and turned to face the room. Surprise, Sarah, she said to herself, lifting a hand to her temple. How long has that been in there hiding? I'd like children. "I want babies." The admission astonished her, and she sat down on the windowsill for a moment to let it sink in. "And a dog," she added. "And a picket fence." Laughing, she hugged herself. "I want it all, every last bit of it."

Do I love him? she wondered. Would I be certain if I did? How do you tell? He makes me happy, that's enough. She reached for her blazer and purse. There was no reason to wait until tomorrow.

Januel's fingers brushed lazily over the soft swell of her breasts. "A drink, *ma belle?*" he asked. With Madeline's murmur of assent, he sighed, satisfied, and breathed in the scent of their damp bodies. "Stay here." Leaning over, he kissed both taut nipples, then rose. "I have a bottle of champagne chilled."

A plum-colored silk robe wrapped around him, Januel moved into the kitchen. He was deeply content physically and thinking of Sarah, reflecting on how very close he was to having everything he wanted. He hummed lightly as he placed two crystal glasses on a tray. Things were falling perfectly into place. Expertly, he buried champagne into a bucket of ice in the center of the tray. There was already a fresh stir of desire building inside him.

The long buzz of the door had him swearing in annoyance. Putting down the tray on a table in the living room, Januel moved to answer. He'd get rid of the visitor quickly. Champagne and women should never be kept waiting.

"Hello!" Sarah tossed her arms around his neck and kissed him enthusiastically.

Shock vibrated through him, but with her cheek resting against his, Sarah saw nothing of his expression. Her hair and blazer were beaded with rain. Recovering quickly, Januel drew her away and smiled into her eyes. "Sarah, what a surprise! Did you finish your work early?"

"Yes." She slipped by him into the room before he could think of a way to prevent her. "I thought we might make that quiet dinner tomorrow a late supper tonight." Smiling, she glanced down at his robe. "I might even be persuaded to be domestic and whip something up here, since you're not dressed to go out." She rubbed the lapels of his robe between her thumb and forefinger. "I hope I didn't get you out of bed."

Januel felt a grim stab of humor. "No. I was just on my way, however." He touched his temple. "I've the most damnable headache. I've taken some medication. Sarah, I'm afraid I'd be poor company tonight. These pills are strong and very effective, but they make one very drowsy."

"Oh, I'm sorry." She laid her palm on his cheek, and some of the tension eased from his shoulders. He could read the concern in her eyes. "Is there anything I can do?"

"No, no, darling." He clasped both her hands in his, bringing them to rest on his chest. "It will be gone in the morning. But I hate to disappoint you this way. Tomorrow." He lifted her hands to kiss them, then smiled. "I shall make it up to you."

"I'll count on it." She brought her lips to his briefly. "I wanted to give you my answer." Over his shoulder, Sarah saw the tray with champagne and glasses. Surprise came first, then curiosity. With understanding came pain. For a second she closed her eyes. "But then, I see you anticipated me." Pride became suddenly, desperately important. She fought to keep her voice calm as she looked back at him. "Should you drink with your medication, Januel? That can be very dangerous." Crossing the room, she lifted a glass and turned back to him. She gave the crystal a critical examination. He saw the fury growing in her eyes and calculated how best to manage it. Sarah tipped the glass toward the bedroom. "You'll need three glasses now, won't you?" Her tone was dangerously controlled.

"Sarah . . ."

"Januel, perhaps I should handle this." Madeline came from the bedroom, magnificent in a thin green robe.

It's worse, Sarah discovered, knowing who. She hurt, and hated it. "Madeline," she said flatly. "Should I apologize for interrupting?" She glanced back at Januel. "Shouldn't someone say something about being civilized?"

Madeline plucked a cigarette from a cut-glass table holder, sighing over it before lighting it. It's a pity, she thought, that the girl's timing had been so poor. "Sarah." She blew out a stream of smoke. "This is, of course, very awkward for all of us."

"Oh, awkward." Sarah rolled the word over her tongue. "Yes, that's a very civilized word." The pressure in her chest told her that her emotions were fighting to take over, but she forced them aside. "I'll go along with awkward, Madeline." It was easier to speak to her than to Januel.

"Januel and I understand each other." Madeline drew on her cigarette, studying Sarah through a wisp of smoke. "We're old friends who are able to give each other a great deal of physical pleasure. It's very simple."

"Simple is shaking hands," Sarah countered. Her own were trembling, and she wished for something to fill them. Sarah knew that nothing showed emotion more clearly than hands. Casually, she tucked them into the pockets of her blazer. "I've no quarrel with you, Madeline. You had no reason not to sleep with Januel. I did, however, think he had a reason not to sleep with you. Loyalty is something I perhaps take for granted."

"Sarah." Januel spoke from behind her as he stepped forward. The look she shot him over her shoulder stopped him.

"Excuse me," she said to Madeline, then turned to face Januel. "I want to know," she began when her eyes locked on his, "why you asked me to marry you this afternoon, then came home and went to bed with another woman."

"Sarah, one has nothing to do with the other."

"Then explain them separately." Her voice was colorless. "Why did you ask me to marry you?"

"Because I want you for my wife." His answer was quick, his eyes clear. "Sarah." He took her shoulders before she could evade him. "Don't you know how I care for you?"

"Oh yes, I think I do. I think I know precisely how you care for me." Her cheeks were as pale as her voice. She wanted to shrug his hands from her shoulders but forced herself to stand still. "Take your hands off me," she demanded quietly.

"Don't be a child." His voice sharpened. "What man or woman is faithful to another? What difference does it make? Our marriage, Sarah, will bring us too much success for us to worry about foolish trivialities."

She tightened her muscles to keep herself from trembling

under his hands. She wanted him aware of no weakness. She wondered, when she searched his face, why she had never glimpsed the callousness.

"*Success*, Januel? Of what kind?"

"Personal success, Sarah, naturally." She remembered how persuasive his soft, gentle tone could be. Now it grated on her nerves. "But also, social, business successes. Think of it, Sarah." She watched him smile. "With the social contacts I have, your career will skyrocket. With the Haladay name behind you and the doors I know how to open in Europe, you could be the most sought after architect of the decade. The Delacroix Center is just the beginning, Sarah. Within a year or two you'll be ready to leave Haladay behind. You won't need him."

"I see." She took a long breath. "But I will need someone to tend to the business end of things, someone who knows how to handle the administrative angles, all those monetary details I like to fluff off. And you're very good at that sort of thing. I've always admired your ability."

"Together, Sarah." He lowered his mouth to hers, kissing her lightly. "The possibilities are endless."

Sarah suffered the kiss, then drew away. "When I need an executive son of a bitch, you're hired. Now, take your hands off me." She watched temper flare into his face. His eyes hardened like glass. "I won't tell you again, Januel," she warned quietly. Her nails dug into her palms. "Take your hands off me."

"Very well." His voice was tightly controlled as he stepped back. "Perhaps it would be best to talk tomorrow when you've had more time to think."

Sarah strolled over to the tray and lifted the bottle of champagne from its bed of ice. She studied the label and nodded. "You have excellent taste, Januel. I've always thought so." She inclined her head to Madeline.

"*Au revoir*, Sarah."

"Good-bye, Madeline." The neck of the bottle was cold on her palm as she strolled to the door. Reaching it, she turned again and aimed one last look at him. "You know, Januel, every woman should have a French lover to write about in her memoirs. I'm going to give you almost a whole page."

As the door closed behind Sarah, Madeline gave a low, appreciative laugh. "You underestimated her, *chéri*."

"Perhaps. I won't again."

Madeline recognized the barely controlled fury in his face and casually crushed out her cigarette. She walked over to him and opened his robe, then slid her hands around his waist. "You lost that one, *mon chèr ami*."

"For now." Januel frowned at the door, then brought his attention back to Madeline. "Just for now."

Chapter Nineteen

WITH HER FEET PROPPED UP ON HER DESK, SARAH wriggled her stockinged toes and studied her water glass. Champagne bubbled inside it. The light from the lamp shot clear through it. She downed the remaining wine in the glass, stretched forward, grasped the bottle, and filled up again. Tremendous coordination, she decided. Incredible dexterity. And zero for brains.

"You can't have everything," she told the champagne before swallowing. She had pulled the pins from her hair and now pushed it back from her face as she saw Byron leaning against the doorjamb. "Hi." She gave him a grin before she lifted her glass again. Rubbing the bottom of one foot against the calf of her leg, she gestured for him to join her. "Don't stand out in the cold, Byron. Come on in by the fire."

Before straightening, Byron ran his eyes from the tip of her bare toes, up the legs the lifted skirt generously exposed, to her flushed face and tumbled hair. She was extraordinarily beautiful and extremely drunk. "What's going on, Sarah?"

After a quick toast she emptied her glass. "I'm celebrating." She smiled again and tossed back her head. "I haven't come up with the proper word for the occasion. You might have one."

Byron walked in, watching her go through the routine of filling her glass. He lifted the bottle and examined it.

"You drink all this yourself?"

"Absolutely." There was a touch of pride in her voice. She drank again. "And if you want some, you'll just have to go out and get your own."

"Gracious to the last." He set the bottle down. She had downed three-quarters of it; he had to admire her endurance. "What are you celebrating, Sarah?"

She pulled her feet from the desk and stood. Vertical, she wavered a bit, then shook her head to clear the haze. With surprising grace, she rounded the desk. "This goddamn floor's leaning, Byron. Faulty braces. You should look into that."

"Of course." As he looked on, she kicked her discarded shoes out of her path and lifted her glass again.

"What was I saying?" She turned back to him and frowned.

"Faulty braces," he supplied.

She giggled. "No, before that. Wait a minute." Sarah combed her fingers through her hair, holding it back from her face while she concentrated. "Oh yeah." She let the hair tumble into her face again. "The celebration. Januel proposed to me this afternoon. From just about where you're standing right now," she added in afterthought.

Byron's eyes were direct on hers, but he didn't answer her smile. "I see."

"No, you don't," she corrected, then poked a finger into his chest. "What do you think about the institution of marriage, Byron? I gave it quite a bit of thought this evening. Quite a bit." She was having trouble with the words and drank again as if to loosen her tongue. "My parents were married, you know. I've known just scads of people who were married. Some of them stay that way.

Some people try it over and over and over again until they get it right. Must be something to it. A lot of people have babies after they're married. Some even have babies before. . . ." Her voice trailed off. "Do you like babies, Byron? I do. But we were talking about Januel," she remembered. "You really should stick to the point."

"Sorry."

"Never mind." She waved a hand at him. "I decided marrying Januel was a hell of an idea. He's got a beautiful face, have you noticed? God, I really fell in love with that face. Like something in a Raphael painting, don't you think?"

"I haven't given it a great deal of thought." The dryness in his tone penetrated the fog of champagne.

Laughing, Sarah turned three quick pirouettes. When she stopped, she tossed down the rest of her drink, pressing a hand to her chest.

"I went to his apartment tonight to tell him I'd decided to marry him." She looked down at the drink in her hand. "My glass is empty again. Where was I?" she asked, looking back to Byron.

"In Bounnet's apartment."

"Oh, yes. I was in Januel's apartment. So was Madeline. You remember Madeline, Comtesse de la Salle, don't you?" As she spoke, she moved to the desk to refill her glass. The champagne popped and bubbled. "I was—how do you say?—*de trop*. Or as Madeline put it, it was an awkward situation." After stumbling over the last word, Sarah laughed and lifted her glass. "We were very civilized, naturally. He explained it all. Januel's a whiz at explanations."

She pressed the glass to her brow a moment. "You see, his fucking Madeline didn't have anything to do with him and me. I didn't realize that, of course, until he pointed it out. I'm afraid my attitude was very provincial." Her voice had begun to tremble, and she swallowed all the wine. "Damn him!" She hurled the glass across the room. It smashed against the wall and scattered on the carpet. "He won't make me cry." She pressed the heels of her hands hard against her eyes. "I swore when he stood there with his hands on me, handing me all that garbage, I'd never cry over him. *Never*."

Byron watched as she struggled. Her breath shuddered in and out again and again before she won control. Stubborn, he thought, and admired her for it. When she dropped her hands, her eyes were wide and bright, but dry. "Well done, Sarah."

She took another deep breath, then glanced around. "I need a new glass." She turned to find one, willing the champagne to anesthetize the pain.

"Enough." Byron took her arm. Her skin was hot under the silk of her blouse. She swayed, then straightened. "I think you could do with some food and coffee."

Blowing the hair from her face, she shook her head. "I promised myself I was going to drink that whole bottle." She held her hands against his chest until she had steadied her balance. "I'm going to drink that whole bottle."

"Suit yourself." With a shrug, he released her. He sat while she located a new glass. "If you're going to make yourself sick, you picked a good brand to do it with."

"Januel's choice," she corrected, pouring. "I ripped it off from his apartment. It was all iced and ready. My salvation." She lifted the glass high to study it. "You see, if I hadn't noticed the bottle and the glasses sitting there, I would've believed the bullshit about his not feeling well. I'd have gone on home, and he and Madeline would've been drinking this now. Here's to my keen powers of observation. I hope like hell he didn't have a spare." Sarah giggled, pleased with herself.

"Were you in love with him?"

The sudden question stopped her glass halfway to her lips. Slowly, she shifted her eyes until they met Byron's. "I wanted to be," she whispered. Her hair trembled with the furious shake of her head. "I was trying to be."

"Then you weren't," he concluded, pulling out a cigarette. "Wanting and trying add up to zero." His shrug discounted her answer.

"He made a fool of me." Sarah drank, then set down the glass with a loud bang.

"A blow to your pride." Byron's tone was unsympathetic as he lit his cigarette. Sarah watched the flame of his lighter flick on then off.

"He hurt me." Her voice steadied with temper. "The son of a bitch really hurt me. And he never cared, never cared about me. It was all a lie." Her eyes were intense on his for a moment. Then she closed them. "Oh, Christ." Sarah pressed a hand to her head as it spun. "I'm awfully drunk."

"Yes," Byron agreed. "I noticed that."

"Not much gets past you," she commented as she opened her eyes again. "It's hard to be mad when you're drunk. That's why I got this way. Oh, well." She shrugged, smiling at him again. "It could've been worse, right? I could've married the bastard. Is that logical enough for you, Byron? You're a logical son of a bitch." She yawned hugely. "I don't guess you're the type of man to take advantage of a woman in my present condition."

He lifted a brow. "Is that a question or an invitation?"

Sarah shrugged again and turned back to the bottle. Brow furrowed in concentration, she shook out the last lingering drops. "I dunno. Does it matter? I doubt I could seduce you at the moment." Tossing her hair behind her shoulder, she turned and watched him over the glass rim.

He grinned. "Wanna bet?"

Laughing made her unsteady. She gripped the table for support as the walls rocked. Her laugh was throaty and appreciative nonetheless as she threw back her head. "Sometimes, Byron, I really like you. I really do."

"And others?" he asked, watching her through a cloud of smoke.

"And others I don't know. You're scary. Tell me about

yourself, Byron,'' she invited as she rested a hip on the desk. She nearly slid off, but steadied herself. "I know almost nothing, after all. I often wonder.''

He watched the remaining champagne sway dangerously in her glass. "Later.''

"I like Rachmaninoff, Ray Bradbury, and the hot dogs at Yankee Stadium. And I like Dylan Thomas and having my feet rubbed." She drained her glass.

"That's fascinating." Byron watched while Sarah absently swung her leg. "It appears you've hit bottom.''

She looked down at her empty glass, surprised. "Don't we have any more?'' She gave the bottle a quick shake, then set it back down. "Shall we send out for some?''

He crushed out his cigarette before rising and moving to her. "I don't think I better have any more. I'm driving.''

"Oh.'' When he took her waist to slide her from the desk, she went into his arms. She was soft, warm, pliant. With a yawn, Sarah rested her head on his shoulder. "Is the party over?'' she murmured.

"It seems that way.'' Her lips brushed his neck. His fingers tangled in her hair, tilting her head back until he could look down at her. Her eyes were heavy, nearly shut. The green glimmered just under her lashes. When he kissed her, her mouth opened to his, warm and willing, with the lingering taste of champagne. The kiss dove far deeper than he had intended.

It occurred to him that he had never tasted her skin. Byron moved his lips over the curve of her neck, finding her pulse. He could smell the rain in her hair. Sarah sighed and leaned heavily on him.

"Take me home, Byron." She could feel the ground swaying under her feet. "I don't want to be here. I want to go home, back to Phoenix.''

"Right now?'' He cradled her head on his chest.

"When I wake up,'' she corrected and gently passed out.

Chapter Twenty

WITH A VENGEFUL HANGOVER POUNDING IN HER HEAD, Sarah sat aboard Haladay's private jet. She closed her eyes against the unbroken white of the clouds. The numbing effects of Dom Perignon were gone, leaving her feeling raw and dingy. But her memory was clear. She remembered everything that had happened the previous evening until she had passed out in Byron's arms.

Sarah's next memory was of waking up in her own bed, tucked in, dressed only in her camisole and panties. It wasn't difficult to figure out how she had gotten there. Making a fool of herself twice in one evening was difficult to swallow.

Worse, she mused, keeping her eyes shut, he hasn't said *anything*. He just sits back there. All Sarah could hear from Byron was the occasional rustle of papers. Otherwise, the cabin was silent. She would have liked to slip back into oblivion, but the hangover, and her own sense of embarrassment, kept her awake. She should never have used her office for a drinking marathon, she admitted. Unprofessional. She had put herself in an unbusinesslike position. Now she had to pay the price.

Byron had gotten her out of bed that morning. *Dragged her out*, Sarah corrected grimly. Not even bothering to knock, she recalled, but using her key to let himself in. *Her key*. Christ. Then, she remembered, he had shoved a cup of coffee in her face and told her to take a shower and pack.

And what did she do? she asked herself. She had done exactly as she was told. She had stood, half naked, guzzling down the coffee, then had crawled off to the shower. Byron had arranged everything. He had settled her hotel bill, checked her luggage, and put her on a plane. She hadn't given a murmur of objection. Not then; she had been too dazed to think of any objections. But now . . .

Opening her eyes, Sarah turned in her seat to watch Byron. He shifted through the papers in his briefcase and never glanced in her direction. He might have been alone. She could let the entire thing ride, she considered, then forced herself to think above the throbbing in her head.

Byron looked well rested and in control. She could say nothing, pretend she hadn't put away an entire bottle of champagne and passed out. That would be the sensible thing. He could go for the rest of his life without mentioning it again. That was just the sort of man he was. For a moment she hated him for it.

"You didn't have to do this, you know," she blurted out.

Byron glanced up and over. His eyes swept her face before he went back to his papers. "You really should get some rest, Sarah. You look like hell."

"Nice of you to point it out." She rose. Her stomach lurched with the movement, but she ignored it. She went to the galley and began to make coffee.

Briefly, he looked up as she passed. He remembered holding her the night before. And how badly he had wanted her. If she hadn't been unconscious, he would have made good use of the sofa in her office. Undressing her in her hotel room and then leaving her to sleep it off hadn't been the easiest thing he'd ever done. Strange that he should be involved with a woman he had never taken to bed. But he was involved, and he didn't like it.

Throughout his life, when he thought of women, he

thought comfortably. They were companions or associates or lovers. He wouldn't place Sarah in the role of companion, and she wasn't his lover. But he was having too much trouble keeping her in the strict category of an associate. No, he was forced to admit, he was never comfortable when he thought of her. And he thought of her more often than he liked.

He would take her to bed, he decided, and flipped over another page. That would end it. Once he had her, he would stop wondering what it would be like. Once he had her, he'd be able to think of her comfortably.

With a quiet oath he turned back the page he had just discarded, annoyed that he hadn't taken in a word that was written on it. His mind centered abruptly on Januel Bounnet.

It was best that Sarah had severed her relationship with him. Best that she had been prepared to leave France. It was no longer necessary for her to be on the site of the Delacroix Center. Her usefulness there was over. Whatever needed to be done now could be done by telephone. Byron, too, had been ready to leave. He felt he had done all he could do in Paris. For the moment.

"You didn't have to arrange all this," Sarah told him as she stood in the doorway of the gallery. "I could have managed."

"Bring me a cup while you're at it."

Setting her teeth, Sarah poured a second cup of coffee before coming back into the cabin. With a cup in each hand, she stood in front of him. "Goddamn it, Byron, I wish you'd say something. I made a fool of myself last night."

He took a cup from her and sipped. "If you know that, what would you like me to say?"

Her cheeks colored with temper. "I'd forgotten how perfect you are."

Their eyes held. "Sit down, Sarah." When she continued to stand, he took the second cup from her hand, then pulled her down beside him. Her head pounded at the movement. "You're not the first person with an unfaithful lover, and you're not the first person to be poured into bed. Forget it."

"You really think it's that simple, don't you?"

"Isn't it?"

"No. No, it isn't." She didn't want to talk to him, but the words were already coming out. "I don't like the fact that I humiliated myself in front of you. I don't like the fact that you know what happened between Januel and me. You're the last person I'd confide in."

"No," he agreed. "But I think the crux of it is that you don't like the fact that he manipulated you."

"He didn't—" she began furiously, then stopped. But yes, yes he had. Byron had hit the nail squarely on the head. She struggled with hurt now as well as anger. "God, you're a hard man, Byron, but you're right. I looked at his face, and I saw a beautiful man. I didn't want to look any further. He sent me flowers, he was romantic. He said things I wanted to hear." She ran both hands through her hair when Byron said nothing. "I enjoyed it—the candlelight, the soft words. I fell for it, and he knew I would. He used me, and I hate knowing I looked right at him and didn't see what he was."

"You would have," Byron commented. "When you got bored with the flowers."

"Maybe. But I'll never know for sure, will I?"

"Why do you need to?" he countered and sipped his coffee. "It's over."

Sarah blew out a breath and sat back. "I *cared*, Byron," she said, frustrated. "I really cared. That makes all the difference."

"Why?"

"It isn't possible to explain emotion, Byron." She sighed. "There's no logic to it." She was silent for a moment, then looked back at him. "Let's put it this way. How would you feel if you'd been used by someone you trusted?"

Byron thought of Max. But in their own ways, they used each other. "The first lesson is not to trust anyone."

"Who can live like that?" Sarah demanded. "I can't. I'd rather be hurt than alone."

"We make our own choices," he said simply, but her words played back to him. *Alone*. She had made it sound like a place—a very cold, very empty place. He'd been living there most of his life.

"Yes, we make choices." Suddenly tired, Sarah closed her eyes. "Then we have to live with them. I chose to become Januel's lover, and when you strip away all the frills, it doesn't really matter why. He hurt me. I'll get over it." Her voice became quieter as she drifted toward sleep. "But God, I hope it's soon."

She opened her eyes a last time and found Byron watching her. Sarah smiled before she closed them again. "You know, Byron, you still haven't told me about yourself."

"No," he agreed and pushed the coffee aside. He didn't want it any more than he wanted to sit next to Sarah and watch her sleep.

Chapter Twenty-one

SARAH ARRIVED IN FRONT OF HER APARTMENT DOOR WITH two suitcases, a garment bag, and a poor disposition. For twenty-four hours she had put nothing into her system but champagne and coffee. It was beginning to wear on her. She had refused Byron's offer of a meal and a ride home after they had landed at the airport. She wanted to put distance between them. She had left herself no barriers, no mysteries; all she could hope for was space.

She wanted to resent him for simply being the one who had been there to listen. She couldn't. Part of her was grateful that he had only listened and offered no platitudes, no advice. Now she just wanted to be away from him, to have time to put what had happened with Januel in perspective.

The key to her apartment was in her purse only because Byron had reminded her to put it there. She frowned as she remembered her pliancy that morning, and slid the key in the lock.

Don't think about it, she ordered herself as she turned the knob. Just think about being home. Think about how good it is finally to be home.

Struggling with her luggage, Sarah pushed open the door and stepped inside. With her elbow, she flipped on the light switch. Everything familiar jumped into view as if she had seen it only yesterday: the old Victorian sofa she had reupholstered in the little shop on the East Side, her maize rug, the oil painting of a bayou she had bought on a weekend in New Orleans, the ceramic frog a college friend had made her a million Christmases ago.

"God," Sarah murmured, setting down her bags. "It *is* good to be home." There seemed to be so much of her here that she wondered for a moment what part of Sarah Lancaster had gone to Paris and what part had remained behind.

Standing just inside the doorway, she stared around the room as she set down her purse. She wanted to touch everything again, to assure herself that this was where she belonged. She turned and glanced at the door across the hall. First she wanted to see Dallas. She blocked out the coolness she had sensed in the last letter. Sarah needed her, needed to assure herself that their friendship had remained as her apartment had. The same. She wanted to laugh, to hug the thin body, to smell the fragrance of the White Shoulders Dallas all but bathed in. She needed to hear something ridiculous and to know she had been loved simply because she was Sarah. Leaving her door open, she walked across the hall and knocked.

When Evan opened the door, he stared at Sarah in stunned silence.

"Hello, Evan." Sarah smiled, trying to be glad to see him.

"Well, Sarah." Recovered enough from his initial surprise, he stepped back, gesturing with the glass of gin and tonic in his hand for her to come in. "I never heard you were coming home."

"It was a last-minute decision. I just got in." She glanced toward the bedroom. "I wanted to see Dallas."

Evan sipped at his third gin. The top two buttons on Sarah's shirt were undone. He counted four others before the shirt disappeared into her jeans. "She went to pick up a couple of things at the store." He forced himself to look back at her face when she turned her eyes to his.

"Oh. I'll come back. I guess I should unpack anyway."

"She won't be long." Evan took her hand before she could turn for the door. "Hang around," he invited. "Tell me about Paris. I've never made it over there. And the project. Word's out that you've made a name for yourself with that one." He smiled persuasively as he saw hesitation in her eyes. "Keep me company. I'll fix you a drink."

"No, really." She shook her head and tried not to think of champagne. "My system's shaky enough from the flight." She noticed that the glass in his hand was nearly empty. "You go ahead."

While Evan freshened his drink, Sarah wandered, pleased to find so many pieces of Dallas in the room; a pair of jade hoop earrings tossed on a table, a bottle of vivid pink nail polish, a glossy gossip magazine. The fatigue she had felt in the cab was replaced by a restlessness, an impatience. She wanted to see Dallas again, to feel she had really come home.

"Sarah?" Preoccupied, she glanced over when Evan spoke her name. He gestured with his glass. "Sure?"

"Oh." Shaking her head, she began another circle of the room. "No, I don't want anything." Feeling his eyes on her, Sarah turned back. "How have things been here, Evan? I've talked to Max several times, and Mugs once or twice, but it was almost all business."

"I don't think you'll find much changed," Evan said. He watched her steadily as he sipped at his gin. When she pushed her hands into her pockets, her blouse tightened over her breasts. The palms of his hands grew damp.

His stare was annoying, but Sarah fought to remain pleasant. "You and Dallas see quite a bit of each other, I suppose."

"Great lady, Dallas," Evan commented, not mentioning that their relationship had been growing shaky over the past few weeks. "I don't guess I ever thanked you properly for . . . bringing us together.'' The light touch of sarcasm in his voice was unmistakable.

"Don't mention it.'' She watched Evan drain his glass. "I'm going to start on that unpacking, Evan. You'll tell Dallas I'm back, won't you?'' As she spoke Sarah turned for the door.

"What's your hurry?'' His fingers wrapped around her upper arm before she could cross the room.

Sarah glanced back over her shoulder at him and kept her voice casual. "I'm wasted, Evan. It was a long flight.''

He put down his empty glass before he pulled her around to face him. Sarah stiffened. "Evan, I—''

"You haven't told me about Paris, Sarah.'' He lifted a hand, then ran his fingers down her hair, all the time keeping his eyes on her mouth. "We've a lot of catching up to do.''

"It'll have to be later.'' She spoke calmly as she attempted to free herself from his grasp. "I'm tired, Evan, and you've had too much to drink.''

"You haven't told me about that French lover of yours.''

"And I have no intention of doing so.''

"I promised myself I'd have you when you got back.'' His fingers tightened in her hair as he drew her closer. "I've wanted you for a year.'' He stared down at her while his voice deepened with annoyance and frustration. "A whole fucking year. I've never wanted a woman for that long before.''

Sarah pressed both hands against his chest. "Evan, I can't cope with this right now. I just can't.'' The words, husky with emotion, only fanned an already outrageous desire. His mouth rushed down to hers.

When she managed to tear her mouth away from his, he moved to her neck while he began to fumble with the snap on her jeans.

"Evan, stop! Don't do this.'' He was dangerously drunk. For an instant she managed to break away, but before she could dash for the door, he had her again, pulling her to the floor. Her legs tangled helplessly with his as she tried to kick him. Pinned beneath him, breathless from the fall, Sarah could only squirm.

"Let me go! Let me go, Evan. I'll scream." She dug her nails into his back and raked down with all her strength. With a quick sound of pain, Evan jerked up his head, staring down at her with feverish, angry eyes. Sarah went for his face, but he caught her wrist. In a swift movement of fury, he hooked his hand in her blouse and ripped it down the front.

Abruptly his expression changed. "Jesus." Shaken, he searched for something to say. "Sarah, I . . ." His head whipped around as the apartment door opened.

It took less than an instant for Dallas to assess the situation—Sarah's wide eyes gleaming with tears and fear, the torn blouse, Evan's expression of astonished guilt.

"Well." Her arms filled with groceries, she pushed the door shut with her back. "Welcome home, Sarah."

"Dallas . . ." Evan groped for words, but his mind was stumbling drunk and confused.

"Didn't waste time, did you?" she demanded. Her voice was quiet, sharp as a needle. Her eyes were on Evan as she walked to them, then shifted to Sarah's face.

Sarah's skin was dead white with bruising shadows under her eyes. Her breath was coming in quick, jerky sobs.

"So you were right all along," Dallas said evenly. "It must be very rewarding to be so goddamn clever."

Sarah closed her eyes, unable to bear anymore. "Oh, Dallas, no."

"Oh, Dallas, no?" Dallas repeated and flung both bags of groceries across the room. They split and spilled and scattered. "Oh, Dallas, no? What the fuck am I supposed to do with that? You were right, Sarah, you were so goddamn right it stinks."

Sarah's eyes were eloquent. "Please, don't."

"Listen, Dallas." Evan tried to struggle to his knees.

"Shut up," she shot back at him. "And stand up, you

bastard. Can't you even keep your hands off her when I'm watching you?''

Wavering, Evan got to his feet. ''Dallas, I'm sorry . . . I've had too much to drink . . .''

''You slimy son of a bitch! You think I don't know how many times you pretended I was her?'' Her voice was hollow with pain. ''I want you to get the hell out of here.'' Her voice rose passionately as she struck out at Evan. The blow staggered and sobered him.

''All right.'' His voice was calm, but his hand shook as he pushed it through his hair. ''You should look after Sarah. I think . . . I think I hurt her.''

''No.'' The word tumbled as Sarah dragged herself to her feet. ''Leave me alone.'' She swayed, and Evan reached out for her arm.

''Sarah.''

''Leave me alone!'' she shouted, clutching her blouse tightly together as she jerked away. Without looking back, she walked to the door. Her hand fumbled with the knob before she managed to open it. Dallas watched her leave, then heard the sound of her door shutting. Stiffly, she turned to Evan.

''Get out.''

''I'm going,'' he said with a nod. He too moved to the door, but paused when he reached it. ''I'm going to tell you something maybe you won't believe.'' He turned to take a long look at her; the tall, almost scarecrowish build, the unruly mop of curls, the deep-set smoky eyes. ''I never thought about anybody but you when we were making love. Not Sarah or anyone else.'' He walked through the door and left her alone.

Chapter Twenty-two

CASSIDY SAT GRUMBLING OVER THE PILE OF CONTRACTU-
al data on his desk. It ran through his mind, as it habitually
did when he was faced with a backlog of paperwork, that he
should never have let Haladay talk him into becoming an
executive.

Executive, he thought. Fancy word for paper shuffler.
Shit shoveler, he thought with more relish. Max, you
bastard. He glared down at a ten-page proposal. When he
answered his intercom, his voice sounded angry.

"Ms. Lancaster would like to see you," Mrs. Fitzwalter
announced in her cultured tones.

"What the hell's she doing here?" he demanded. "Don't
keep her waiting out there!" he shouted. "Send her in."

"Right away, Mr. Cassidy."

Cassidy clamped a smoldering cigar between his teeth
and glared down at the papers.

Sarah walked in and threw her arms around him. Blush-
ing and pleased, he returned the hug, patting the back of her
shoulder with his thick hand.

"Well, well, Sarah Lancaster, welcome home. Here
now, let's have a look at you." He drew her back by the
shoulders and smiled down into her face. His full red brows

lifted. "Girl, you're worn out. What are you doing in here?"

"Looking for work."

"Go home and go to bed."

"I tried that." Sarah smiled. "I need to work, Cassidy." Turning back, she lifted her hands in entreaty. "Put me to work, give me an assignment. Anything."

"You haven't taken a vacation in the year you've worked here," he pointed out.

"Next year. The timing's just not right. A tree house, Cassidy," she continued. "I don't care what it is."

He folded his arms around his chest and aimed a level look. "I've gotten no reports of trouble on the Delacroix project."

Sarah sighed and moved over to his drawing board. "The center's going beautifully. It's my life that isn't doing so well at the moment."

"Seems to be a lot of that going around." He studied her profile with narrowed eyes. "Evan's asked for a transfer to the Houston office."

Sarah turned around to face him fully. She saw the question, but refused it. "I need to work, Cassidy."

He frowned. "You want work?" Nodding, he moved to the papers on his desk and began to rummage. When he came up with the file, he held it out. "You got work. Here's the program and all pertinent data on a library projected on a site on the Navajo Reservation up north." He didn't add that he had given serious consideration to taking the assignment himself. It would be a challenge.

"Terrific."

Cassidy watched as she opened the folder. "Byron will be the engineer on this one." He caught her start of surprise; but misconstrued it. "He gets his hands dirty now and again, and this job's a particular pet of his."

"I see." Sarah remembered her vow to avoid Byron Lloyd for the next six or seven months. She sighed. You can't have it both ways, she decided. "I'll get started right away," she told Cassidy and moved to the door.

By noon the next day Sarah had several substantial concepts in mind for the design. After a brief conference with Cassidy, she was anxious to begin her preliminary drawings.

Mugs glanced up from her typewriter as the double glass doors slid open. Sarah strode through.

"Hi, Ms. Lancaster. Your lunch is here"—she tapped a white paper bag on her desk—"and—"

"Listen, Mugs," Sarah interrupted. "For the next couple of hours hold anything that's not vital to national security." She pushed open her office door. Maxwell Haladay stood inside, scowling at her Dali print.

"What the hell kind of picture is this?"

"Surrealistic," she answered, closing the door at her back. She grinned. "Want some lunch?"

Max glanced down at the bag. "Whatcha got?"

"Fresh out of caviar," she apologized, then motioned for him to sit. "How about tuna on whole wheat?" She heard the negative grunt as she rounded her desk. "There's a Diet Pepsi and a raisin cookie," she offered with a quick peek in the bag. The grunt became one of disgust.

"Any pickles?"

"Sorry."

At first glance, one would have thought how well Haladay looked. His skin was brown, his hair thick and magnificently white, his eyes sharp under his full black brows. Sarah looked deeper. There was a thinness at his neck that had not been there before, and fleshy folds of age. His face was more narrow, less firm. Time was catching up with him, Sarah thought with a stab of pity.

"Well, you can share or you can watch me eat," she told him as she spread her lunch on her desk. "I'm starved." Sarah bit into half the sandwich while offering the other half to Haladay. He waved it away.

"I ate my share of tuna fifty years ago." He settled back in the chair to study her. He too saw changes; a hint of sadness that seemed just under control. "Byron called me about Lafitte. He was a good man."

Sarah nodded, remembering.

"When you're around construction sites long enough, you see accidents. A lot of good men die for buildings. Sarah, not a thing in the goddamn world's going to change that. Take it from a man who's been there for better than half a century. Jesus." He shook his head at his own statement. "That's too goddamn long."

"Not for you," Sarah corrected and smiled again.

His mustache rose with his grin. "You and Byron think alike."

Surprise was almost comically obvious on her face. "We do?" She frowned.

"Reports on the center are all favorable at this stage," he began, taking note of her frown. "You managed to impress Byron—not a simple task. Bounnet's reports are all positive." Deliberately, Sarah took a bite of her sandwich. Haladay observed the slight fluctuation in her color. "Ceseare has nothing but praise for you."

"Do I get a raise?" Sarah demanded with her mouth still full.

"Five thousand a year."

Her brows shot up in surprise. Silently she watched him while she chewed and swallowed. "You don't piddle around, do you?" She liked the wolfish grin he gave her.

"If I make it comfortable enough for you, you won't be itching to start out on your own too soon." Sarah watched his grin fade. "Young people are restless. In too much of a hurry to begin. They don't look at the end. They don't even look at tomorrow. You're an architect, you've got to think about tomorrow." His eyes were suddenly, fiercely on hers. "We have that in common."

For a moment his eyes rested on her face. There was something in the look that puzzled her.

The freehand drawings for the library kept Sarah in her office long past five o'clock. The ideas were spinning through her head. She wanted to get them onto paper.

Next week, she thought, I'll go up and take a look at the site firsthand. But these are right. She caught her bottom lip between her teeth as she concentrated on the line of the roof. *These are right.*

"Sarah."

Sarah sucked in her breath, dropped her pencil, and whirled on her stool. Dallas stood in the center of the room, her long, thin hands hidden in the pockets of her white linen slacks. She watched the surprise fade from Sarah's eyes. There was neither the wariness nor the aloofness she had expected in its place. Taking a deep breath, she came closer.

"I'm sorry. I knocked." Dallas shook her head as she found herself already floundering. "I'm sorry."

"It's all right," Sarah told her, recognizing what the apology was for.

"No, it's not." Dallas took another step toward Sarah, then turned away. Her movements were jerky and nervous. She drew her hands from her pockets to hug her elbows. "No, it's not all right. It's taken me days to work up the nerve to face you. Oh, Christ, Sarah, I don't know how I could've said those things." She turned back, and her eyes were large and dark with tears just beginning to slip out. "I don't know how I could've been that way."

"Dallas . . ."

"No." She shook her head furiously. "Jesus Christ, Sarah, I knew you were scared to death, I knew the son of a bitch had hurt you, but I . . . oh, *shit!*" She brushed impatiently at the tears. "I wanted to kick you both. I couldn't stop, not even when I saw what it was doing to you. Oh, God." She turned away again. "I still don't believe it. It was worse, a hell of a lot worse than what Evan did, because I was supposed to be your friend. You should've been able to count on me.'' She sat on Sarah's desk, then rose again immediately, unable to settle. ''I'm not doing this the way I wanted to.'' She looked around once, eloquently. ''Sarah,'' she said with a sigh as the tears began to spill again.

''Dallas, please.'' Sarah came off the stool and moved toward her. ''You don't have to do anything.''

''No, no.'' Dallas held up a hand to stop her, then pressed her fingers to her eyes. ''Give me a minute.'' She didn't want forgiveness through sympathy. Forcing back the tears, she breathed deep. ''Listen . . .'' After dropping her hands, she looked directly into Sarah's eyes. ''You were right all along, and I knew it months ago. I couldn't stop. I was in love with him and I lost perspective. It got to be pretty easy to convince myself that if it hadn't been for you, he'd have loved me back.'' She dragged both hands through her hair. ''It wasn't easy living with the fact that you'd been right about everything and that Evan wanted you a hundred times more than he ever wanted me. The things I said when I walked into the apartment were ugly, and the only excuse I have is that I was hurting.'' She swallowed hard. ''I'm sorry, Sarah.''

Sarah let the silence take a beat. ''Want a drink?''

''Yeah.'' Dallas let out her breath on the word. ''Oh yeah.''

After moving to a small lacquered cabinet, Sarah rummaged inside. She took her time, giving Dallas the space she needed. As she poured two hefty glasses of vermouth, she heard Dallas gently blow her nose. ''You know my opinion of men?'' Sarah questioned, then walked across the room to offer a glass.

''Uh-uh.'' Dallas took a good swallow of vermouth and shuddered.

''They stink,'' Sarah said mildly before she too drank. ''They absolutely stink.''

"Yeah," Dallas agreed and finally smiled. "Oh yeah."

"Of course, this opinion is subject to change at any time." Sarah smiled back, the slow smile that touched every portion of her face. Dallas's eyes flooded with tears.

Setting down her glass, she threw her arms around Sarah. "Oh, God, I'm so glad you're back. I'm so glad."

"I missed you," Sarah told her.

"Welcome home," Dallas muttered, then drew away to fumble for a tissue.

"Thanks."

After a moment Dallas took a deep breath. "I've made a real ass out of myself."

"That's funny, so did I. In Paris. To men," Sarah said, raising her glass. "The lousy bastards."

Dallas picked up her glass. "Want to get drunk?"

"Oh no." Sarah shook her head. "I did that in Paris too." She looked down at her glass and shrugged. "It really didn't help a hell of a lot either." She pushed away thoughts of Januel. She wasn't ready to talk about him yet. "You know what you need," she said suddenly, bringing her eyes back to Dallas. "A date."

Dallas made a sound between a snort and a laugh. "Fuck men," she said briskly, then shook her head. "Freudian slip. That's not at all what I meant. I'm taking a vow of celibacy."

"How many choices have you got?" Sarah reminded her. She set down her glass and laid her hands on Dallas's shoulders. "Birdwatching would really bore you, and you're just too thin for football. Stick with what you do best. Work Evan out of your system." When Dallas opened her mouth to protest, Sarah lifted a brow. "All the way out," she added.

"Maybe you're right." She studied Sarah for a moment. "What happened in Paris, Sarah?"

"Not now." She squeezed Dallas's shoulders before she released them. "I've got to work a few things out of my system first too." She gestured toward the drawing board and grinned. "I just go about it differently. Listen. Let's go to Vegas next weekend. You keep telling me how crazy it is. I want to see it. We'll win hoards of money and I can watch you pick up men."

"Okay." Dallas grinned as she rose. "I know this blackjack dealer . . . he's got the ace and jack of spades tattoed on his left cheek." Her grin widened. "Of course, you can't see it when he's wearing his tux." She ran her tongue between her teeth as she remembered. "You know what I'm going to do?" she said, then turned to find Sarah smiling at her. "I'm going to call Dennis and see if he'll let me buy him dinner. Chinese. I have a lot of making up to do there too."

"Save me some ribs and an eggroll. I can have them for breakfast."

"You got it. Anything else? Want some sweet and sour pork?"

"No rice."

On her way to the door Dallas turned back. "I love you, Sarah. I really do."

Chapter Twenty-three

IT WAS JUST AFTER SEVEN WHEN SARAH PUSHED BACK from her drawing board. The preliminary sketches satisfied her. She stretched as she paged through them.

Well, Byron won't find anything to complain about here, she thought with satisfaction. He can take a look at them Monday. Then I'll drive up to the site. Shouldn't take more than half a day. She spread the drawings out again. She nodded, pleased. They're really very good. After a quick glance at her watch, Sarah picked up the phone. Why wait until Monday? she asked herself. He's probably still in his office. Mugs says he usually works late.

"Byron Lloyd."

"Sarah Lancaster," she returned very professionally and straightened on her stool. "I've just finished the preliminary sketches on the library. I thought you might like to have them over the weekend."

"That was quick!" Byron said. "Bring them up. I'd like to see them. I'll release the elevator."

"Don't bother. I can take the public one."

"I'm not in my office. The phone rings through directly to my apartment when it's shut off there. You can't get to the top floor in the public car."

Damn impulses, she thought bitterly. "I had no intention

of bothering you at home, Byron. They'll wait till Monday. I—"

"Bring them up." He cut her off, then broke the connection.

Sarah slammed down the receiver. Sliding the sketches into a file folder, she reminded herself that it was her own fault. She should have waited until Monday.

Bring them up, she repeated silently and scowled at the numbers flashing above the door. No *please* and *thank you* from Byron Lloyd. No *would you mind* or *why don't you*. Why clutter up a conversation with manners? Forget it, she advised herself. In and out, then I won't have to think about him until Monday.

After stepping into the hall on the top floor, Sarah moved to the adjoining vestibule. Her professional curiosity took over. She was forced to admit that she had wondered how Byron Lloyd lived. She admired the open flow of space between the vestibule and the living quarters. The absence of doors gave the space an unrestricted look. No bars, she thought. A skylight slanted overhead.

Byron watched her enter. He silently crossed to her. She wished briefly that he still wore his suit jacket and tie. They made him seem more professional.

"The file." She held it out. "All the sketches are inside."

Byron took it from her, then moved to the sofa. He opened the file without glancing at her. "Pour yourself a drink."

Sarah's brows arched high at his offhand hospitality. "Thank you, no, Byron. I really can't stay."

"Pour me one while you're at it."

Sarah's mouth opened and closed twice before she managed to control herself. She moved to a chrome and leather bar that took up an entire wall. The shelves were fully stocked and backed with mirrors. In the glass Sarah could see Byron as he sat on the couch. She yanked down a bottle of bourbon, found a glass under the bar, and poured.

Without replacing the bottle, Sarah stalked back across the room.

"Only because you asked so nicely. Just remember, I'm an architect, not a bartender." Slamming down the glass, Sarah turned to leave. Byron grabbed her wrist and pulled her down on the sofa.

"Are you annoyed, Sarah?"

"What," she said and tried to control the anger in her voice, "have you done that could possibly annoy me? Besides being rude?"

In answer, he smiled. In his eyes was a recklessness she had never seen in him before.

"I'm going," she said quickly. When she stood, his hand still held her wrist. Slowly he rose to stand beside her.

"No," he corrected. "You're not."

He saw the change in her face—understanding, more anger.

"I'm going home, Byron. Business hours are over."

"Exactly why you're not going anywhere. Not this time." He moved his hand from her wrist to her waist and pulled her against him. "This has nothing to do with business. This time it's just you and me, Sarah."

"You've no right—"

"Take down your hair."

"Go to hell." Sarah pushed against him, but he brought her closer. He laughed and swept his free hand through her hair, scattering pins. It fell heavily. Furious, she tossed back her head. "Nobody holds me unless I want them to."

"I know." His other arm came around her.

In a desperate attempt to be free, Sarah hooked her foot behind his and shifted her weight. Byron countered the move. With a gasp of surprise, she clutched at him as she began to fall. He tucked, cushioning her as they went down. He rolled, then pinned her beneath him.

Winded, Sarah lay still. Her breath came in quick pants as she gripped his shoulders. "Bastard," she managed, but there was no force to the oath.

Byron brushed at the hair that had fallen over her face. Her skin was warm under his fingers. He could feel desire fighting with the temper in her eyes. She wanted him, and he knew it.

Slowly, his eyes open and on hers, he lowered his mouth. Her lips were soft and silky. Sarah's fingers tensed on his shoulders, but he kept his mouth only a whisper on hers. He traced its outline with his tongue and waited. He could feel her breath beginning to shudder in his mouth. Gently he caught her bottom lip between his teeth, then let his tongue move over its fullness. Sarah's eyes clouded, the lids fluttered as she moaned. He'd waited long enough; Byron savaged her mouth.

She learned that desire could be overwhelming. She was clinging, burning up, then she was tugging at his clothes, desperate to touch him. The urgency was new to her. When her dress was in a heap beside them, she fumbled with his belt as he pulled the chemise down her body. His hands seemed to be everywhere at once, learning all there was to know of her while hers shook, reaching for him.

"Now," she whispered, and before she could demand again, he was inside her.

The climax came instantly—a deluge of sensation. It took her breath away. Sarah clung tighter, gasping for air. Then, weak and dazed, she lay beneath him.

Byron's face was buried in her hair. She could hear the long, deep breaths he took. Though his full weight was on her, she lay still and separated each individual sensation.

His heart thudded against hers. His breath was warm against her throat. The carpet was soft on her back while his body was hard. His skin was damp. So was hers. Sarah felt him shift as he lifted his head to look down on her. Slowly she opened her eyes. Hers were heavy, his guarded.

Studying her, Byron tried to deal with his own reaction. He had never lost himself in a woman to this extent. When he had made love with her, he had known a vulnerability he had never experienced. Total involvement. Sarah lifted a hand to his cheek.

"It's never been like that for me before." Her husky whisper disarmed him.

Damn the woman, he thought and crushed her mouth again. She was totally his, but he could feel the strength of her. He'd been wrong to think she had surrendered. Perhaps, strangely enough, the surrender had been his. After the kiss Sarah smiled up at him. Byron shifted from her, but when she started to sit up, he lay a hand on her shoulder.

"No, I want to look at you."

Her hair fanned out around her. Her mouth was soft and swollen. Her skin was pink and warm from his hands.

"Exquisite," Byron murmured, then brought his eyes to hers. He felt her skin leap as he ran his hand along the journey his eyes had taken. Her instant response fired him. He cupped her breast in his hand. Bending, he caught her nipple between his teeth and felt the tremor pass through her. "Spring," he murmured, tasting. "You smell always of spring." He felt her hands move over his shoulders to caress his neck.

Her long artist's fingers tangled in his hair. The need for her was rebuilding rapidly. When he lifted his head, her eyes met his directly, looking far inside—not in search, but in intimacy. He wondered what she saw, what she knew, and in a move of pure instinct he began to draw away. Sarah urged him closer as she smiled. His mouth was on hers before any thought could register.

He kissed her slowly, deeply, with a gentleness she had not expected. Again and again, their lips met, their tongues exploring. His hands were still as all desire was concentrated in the kiss. Her heart beat fast and steady under his. The tasting was long and luxurious.

Over her cheeks and closed lids, over her hair and ears, his mouth began to move. Still his hands touched only her hair as he trailed his lips down to her throat. He could feel her pulse skip, then race as he nipped at it with his teeth. The lowering sun turned her skin to gold and tossed shadows into the room. Sarah stroked the length of his back and marveled at the sensations he could create for her with only his mouth.

He continued his journey down until his tongue flicked lazily over her nipples. Sarah's breath caught and a sudden searing heat flashed into her stomach. He lay hard and erect against her thigh, and though her hips moved, he continued to savor her breasts without hurry. One, then the other, grew taut as she arched against him. Slowly he traced his tongue down her ribcage to her waist.

He was leading her, setting the pace. His own passion was banked. He trailed his lips and tongue over her stomach, then lingered as they passed through her springing mound of hair. Sarah moaned and clutched at his shoulders, but still he moved with aching slowness. With the tip of his tongue, he traced the crescent of the birthmark on her thigh.

She had lost herself and was aware only of rising pleasure and driving need. Nothing had ever taken her so far. No one had ever shown her how much there was to have.

He watched her face as he entered her. The light was dusky as the day ended, sending a mystery of hollows and shadows over her features. Her eyes were closed, her lips trembling with each breath. He took long, slow strokes and saw flickers of pleasure and passion run over her face. The pulse at the base of her throat hammered visibly.

Control slipped and was lost. He felt himself drowning in her but was helpless to prevent it. Caught, he increased his pace. His mouth swallowed her gasps of pleasure. They rose together, peaking on a desperate arch that left them both exhausted.

Byron rolled from her, wanting to be able to separate himself again, but Sarah moved with him. Warm and soft, she cuddled against him, kissing his shoulder as her arm stretched across his chest.

He turned his head to look at her and found her watching him. Her eyes moved him; their directness, their humor, their generosity. Tomorrow was soon enough for thinking, he decided. Tonight he needed to fill himself with her. He rose, lifting Sarah into his arms. Her hair floated down to trail beneath her.

"I want you in my bed," he said, and took her.

Chapter Twenty-four

Byron moved from sleep to wakefulness instantly. A lifetime of early rising had trained both his body and his mind to leap awake rather than drift. He opened his eyes, immediately alert.

Sarah was curled on her side, her head settled in the curve of his shoulder, her hand balled in a loose fist as it rested on his chest. He could feel the softness of her breast against his ribcage. Her heartbeat was as slow and regular as her breathing. The feelings that warmed inside of him disturbed him. Never had he guessed that his need for her would be so tenacious. When she sighed, her breath whispered over his skin. He wanted her, wanted to arouse her before she was fully awake, to feel her stir under his hands. Annoyed that a long night of loving hadn't been enough, he banked down the urge. He released himself from the tangle of Sarah's limbs and hair, then rose. She stirred once, then murmured his name before she lay still again. He swore and turned to the bath.

As Byron showered he reflected that he had made love with women more skillful, more adventurous, more demanding, but never one so giving. There was an openness about her that was dangerous because it invited openness in return. In order to regain his perspective, he felt it would be necessary to keep Sarah at arm's length. Without uttering a sound, she demanded emotional involvement.

When he returned to the bedroom, Sarah hadn't moved. She lay still on her side, with her head settled near the indentation he had left on his pillow. Her face was peaceful in sleep. On her bare shoulder, he saw the faint mauve shadows made by his own fingers. They reminded him of a fragility he continually forgot whenever he confronted her. Frowning, he bent to draw the sheet over her. Her lashes fluttered, lifted, dropped, then lifted again. Beneath them, her eyes were dark and unfocused. She stared at him, or through him, without the slightest change of expression. Sarah did not leap into mornings. Gradually her eyes focused, then warmed before the smile moved her mouth.

"Good morning." Her voice was thick and husky with sleep.

"I'm sorry. I didn't mean to wake you."

"It's okay." She yawned carelessly. "I won't be awake for at least an hour." Arching her back, she stretched under the sheets. "My system's programmed to sleep late on Saturdays. Have you been up long?"

"Not long." He dipped his hands in the pockets of his robe.

"What time is it?" Disoriented, she looked around for a clock.

"Seven fifteen."

Her eyes widened. "In the morning?" Shocked, she turned her head to the window, then back again to Byron. "Good God." She put both hands over her mouth and yawned again.

"Do you want some coffee, or are you going to lie around in bed all day?"

Sarah sat up, not bothering to tug up the sheets. The movement was natural and unselfconscious. Her hair fell over her, spreading over her shoulders and back, dipping over her breasts. "You haven't made it yet or I'd have smelled it."

Her skin was creamy against the masses of fawn-colored hair. She locked her arms around his neck and kissed him. Instantly his mouth was avid on hers. He pressed her to him. There was a hunger in him still unsatisfied. Because she sensed it, Sarah was surprised when he drew her away.

"Can you come up with an extra robe and a toothbrush?" She kept the request and her smile casual.

"Before or after coffee?"

"Before." He saw her teeth nip at her bottom lip. "But preferably as close to the same time as possible."

Byron moved to the closet and pulled out a dark blue robe. "The bath's through there," he told her as he passed her the robe. "You'll find an extra toothbrush on a shelf in the medicine cabinet." He watched her gather her hair into her hand and toss it behind her back before she belted the robe. "I'll put coffee on."

He was being polite, she noted, as if they had just shared afternoon tea instead of a night of wild loving. "Thank you," she said at last. With a nod, he turned and left her.

Sarah was surprised at how much his coolness hurt her. Men, she thought philosophically, then shook her head. If she had really known any man, she had known Benedict. She moved into the bathroom to frown at herself in the wide mirror above an inlaid double sink.

She was aware that it had been the romantic in her who had responded to Januel, the idealist who had been disillusioned. Now there was Byron. Or, more to the point, she thought as she located a tube containing a fresh toothbrush, there's been Byron for some time. It did no good to deny the fact that she had been thinking of him for over a year. Wanting him for over a year.

But I'd better take a few steps back, Sarah thought. My emotions are taking over again, and I can't let them. His aren't involved. She tightened the belt at her waist and followed the scent of coffee. Byron was pouring when she entered the kitchen.

"Ah, perfect timing." Sarah smiled, resisting the urge to

rub at a headache building in her left temple. It was a sign of stress she tried to discount.

There was a Formica counter in the center of the room, and she sat down on a stool. Byron set a cup in front of her, but remained standing as he drank.

"This is quite a place you have up here, Byron." Sarah's eyes wandered the room as she added cream to her coffee. She drank, holding the cup in both hands. The sleeves of the robe fell back to her elbows. "You have complete privacy, yet easy access to the building. Of course"—her eyes came back to him—"I'm sure the convenience means you work too hard and too long and too often."

"Wasn't it you who called a bit past seven from your office last night?"

Sarah grinned. "But I can be lazy too." She shot him a look. "Particularly on weekend mornings. I don't think you know how to do nothing and enjoy it."

He liked the look of her: her delicate hands holding the cup, her slender body lost in his robe, her face naked of cosmetics and beautiful in the strong morning sunlight, her hair rumpled from the night. There was a naturalness in her being there that disturbed him nearly to the point of temper. He turned his back on her and moved to the refrigerator.

"Want some breakfast?"

"Do you cook? Yes, of course, you do." Sarah laughed and pressed her fingers against the growing headache. "And very well without a doubt. You'll put my eggroll and ribs to shame."

"I beg your pardon?" Setting a carton of eggs on the counter, Byron turned to face her.

"That was what was on my menu for this morning. Dallas was going to bring me a Chinese doggie bag from dinner last night."

Byron's eyes narrowed. "Didn't you have dinner last night?"

"Mmm?" Smothering another yawn, Sarah shook her head. "Uh-uh."

"Why the hell not?"

The edge in his voice caught her full attention. She met his eyes with a half smile. "I was distracted."

"Damn it, Sarah, you might have said something."

She laughed at that. "I wasn't thinking much about food last night. Oh, stop looking so glum, Byron. I'm hardly teetering on the brink of starvation." Slipping from the stool, she moved to the stove to pour more coffee.

He pulled bacon from the refrigerator.

"Byron, I don't like eggs." She sighed and glanced around the room. "Got any peanut butter?"

"Not since I was twelve."

"You were never twelve." She took her coffee back to the counter. "Well, then, I'll have some bacon, but the eggs are all yours."

Sarah watched him cook. His movements were economical and sure. The scent of bacon mingled with that of coffee. When he set a platter of bacon and eggs on the counter, she lifted a slice and crunched into it.

"You did that very well," she told him when he added toast and butter. "I admire anyone who can cook an entire meal without a mishap." She took a bite of toast. "Everything I cook tastes the same," she added with her mouth full. "Terrible."

"That explains why you're so thin."

"I'm not thin," she disagreed as she chose another slice of bacon.

Byron merely lifted an eyebrow and filled his plate.

"Slender," Sarah continued, gesturing with the bacon, "is entirely different from thin. My father was thin." She sighed, remembering. "Dallas is thin."

Byron listened to her ramble as he ate. His robe had worked its way open at the throat, revealing a hint of breast. Byron poured more coffee. He was annoyed with himself for wanting her, more annoyed with Sarah for unconsciously arousing him.

"What happens when you sleep with a man who doesn't

cook?'' Byron expected her to respond with anger, but he saw only a look of stunned hurt. ''I doubt Bounnet is much of a cook, but I suppose he can dial room service well enough.''

Sarah's eyes locked on his. A pressure was building under her ribs. The headache was back in full force. ''I wouldn't know,'' she said calmly. ''Januel always refused to spend the night with me. He used my reputation as the reason, and we both know I was foolish enough to buy that. The same way I was foolish enough to think that you and I had shared something here.'' She unfolded her legs and pushed from the stool. ''If you don't mind, I'd like to shower before I go.''

Sarah walked into the living room and gathered her clothes. Her movements were swift and jerky. As she turned with her dress and lingerie crumpled in her hand, she walked into Byron. He took her arm as she tried to pull away, and with his free hand he held back her chin. He could feel her tremble with the sobs she was trying desperately to control. Guilt made him only more unreasonably angry.

''Goddamn you, let me go!'' Sarah fought against his hold, hating herself for letting him see her cry. ''Don't touch me.''

''Still hung up on Bounnet?'' Byron demanded. ''Do you still need the flowers, Sarah, and the lies?''

She stopped struggling. ''He could take lessons from you, Byron, on how to humiliate.''

Byron's grip loosened and she jerked away. In silence, he watched her walk from the room.

Sarah made certain all traces of tears were gone before she walked into the bedroom. The silence was so complete that as she slipped her arms into her jacket, she thought Byron had left. That would make it simpler, she decided, and lifted her damp hair over the back of her collar. *Oh God*. Briefly, she squeezed her eyes shut. How could I let this happen to me? Taking a long breath, she moved to the living room to retrieve her purse and shoes.

Byron was sitting in a chair. He was dressed, looking cool and totally at ease in a smoke-gray suit. There was no trace of the man who had loved her the night before. For a moment Sarah stood under the square of sunlight, then she quickly turned away to slip into her shoes. She headed for the vestibule without a word. Byron's hand closed over hers.

Sarah jerked back. She hadn't heard him move.

"I'll drive you home."

"No." She lifted her free hand to their joined ones and pushed. "I have my car."

"And I have your keys." He pulled her into the elevator before she could react.

"You had no right to go into my purse." Again, she tried and failed to pull her hand from his. "Give me my keys and leave me alone."

She turned away and looked straight ahead. *I will not humiliate myself with another scene,* she thought. They walked across the parking complex to Sarah's car, the only sound the echo of their footsteps.

Throughout the drive to her apartment building, Sarah remained silent. It gave her some satisfaction to know that Byron would be forced to take a cab back to his own apartment, a small inconvenience nonetheless. When he parked in front of her building, she held out her hand, palm up, for her keys. Byron ignored the gesture and stepped from the car. He took her arm as they moved to the entrance. Going directly to her apartment, Byron drew her keys from his pocket and unlocked the door. Sarah reached to retrieve them, then found herself inside the apartment with Byron. Again, he held the keys in his hand.

"I don't believe I invited you in," she said. "We have nothing to say to each other on a personal level. Business hours begin at nine a.m. on Monday."

Byron released her. He began to wander aimlessly about

her living room. Something in the way he moved alerted Sarah. The recklessness was back.

"Pack." It was an offhand command. Byron picked up a bowl in delft blue and examined it. "You'll need enough for two weeks."

Angrily, Sarah snatched the bowl from him. "What are you doing, shipping me to Alaska to design igloos?"

Byron studied her furious face. "No," he said calmly. "I'm marrying you."

The bowl slipped through Sarah's fingers to smash on the floor between them. "You must be out of your mind."

He lifted a brow. "Where's your bedroom?"

Sarah shook her head again.

Byron's eyes narrowed. Without speaking, he moved to the hall and into her bedroom. Sarah followed him and found him searching through her closet.

"What are you doing?" she demanded. She rushed to him and tugged on his arm. "What the hell are you doing?"

"Here." Byron pulled out an ivory dress, high and lacy at the neck, with long, full sleeves. "This should do."

"Do what?"

"Do for a wedding dress. I assume you'll want to wear one."

"For God's sake, Byron, what are you talking about?"

"Put that on." He tossed the dress onto the bed. Turning back to her closet, he began to select more clothes.

"Byron . . . Christ." A headache was pounding through her skull. With both hands pressed to her temples, she watched him draw clothes from her closet. "Stop this. Stop it!"

"I'll dress you if necessary, Sarah, but you'll probably be more comfortable doing it yourself." His back was still to her as he tossed clothes over his arm.

"Byron, you can't . . . you simply can't force someone to marry you. It's ludicrous."

"The hell I can't." He threw the clothes into a chair. "Why?"

In one stride Byron had caught her to him. His eyes bored into hers. ''I want you, and by Christ I'm going to have you. There isn't another man who's going to put his hands on you.'' He released her abruptly. Sarah staggered. ''Change,'' he ordered as he pulled open a drawer of her dresser.

''No.''

He whirled back, but instead of retreating, she advanced on him.

''I don't take orders from you outside of Haladay.''

''You do now.'' He tossed her lingerie on the bed. ''You can change, or we'll go the way you are.''

''You're not a stupid man, Byron.'' She spoke calmly, though her knees were beginning to tremble. She had seen his temper before, but this time he looked ready to murder. ''You know damn well I'm not going to change my clothes because you're having a tantrum.''

''Sarah—'' He grabbed both her arms but found that anger and emotion left him unable to speak.

''What are you going to do, beat me? Is that what you do when shouting and intimidation don't work?'' She put both hands on his chest and pushed away. Now she was just as furious as he. Something was building inside of her that she was afraid to acknowledge. ''This morning you went out of your way to make me feel cheap, and now you expect me to slip on a dress and run out and get married? No, you're not stupid, Byron. You're crazy.''

''I said''—his voice was icily calm—''I'm going to marry you.''

''Why?''

''Change your clothes, Sarah.'' He had to curl his hands into fists to keep them off her.

''I asked you why.''

''Because I want you.''

''Not good enough.'' Some of the anger was draining. Fear was growing in its place—not fear of him, but of what was happening inside her. ''You had me last night,'' she

216

continued. "You didn't seem very pleased about it this morning."

Byron turned away, fighting for control. "Don't push me, Sarah."

"Push *you?*" she tossed back. This time she stalked to him and grabbed his arm. "Push *you?* You son of a bitch. You stand there and say that to me after you order me to marry you? You don't ask if I want to, you don't ask how I feel!"

"I don't care how you feel." They were holding on to each other now, both of them trembling with rage—and something more. "I know how *I* feel."

"Then how do you feel?" she demanded, clutching his jacket in both hands. Her eyes were intense on his. "Tell me!"

"I'm in love with you, damn it!"

Then there was silence. They stared at each other, stunned. Very slowly, Sarah released her hold on his jacket and took a step back. She felt as though she had run for miles—short of breath, light-headed, exhilarated.

"My God," she managed. "I think you mean it."

"I don't want to." His voice was still a long way from calm. "I'll tell you that right now. I don't want to."

"No." She laughed, but it was a dazed sound. "No, I can see you don't."

"I've wanted you from the beginning."

"I know that." The light-headedness was passing. Now there was shock. How long had she waited for this without even being aware of it?

"When I came to Paris and saw you again, I knew—I knew it had gone past just wanting you, but I didn't want it."

"You still don't."

"No, I don't want to be in love with you." He reached out to touch her hair, then his fingers closed over it convulsively. "But I am."

"Would you like to know how I feel?"

"No," he answered quickly, and the anger came back to his eyes. "I told you I don't care how you feel."

"But I do, and I'm every bit as selfish as you are, Byron." Sarah held up a hand when he would have interrupted. "No, you're going to have to hear it, then you're going to have to deal with it." She moved away from him again before she continued. "I was going to marry Januel because I discovered all at once that I wanted a family, a home. I wasn't in love with him, but I wanted to be. At least I wanted to be in love with the man I thought he was."

"I don't want to hear about Bounnet, Sarah," Byron said, dangerously calm.

"It has nothing to do with Januel, Byron," she countered, "but with me. I learned that love means a great deal more than romance. Though I suppose I'll always want to hear a few soft words now and again. I still want a home and a family. I think, next to loving, that's the most important reason for marriage. "And . . ." She paused as she stepped to him again. "I promised myself after Januel that I'd never marry a man I wasn't in love with."

"Sarah—" Byron took her arms again, ready to explode.

"I'd like you to rephrase your initial question now," she told him calmly.

He stared at her. He had to force himself to lighten his grip on her. Who the hell was she to make him feel like a foolish teenager? There were a dozen other women who— Byron stopped himself, knowing there was no other woman. There was only Sarah.

"Will you marry me, Sarah?" he asked her, then saw the smile before her arms drew him to her.

Dallas groped for the ringing phone with one hand and kept her eyes firmly shut. The body of the phone fell to the floor with a crash, but she managed to keep a grip on the receiver. Beside her, Dennis mumbled in complaint.

"Yeah," Dallas breathed into the phone as she settled back against her pillow.

"Dallas, it's Sarah."

"Mm-hmm." She pushed her hair off her face before she started to drop off again.

"Dallas, wake up. It's important."

"Okay." Obediently, Dallas opened her eyes and stared glazedly across the room. "I'm awake. Did you want your breakfast? What time is it?"

"About ten thirty, I think."

"Oh, shit." Dallas crossed her eyes again. "You can have breakfast for lunch. I've only been asleep for about three hours. Call me back."

"No, Dallas, don't hang up!" Sarah let out a frustrated breath. "I'm in Vegas."

"Vegas," Dallas muttered. "I thought that was next weekend. We didn't go to Vegas yet."

"No, *I'm* in Vegas." Sarah shifted inside the phone booth. The clinkity-clink of the slots penetrated the glass. "Dallas, listen. Okay?"

"Yeah." Dallas yawned.

"I'm getting married in about fifteen minutes."

"Okay." As she was finishing her yawn, Dallas's eyes shot open. *"What!"* She scrambled into a sitting position, annoying Dennis by pulling the sheet from his back. He grumbled and turned over. Dallas shook her head to clear it. "What did you say?"

"I said I'm getting married in about fifteen minutes. In one of those fix-'em-up-quick chapels. I think it has a drive-in window."

"You're kidding. Married? In Vegas?"

"I'm in a phone booth outside the casino at the MGM," Sarah told her. "I wanted to let you know before—"

"Sarah, who? Who the hell are you marrying at the drive-in window in the chapel in Las Vegas at ten thirty on Saturday morning?"

Sarah adjusted the brim of her hat. "Byron Lloyd."

"Holy shit."

"Yes, well I knew you'd be pleased."

"When? How?" She raked her fingers through her hair. "Jesus Christ, Sarah, talk to me!"

"It's all happening rather quickly," Sarah began. "Just this morning, really. I'll have to fill you in when I have more time. I didn't want you to worry. I'll be away for a couple of weeks."

"But, Sarah, I didn't even know you were seeing him . . ."

"I wasn't . . . not really. Oh, Dallas, it's so bloody complicated. It just *happened*." She looked through the glass, but there was still no sign of Byron. "Please, wish me luck or congratulations or whatever the hell it is you're supposed to wish somebody who's getting married. I'm scared to death."

"Well, of course I do." Dallas shifted, found one of Dennis's socks under her, and tossed it on the floor. "But is this what you want? Are you okay?"

"Yes, it's what I want, and no, I'm not okay. I've never been so nervous in my life. It's ridiculous, but I feel like an eighteen-year-old virgin."

"Sarah." Dallas's fox-colored brows lowered. "Are you in love with him?"

"Oh, God, yes."

Her expression lightened. "That's great. I can't believe it."

"Neither can I. I have to go. I think they run these marriages through like Coke bottles in a factory."

Dallas felt her eyes fill and sighed. "Good luck, Sarah. Be happy."

Sarah's smiled as she spotted Byron. "I'm giving it my best shot."

Chapter Twenty-five

The DESERT WAS MORE VAST THAN SARAH HAD IMAGined. There were saguaro cacti, many-armed and as tall as a house; and cholla, grotesque and bushy. There were hawks and roadrunners, and although she did not see them, she knew there were snakes and lizards of all descriptions. There was also more color than she had expected: browns and golds and whites and grays along with the yellows and greens of the cacti. There were mesas and buttes and ridges, the angles and shapes wonderfully varied. Pillars of rock seemed to rise up out of nothing, sheering off into a sky so impossibly blue it might have been painted with a brush. The air was as dry as bone. She sat, gathering impressions, as Byron drove north.

Five minutes, a form, a few words, and payment in full. MasterCard welcome. Sarah was amazed that it had taken so little to bind her legally to the man at her side. She glanced down at the ring on her finger. That too had been a surprise. It was thin and silver, crusted with diamonds and emeralds. She hadn't expected Byron to take the time to buy anything more than a plain gold band.

Now, after a quick flight back to Phoenix, they were driving northeast. They would spend two weeks in Byron's home on the verges of the Navajo Reservation. Sarah found it odd to think of Byron with a home. The penthouse with its clean sophistication was easy to accept, but a home in the desert, away from the city, was more difficult. But then, she herself had often thought how many aspects there were to Byron Lloyd. She ran her thumb over her wedding ring and sighed.

"Tired?" Byron asked, glancing briefly from the ribbon of road to look at her.

Sarah smiled and shifted in her seat to face him. "No." His jacket and tie had been discarded, and his shirt sleeves were rolled to the elbow. She could see the muscles play in his forearm as he held the wheel. "It hardly seems real." After lifting the nosegay of lily of the valley and breathing in its scent, she smiled again. "These are."

"They suited you." Byron looked over again, watching her as she buried her face in the tiny blooms. He remembered the expression of surprise and pleasure on her face when he had handed her the nosegay.

He knew he would always be able to imagine her like that—with her eyes warm and alive between a spray of lily of the valley and a schoolgirlish straw hat. "I didn't thank you for the ring." She lowered the flowers to her lap. "I was surprised when I looked down and found it on my finger. It's beautiful." She studied it again, spreading her fingers. "It was clever of you to pick the right size while you were about it."

"I know your hands very well."

Curious, she lifted a brow as she turned to face him. "Do you?"

"They're narrow, very finely boned, with just traces of blue veins showing under the skin. Your fingers are long, very slender, with the nails always short, rounded, and unpainted. They're the sort of hands one sees tucked into the sleeves of a habit or holding a paintbrush."

Sarah frowned down at her hands. "How odd," she murmured before she looked back at him. "I never would have thought you'd notice something like that."

"I've noticed everything about you."

Sarah studied him another moment before she sat back in her seat. "Do you know, Byron, this all seems unreal. Twenty-four hours ago I'm sure neither of us had any notion of what we'd be doing today. Dallas was stunned when I told her. It occurs to me everyone else will be too."

"That shouldn't bother you," Byron remarked dryly.

"No, I like stunning people. I wonder what Max'll think." She twisted her head to Byron again. "Will he approve, do you think?"

"Shouldn't he?"

"You're very important to him," she replied. "He might be annoyed that you didn't discuss it with him."

"I don't discuss everything with Max."

"No, I don't suppose you do. Still, I imagine he'll have something to say about our eloping. That's what the papers will call it once it leaks out. 'Haladay V.P. Elopes with Architect.'" Sarah laughed. "That's what you get for being an important person."

"And for marrying one?"

"Oh, I'm not important yet," Sarah disclaimed airily. "Next year. Oh, Byron, look at those colors!"

To the east was a line of cliffs, but the desert stretched before them. Red was dominant, but with it were shades of pink and purple, gray and white and brown. She could see for miles, the clarity of air was so perfect. Some distance ahead, she spotted a huddle of buildings.

"You should see it in the spring," Byron commented and brought her attention back to him.

"What?"

"The desert in the spring," he explained. "The flowers are incredible. Poppies surrounding ocotillo, desert marigold, cactus flowers of all descriptions. I've seen white primrose scattered over sand dunes like someone dropped them by mistake."

"It seems impossible," Sarah murmured. "Do you come back here often?"

"Every couple of months."

Not often enough, Sarah thought suddenly. No, not often enough. Something here is good for him, but he forgets it for long stretches of time.

The huddle of buildings turned out to be a town that Sarah found perfect. There was a diner with a wide glass window in front, and a two-pump gas station where she could hear tinny country music scratching its way out of a portable radio. There was a clapboard general store with a large wooden sign proclaiming it. It was here that Byron stopped the car.

"We'll need some things . . ." he said.

Sarah was already out of the car and looking everywhere.

"It's plopped right down in the middle of nowhere," she said when Byron joined her. "It looks like it's been here forever. The sun's turned all the buildings the same dusty gray."

"Come inside." He took her hand. "You shouldn't stand in this sun for long."

When Byron pushed open the door, it gave a creak, then a jingle of bells. Inside, fans swirled the air and managed to give some assistance to a spitting window-unit air conditioner. Behind the main counter a man sat smoking a hand-rolled cigarette and reading the sports section of a Phoenix daily. He was middle-aged, nut brown, and thin as a reed. When he saw Byron, his expression sharpened.

"Well," he said and drew consideringly on his cigarette.

"Hello, Deerfoot." Byron crossed the linoleum floor.

"How long you staying?" The question was asked as his eyes drifted to Sarah. She smiled, sensing the grudging affection he directed toward Byron. Through a plume of smoke he watched her.

"Couple weeks." Byron noted the exchange between his wife and the shopkeeper and said nothing. "We'll be needing some things."

Deerfoot scratched his upper lip and shifted more comfortably on his stool. "Guess you know where everything is," he commented. "Ain't moved nothing."

Sarah waited until Byron had moved out of earshot, then approached the counter. "Got any Oreos?" she asked in undertones. "I'm starving."

"Third aisle down on the right, top shelf."

She cocked a brow. "Double Stuf?"

When he grinned, she felt a definite victory. "Yeah."

"I'm Sarah," she said and extended her hand.

Deerfoot stood, wiping his hand on the seat of his jeans before he accepted it. "John Deerfoot, ma'am."

"Nice to meet you, Mr. Deerfoot."

The store was perhaps twenty by twenty-five feet, with all available space given over to merchandise. There were pots and pans, kerosene lamps, hunting knives, hand-painted flowerpots, light bulbs, stationery, sewing thread, hairpins, and, Sarah decided, everything else imaginable. There were all manner of canned goods and dry goods, refrigerated dairy products, beer and soft drinks. She watched Byron choose a carton of eggs, a half gallon of milk, and a pound of butter.

"I'm rather fond of grape Nehi," Sarah ventured, eyeing a carton through the glass.

"Help yourself."

"You know, Byron," she began as she slid the door aside, "we haven't discussed the domestic aspects of our relationship."

He glanced down at her as she lifted out the carton of soft drinks. "I imagine we'll be able to muddle through."

She laughed and shot him a look.

Deerfoot rang up the order, bagging as he went along. When he came to Sarah's cookies, he handed them to her. "No charge," he said and was pleased when her lips curved.

"Thank you, Mr. Deerfoot."

As the cash register rang up Byron's change, Deerfoot

spoke in a low, rumbling tongue Sarah took to be Navajo. Byron answered, lifting the bags of groceries. When they reached the car, he turned to her.

"How do you manage to charm all men instantly?"

"Do I?" She smiled at him, opening the door so he could deposit the groceries in the back.

"You know damn well you do." He caught her chin in his hand to study her. "Deerfoot said your smile was worth more than all the gold in the mountains."

"He did?" Touched, Sarah glanced back at the storefront. "That was very sweet. What did you say to him?"

Byron stared down at her a moment, then his thumb traced her jawline. "I said some things are without price." He saw the change in her eyes, the darkening, the shifting of green that meant her emotions had been stirred. He bent to kiss her, feeling her mouth soften under his.

Moments later they were speeding down the narrow two-lane highway. Dry desert air rushed through the windows. "Want one?" Sarah asked as she broke open her bag of Oreos.

"Not without milk."

"We've got grape Nehi," she reminded him, twisting to pluck a bottle from the back.

"That," he said definitely, "is disgusting."

"No, really it's pretty good." To prove her point, Sarah washed down half a cookie with a generous swallow. "And it's a very unique wedding lunch."

Byron looked dubiously at the bag of Oreos and bottle of grape drink. "I suppose I should've stopped to feed you."

"I'm not a horse," she pointed out. She held out the bottle, and after a moment's hesitation he accepted. It had been a long, hot drive. Sarah grinned at his expression after he had swallowed, but said nothing. "Is it much farther?"

"About a mile." Byron passed the bottle back to her.

"You grew up near here, I suppose."

"On the reservation. My mother teaches on the reservation."

It wasn't the information that surprised her, but the fact that he had volunteered it. She knew he was very close about the part of his life that was connected to the land now sprawling around them. Sarah munched on an Oreo and studied Byron's profile. "What sort of teacher is she?"

"English. She specializes in English literature."

"Ah, so she did name you after Lord Byron." Sarah took another generous swallow of the Nehi. "I'd wondered about that. Is the site for the library far from here?"

"About ten miles north."

"Then we'll—" Her attention was captured by the house they approached.

White and cool and dry, it faced the east. It was tri-leveled, with each level turned in a different direction. Each was terraced and, Sarah guessed, roughly forty feet in length excluding patios. The flowers astonished her. She recognized impatiens, marigolds, geraniums, and pansies.

There was a carport on the far north side, but Byron stopped directly in front of the house.

"Byron, it's beautiful. It's perfectly beautiful. Did Cassidy . . ."

"Yes. I suppose you can see his signature all over it."

The smile she gave him was filled with pleasure. "I know it's a cliché to say it's like a mirage, but I'm saying it anyway. And it's wonderful."

Byron held her eyes a moment before turning to deal with the groceries. She tucked her nosegay into the sash of her dress.

"Let me help," she offered.

"No." He straightened, one bag in each arm. "I'll come back for the cases."

With a shrug, Sarah moved ahead of him to the wide stoop at the main entrance. There was a vivid red and gold celosia edging it. Sarah could smell heat and a vivid mixture of floral scents. She felt Byron's hand on her shoulder. Turning to him, Sarah saw that he had set down the bags. He put the key in the lock, pushed open the door, then lifted

227

her off her feet. Stunned, Sarah stared down at him as he carried her into the house.

"Oh, Byron," she whispered as she lowered her mouth to his. "I love you." Byron felt a surge of happiness rush through him as she rested her brow against his. He kissed her again, slowly, before he set her on her feet.

"We should put the food away," he said, then ran his hands down from her shoulders to her wrists before he turned to get the bags.

Sarah wandered around the room. It was dim and cool, with slatted blinds drawn over wide windows. There were two low sofas in eggshell with dark brown pillows. The floor was hardwood, covered only with a hand-tooled Navajo rug. Sarah noticed the local pottery on the glass tables and the Toulouse-Lautrec over the stone fireplace. She slipped out of her shoes and felt at home.

"It's so cool," she commented. "Surely you don't leave the air conditioning on when you're not here."

"I called ahead this morning," he said. Following him, Sarah found herself in the kitchen. The blinds had been drawn here, allowing a flood of sunshine in. From the window, Sarah could see the terrace and its tangle of plants against the backdrop of desert and mesas.

"How do you stand leaving it?" she murmured. She turned back to face the room as he stored the fresh produce in the refrigerator. "You'll have to tell me where things go." She looked around at the oak cabinets. Then she peeked into a bag and lifted out a pound of coffee. "I make fairly adequate coffee. Would you like some?"

"Later." When he closed the refrigerator, he saw her frowning down at the coffee and a loaf of bread. He took them, setting them on the counter. "Later," he said again as she lifted her eyes to his. "I'll show you the house."

"I'd like that."

The second level held a small guest room and bath along with what Sarah would have called the library. Its walls were lined with books. It was furnished with two chairs, a

desk, and a daybed. Here Byron worked. He might leave
Phoenix from time to time, but it was very rare that he left
Haladay. The terrace could be seen through the line of
windows in back of the desk. They moved to the third level
on an open staircase.

Here was a sitting room with a bar, a stereo unit, a chess
set in teakwood. The paneling was dark, the beams exposed
in the ceiling, the chairs deep and comfortable.

"Does Max come here?" Sarah asked suddenly. "I can
picture the two of you playing chess at that table."

"He does and we do." When he held out a hand, she
slipped hers into it. They moved across a narrow hall and
into the bedroom.

The slats of the blinds were tilted, allowing slices of
sunlight to filter through. It was a wide room with an
antique chifforobe and a brass bed that gleamed dully in the
dim light. There were tall doors in stained glass that she
knew must lead to the terrace. Now they were closed, and
the sun fell through them in colorful patches onto the floor.
There were candles in chunky pottery holders beside the
bed and a Tiffany lamp.

Byron let her wander, watching as she touched and
studied. He had wanted to see her here, wanted to know
how it would feel to see her among his things, his private
things.

"It's lovely, Byron, a lovely house." She glanced
toward the stained glass doors. "I'd like to go outside. The
view from the terrace at this level must be incredible."

In silence, Byron walked to her. He took her hat, setting
it on a ladder-back chair before he ran his fingers through
her hair. His eyes never left hers. He took the nosegay from
her sash, then set it on the bedside table before untieing the
bow. With a whisper, the silk dropped to the floor. Sarah's
heart began to pound in her throat. Byron pulled down the
zipper at her back, easing the dress over her shoulders until
it too floated to the floor.

She wore only a white silk teddy laced from the vee of the

229

bodice to the waist. He knew he could hook his hand in the top of the lacing and rip it from her with one smooth jerk. His eyes stayed on hers as his fingers took the silk.

"You're trembling," he murmured.

"I know." Sarah swallowed as her voice came only in whispers. "I know it's silly, but—" He stopped her words with a kiss.

It was long and luxurious and deep. He heard her soft moan and felt her instant and complete response. He knew he could take her where they stood—quickly, fiercely. His blood began to pound at the memory of what it was to have her. The softness, the taste. Drawing her away again, he looked down into her face. Her eyes were heavy, already clouded, her head tilted back in invitation. Byron brought both hands to her bodice and began to undo the lacing. Her breath was soft and shuddering in the silence of the room. She felt as though it were the first time, all nerves and needs.

With aching slowness, he unlaced her until the teddy was parted to the waist, just covering the peaks of her breasts. With his hands under her arms, he lifted her to sit on the bed. Then, carefully, he unhooked her stockings. Barely touching her, he slid them over her legs. Byron straightened to take off his shirt, and she managed to shift herself to a kneeling position on the bed.

"Let me do that." Her voice was low and husky, trembling like her hands when they reached for the buttons. She lowered her eyes to them, concentrating on the simple task that was suddenly so difficult with her breath struggling in her lungs. When she fumbled, he took both her hands in his, lifting them to his lips.

Sarah threw her arms around his neck and found his mouth with hers, then pulled him onto the bed. He slid the thin wisp of silk from her until she was naked beneath him. He could feel her muscles respond wherever he touched her until her whole body pulsed. She was all giving, all asking.

Between them, they freed him of his clothes until they

were at last flesh to flesh. The need to take her burned inside him, but he continued to caress with hands and mouth, aroused by her absolute response to him. His fingers slipped inside her to find her wet and warm and incredibly soft. Her breathing was shallow and rapid as she went where he and her passion guided her. When he knew the need would overpower him, he pushed her knees high and entered her.

Sarah's breath caught on a moan as he took her rapidly, rhythmically. Through a haze, she could hear him speak her name before all of her senses concentrated into one. She felt only the hardness of him inside her, the sharp heat of his mouth against her neck, the dampness of his flesh against hers. There was a blaze of almost intolerable pleasure as he kept her positioned to receive as much of him as possible. With a shudder, he was empty and laid his full weight on her. She only wrapped around him tighter, welcoming the continued closeness. He lay still, staying inside her.

Sarah watched the pattern of the squares of colored sunlight on the floor and knew that nothing would make her regret the decision she had made. When the time came and he hurt her, as he was bound to, she would remember this moment. No regrets, she told herself, shutting her eyes. I'll take what I need now and pay for it later.

Slowly, lovingly, she began to kiss his neck where her face was nestled. He stirred, and, feeling the beat of his heart increase against hers, Sarah ran her hands down to his hips. His body tensed where her fingers trailed. Incredibly, she felt him growing inside her again. She cried out when he began a fierce rhythm, and his mouth came savagely down on hers. His desperation shot through her, and where she had thought herself powerless to give more, she gave. As he asked, she found. When at last he was sated, he lay still for a moment, as breathless as she. Without speaking, he shifted from her, then drew her close against his side.

For the first time in years Byron slept while the sun was high.

* * *

The pattern of the colored patches on the floor had shifted when Byron awoke. From the angle of the sun, he estimated it to be near five o'clock. When he turned his head, Sarah's face was less than an inch from his. She was deeply asleep, curled into him much as she had been that morning. For a moment he lay still, looking at her. She barely stirred when he drew away, and he moved lightly, rising from the bed and pulling a robe from his closet. Soundlessly he left the room, shutting the door behind him. He went directly to the phone across the hall and remained standing as he placed the call.

"It's Byron Lloyd," he said briefly into the mouthpiece and waited. In moments he heard the click of an extension.

"Byron." Haladay's voice boomed from Phoenix.

"Max." Byron found a pack of cigarettes in a drawer, opening them as he spoke. "I'm in the desert. I'm taking a couple of weeks." He struck a match, then pulled smoke into his lungs. The tobacco was old and strong.

"That so?" Haladay said with idle curiosity. "Business or pleasure? Any trouble with that library project?"

"No trouble. I'll check out the site again while I'm here and handle a few other things by phone. I'll get in touch with Kay and Cassidy on Monday." He paused, then drew deep on the cigarette again. "Sarah's with me. We were married this morning."

The silence that followed was absolute. Byron walked to the window and pulled up the blind. Sunlight catapulted into the room. He could see an ocotillo still stubbornly blooming. Before he spoke again, he turned away.

"We flew to Vegas early this morning. I want a couple of weeks with her. Here, alone."

Haladay's voice was quiet, the tone Byron knew he used when he wanted his thoughts to remain his alone. "You never told me you were going to marry Sarah."

"No." Byron stared down at the chessboard. "I had no intention of marrying her until this morning." He blew out a stream of smoke, frustrated, annoyed with the irresistible compulsion to defend himself. "If I had, it still would've been between Sarah and me. We're not children, Max."

"Then why the hell did you run off like a couple of teenagers?" Haladay demanded.

Byron took a last drag, then crushed out the cigarette. "We were married quickly and quietly."

"I believe we have a great deal to discuss."

"Yes, when I get back."

"I want to talk to Sarah."

"When we get back."

He heard the old man sigh gustily into the receiver. "We'll talk."

"Two weeks," Byron said before he hung up. The door of the bedroom opened.

"Byron?"

Sarah came into the hall. Her hair was tousled around her, and she pushed at it as she glanced around. Sleep had flushed her cheeks and made her movements languid. Blinking against the sunlight, she found him. With a smile, she held out her hand.

He went to her.

Chapter Twenty-six

THE DAYS PASSED—SLOW, SUN-FILLED DAYS WITH cool, clear nights. Sarah lived for the moment, putting all her energies into each second without giving tomorrow a thought. She learned more of the physical aspects of love than she had thought possible. True passion was infinitely more demanding than she had ever realized, and Byron's need for her seemed insatiable.

They ate and they slept and they made love. There were no outside disturbances. Their world was insular and completely their own. They drank wine in his hot tub, sunned naked on the terrace, and made love under the searing sunlight. They talked of nothing important. Though Sarah knew this was only an idyllic moment out of their lives, she relished it. Perhaps she relished it because she knew it would be brief, like the flowers that explode in the desert in the spring. The time would come when they would have to return to Phoenix and the responsibilities of marriage. A week passed, and the life outside themselves was very remote.

Sarah woke and the blinds were still closed. She stretched, touching the empty pillow beside her with her fingertips. Almost invariably, Byron was up long before she was. Now and again, he woke her or lay beside her until she stirred. With a last, lazy stretch, she rose, plucking a short white robe from a chair. Belting it loosely, she pushed open the doors to the terrace and stepped outside. Instantly the scent of flowers greeted her.

Plucking pansies from the border of the terrace, she marveled at the new course her life had taken. A wife, she mused, and wondered how it would feel to truly be one. For now, she felt only like a lover. She tucked the flowers behind her ear, satisfied with the moment. It was too soon to think about forever, too late to think about tomorrow. There was only now. Using the railing as a barre, she began to do the morning exercises that had been part of her life for twenty years. With her thoughts drifting away, she positioned her feet and did a deep plié. Her arms moved lightly with the motion as she stared out at the sweep of the desert.

Byron stopped at the doorway to watch her. Each gesture was slow and graceful. She was humming lightly to give rhythm to the motions, but he could see by her eyes that her thoughts were far from her body. There was a hint of a smile on her mouth as her muscles responded effortlessly to command. She pliéd again, the skirt of the robe floating up, then down with her. It was just separated at the front, a narrow strip of space between the panels. The sun poured down over her, drawing out the lighter shades of her hair until they shimmered nearly white.

He liked to watch her like this, when she was lost in herself, unaware of him. The simple, unpretentious grace of her body awoke in him an unexpected tenderness.

With her toe pointed, Sarah lifted her leg in front of her, then swiveled it from the hip to the side before slowly taking it to the back. He thought her joints must be liquid to allow her that sort of freedom. Her back remained straight, her eyes dreaming. She bent her leg at the knee into an attitude position, holding it there, then straightening again, bringing it back to the side then to the front before coming back to the first position. It was a movement of absolute control. When she turned to work her other leg, she saw Byron in the doorway.

She smiled. He wore only cutoffs, and though she knew his body intimately, it still aroused her to see it. But it was his eyes that held her. There was nothing casual in them, as there was in his attire. For an instant she had a sense of her power over him. It rose in her, fast and hot, and showed in her eyes. She waited for him.

He came to her, taking her hair in both hands as she tilted her face up to his. She read the struggle on his face, a resistance. Placing her hands on his hips, she ran them slowly up his stomach and chest to his shoulders. She felt his muscles quiver along the way. She savored the power she had over him, then touched her mouth to his.

Instantly he pulled her against him. She thought she tasted a trace of temper with the desperation, then he swore and pulled his mouth away. With the calm of understanding, she stared up at him. He wanted to turn away, to walk away, to prove to himself he could, then she was against him again. The need for her grew unreasonable. He ravaged her mouth again and again, wanting more and still more. Through the thin silk of her robe, he could feel every line of her body. It wasn't enough. He pulled it from her, then ran his hands over her skin, feeling the curve of her back, the long narrow bones of her hips. He knew she was pulling him in, drawing him into her emotionally as she did physically when they lay together.

"Sarah." His teeth found the sensitivity at the curve of her neck. He felt her tug at his cutoffs before her slender fingers took him. He shuddered once before his mouth began to rush over her face. "Christ, will I never get enough of you?"

There was something desperate, something savage in the words before he swept her into his arms and carried her inside.

* * *

The morning had drifted into afternoon before Sarah sat up in bed. "You know what I'm going to do?" she demanded and flipped her hair over her shoulder.

"Mmm?" Byron lay on his back with his eyes on the ceiling.

"I'm going to cook dinner tonight."

He shifted his eyes to Sarah's and lifted a brow. "Oh?"

"There's no need to look so skeptical," she said dryly. With an easy movement, she turned and straddled him, then gave him a narrowed look. "I'm going to do much better than the grilled cheese sandwiches I burned a couple of days ago. You're not the only one who can cook a decent meal, you know."

"Were you aware that you have a very strong competitive streak?"

"Yes. I'm going to make chicken fricassee and lemon meringue pie. Have you got a cookbook?"

"Probably."

"Good. Then you can go to town and get some more eggs and milk. And don't forget the Oreos." She leaned down to give him a long kiss. Her hair curtained them as she pressed her brow against his.

"Anything else?" he asked as he ran his hands over her breasts.

"I'll give it some thought . . . after I drive you crazy."

True to her word, Sarah found a recipe for chicken fricassee and set to work after Byron drove off to town. She plowed ahead, content, with Beethoven pouring through the kitchen speaker.

She had braided her hair on either side of her head, with red ribbons at the ends. Flour dusted over her cutoffs and white shirt. From time to time she muttered to herself, brows lowered as she read from the cookbook. Her absorption was absolute. When she looked up to see a woman in the kitchen doorway, Sarah merely stared, caught totally off guard.

She had a quiet face with dark, liquid eyes and a full mouth. Her hair was pulled straight back, secured at the nape of a long neck. But for a few wisps of gray, it was a shimmering, radiant black. She was tall and slender and wore a simple shirtwaist dress in the palest of blues.

"Hello," Sarah said with a smile.

There was a smile in return, singularly charming and serious. "Hello." She stepped into the room. "I knocked, but you apparently didn't hear me. I heard the music, and the door was unlatched. I'm Catherine Lloyd."

Sarah put the bowl on the counter. "Byron's mother." She came forward, extending her hands, then stopped and glanced down at her flour-covered palms. "Oh, I'm a mess," she apologized, brushing uselessly at her cutoffs. With a laugh, she looked up at Catherine. "I've backed myself into a corner, you see, and swore I'd make dinner. I'm a dreadful cook and Byron is so damnably perfect."

Catherine smiled. The impulsive gesture of welcome had touched her. "He always was, I'm afraid," she returned. "At times almost calculatingly so."

"It's wonderful meeting you." Sarah motioned to a kitchen stool. "Please, sit down. Would you like some coffee?"

"I'd like that." Catherine moved to the stool, then watched as Sarah rinsed her hands in the sink.

"Byron went into town," Sarah told her as she began to fiddle with the coffeepot. "He should be back soon."

"I hope it's not too soon for visitors," Catherine began. "When Byron called me to tell me he was married, I thought a week's wait would be acceptable."

"You didn't have to wait," Sarah said. "I've wanted to meet you, to talk to you, very much."

Catherine looked at her a long moment before she smiled. "Byron didn't tell me your name."

Sarah walked to Catherine and stretched out her hands. "I'm Sarah. I love Byron very much."

Catherine accepted the hands. "Hello, Sarah. I'm very

glad you do.'' She squeezed Sarah's hands before releasing them. "Can you talk while you cook? I'd like to learn about my son's wife."

"I can talk much better than I can cook," Sarah told her. "What would you like to know?"

"Where did you meet Byron?"

Sarah put a lid on the skillet of chicken. "In his office when I came to Phoenix for an interview last year. He hired me for Haladay. I'm an architect."

"An architect," Catherine said, surprised.

"Yes. I thought him very formidable and reserved. But I could never stop myself from wondering what he was like . . . really like. There's so much he keeps under the surface." She lifted her eyes to Catherine's.

Seeing the unspoken question, Catherine nodded. "Always. He's very cautious of giving his trust or affection. I believe Maxwell Haladay is the only one to whom he's given both. Perhaps, to a certain extent, John Cassidy. He was a difficult boy to understand, and he grew into a difficult man. At times, perhaps unfairly, I blame Maxwell Haladay for that."

"Max?" Sarah repeated, puzzled. "Why?"

"He gave Byron exactly what he wanted." She sat in the direct sunlight, and Sarah saw that her face was smooth, almost lineless, and the shape of Byron's. "He saw the man," she continued, "and forgot the boy."

Sarah went to a cupboard. "It's difficult for me to imagine Byron as a boy. He's so self-sufficient, so controlled." She shrugged as she put cups and saucers on the counter. Catherine saw the thin circlet on Sarah's finger and, like her son, found the hands exquisite. "Max depends totally on Byron now in business and, I believe, personally," Sarah went on. "He's quite brilliant, both as an administrator and as an engineer. Though I'd never tell him that." She grinned.

The coffee began to perk. Sarah brought the pot to the cups. "How do you take it?"

"Black." Catherine waited until Sarah had taken a carton of milk from the refrigerator and added some to her coffee. "I never expected Byron to marry."

Sarah slid onto the stool opposite her. Her eyes were direct. "No?"

"He never knew his father. He left when Byron was less than a year old. Byron's father hated being poor." She lifted her coffee and sipped. "So did Byron. It was difficult for him being without a father, being of mixed heritage, being poor. More difficult perhaps because he was very quick, very bright. He understood too much too soon." Her eyes came back to Sarah's. "He had a dreadful temper. It was a problem in school for some time. Fighting. Black eyes, bloody noses, torn clothes."

"Byron?" Sarah murmured, astonished.

"Oh, yes. He was easier to understand when he rebelled, when he was angry. I lost him when he discovered ambition. Of course, it was inevitable." She lifted her cup again, giving Sarah one of her serious smiles. "He learned to harness the energy, the emotions, the temper. I've often wished he hadn't been quite so good at it."

"He seems more open here, in this house." Looking around, Sarah gestured widely with her hands. "He needs this part of his life as much as he needs Haladay."

"He always has," Catherine murmured. "And what about you?" Their eyes met again. "What do you need?"

"Byron," she said instantly, then shook her head and smiled. "Of course, it's not that simple. I need him, need what I think we might have together." She held the cup in both hands, looking at Catherine over the rim. "And I need Haladay. We share ambition. I don't know if that'll make our lives easier or more difficult."

Catherine studied her in silence for some moments. "Shall I tell you you're not what I pictured when I learned Byron had married? Oh, I expected someone beautiful. And someone intelligent. But . . ." She laughed a little before setting down her cup. "I had expected to find someone very cool, someone *suitable*. Tell me, Sarah, would you know how to write a menu for a dinner party of fifty?"

"I wouldn't have the vaguest idea."

Catherine reached across the counter to take her hands. "I'm so glad. He's my only child."

They heard the front door open. Sarah smiled slowly, completely, before she turned to greet Byron. "You were quick," she said, meeting him at the kitchen doorway. "We have company." Taking the bag from his hand, she stepped aside.

He glanced over the disarray of Sarah's cooking and saw his mother. Sarah's watched surprise flicker briefly in his eyes. He didn't smile, but crossed to her, studying her face before he kissed her cheek. "Mother."

Sarah frowned at the tone of the greeting, but Catherine appeared to accept it. "Hello, Byron. I hope you don't mind that I came. I wanted to meet your wife."

"Of course not." She looked, he thought as always, beautiful and much too young to be his mother. Then he remembered, as always, that she had been barely sixteen when he was born.

"We were having coffee," Sarah told Byron. "Would you like some?"

"Yes." He turned away to get a cup.

"You'll have to take your mother out on the terrace," Sarah began casually as she set the pot on a tray, "while I finish making dinner. With any luck we should be able to eat by six." She smiled at Catherine as she slid her cup and saucer onto the tray. "We've got some Chablis, don't we, Byron?"

"Yes." He ran his hand down one of her pigtails. "We have some Chablis."

"If I'm staying for dinner," Catherine said, glancing around at the chaos, "perhaps you'll allow me to help with this."

Sarah blew out a long breath as she followed Catherine's gaze. "No, that would be cheating, I suppose. I wouldn't mind that, except he'd know about it."

"Glad to see you have scruples," Byron said. He took the tray as she handed it to him.

"If I had told you I failed home economics in school, would you still have married me?"

He smiled. "No."

Moving past him, Sarah opened the terrace door. "It's lovely on the terrace," she told Catherine. "Perhaps you can persuade Byron to tell you how wonderful I am while I'm not around to be embarrassed."

During the next hour Sarah did what she could in the kitchen and gave the two on the terrace their privacy. When she joined them with the offer of more coffee, Byron took her hand and pulled her down to a chair.

"Byron tells me you're a very good architect." Catherine watched Sarah's brow arch as she shot him a look.

"Terrifying praise indeed," she murmured, "from an engineer."

"You'll be working together on the library for the reservation," Catherine went on.

"Yes." Sarah's professional interest perked up. "Do you know the site? It isn't far from here, is it?"

"I'll take you before we go back," Byron said.

Sarah smiled at him and sat back, folding her legs into the lotus position. "Let's eat out here," she suggested.

The meal was surprisingly good. Sarah thought she could see Byron relax. He was not completely comfortable with his mother, but she sensed that the bond between them was strong nonetheless.

Around them, the desert changed colors with the lowering sun. Shadows lengthened on the terrace. To the west, the sky was pink and cloudless. They remained outdoors as the air cooled with evening.

"I'd like to help you with the dishes," Catherine said as she rose.

Sarah agreed. "Thanks. I'd rather not ask Byron," she said as if he weren't sitting beside her. "He's so organized when he cooks; he'll be shocked by the mess in the kitchen."

He said nothing, only pulling out a cigarette and lighting it as Sarah stacked the dishes.

The sun was slanting low through the windows by the time the kitchen was set to rights. Sarah carried another tray of coffee into the living room to find Byron starting a fire.

He stayed where he was, crouched by the hearth, while his eyes shifted from his wife to his mother. Catherine smiled, touching Sarah's arm lightly before crossing to him. "I can't stay any longer." She reached a hand down to him and he took it as he straightened. "Honeymoons are for two."

Byron squeezed her hand, warm from kitchen work and rough from gardening. "I'm glad you came," he told her.

"So am I." She spoke again, quietly, in her own tongue. Byron lifted his hand, holding it against her cheek as he answered her.

Sarah lowered the coffee tray to the table as Catherine walked back to her. She took Sarah by the shoulders and kissed both of her cheeks. "I have given my son my blessing. Be happy." She squeezed Sarah's shoulders lightly before turning away. Byron moved to the door with her, and she paused to look up at him again. "You've chosen well. I am pleased with you." She walked outside as the sky exploded with sunset.

"Your mother is a beautiful woman."

He stood where he was. "Yes, I know."

Sarah lowered herself to the floor in front of the fire. "She's very proud of you." She tossed both braids behind her back as she kept her face lifted to his. "You're very lucky to have her."

Byron stared down at the fire. "She was fifteen years old when she got pregnant, sixteen when he left her. She never had a chance."

He, Sarah noted. Not *my father*. "A chance for what, Byron?"

"To have a choice."

"Who are you blaming?" Sarah asked him. "Your mother, your father, or yourself?"

He turned sharply but bit off the words before he said them. Sarah was looking at him, not with pity, not with reproach, but with love. "All of us, I suppose." He lifted the poker and jabbed it at a log. "She won't let me give her money."

"She doesn't need your money, Byron." Sarah rose and, wrapping her arms around his waist, rested her cheek on his back. "You found your way out because you had to. She stays for the same reason."

"I've never understood her," he murmured. It was difficult for him to speak of his mother. Yet with Sarah's arms around him, he found the words coming. "She was a child; she didn't have to keep a baby. She didn't have to put herself through all the years of struggle."

"She loves you. That's why she kept you, and that's why she let you go."

He turned and faced her. "How do you know that?"

"Because I love you too."

Chapter Twenty-seven

Good morning, Ms. Lancaster—Ms. Lloyd," Mugs corrected, rising as Sarah stepped in front of her desk. She held out a yellow rosebud. "Welcome back."

"Thank you, Mugs." Taking the flower, Sarah leaned over and kissed the freckled cheek. "And Ms. Lancaster's fine in the office."

"Yes, ma'am. Mr. Haladay wants to see you at ten."

"Oh." Sarah took a quick glance at her watch. "All right. Buzz me, will you?" She shifted her briefcase to her other hand. "Anything else I should know?"

"The latest reports on the Delacroix project are on your desk."

Before Sarah could turn to her office, the glass doors of the reception area opened. Dallas strode in and took Sarah by the arms. "Hiya, Mugs. Your boss is going to be busy for a while." She steered Sarah into her office and shut the door. "Okay," she said. "Let's have it. How the hell did you end up married to Byron Lloyd? You are married, aren't you?" She grabbed Sarah's left hand, then let out a long breath as she stared at the ring. "Christ, you *are* married."

"That's what the man told us in Vegas. Why don't we sit down?"

"Yeah." Dallas sighed, dropping Sarah's hand. "Yeah, maybe we better." She sank into a chair. Crossing her arms, she studied Sarah critically. "Good God, you look fantastic!"

"Thanks." Sarah set the rosebud and briefcase on the desk beside her. "I feel that way too."

"What," Dallas began after a pause, "the hell happened?"

Sarah took a deep breath as she moved to the window. "I don't know how to explain it." She stuck her thumb into the dirt of an ivy to check for moisture.

"Don't let that stop you."

"I've been in love with him for a long time," Sarah murmured. "It isn't one of those things that I could pinpoint the moment and say—yes, that's when I fell in love with Byron. It just was."

"I didn't even think you liked him very much."

Sarah laughed. "I didn't always. I don't always. Byron isn't an easy man to like, or to love." She sat on the edge of her desk. "I was attracted to him right from the start. I could never seem to get him off my mind."

Dallas listened in silence. She's trying to explain this to herself as much as me, she decided.

"When I went to Paris and met Januel," Sarah continued, "I think I wanted a fairy tale. He gave it to me, and there was nothing real about it. The whole time I was with Januel, I caught myself comparing him with Byron. Then when he came to Paris too, I . . ." She shook her head. "God, he confused me, Dallas. He can be so reserved, and then so physical. He's so many different people, I doubt I'll ever understand him completely. Perhaps that's part of his attraction for me."

Dallas ran her hand through her shock of curls. "Do you mean you decided to get married while you were in Paris?"

"Not to Byron, to Januel."

"Once more," Dallas requested. "With clarity."

Sarah told her quickly and briefly of her last days in

Paris. It wasn't until the story was complete that Dallas moved. Slowly she rose from the chair.

"And you came to see me right from the airport." She took a shaky breath. "Evan and I gave you a hell of a greeting."

"Dallas—"

"At least Evan had gin for an excuse. I haven't any."

"Dallas, please." Sarah took her hands. "Just be my friend. I love Byron so much, it's a little scary. I'm going to need a friend."

Dallas pulled Sarah into her arms. "Oh, shit," she muttered. "I'm going to get sloppy. I know I'm going to get sloppy."

"Good. There was nobody to get sloppy for me in the Tie the Knot Quick Chapel."

Dallas sniffled and drew Sarah away. "It wasn't really called that."

"It should have been."

"So what happens now?"

"I'm not sure. Byron and I have a lot of adjusting to do, I suppose." Dallas saw the crease form between her brows. "Honeymoons and marriages are entirely different things. I don't think it's going to be easy for either of us. And mixing business and a marriage . . ." She trailed off, then walked back to the window. "Byron and I will be working on the Navajo project together."

"And?" Dallas prompted.

"And I think we'll work well together. I hope we will."

"But?" Dallas prompted again, and Sarah laughed.

"You really do know me, don't you?"

"Enough to know what it means when you get that look on your face."

"I've been thinking that I should consider starting my own business," Sarah mused.

"Leave Haladay?" Dallas moved over to her. "Why?"

"I want to build as Sarah Lancaster, not as Byron Lloyd's wife, the architect."

"Oh," Dallas said, stretching the word into three syllables. "What does Byron think?"

"I haven't said anything to him yet." Sarah shrugged. "I'm not completely certain it's what I want to do. I guess I'm keeping my options open. I don't want my profession to interfere with my marriage, and I don't want my marriage to interfere with my profession." Sarah laughed again. "Maybe I'm right back to that fairy tale. I want it all, Dallas. Maybe if I want it all hard enough, I'll get most of it."

"I don't like to give advice," Dallas began.

"But?"

She grinned and hugged Sarah again. "Let things settle for a while before you do anything. Rome wasn't built in a day."

"Blame that on the engineers," Sarah told her.

They both turned as her office door opened. Sarah's smile grew wider as Cassidy lumbered toward her.

"Well, so it's Sarah Lloyd now, is it?" He put his hands on her shoulders. "Here, let me look at you." He frowned with the critical survey.

"Well?" Sarah lifted a brow.

"Not too bad. The two of you move pretty fast."

"It certainly looks that way. Do you approve?"

"You're what he's needed for quite some time." He rubbed his hands up and down her arms briskly before releasing her. "I hope he's as right for you as you are for him."

"He is," Sarah assured him, pleased. "Have you seen him this morning?"

"He went directly up to Max."

"Oh, I see." Sarah frowned as she glanced at her watch. "I'm supposed to go up myself at ten." She gave Cassidy a level look. "How is Max?"

"You surprised him," he said briefly. "Max isn't often surprised." Cassidy turned to Dallas and cocked a brow.

"I'm having a bit of trouble with a requisition I sent down a few days ago. The one for the door."

Dallas's animated, angular face became utterly impassive. "Yes, I know about that. I sent it back up for justification. Have you sent me the paperwork?"

"I want it," Cassidy shot back. "That's the justification."

Dallas folded her hands. "I'm afraid that's less than adequate. I'll need a justification before I can purchase the door from the Debilleri firm in Rome. The cost exceeds the limit, and therefore we're required to have bids. There were no quotes in the requisition you sent me. You might, of course, justify the Debilleri firm as the best or sole source."

"Bullshit."

Dallas sighed and turned to Sarah. "Architects never give the least consideration to fraud, abuse, or waste. And neither," she added, "does almost anyone else, which is why I've dedicated my life to it. Send me the paperwork and you can have your Italian door," she repeated to Cassidy.

"Justification my ass," Cassidy muttered and stalked from the room.

"You see?" Dallas gave a weighty sigh. "Fraud, abuse, and waste. Everywhere."

Sarah thought it best not to tell Dallas about the requisitions she was planning for the library project. "You better get to your office and make sure nothing slips by," she suggested. "I've got to get upstairs."

"Yeah," Dallas murmured absently as they left the office together.

Byron and Haladay rose as Sarah came into the room. She exchanged a look with Byron before her eyes drifted to Haladay. There was tension here, and she sensed it instantly.

"Hello, Max."

"Hello, Sarah." Was he thinner? There were folds under his eyes that hadn't been there before. "I'm told congratulations are in order."

"Yes." She took a step closer until she stood between the two men. "Are you going to wish me happy, Max?"

She saw Haladay's eyes shift over her head and wondered if he resented her claim on Byron.

Haladay brought his gaze back to her face. "I wish you happy, Sarah."

She smiled and held out her hand. "Thank you, Max."

He took her hand lightly, quickly. "I have something for the two of you."

"A present?" Sarah turned to Byron as Max crossed the room. The tension wasn't only in Haladay, she noted, but in Byron as well. Adjustments, she thought. It seems we're going to have to begin already.

Haladay took a canvas from the table at the far end of the room. "A present's traditional, isn't it?" He smiled as he handed it to Sarah.

"Oh, Max, it's wonderful!"

"Better than that thing you've got hanging in your office," he muttered.

Sarah laughed as she looked up at Byron. "Max prefers Cézanne to Dali." She handed the canvas to Byron, then kissed Max's cheek. "Thank you."

The old man sighed. "There's some champagne in the refrigerator behind the bar," he said briskly. "Open it, and don't pour me any of that goddamn sherry."

There were times when Byron made love with her that Sarah felt his need for her was desperate. She thought, as she had thought the first time they had been together, that no one had ever wanted her to this degree. It was total, almost unreasonable, and as weeks passed there was no change in it. Not in bed. Yet she sensed the same anger in him, the same desire to hold himself back. He wasn't a man to give love easily or to accept it. What he had told her the day they were married still held true. He didn't want to love her. Sarah had to remind herself that she had walked into her marriage with her eyes open. She wanted Byron and would have to be patient until she had him completely. But Sarah didn't have much patience.

Work on the library consumed her professional hours. Because the project became personally important to her, she rejected the use of a draftsman and completed the blueprints herself. She and Byron worked head to head. It was during this time that she became fully aware of his skill. Though she had often fought tooth and nail with engineers—and Byron was no exception—she admired his sharp, meticulous knowledge of his field. Professionally they were well matched; the creative and the practical balanced each other.

With a cup of cooling coffee in her hand, Sarah looked over the blueprints on her desk. The library was part of both of them. For now, she mused, this is as close as he'll let me get to his past. She remembered their conversation after his mother's visit. He had opened up then, briefly, but she knew it had been an important step. It could take weeks, maybe months, until there was another. With a sound of frustration, she set the coffee aside. Weeks or months or years, she thought. Christ, can I wait that long without pushing?

She didn't want him to change. No, she wouldn't have fallen so deeply in love with him if he had been any different. She wanted him to let her know who he was. She wanted him to trust her. Glancing back down, Sarah studied the blueprints again. There had been a solidity between her and Byron when they had discussed stats and stress points. There was complete, consuming need when they made love.

It's not enough. Suddenly tired, she pressed her fingers to her eyes. It's just not enough for me. And I don't think it's enough for Byron either.

When the buzzer sounded on her desk, Sarah pushed away thoughts of Byron and answered. "Yes, Mugs."

"A Mr. Bounnet to see you, Ms. Lancaster."

"What?" Sarah paused in the act of tightening her left earring. "Who?"

"Mr. Januel Bounnet."

"Januel," she murmured, then gave a low, astonished laugh. Well, I'll give him points for nerve, she thought. "Send him in."

Sarah stood behind the desk, not bothering to tidy the blueprints or papers. When he entered, she noted how marvelous he looked, absolutely right in the expensive suit and silk tie. His face was as romantic and beautiful as ever. She was surprised to find that she felt no pain or discomfort —only curiosity.

"Sarah!" Januel smiled as he crossed to her to take both of her hands in his. "How beautiful you are."

"I was just thinking the same about you." She removed her hands. "I didn't expect to see you in America, Januel. Is there a problem with the center?"

"No. I'm sure you've seen the reports. It's progressing well. I didn't come to see you to discuss business, Sarah."

"No?" She smiled, but he noted that it wasn't in pleasure, but in amusement. He had to concentrate on keeping annoyance from his voice. He didn't care to be laughed at.

"I heard the most extraordinary thing." His eyes still smiled at her, warm and appreciative. "That you and Byron Lloyd are married."

"Is that extraordinary?"

"My love . . . Sarah," he corrected when she lifted a brow. "Perhaps I should say unexpected."

"Perhaps you should," she agreed simply and waited for him to continue.

"Please." Januel spread his hands. "May I speak frankly?"

"Oh, by all means."

The sarcasm in her voice brought on a quick flash of irritation. "Sarah," he said, softening his tone, "how can I apologize for being a fool?"

"Any way you like."

He shook his head with a quick laugh. "You won't let me off easily, will you?"

"Why should I?" she countered. "You were despicable. How's Madeline?"

He laughed again. "She said you would ask. I'm to give you her best. Sarah . . ." The appeal was in his voice and his eyes. "I was wrong, terribly wrong. What I did, what I said, was unforgivable. I misjudged what would be important to you. A small excuse, I know, but I hope you'll believe that I did care—do care, very much. Is it too much to ask that we might be friends?"

"Yes," Sarah told him. "Entirely too much."

"But perhaps you will not hate me?" His smile was charming. It amazed her that he still expected her to see no further.

"I don't hate you, Januel," she said honestly. "Though it was unintentional, you did me a favor. Just don't ask me to thank you for it."

He came around the desk and took her hand again. "You are happy with your marriage?"

"I'm happy with my marriage."

He sighed and brought her hand to his lips. "Sarah, if—"

Coming in at that moment, Byron saw Sarah's hand in Januel's, saw the warm, intimate look the Frenchman gave her, saw Sarah's smile. Closing the door at his back, he crossed to the center of the room.

"Take your hands off my wife."

"Byron!" Stunned, Sarah stared at him. Her hand was released immediately, so immediately that she might have laughed if she hadn't recognized the look in Byron's eyes. "Januel was—"

"Don't ever put your hands on my wife again." Byron

253

cut off Sarah's explanation without a glance in her direction. His eyes were all for Januel.

"My apologies," Januel said stiffly as he walked to the door.

"How could you?" Sarah demanded the moment they were alone. "How could you be such a fool?" She pushed her chair aside and crossed to him. "Don't you ever say *'my wife'* again as if I were an expensive tie."

Byron took the lapels of her jacket in either hand and pulled her against him. "I won't tolerate you holding hands with that son of a bitch. Understand?"

"You won't tolerate?" she tossed back. *"You* won't tolerate? Listen to yourself. Can't you hear how ridiculous that sounds? You act as if you had walked in on us while we were making love."

"I don't want to see him around you again. I had to watch him put his hands on you in Paris. I had to lie in bed and know he was with you in the next room. I don't have to watch him pawing you now."

Sarah struggled to keep calm. "No one paws me, Byron, not even you. And it's a little late in the day to throw a former lover in my face. Yes, I slept with him. If you'd wanted a virgin, Byron, you should have looked elsewhere. We've both had lovers. Do you want me to make you a list of the rest of mine?"

He had to tighten his grip on her jacket to keep from striking her. He couldn't see the right or wrong of it. Didn't want to see. "Not him," he said with low fury. "Not Bounnet. You keep the hell away from Bounnet."

"Byron, I—"

He cut her off by flinging her away into a chair before he stalked from the room.

Chapter Twenty-eight

FOR A FULL TEN MINUTES SARAH SAT PERFECTLY STILL IN the chair. She wanted the trembling to stop before she tried to think.

It hadn't been simple jealousy. It had been rage. She couldn't understand it. If anyone knew Sarah's true feelings about Januel, it was Byron. He had seen her put the relationship behind her before they had gotten married. But, she recalled, his attitude toward Januel had been far from friendly all along. Looking back over the weeks in Paris, Sarah didn't believe that Byron's dislike of Januel had anything to do with her. At least not initially.

Shaking her head, she pushed herself out of the chair. That wasn't really the issue. Byron didn't trust her, and that hurt. With this scene, he had put her in the category of a possession rather than a person. That infuriated her. And that, Sarah decided, was going to change quickly.

If he had wanted a tidy little wife who would follow orders and offer no complaints, he should have married someone else. Loving him didn't mean she had to stop being Sarah Lancaster. She began to think that her notion of moving on from Haladay and starting her own business might be the answer.

Separate our professional and married lives, she mused. If she didn't work for him, it might take some of the strain off their personal life. And, she admitted, if she didn't work for him, she wouldn't have the nagging doubt that she would be given a plum assignment because she was Mrs. Byron Lloyd.

She intended to get to the top, but not on anyone's coattails. She intended to make her marriage work, but not at the sacrifice of everything she was.

Sarah walked to the phone and punched a series of buttons. Fifteen minutes later she walked into Haladay's office.

"Max, I appreciate you seeing me so quickly."

He leaned back but didn't rise. "It sounded important."

"I think it might be." She was nervous, she discovered, more nervous than she had been the first time she had come into his office.

"Sit," he said and gestured. "Is there a problem on the library project? The prints look good."

"No, it's not that." Because she didn't know how to begin, Sarah dove straight in. "Max, I'm thinking of resigning."

"What?" His brows drew nearly straight. "What the hell are you talking about?"

"I'm considering opening my own firm. I had thought of doing it once before but—"

"What kind of bullshit is this?" he demanded.

"It's not bullshit, Max."

"You have complaints?" he asked her, still scowling. "Your salary? Your assignments?"

"No." Sarah shook her head. "No, it's nothing to do with that. No one who works for you could complain about the way you run your business, Max, or the way you treat your employees. This is personal."

"Now what the hell is that supposed to mean?"

"I don't want to work for Byron."

Max sat back at that and blew out a long breath. "Why?"

"Because I want to stay married to him. And because I want to be independent of him."

"Am I supposed to know what that means?"

Sarah laughed. "No. Max, I love him. I don't want to lose him. I don't want to lose myself either."

"That doesn't tell me why you want to go off on some harebrained scheme, setting yourself up in business."

"Harebrained," Sarah repeated, both brows rising. "Don't you think I could do it?"

Max frowned as he studied her. "Yes, I think you could do it," he admitted. "But I don't think you need to. You have all the goddamn creative freedom you need here. I couldn't keep men like Cassidy working for me if I put chains on them." He stopped, lifting a pencil and tapping it on his desk. "What does Byron think of this idea of yours."

"I haven't discussed it with him yet."

"Why the hell not?"

"Because I don't want to discuss it with the vice-president of Haladay," she returned evenly. "I want to discuss it with my husband. I'm coming to you first because you own the company. I'll talk to Byron, but not during business hours."

"I see," Haladay mused, and began to. "I wouldn't have wanted my wife working for me," he told her. "I wanted her home and my dinner hot when I got there." He shook his head, then focused on Sarah again. "But you're a different kind of woman, aren't you, Sarah?"

"Yes," she answered and smiled. She had always wondered if he had loved his wife. Now she saw that he had.

He set the pencil down and folded his hands. "I never had a son," he began briskly.

"Didn't you, Max?"

The words stopped him. Their eyes held a moment before he nodded. "Yes, you're a very smart woman. Byron's everything I would have wanted in a son. The first time I saw him, he was young and tough and hungry. I thought—

Christ, he could be me thirty years ago. But he was smarter, brighter. I made an investment in that boy, but it wasn't only for the business. It paid off.''

His look became sharper. ''I didn't like it one damn bit when he told me he'd married you.''

Sarah's eyes didn't waver. ''I know.''

''I didn't like it,'' Haladay continued, ''because it told me he'd taken a step back. If he'd have married someone like my Laura, I wouldn't have batted an eye. Goddamn it, Sarah, I look at you and see myself all over again.''

''Is that so bad, Max?''

He gave a long, tired sigh. ''I'm an old man. Goddamn it, I'm an old man and I'm not ready to be. You're the woman Byron needed, and it was time he took a step back from me. But I'll tell you this—Haladay isn't prepared to lose one of its best architects.''

''Max, I appreciate it, but—''

''Don't appreciate it,'' he snapped and felt a twinge in his chest. ''Think about it. I made an investment in you too. You settle this with Byron. I want to see both of you in here at eight o'clock tomorrow morning.''

''Yes, sir,'' she said primly and watched his mustache twitch.

''Goddamn it, Sarah, get out of here. I've got work to do.''

She rose, but paused at the door. ''Max, whatever I decide, I appreciate you talking to me like this.''

It was after seven when Sarah heard the elevator doors open and close. She didn't rise from the sofa, but waited until Byron entered the penthouse. He saw her, said nothing, and went to the bar to pour a drink.

''Byron, there's something I'd like to discuss with you.'' Her voice was cool, but she could put no warmth in it. She discovered she was still angry.

''Go ahead.'' He lifted his drink but stayed where he was.

And so is he, Sarah thought. "I've been giving some thought to leaving Haladay and starting my own firm."

He said nothing for a moment, banking down on a furious retort. "Why?"

"There are a couple of reasons." Sarah felt a surge of frustration. Why were they talking like strangers? "Byron." She rose and took the first step. When he didn't move toward her, she stopped. "I don't think we should work together."

"Haladay has a full engineering staff." He drank down two fingers of bourbon.

"Damn it, you know that's not what I mean."

"Why don't you tell me what you mean, Sarah," he said coldly. "I don't like guessing games."

"Oh, God, you're a bastard, Byron." She turned away, struggling for control. "I don't want to work for you because I don't want you to think of me as an employee when we're here."

"What makes you think I do?"

"Orders, Byron," she said, turning back to him. "Orders. You told me once you don't tolerate orders. That was in a business situation, and you were perfectly right. Now I'm telling you: I won't tolerate them in our marriage."

"So." He studied the liquor in his glass before he drained it. "We're back to Bounnet."

"No!" Infuriated, Sarah went to him. "We're back to you and me because that's all that matters. I won't go on having you juggle me and Haladay. I'm not asking you to make a choice. At this point there's little doubt of who'd come out on top."

"I don't know what the hell you're talking about."

She was getting to him now. Sarah saw the anger beginning to break through the ice. She pushed further. "I think you do, Byron. And I think if it isn't possible to keep our marriage separated from what we do downstairs, then one of us has to make a change."

"Just what sort of a change do you have in mind?"

"I've learned enough to handle a small business of my own," she began. "I've built up a reputation."

"Both of those things have come from Haladay," he said shortly and poured another drink. He didn't like the feeling that he was losing something—losing it while he grabbed for it with one hand and pushed it away with the other.

"I'd never deny that."

"What would you prove, Sarah?"

"That I could do it."

"You're tossing away a hell of a lot for ego," he commented.

"It's not ego, Byron." She ran a hand through her hair. "Oh hell, maybe it is, partly. But I also know that unless there's a change, we won't make it together. You've been tense ever since we got back to Phoenix. You still don't want to love me, Byron. It's hard for me to accept that. And I think the longer it goes on, the easier it will become for you to stop. I'm wondering if some distance on a professional level might not help close some of it in our marriage."

"I never lied to you."

"No," she said simply. "You never lied to me."

His fingers tightened around the glass. He wanted her so much in that instant he could have shouted out in rage and frustration. He should have been able to control it. He had always been able to control his emotions—since he had left the reservation, since he had begun the long climb. Sarah was changing it all.

Abruptly he tossed the glass behind the bar. Even as it shattered he dragged her into his arms. He hurt her, he knew it. Somehow he wanted to. "I need you. Damn you, you know I do."

"Byron—"

But his mouth was on hers, rough, desperate, angry. He pulled her to the floor, and she remembered the first time they had lain there. Then, he had been reckless, confident. Now he was savage and out of control. The fierceness of his need was overwhelming, driving them both. He had no patience with buttons and zippers now. Sarah felt her blouse rip.

He wanted her skin—naked, hot. He wanted her hands on him. She was still pulling at his clothes when he dove his fingers inside her. Sarah arched and cried out with the first climax, but he was relentless. Here, he would have her here, then he would find his control again.

She was shuddering, moaning mindlessly as his fingers worked inside her. He told himself he was leading her as his mouth sought her breast. Then he was lost in the taste of her, groaning as the need built. He couldn't get enough, and he knew, with a final flash of fury, that he would never get enough. Then her hands were on him. She pulled him inside her.

Sarah lay still, though her breathing was far from steady. Beside her, Byron was silent. He hadn't drawn her against him. When she turned to him, reaching out, he rose. Still dazed with passion, weak from the demands of it, Sarah watched him as he dressed.

"Byron, where are you going?"

"Out."

"Out?" she repeated stupidly and sat up.

"That's right." He buttoned his shirt without looking at her.

Her thighs were still damp from him. Sarah shook her head in confusion. "Why?"

He said nothing as he moved toward the archway.

"Byron," Sarah called after him. Though a pain twisted in her stomach, her voice was steady. "Don't do this. I need you too."

He continued through the archway without stopping. Sarah heard the rumble of the elevator.

She lay on her tumbled clothes and wept.

Chapter Twenty-nine

Uncharacteristically, Sarah woke before Byron. She drifted awake slowly. Weeping had left her groggy. Twisting her head, she saw Byron beside her. It occurred to her that she had never seen him sleep before. He was always awake before her. She wanted to touch him, to turn to him. But he had walked away from her. She turned away. At her movement, Byron was instantly awake. He sat up as she did and took her arm.

"Sarah."

She stopped, unresisting. "I'd like to shower first. Max wants to see us at eight."

He had an irrational urge to shake her, but instead he let her go. The bathroom door shut quietly behind her.

They dressed in silence. Sarah slid the last pin into her hair as Byron buttoned his shirt. "I'm going down now," she said.

"I'll be down in a few minutes," he answered tonelessly.

Byron watched her walk away. He heard the rumble of the elevator.

Sarah told herself not to think as she pressed the button for Haladay's floor. She wouldn't think or feel, not until she had to. She didn't want to plan what she would say to

Haladay. She didn't want to admit that at this moment she had no plans. As the elevator doors opened, Sarah took a deep breath, then stepped into Haladay's office.

He was sprawled facedown on the floor in front of his desk. She mouthed his name, but no sound came out. Then she shouted for him and ran across the room.

Her breath hammered in her throat as she knelt beside him. She pushed, but his weight resisted her effort to turn him over. Setting her teeth, Sarah pushed again. As she managed to shift him to his back, his hand brushed her thigh. Instantly Sarah recoiled. It was cold. She recognized death before she looked into his face.

Her stomach lurched. She shook her head, refusing it. "Max." She took his shoulder and shook it. *"Max!"*

Scrambling up, Sarah dashed to the phone on Haladay's desk. Her fingers fumbled over the numbers twice before she heard it ring. "Byron," she said the instant she heard the answering click. "Byron!"

"Sarah?"

"Come quickly." Letting the receiver drop, she went back to Haladay. She ignored the answer on his face and felt for his pulse in his wrist, then his throat. Desperately she tugged at his tie to loosen it. Her heart was pounding against her ribs, and she swore at her hands when they shook.

When Byron found them, she was opening the buttons of his shirt. In seconds he was across the room, pushing her aside. It took only one glance to tell him it was useless. Still, he felt for a pulse as Sarah had. Haladay's flesh was cold under his fingers. He could hear Sarah's ragged breathing as she knelt on the other side of the body. In a quiet movement Byron reached across and closed Haladay's eyes. Sarah's protest stumbled out.

"No, Byron. No, no, there must be something . . ." She swallowed a fresh wave of nausea. "There must be something we can do."

For a moment they knelt in silence with Haladay between them. "He's gone, Sarah. He's been gone for hours. There's nothing we can do."

He watched her face crumble with his words before she lay her head on Haladay's chest.

Sarah stood straight and silent during the graveside service. She saw the adjoining headstone and thought dully that Laura Winters Haladay had stayed at home and kept supper warm. When she and Byron were alone at the grave, she laid a carnation on the coffin. Wordlessly, Byron took her arm to lead her away.

They settled in the back seat of the limousine, cut off from the driver by a soundproof shield. Sarah spoke for the first time in an hour.

"When my parents died I was angry and sad. But more than anything, I was guilty. They were good people. They had given me a very secure childhood. I loved them both and took them for granted. Then they were dead, and I realized I'd never told them how much I loved them."

She sighed and looked out of the window. "The day before Max died I was in his office. I felt so close to him for those few minutes. And he said—" Her voice broke and she shook her head and controlled it. "He said he was an old man, but he wasn't ready to be one. He looked so fierce trying not to smile when he told me to get the hell out, he had work to do. I didn't even know that I loved him. Now he's dead."

Byron said nothing. Sarah had seen no grief from him. If he felt any, he kept it to himself. He was more remote from her now than he had been the first time she had walked into his office.

She drew a deep breath. She was tired of fighting. "I don't want to go to the board room, Byron. I don't want to hear the reading of the will."

"It's important that you're there." His tone was flat and

final. "There are reasons why this has to be done quickly. A change of power in a company of Haladay's size is always a dangerous period. There are loans and suits and contracts, hundreds of major and minor things to be seen to. Once the will's read, the transition can begin."

"It has nothing to do with me." She leaned her head back against the seat.

"It's necessary that you be there."

He turned away and they took the rest of the journey in silence.

The board room smelled of leather and furniture polish. The walnut table that dominated the room was twenty feet in length. There were high-backed chairs with cushioned seats and Waterford crystal glasses beside each place. Heavy damask drapes were drawn over the window. Cassidy opened them with a quick tug and sunlight spilled into the room.

Sarah saw that his grief took the form of anger and sympathized. She watched Kay Rupert quietly filling the water glasses. When she had finished, she sat at the base of the table and folded her hands. At her elbow was a pad and pencil. Her eyes flickered over Sarah before they turned discreetly away.

Almost everyone else in the room was a stranger to her. She recognized two of the board members, but the other three men in dark suits and solemn faces were unknown. She sat between Byron and Cassidy and looked beyond them.

Greenfield was Haladay's attorney and, with Byron, executor of the will. Though she knew it was irrational, Sarah disliked him because it was he who held the will in his hand. He cleared his throat as he took his place at the head of the table. His voice was soft and surprisingly rich. Sarah tuned it out almost immediately.

Now and again, as the monologue droned on, she heard a

snatch of some technical passage; a scholarship fund, an endowment. She found them impersonal, remote from the Maxwell Haladay she had known. She hated Greenfield's soft, expressionless voice. Fatigue made it more and more difficult for her to turn into herself and block him out. When Cassidy reached down to lay his hand on hers, she gripped it, grateful for the simple human contact. But even as her shoulders relaxed, they tensed again as she heard her name.

"To Sarah Lancaster Lloyd, I bequeath my wife's jewelry, herein itemized, my property in Cornwall, and the house thereon and its contents. Also to Sarah Lloyd, I bequeath fifty percent of my interest in Haladay Enterprises."

Sarah didn't hear the murmur of voices around her as she frowned at Greenfield. What had he said? She glanced at Byron, but found no answer. His face was calm and closed. Cassidy's hand was still over hers, so she turned to him. He reached his other hand to her shoulder.

"Relax, Sarah," he murmured.

"What did he say?" she demanded, then turned to Byron again. "What does he mean?"

Without speaking to her, Byron rose, taking her by the arm. "If you'd continue," he said to Greenfield, "with the specific terms of the disbursement of the bequests, I'll be a few moments."

"Yes, of course."

Byron led her out and closed the door behind them. When they entered a large reception room, she pulled impatiently out of his hold. "Byron, I want to know what's going on."

"Max left you his wife's jewelry, his Cornwall property, and half of his sixty percent share of Haladay Enterprises," he said simply. "I'd estimate that at somewhere in the neighborhood of fifty million in cash value."

"Oh my God." She couldn't take it in. Her mind refused to. "Why?"

Byron lifted a brow. "Because that's what he wanted."

"That doesn't make sense, Byron. I worked for the man for a year and a half. Why should he leave me anything?"

"Max never felt he was obliged to give explanations. You'll be able to do what you please with the personal estate. As to the stock . . ." He paused to flick on his lighter. "That depends on how involved you want to be with the company."

Impatient, Sarah rose. "Byron, this is ludicrous. I don't have any right to the property or the stock."

"Max gave you the right," he countered. "And the responsibility."

She stopped what she had been about to say and studied him. "You knew about this," she said slowly. "You knew he'd done this."

"We discussed it," he told her briefly, then turned away. "Wait here."

Without giving her a chance to speak again, he strode to the double doors and into the board room. Sarah stared after him. What game was going on here? she wondered. And why had no one told her the rules? Sarah heard the doors open again and turned. It was Kay Rupert, not Byron, who came out.

"Mrs. Lloyd, Mr. Lloyd asked me to take you upstairs. He'd like you to wait for him up there. You won't have to see any reporters or answer any questions."

"I see." Sarah glanced at the closed doors again. "You needn't come with me, Kay. I'll be fine."

"Mrs. Lloyd." Kay smiled as she opened the doors to the corridor. "I always follow the boss's orders. That's the way he wants it."

"All right then." Annoyed, Sarah watched Kay slip a key into the elevator.

"Let me fix you a drink, Mrs. Lloyd." Kay gave her a sympathetic smile as they stopped at the penthouse. "You look like you could use one."

Sarah started to snap that she wanted to be alone, then

stopped herself. The woman was only trying to help. "Thanks, I'd appreciate it. Would you like one?"

"Not while I'm on duty. Brandy?"

"Yes, that's fine." Sarah sat on the couch and tried to think.

In the mirrored back of the bar, Kay watched her. She felt the bitter taste of fury lodge in her throat. Sarah was sitting in her place, the place she had worked for. Ten years, Kay thought furiously. Ten years I've waited, and in less than two, she has it all. She poured the brandy and brought it to Sarah.

"You must be surprised at the way things worked out," she commented.

"Surprise," Sarah murmured as she accepted the snifter, "isn't the word I had in mind."

"Mr. Lloyd should be pleased."

Sarah glanced up. "Why?"

"Well, after all, he'll have controlling interest in Haladay now. He had twenty percent already, and Mr. Haladay left him twenty more. The addition of your thirty shares gives him seventy. Of course, I don't know why Mr. Haladay didn't simply give him the stock to begin with, but . . ." She trailed off and shrugged. "I only hope they patched up their disagreement before Mr. Haladay died."

"Disagreement?"

"Yes, it was too bad they had to argue on the night he died, isn't it?"

"What the hell are you talking about?" Sarah had risen, but Kay kept smiling.

"Didn't you know?" Her voice was as light and professional as ever. "I thought Mr. Lloyd would have mentioned it to you. I had to work late that night. I was taking some papers up to Mr. Haladay's office when I heard them arguing. Of course I didn't stay to listen. I put the papers on his secretary's desk and left. But Mr. Haladay was furious. He has a carrying voice."

"Byron wouldn't fight with Max," Sarah insisted, thinking of his heart. His heart, and the heart attack that had killed him.

"Oh well, I'm sure it was just a disagreement." Kay enjoyed watching the horror grow in Sarah's eyes. "Mr. Haladay sometimes got overexcited. I'll go now. I'm sure you'd like to be alone."

Sarah sat down again as Kay disappeared into the vestibule. Fifty million dollars, she thought numbly. Thirty percent of Haladay. Oh my God. Byron fighting with Max on the night he died. No, he couldn't. Sarah told herself. He wouldn't upset Max, knowing how bad his heart was. Byron has more control than that.

She remembered how he had left her that night—how he had made love like a driven man, then left her. No, no, no! She tried to block out her own thoughts. He wouldn't have taken his anger down to Max. He would have had no reason to. Kay was mistaken. Mistaken or lying.

When she heard the rumble of the elevator, Sarah was on her feet and waiting.

Byron noted the rigid stance and the untouched brandy. "You should drink that and go to bed."

"How long have you known what Max was doing in his will?"

Byron crossed to her, picked up her brandy, and drank it himself. "As far as you're concerned? Six months ago with the stock, two weeks ago with the rest of it."

Sarah let out a long breath. "All right, Byron, why did Max leave me the stock?"

"He knew you. He knew you were smart, ambitious, and strong." Byron set down the brandy and removed his tie. "He wanted Haladay in strong hands, and he wanted to make certain no one had too much of a cut."

Goddamn it, Sarah. I look at you and see myself all over again. Sarah could hear Haladay say it as if he stood in the room with them. The sudden fierce wave of grief had her turning away.

"I wish he had told me himself," she murmured. "I wish he had talked it over with me first."

"Max did what he wanted to do. He always did."

Sarah nodded, then turned back. "You'll be president now."

"The board will vote on it." He stared down into the brandy. "But yes, I'll be president."

"And with my thirty percent, you'll have controlling interest."

He looked up at her now, his eyes guarded. "The mathematics of that will occur to some people."

"I wonder, Byron, just how badly you wanted it."

His hand tightened on the glass. "Go to bed, Sarah."

"Did you go to see Max the night he died?"

She saw the change in his expression, but it was too quick to read. His face was closed when he spoke again. "Yes."

Sarah felt the headache begin as a slow, steady throb at the base of her neck. "Why?"

"That's my business."

"Did you argue with him?"

Byron said nothing, but his eyes never left her face.

"Damn it, Byron, tell me. His pills were still in his jacket pocket. If he'd been arguing, upset—"

"I told you to go to bed, Sarah." He loosened his grip on the snifter, knowing it would shatter in his hand.

"He gave you everything!" she shouted, infuriated by his coldness. "You were the son he always wanted. He loved you. Don't you care? Don't you have any feelings, Byron?"

"My feelings aren't your concern, Sarah."

If he had struck her it would have been less painful. Byron heard her suck in her breath, then let it come trembling back out. "No, you won't let them be. And I can't live with you knowing that. I took a chance . . . I lost." She let out another shuddering breath. "I thought you'd start to trust me, start to let me in. But you won't. I'm not satisfied with half a marriage, Byron. I want all or nothing.''

Byron shrugged, then drank. "That's your privilege."

Turning, she went to the bedroom to pack. When she came back out, he was gone.

Chapter Thirty

SARAH STOOD TWENTY STORIES ABOVE THE TRAFFIC AND watched it pour over the streets. She didn't feel like she had come home, not the way she wanted to feel it. She simply felt in between. She was stuck in a clock that moved neither forward nor back.

What was it Dad used to say? *A stopped clock's right twice a day.* Not this time, she thought with a sigh. She didn't hear the door open behind her or the sound of her name. The hand on her shoulder had her spinning around.

"Oh, Benedict." She fell into his arms and clung.

All that was familiar about him flooded over her; his scent, the texture of his beard against her cheek, the soft, lightly Bostonian sound of his voice. She wanted to bury herself in it and forget. But she wasn't certain that, even if she could turn the clock back to the last time he had held her, she would. He held her until she was ready to let go.

Slowly Sarah drew away to look at his face. After lifting both hands to his cheeks, she smiled. "Benedict, it's so good to see you. Pat told me I could wait for you in here."

"Sarah, when did you get into town?" He spoke lightly as he led her to a chair, but his professional eye had noted her pallor. And she was thinner, he thought.

"Last week. You were away." She smiled again as she

sat in an overstuffed chair. "So I decided to park on your doorstep the morning you were expected back."

"I wouldn't have gone if I'd known you were coming."

"No, I know you wouldn't have, Benedict."

"I read the papers." He stretched out in the chair beside her. "You've been busy. The Delacroix Center, a surprise marriage to Byron Lloyd, then your equally surprising inheritance."

"A banner year," she murmured.

"Tell me about it."

"I found someone I'm not so compatible with, Benedict."

"Congratulations."

She laughed, then sat back in the chair. "Oh God, that's why I came back here. I needed to laugh." She leaned forward again and took his hands. "I love him, Benedict, and I think—no, I know he loves me, but it doesn't seem to be enough."

"Why?"

"He won't let me in." She squeezed his hands in frustration, then dropped them. "For the first couple of weeks after we were married, he started to, and then he shut off again. He's always pushing me back. He really hates loving me, if you can understand that. Maybe you have to know Byron to understand that."

"You know him," Benedict said. "Do you understand it?"

"Yes." Sarah leaned back again and let the words come. "He's full of emotion, not all of it pleasant. There's a lot of bitterness, anger, from his childhood. He kept a leash on his temper for a lot of years. I seem to snap it too often. Byron doesn't trust emotions. He didn't want to be in love with me; he told me so. I think one of the most difficult things he ever did was admit to himself, then to me, that he was in love with me. It gave me a hold."

"But he did tell you."

"Yes." Sarah smiled, remembering. "In his own way.

At Haladay he has the control; he knows how to use it. In our marriage the control was balanced between us, and that didn't suit him. He's a man who doesn't relax often enough, who doesn't trust, and yet he can be gentle. I don't know, Benedict. If I had to sum Byron up in one word, I'd use complicated. It covers the most ground.''

"I've never known you to back away from a complication, Sarah."

"I backed away from this one," she said quietly. "I ran away from it. The night before Max died, Byron and I had a very serious row. He left the penthouse, and I learned later that he'd gone down to Max's office. They'd had an argument.'' She felt her stomach muscles tighten, but forced herself to continue. "After the will was read, and I suddenly found myself owning a thirty percent share of Haladay, I demanded explanations. I didn't like the ones I got.''

She rose now, unable to sit any longer. "Byron had known about the stock. And, after thinking it over for a while, I can accept Max's reasoning. He was a selfish man when it came to that business. He wanted it to keep running his way even after he was gone. He chose people he was sure of. Anyway, I wasn't thinking as straight as I might have been. I really cared about that old man, and listening to that damn lawyer in his three-piece suit reading the will . . . well, someone planted an idea in my head, and I went with it. I'm ashamed to say I was easily manipulated.''

"Your defenses were down, Sarah. You're not invincible.''

"Yes, that's what I've been telling myself." She stared out the window. "It hasn't been helping. I brought up the stock to Byron again. Maybe if he hadn't been so cool, if he had understood how badly I wanted his support just then. But we missed each other's needs. We do a lot of that. I all but accused him of plotting to gain controlling interest of Haladay with the addition of my stocks.''

"Did you believe it?"

She turned, and her eyes were filled with grief and regret. "I wanted to hear him tell me no. I wanted him to say 'Sarah, I love you. You're more important to me than stocks or Haladay.' And when he didn't, I asked him about the argument with Max. I wanted to shake him. I wanted to see some emotion. He'd blocked himself off completely since Max died—no grief, just nothing. He told me that his feelings weren't my concern. That's when I realized that I couldn't go on in a relationship where I'd never be able to feel any closeness, any real bond. Love just isn't enough. Not for me."

"What have you decided to do?"

"I haven't made all my decisions yet," she told him. "I think I need a little time before I make too many. I did go to the lawyer before I left Phoenix. I transferred my Haladay stock to Byron."

"Is that what you want?"

"Yes." She drew a deep breath. "Yes, the stock could be important to Byron. It's not to me."

"What do you want for yourself, Sarah?" He rose and went to her.

"What I always wanted. To build. To be successful. I want Byron, too, but I don't think that's possible. Not the way I want him. So I have to concentrate on the first two." She swallowed, then went into his arms again. "But I don't feel very strong right now. I'm afraid I'm going to find myself on a plane back to Phoenix ready to settle for whatever he'll give me. I love him so much, Benedict, and I'll hate myself if I go back to him."

"Sarah." He drew her away until he could look into her eyes. "Give yourself a little time. The strength'll come back; then, whatever decision you make will be the right one."

"Are you sure?" she demanded and managed a weak smile.

"I'm sure about you. Do yourself a favor. Get away for a

while. Not here, not New York. There are too many memories here for you."

"Yes," she agreed. "I've been finding that out."

"Why don't you go skiing? It was always one of your favorite things."

"Skiing?" She thought about it a moment, then her smile was stronger. "Yes, I think I'd like that, but Vermont's no good this time of year."

"You're a few weeks ahead of the season." Benedict gave her a friendly kiss on the nose. "Go to Saint Moritz."

"Saint Moritz?" Sarah laughed. "Go to Switzerland?"

"Why not?"

She opened her mouth, but could find no reasons. "Why not?"

Sarah took the slope with confidence, reveling in the speed and the sting of the wind. The world was white, open and free. Her muscles were responsive, tight and ready for each twist, each turn. Her breath vaporized and was lost behind her. She stopped at the bottom of the run with a spray of snow. Laughing, she pushed her goggles on top of her head.

"Showoff." Dallas walked over to her. "Nothing more disgusting than a showoff, especially when they're good."

"Hi." Sarah bent to remove her skis. "I thought you had a lesson with that blond hunk this morning."

"I did. We're finished." She watched Sarah maneuver skis and poles. "You've been buzzing around the Alps for over three hours."

"Oh, I'm sorry." Sarah tossed back her head to glance at Dallas as they began to walk. "I didn't realize."

"Don't apologize. Jens kept me busy. You know . . ." She took a deep breath of the thin, pure air. "I've always needed a filthy rich friend. It's so nice to have someone call you up out of the blue and say 'Pack, we're going to Saint Moritz.'" Dallas grinned. "It sort of adds something to your day."

"It's a change from sun and cactus." Sarah shifted the skis on her shoulder. "How about some hot chocolate?" She inclined her head toward a tiny café. "Did you manage to move on the skis today?"

"Just barely." She waited for Sarah to stack her skis and poles outside the door. "Jens seems to enjoy picking me up."

"Have you decided how slow a study you're going to be?" Sliding inside a booth, Sarah pulled off her scarlet ski cap and gloves.

Her face was flushed with cold and excitement, her eyes eager again. Her grin as she ordered was spontaneous and unstrained. Two weeks ago, Dallas mused, she looked ready to sink. There had been a touch of desperation about her when they had set out on the trip. It had faded, and the strength was coming back. Dallas had watched it grow by degrees each day. She took a deep breath, deciding the time was right.

"You know, Sarah, you look great. You really do."

"Thanks." She pushed loose hair behind her ear. "I feel pretty good."

"You know I'm going to have to go back." She paused while Sarah's eyes came to hers. "I'm going to have to leave Sunday."

"Dallas, can't you take another week?"

"I have to go back." She reached out and touched her hand. "And you have to decide where you're going."

Resting her elbows on the table, Sarah made a steeple of her arms and interlaced her fingers. As she leaned her chin against them, her wedding ring came into her line of vision. She stared at it a moment, then shifted her eyes to Dallas again.

"You're right, I've hibernated long enough. I'd like to say I could just travel for awhile, just play." The waitress set their cups on the table. Sarah glanced at the steam rising from the chocolate and cream. "But I know I can't. That's just not possible for me. I have to get back to work. First

277

decision," she said with a sigh, then lifted her cup. "Second decision: where?" She sipped chocolate and thought. "I suppose I should go back to New York. I'm comfortable there. I'm in a position, thanks to Max, that allows me to build what I want, when I want. And with the work I've done at Haladay, particularly the Delacroix Center, to my credit, it shouldn't be too difficult to find clients."

"What about Byron?"

Sarah's eyes focused again. They stayed steady on Dallas's. "I don't believe I have a decision to make there. I'd like to cop out and say I made a mistake by marrying him, but I'm not certain I did. And I promised myself once that I wouldn't have any regrets about the time we spent together. I loved him." She shrugged, taking up her cup again. "I love him. If I didn't, we could probably live together very successfully. But as it stands, that's just not possible. I've accepted that."

Dallas shifted her gaze to Sarah's hand. "You're still wearing your wedding ring."

"You know me too well," she murmured, setting down her cup. "I will accept it," she corrected. "It's just going to take a bit longer. Right now I have to get back to work, and the rest'll follow."

"The press is going to be crawling all over you when you get back to the States."

"To hell with them." Sarah shrugged with a trace of her usual arrogance. Dallas smiled seeing it. "The publicity will make it easier for me to snap up a few contracts. I should think they'll have gotten most of the 'Surprise Heiress' routine out of their systems by the time I get back."

"There's nothing the press likes better than a beautiful face, a fairy tale story, and big bucks. You've already been recognized here once or twice."

"They'll get bored when they realize I'm more interested

in cantilevers than glass slippers. Come on." She slid from the booth. "Let's go hit the sauna."

The stars were out. Sarah walked away from the resort lights and let the moon guide her steps. There was a three-quarter slice of it in the sky and the glow fell generously on the snow. Sarah kept her hands in her pockets and walked. She had left Dallas to flirt with a trio of tourists from the south of Italy. Language, Sarah had mused, gave Dallas no problem at all, especially when the tourists were all male. Lifting her face to the sky, she watched a roll of clouds shift over the stars. They held snow, she was certain. There'd be fresh powder in the morning.

Benedict's prescription had been precisely what she had needed. And with Dallas for support, Sarah knew she'd come over the hump. What was left was to move ahead. And I will, she promised herself. I'll have to see Byron again and make the break clean before I move back to New York. After that I'm going to be very busy. I should finish up my obligations . . . the library in particular. She sighed, then gave herself a moment to consider. I think I'll be able to handle it now. Once we dissolve our personal relationship, I should be able to handle our professional one.

Oh, bullshit. She shook her head and kicked at the snow. I'll never be able to deal with Byron personally or professionally without making a total ass out of myself. There're a lot of things I can do, a lot of adjustments I can make. That simply isn't one of them. What I have to do is turn my files over to Cassidy and let him take over. I have to have my things shipped out from Phoenix and set myself up in Manhattan. The lawyers can handle whatever needs to be handled between Byron and myself. *Coward*, she thought grimly.

She stopped at a ridge and stared out over an expanse of mountain and space and snow. It was cold, beautiful, and forever. It made her think of the desert. Shivering, she turned from it.

Someone walked toward her. In a shaft of moonlight she saw his face. "Januel?" Surprised, Sarah waited for him. His face was pale and exquisite in the night light.

"Sarah." He took her hands in a warm clasp. "How wonderful to find you here."

"What in the world are you doing here?" She allowed her hands to lie in his as she searched his face.

"Getting away from the office," he returned with a brilliant smile. "Things have been in such utter chaos, I wanted a few days to myself." His smile faded as he looked down on her. "Such a tragedy. There wasn't time to speak to you at the funeral, and I left for France almost immediately afterward. Of course, the news of your inheritance from Haladay stunned everyone."

"Including myself," Sarah countered, removing her hands. She dipped them back into her pockets and began to walk along the edge of the ridge. "I'm just beginning to get used to it. I only wish I'd had more time with him."

"I must tell you, there is much speculation about you at the moment. You dropped out of sight right after inheriting a large portion of one of the biggest companies in the world, and a healthy personal estate."

"I'm eccentric," she answered lightly. "It's simply that a greater number of people know that now."

Januel gently took her hand as they walked. "Byron, on the other hand, has been quite visible in this, shall we say, transition period."

"Byron is anything but eccentric," Sarah murmured. The clouds grew thicker.

"He is president of Haladay now."

"Naturally."

"It seems a bit odd that you're not by his side."

Sarah continued to look straight ahead. "I should think that's our business, Januel."

"Of course, *chérie*. I wouldn't say anything if I hadn't

been worried for you." He stopped her by taking her other arm as well, turning her to face him. "Sarah, I hate to think of you being unhappy. You must know how very much I care for you."

"Januel." Her voice and eyes were steady. "I appreciate your concern, but it isn't necessary."

"Sarah." She stiffened at the caressing note in his voice, but he continued. "I was devastated when I learned you'd married Byron. I can only blame myself for being a fool and driving you away from me and into his arms. We can still be together. I know your marriage was an impulse; it can be easily ended."

"My marriage is my business," Sarah countered. "Whether I maintain it or end it is for me to decide. I have no desire to *be* with you, Januel, and I find this conversation very distasteful."

"Sarah, don't punish me any longer." His grip on her arms tightened as she started to pull away. "We could have so much together."

"I'm sure we could," she agreed and stood still in his arms. "With a few million dollars to keep us comfortable. You can only make a fool of me once, Januel. You're a parasite and an opportunist."

His eyes kindled. "And what is your husband?"

"I won't discuss Byron with you. Let me go."

"Why are you here?" he continued, pulling her closer as his temper frayed. There was a desperation in his voice that surprised her. "Thousands of miles from him. I came the moment I learned where you were. This time you'll listen to me. Be realistic, Sarah. Your marriage with Byron is over, and was nothing more than what I offered you months ago."

Their faces were close enough so that the clouds of their breath mingled.

"You and I together can take over Haladay. A few years, that's all we need. I know what has to be done and how to do it; I need only your leverage. And we can take it so much further, have so much more." His words rushed out in excitement, but she concentrated on his eyes. "Byron's a fool, as Haladay was. Too scrupulous, too exacting. There are profits to be made that he will ignore."

"What are you talking about?" She stared at him, looking deep. "You're talking about altering specs?"

"There are degrees of alteration, degrees of bending the laws. You're not so naive that you don't know this is done every day. Certain sacrifices have to be made to stay under budget."

"Sacrifices? Have you done a lot of sacrificing, Jan005? Were there sacrifices on the Delacroix Center I wasn't informed of?"

"The center is a success. What difference does it make?" Angry, he shook her. "I have no time for moralizing. I need your support."

"Is that why Byron came? Is that why he stayed so long in Paris? Did he find out what you'd been doing? Did he tell Max?" She pressed her hands against his chest. "He'd have fired you on the spot. You're worse than a parasite. You're a cheat, a thief."

His grip tightened and his face grew hard. "I'm a realist, Sarah, and I'm good at my job. You're too honest to say otherwise. I need your support against Byron. I need to cement my position quickly."

"Your position?" she tossed back. "You'll have no position when Byron finishes with you. I only wish Max had had the pleasure of ruining you."

"He would have, but his temper betrayed him. He should have known better than to lose it with his heart in such poor condition."

"What are you saying?" She froze, and her fingers gripped at his jacket. "You were there? You were with Max?"

"He was furious," Jan005 told her. "I think surely he would have struck me, but it was too late. There's no need to look at me with such horror. There was nothing I could do. He was simply dead.''

Her eyes were wide. "You left him. You left him lying there alone, all night." The words tumbled out. "How could you? You told no one, you called no one. You just left him there on the floor."

"What good would it have done to have called anyone? What an impossible situation it would have put me in. He was dead," he repeated, shaking her again. "His own temper, his own stubbornness killed him."

"And you left him." She struck him hard once, then again. "You left him. You bastard, take your hands off me." She would have slapped him again, but he stunned her with the back of his hand.

"Stop this. I tell you there was nothing to be done." His words rang out into the air and fell into the darkness behind them. "How can you blame me for the weakness of his heart, for the temper he failed to control? I had to think of my own position."

"You altered specs." Her breath raged in and out of her lungs. The side of her face stung from his hand. "You took advantage of his name, his reputation. I'll make you pay for that. Damn you! Damn you! He lay there all night on the floor!"

"Sarah, be reasonable." He realized that he had said far too much too soon. "I panicked. I wish it had been otherwise. He died so suddenly, right before my eyes. You must understand what a state I was in."

"No, no!" She pushed against him again. "You killed him with your cheating, then you left him. He might still have been alive. There were pills in his pocket." Remembering brought tears, and Januel's face blurred through them. "You didn't even try. His tie was still on. I loosened it myself when I found him. You never tried to revive him. It's the same as murder. The same!"

"No!" Januel shook her, trying to make her swallow the words. "I tell you that is not so. You must not say it."

"I will say it!" She began to struggle more violently. Snow slid under her feet. "I'll say it, and they'll listen. Let me go! Stay away from me!" She swung back, losing her balance with the force of the movement. Sarah screamed once as she fell backward over the edge of the ridge. There was an echo, then silence.

Januel stared in shock. Slowly he backed away, then turned and ran toward the lights of the resort.

Chapter Thirty-one

IT WAS THE SNOW THAT WOKE SARAH. IT FELL ON HER face, dry and cold. There was no moon now. She could see only dark and snow. Her head throbbed as she tried to sit up. Groggy and dizzy, she lifted a hand to the back of her head and felt the matted hair where the blood had flowed and then congealed in the cold. Memory flooded back. Terror replaced the dizziness.

Snow swirled around her and flew into her eyes. Cautiously, she groped out with her hand, then shuddered violently when she found that the edge of the ledge was only inches from where she lay.

"They'll be looking for me," she said out loud. Her voice sounded hollow, smothered by the snow, but she clung to it as a point of orientation. "They'll find me. I'm not that far away from the lodge. I just have to be still."

She curled herself into a tight ball with her back against the cliff wall. She shook with cold and shock. Already a fine layer of snow covered her. She wondered, as she strained her eyes to see, how far she had fallen. Not far, she told herself. It can't be far or I'd have more than a bump on my head. Hysteria rose in her throat and she tried to swallow it.

Someone will come soon. Dallas will tell them. . . . But

she remembered she hadn't told Dallas she was going out. She won't miss me until morning, and even then . . . oh my God. Sarah huddled closer within herself. A night's exposure on the face of a cliff left a slim chance for morning. Januel will tell someone. They'll come. They won't leave me here alone. He *will* tell someone. Panic was bubbling again and she set her teeth against it. She steadied herself and watched the snow. Don't sleep, she told herself. You won't hear them calling for you if you fall asleep.

Taking deep breaths, she tried to think logically. One step at a time. She should stand and see how far she had fallen. Maybe she could climb up. Even the thought of it sent queasiness rolling through her stomach, but with her eyes glued on the darkness in front of her, Sarah stood. She kept her back pressed against the wall until her legs steadied. The dizziness returned, and she waited for it to pass. Carefully she turned to face rock.

The snow hurled itself into her eyes, but she continued to look up, trying to make out the shape of the cliff above her. With her hand she began to feel, cautiously at first. She thought, but couldn't be certain, that she could feel the edge with her fingertips. She stood on her toes and stretched, gripping the wall with her other hand.

A loosened rock gave way in her fingers and, terrified, she pressed against the cliff. The stone was cold against her cheek. Snow and wind battered against her as she clung to the side of the cliff. She lowered herself again as her head swam. She bit her lip hard.

"Now, that's healthy," she said aloud. "Good healthy fear of fainting. I can't faint because I might not wake up. Oh God, how long have I been here?" she asked herself desperately.

She buried her face against her knees. Don't think, don't think! Just wait.

She began to drift again, but this time she didn't notice. Dimly she heard her name and only settled deeper, pillowing her head with her hand. The snow came like a cloak and insulated her. Sarah shifted and murmured. A voice came again, closer now, with an urgency that caused her to blink her eyes open. She waited until she heard the call again. "I'm here!" she yelled, pitching all her strength into her voice. "I'm here!"

"Sarah! Keep calling, I'll find you."

Wind blew the snow into her face, and she brushed it off, trying to see beyond it. "I'm on a ledge. I don't think I'm down very far." She pressed the heels of her hands against her eyes, casting her mind back in a desperate attempt to reorient herself. "It's north of the lodge, five hundred, six hundred yards. Can you hear me?"

"It's all right, I'm coming. Just keep talking."

"You're getting closer. I can't see anything, but . . ." As she looked up into the snow and dark, Byron's face appeared above her. He seemed to loom from nowhere, just beyond the reach of her hand. The tears started instantly. "Oh, God, Byron."

"Are you hurt, Sarah?" he said sharply as she only looked up at him. "Are you hurt?"

"No, I . . ." She reached fingers to the back of her head. "I hit my head, I think. I can't feel anything."

"Stay very still. I'll go back and get a rope."

"*No!* Don't leave me!" The hysteria was back. "Don't go, please, please don't go. Don't leave me here." She rested her brow against the cliff wall and wept violently.

"All right. All right, Sarah. *Sarah!*" His tone had the effect of quieting her weeping, but she continued to stand with her face against the cliff. "I won't leave. You have to keep calm, Sarah. I'll get you up, but you have to help me." She lifted her face to his. "Good, that's good." His stomach tightened as he saw the terror in her eyes. "Now, do you know how wide the ledge is?"

"I . . ." She swallowed, then pressed her lips together tightly before trying to answer again. Little bubbles of hysteria tickled her throat. "When I woke up, I was lying on it. I had only about eight inches to spare."

Byron swore, but against the force of the wind Sarah didn't hear. The snow was falling thickly, and he saw that she was covered with it. He looked back to measure the distance to the lodge, then went from his knees to his belly.

"All right, now listen to me. I want you to reach up your hand as far as you can. Don't step back. Stand close to the wall and reach up. I'm going to pull you up. Do exactly as I say. Trust me, Sarah."

His voice was cold and she did her best to respond to it. She began to shiver again, but reached up. On the edge above, Byron lay prone. He had dug down, using his boots to gain a toehold in the rock beneath the snow. He leaned into space and stretched out for Sarah's hand. Their fingers brushed, then parted as she pressed herself against the wall again.

"I'm sorry."

He could barely hear her with her voice muffled against the rock and clogged by tears.

"I'm sorry. I'm so frightened."

"Just reach up, Sarah. Give me your hand. Give me your hand, Sarah."

Again she reached up and their fingers touched. Quickly his fingers curled under hers; firm, steady. He could feel her trembling. "Use your other hand on the wall; balance yourself. Try to get a toehold with your foot if you can. I'm going to pull you up. Help me, Sarah."

Her breathing hurt her throat. It was cold and jerky and her lungs felt unable to deal with it. She gripped the rock with her free hand, concentrating on the contact with Byron as she scrambled with her feet for support. She felt him lift her a precious inch. Her boots clattered and scraped, and in panic she looked behind her. There was nothing but emptiness.

"No! No! Look at me, Sarah, look at me. Don't look down." She turned at his command and focused on his face. "Just look at me, straight at me. I need your other hand, Sarah. You have to give me your hand."

Sarah stared at him. Suddenly, vividly, she remembered the sensation she had experienced the first time she had walked into his office. The cold, the blinding white, the fear. Dizziness washed over her in waves.

"Sarah, goddamn it, you're not going to faint. Do you hear me? Goddamn it, you're *not* going to faint!" Terror rose inside his chest. "Give me your hand. Look at me, damn you, and give me your hand. Sarah, for Christ's sake, I need your hand."

She heard him dimly, in a dream, in the past. She lifted her hand toward the sound of his voice. He gripped it painfully, crushing her fingers before he slid his hold to her wrist. Using every muscle, Byron crawled back on his belly, pulling her up inch by slow inch. He could feel her pulse under his hand. He dragged, no longer certain she was conscious. His back strained as he dug in and pulled her higher. Snow whipped into his face and blinded him.

He pulled, coming to his knees as he brought her to the edge. For an instant they teetered, poised between the dark and the snow. Then, with one final effort, he had her in his arms rolling away from the border.

Sarah could feel his mouth on hers, cold and desperate, but the words he said were lost. There was a haze surrounding her even as she felt the solidity of his body over hers. His hands moved over her as if to assure himself that she was there, whole and safe.

"It was Januel," she murmured, dipping into semiconsciousness, then back again as the snow revived her. "He left Max. Just left him. I fell . . . I slipped. He altered stats. . . . Did he tell you I fell? He left me." She felt herself go weightless as Byron lifted her. "He didn't call for help . . . he just left him, all night. Byron, don't leave me. Don't go."

The snow swirled around them as he gathered her closer in his arms and walked toward the lights.

* * *

Sarah stared at the ceiling, lost for a moment between wakefulness and sleep; then her eyes shifted toward the window.

Byron stood silhouetted against the door, his back to her, his hand resting on the sill. There was something weary in the way he stood that made Sarah curious. It occurred to her that in the time she had known him, she had never seen him appear tired. He seemed as she had once wished Haladay. Indestructible.

"Byron." She thought she had only spoken his name in her mind, but she must have said it aloud because he turned instantly to look at her. Quickly he came across the room, but there was a hesitation before he reached out and lightly touched her cheek. He drew his hand away and put it into his pocket.

"How do you feel?"

Sarah took a deep breath and tried to find out. "A bit battered, I think," she said after a moment. "And groggy. And alive." When she started to sit up, Byron laid a hand on her shoulder.

"Don't." He lifted it again immediately when she looked at him. "You should try to get some more rest."

"I'd really like to talk." Gingerly she pushed herself all the way up.

"The doctor said you could have some tea when you woke if you'd like." He watched her shift the pillows behind her back and kept his hands in his pockets. "There's medication if your head hurts badly. He seemed to think it was a mild concussion, but wanted you to have X-rays this afternoon. You've got some bruising." The hands in his pockets were fists. "Nothing's broken."

"That's good news." Sarah settled back. "I wouldn't mind some tea, but I'd just as soon skip the medication. I'm floating a bit as it is."

"I'll fix it." He turned to move through the archway and into the tiny kitchenette in Sarah's suite.

She sat silently, cushioned with pillows and bundled by

the quilt, watching the dawn grow. The snow had stopped some hours before and the sun was pushing away the darkness. She wondered if she had imagined it all, then explored the back of her head with her fingers. The lump and the dull pain told her she hadn't. She closed her eyes. She remembered it, but distantly, like a nightmare that had been horribly vivid at the time but vague in the morning. Byron brought her the tea in a cup and saucer and set it beside her. She looked up at him with a smile.

"Thanks. I don't remember much of what happened after you found me and pulled me up." She let out a quick breath. "Actually I don't really remember much of that; the details are hazy." Her eyes narrowed as she studied him. He was unshaven, his hair and clothing disheveled. He hasn't slept, she thought. He spoke before she could comment.

"You fainted," he said. "I carried you back here. The house doctor examined you."

"You don't change," she murmured. Carefully she moved to pick up her tea. "Try to elaborate a bit for those of us who missed the last act. I don't know how much I told you about Januel, but—"

"I knew about the stats, the kickbacks," Byron interrupted curtly. Sarah said nothing and sipped her tea. It was warm and sweet. He watched her take the cup in both hands, then turned away to light a cigarette. "One of the reasons I went to Paris was to investigate a report Lafitte had sent me. It took some time to trace the problems through channels and back to Bounnet. He covered himself very well."

"Yes, I imagine he did," Sarah commented. "Self-preservation is number one on Januel's list." She sighed and looked down into the dark amber tea.

"Lafitte wouldn't be dead if the bolts for the grid hadn't been inferior grade."

"Oh my God."

Byron turned to see the shock race into her eyes. "Only

some of the plumbing, only some of the lumber. He might have continued to get away with it for some time if he hadn't gotten greedy with the center. Lafitte picked up on some things and contacted me.''

"Poor Paul. And Max." Her eyes darted back to Byron. "He was with Max when he . . .''

"I know. You told me. I've dealt with it.''

"But how?'' Sarah sat up straighter. Impatiently she pushed at her hair and he saw the ring flash on her finger.

"I said I dealt with it,'' Byron repeated and blew out an angry stream of smoke. "Leave it.''

Feeling the rebuff, Sarah lowered her eyes. Her cheeks were nearly as white as her pillowcases, but he could just see a mauve tracing along the right bone. He remembered the scattering of bruises over her body, which he had found while undressing her. And she'd been thin, thinner than she should have been.

"Are you hungry?''

Sarah looked up at him. "I never eat breakfast,'' she said and smiled. When he didn't respond, she set the tea aside. "Byron, please, I don't know what to say to you.'' She reached out, taking his hand. "I don't know how . . .'' With a frown, she looked down. The skin on the back of his hand was broken, the knuckles raw. "What have you done to your hand?'' Appalled, she took it in both of hers. "Have you been fighting?'' she said incredulously as she brought her eyes back to his. The question seemed absurd for a moment, then she thought of Januel. "Byron . . .''

"I'd have killed the son of a bitch if I'd had a few more minutes.'' He spoke matter-of-factly as he crushed out his cigarette in an already overflowing ashtray. "As it is I only managed to break his jaw and his nose and maybe a few ribs. He doesn't look as though he belongs in a Renaissance painting anymore.'' Her horror-stricken expression infuriated him. "He'd have let you die out there.''

Sarah ran her fingers through her hair. "But didn't he tell

you where I was? I thought . . . how did you know?'' She stopped for a moment as a thought came to her mind for the first time. "Byron, what are you doing here?"

He tucked his hands back into his pockets. "Dallas called me."

"Dallas?" Sarah echoed him blankly. "Dallas called you?" She paused, then nodded. "I see. I'd say she shouldn't have done that, but as I'd probably be dead now if she hadn't, I won't."

"You weren't in your room," Byron went on. "You didn't seem to be anywhere. The desk clerk remembered you'd gone out sometime after dinner, but he didn't know if you'd come back in. I went to look for you."

"I'm very grateful you did." She tossed back the sheets.

"You're not to get up," Byron said, moving to her again.

"I want to see if I can stand without falling on my face." She managed by putting partial weight on the bedpost. She could feel the remnants of the drug. Her nightgown was like a little girl's, long and full with fussy smocking at the breast. Byron felt an impossible stir and turned away.

"I'll get your robe." He brought her a thick chenille and helped her slip into it.

"Byron." Sarah kept her eyes on her hands as she tied the belt. "I know we didn't part on very easy terms. I'd like to apologize for the things I said to you before I left."

"I don't want your apology."

"Byron, please . . ."

"You were justified. You mentioned Kay last night when you were moving in and out of consciousness. I'll take care of that when I get back to Phoenix."

"I shouldn't have said those things." She shook her head and took a step closer. "I didn't believe them."

"I don't know why you shouldn't have believed them. As for Max, I wasn't completely certain until last night that I hadn't been responsible." His eyes were impassive and set on hers. "I'd gone to see him. He was under a great deal of strain. We disagreed about certain things. I thought he was all right when I left him, but . . . then I couldn't be certain."

Sarah thought of what he must have felt those days following Max's death. What he must have felt when she had stood there demanding answers. "Oh, Byron." Sympathy roughened her voice as she reached out to him.

"Don't touch me!" He snapped at her as he jerked away.

Her eyes round with shock, Sarah whipped her hand behind her back.

She sat back on the bed, gripping her hands together in her lap. "I suppose it's best if we settle what we have to. I realize I should've done all that before I left Phoenix, but I wasn't thinking about anything but getting away."

"Yes, I'm aware of that."

"Have you . . . started divorce proceedings?"

"No."

She bit her lip, then spoke calmly. "I'd rather you took care of that, Byron. I've decided to go back to New York, and with relocating myself personally and professionally, I'll be pretty swamped. In any case, you're more used to dealing with lawyers than I am."

"No."

Sarah opened her mouth, closed it, then stared at his back. "No?"

"That's what I said." He turned back to her. She lifted her hand to her head and tried to read his expression.

"I know that Greenfield is officially my attorney because of the estate, but I really don't know him," she said. "The only dealing we've had is when I signed those papers to turn the stock over to you."

"I tore them up."

Sarah stopped rubbing her temple. "What?"

"I tore the fucking papers up."

"The transfer papers?" Sarah's brows lowered in confusion. "Why did you do that?"

"I don't want your goddamn stock."

Sarah studied his face. A muscle twitched at the corner of his mouth as he kept his jaw tight. "Byron, I don't understand. I thought you'd want a controlling interest."

"I don't want your goddamn stock!" he shouted at her. "You stupid idiot, I don't need your thirty percent to run Haladay. You're going to understand that." His eyes were hot, burning into hers as she stared up at him.

"I never thought you did, Byron. I simply thought the stock would mean more to you than to me, since I won't be with Haladay anymore."

"The hell you won't." Livid with rage, he continued before she could speak. "Max gave you the stocks because he wanted you to have them. He hired you because he wanted you for Haladay. You're not going to turn your back on that or on him now."

Sarah remained silent for a moment. "You really loved him, didn't you?"

"Yes, I loved him." The words came out on a rush of pain and grief. "And I'm going to see to it that he gets what he wanted."

"I see. That's why you tore the papers up. That's why you want me back in Phoenix."

"Yes. No." He turned and stalked to the window, staring out for nearly a full minute before he spoke again.

"In the desert, when we were alone, I lost myself in you. I told myself it was all right, because once we were back in Phoenix, I'd be able to control things again. It didn't quite work that way. You could take me back with a look." He whirled back around.

"I fought that, every chance I could. I knew every time I hurt you, but you wouldn't turn away and make it easy on me. You weren't supposed to be so damn important, you weren't supposed to make such a difference. You weren't supposed to be able to hurt me the way you did when you walked out on me."

"Byron—"

"Shut up!" He came to her and gripped her shoulders.

"Shut up!" His eyes blazed. "I got through almost a week, then I went crazy trying to find you. When Dallas called I was on a plane within an hour. And I was almost too late. Do you know how I felt when I looked down and saw you on that ledge? I almost lost you. If you'd fainted before I'd gotten a good hold . . ." He gripped her tighter because his voice was shaking. "I'm taking you back. Just as soon as you can travel, you're coming back with me. There's not going to be any divorce."

Sarah drew out of his arms and turned away. Her heart was thudding again, as it had on the ledge. But not with fear now. "And what if I file for divorce, Byron?"

"Then I'll fight you with everything I have," he said furiously. "You'll need a fucking fleet of lawyers before you get a divorce from me."

"Oh, Byron, you son of a bitch!" She was smiling brilliantly as she whirled back to him. "That's why I'm crazy about you." She was in his arms, her mouth locked on his before he understood what she had said. She could feel the jerkiness of his heartbeat as she pressed against him.

"Sarah. Oh God, Sarah, I love you." His lips ran wildly over her face and hair. "I love you."

She laughed and pulled her face back. She wanted to see his eyes. The guards were gone. "Yes, but do you want to?"

"Yes, Christ, yes." He pulled her close again and just held her. "I've never wanted anything more."